THE MONEY GUN AND TRAPP'S MOUNTAIN

A Robert J. Randisi Classic Western Double Draw

ROBERT J. RANDISI

WOLFPACK
PUBLISHING
— EST 2013 —

The Money Gun and Trapp's Mountain: A Robert J. Randisi Classic
Western Double Draw
Paperback Edition
Copyright © 2023 (As Revised) Robert J. Randisi

Wolfpack Publishing
9850 S. Maryland Parkway, Suite A-5 #323
Las Vegas, Nevada 89183

wolfpackpublishing.com

Paperback ISBN 978-1-63977-768-6
eBook ISBN 978-1-63977-767-9

THE MONEY GUN AND TRAPP'S MOUNTAIN

THE MONEY GUN

TROUBLE BREWING

"They look mad," Tall Fellow said.

"If we go for our guns there's going to be a blood-bath," Faulkner said.

"So what do we do? Turn and run?"

"Then they'd start shooting for sure," Faulkner said.

Faulkner and Tall Fellow stood their ground and waited as the group approached. They became aware of people behind curtains and windows, staring out, watching. And the street had cleared. There were only the two of them, plus the eight or ten lawmen approaching.

As the group came closer Faulkner spotted one man in the front and decided to key in on him. He looked the most comfortable wearing the tin star.

"I think Sunday and his gang hit the bank," Faulkner said, "and these boys want to take it out on us."

"That ain't fair," Tall Fellow said.

"Let's see if we can convince *them* of that..."

CHAPTER ONE

CENTER, MONTANA, 1898

Faulkner rode into Center, Montana, on an eight-year-old bay mare that had seen better days. He figured once he completed his business there he'd see about buying a new horse. He bought and used horses the way he did his saddle, saddlebags and bedroll. They were all things he needed, but the need was not specific to any one item. A horse was a horse, and to illustrate that fact, he never named his mounts. His friend Henry Tall Fellow had once advised him never to name something you might one day have to eat.

Center was no different from any of the thousands of towns Faulkner had been to over the past twenty-two years. Not large, not small, it was not near a mine or adjacent to rich grazing land. It did not have the growth potential that many of the boom towns had. It was stuck right where it was in its development, and while it would probably never grow any larger, there was a chance that it would begin to die when people realized that and chose to leave.

The buildings that lined Main Street were worn and faded. Even where some folks had slapped on a fresh coat of paint in an attempt to hide or cover the despair, it bled through.

Faulkner found his way to a livery stable, which, in keeping with the tone of the town, looked as if a stiff wind would blow it over. He was going to need to stay over a night, though, to complete the task that had brought him there, and the condition of the place did not alarm him enough to send him looking for something better. He very much doubted there was something better.

He dismounted in front of the livery and walked the animal inside. A stringy fellow, who could have been anywhere from fifty to eighty, walked toward him, carrying a bale of hay.

"You wanna leave your horse?" the man asked.

"Just overnight," Faulkner said. "I should be out of here by morning."

"Don't know why you'd wanna be here in the first place," the man muttered. He tossed the hay into a stall and wiped his hands on his backside as he came closer and eyed the mare.

"Don't look like such a much," he said.

"She ain't," Faulkner said. "Fact is, my intention was to buy a new horse, but this town doesn't fill me with much confidence to that end."

"Town don't matter," the livery man said. "Fact is, I got me some good stock out back you can look at if you've a mind to."

"Good stock? You sure?"

"I been at this a long time, friend," the man said. "I know good horseflesh when I see it. This ain't it. Oh, she mighta been once, but she's plumb wore out, and she shouldn't be. What is she, eight?"

"Yep."

"She's been rid hard in her life," the man said. "That from you?"

"Last couple of years," Faulkner admitted.

"You're hard on a horse."

"Can't deny it."

The man took off his hat, scratched the full head of gray hair he still owned, then replaced the worn hat.

"Maybe I shouldn't sell you a horse, but fact is I can't be choosy. You wanna look at 'em, ya can."

"In the morning," Faulkner said. "What's your name?"

"Thatcher."

Faulkner handed the stable man the mare's reins. Thatcher eyed the saddle with some distaste.

"Looks like you might be needin' a new saddle soon, too."

"That's true enough."

"Well, ya ain't gonna find that here, that's for sure. You

want my advice? Stop off in Laramie. They got some good tack there for a man who needs it."

"I'll keep that in mind. Is there a good hotel in town?"

"No."

"A decent one?"

"Hell no. Tell ya whatcha do. Keep goin' here for a block past us and you'll see a two-story house that looks like it don't belong in this town 'cause it's too well cared for. That's the widow Gentry's rooming house. If you want a good night's sleep, that's the place to get it in Center."

"Well, I'm much obliged, Thatcher," Faulkner said. "Fact is, I think I'm going to be in need of a good night's sleep."

"You can't be in this town on business," the older man said.

"Oh, but I can."

"What kind of business would bring ya to this godforsaken town?" Thatcher wondered.

"You'll know all about it by tomorrow," Faulkner told him, and he walked out. He turned in the direction recommended by the livery man.

————

THATCHER STARED AFTER FAULKNER, noticed the man's well-cared-for weapon and the way he wore his gun belt. Also the way he stood in general, confident-like. He wasn't so much to look at, his clothes covered with trail dust, his face kind of plain, but there was an attitude about him. Thatcher had been around men like that a good long time, prided himself on being able to spot them. This one didn't look the part at first glance, but

Thatcher looked more than once and knew what he was looking at.

Shaking his head, he pulled the horse along and muttered to himself, "Money gun."

CHAPTER TWO

Faulkner found his way to the widow Gentry's boardinghouse with no problem. Thatcher had described it perfectly. It was the only building in town that didn't reek of age and exhaustion. As he approached it he saw a small boy in front, maybe eight or nine years old, with blond hair. He was just standing, staring down at the ground. As Faulkner got closer, the boy didn't move a muscle.

"What are you looking at?" Faulkner asked.

"Nothin'," the boy said.

"You live here?"

The boy nodded.

"Your name Gentry?"

Now the boy looked up.

"Billy Gentry. How'd you know?"

"Lucky guess," Faulkner said. "I guess your grandma would be the widow Gentry who runs this house?"

"No, sir," Billy Gentry said, "that'd be my ma."

Faulkner had gotten the impression from talking to Thatcher that the widow Gentry was an older woman. Given the age of this boy, the lady was apparently a young widow.

"Would you know if she's got any rooms for rent?" he asked the boy.

"She's got plenty," the boy said. "She says this town ain't good for nothin' and that we may have to sell the house and move."

"That a fact?"

"Only she says a body'd have to be crazy to buy this house in this town. Mister?"

"Yeah?"

"Does that mean my pa was crazy? I mean, he bought this house in this town."

"Son, I'll bet when your pa bought this house this town was a mite more prosperous than it is now."

The boy screwed up his face.

"What's prosp-prospish?"

"It means the town probably had more people back then, and was in better shape."

"Oh. So he wasn't crazy?"

"I don't think so. Your ma home?"

"Yes, sir. Just go on up and knock on the door," Billy said. "She'll open it for ya."

"I'm much obliged for the information, Billy," Faulkner said. "You can go back to what you were doing."

"I wasn't doin' nothin' but starin'."

"And a fine job you were doing, too."

Faulkner walked past the boy and tousled his blond hair on the way. He mounted the steps and knocked on the front door.

"Yes?" The voice came from behind a screen, but moments later a woman appeared. She was tall, blond, built along angular lines, thirty but looking forty because she'd been working hard all her life. A handsome woman nevertheless.

"Mrs. Gentry?"

"Yes?"

"That fine young man out front told me you might have a room for rent," Faulkner said.

"Fine youn—oh, you mean Billy? Did he bother you?"

"Not at all," Faulkner said. "Truth be told he was very helpful, and real polite. You should be proud."

"I am, most of the time," she said, "but he is an eight-year-old boy."

"I understand."

"So you want a room? For how long?"

"Just overnight," he said. "I'll just be in town long enough to see to my business."

"Well, whatever your business is, it's no concern of mine. If you follow me I'll show you a room, and you can have it if you like. It'll be a dollar for the day."

"That's fine."

She allowed him to enter, let the storm door slam and led him down a hall.

"I'll need another dollar if you want to take your meals here," she said. "I only have two other boarders now, but I'm cookin' breakfast and supper."

"That sounds fine," he said. "I'll be here for supper, but will probably be gone before breakfast."

Over her shoulder she said, "It'll still be a dollar. If you tell me what time you'll be gettin' up in the mornin' I can have somethin' ready."

Faulkner doubted she'd want to feed him, as by morning everybody in town would probably know what his business had been, but he said, "That's right nice of you, ma'am. I'll be sure to let you know."

She showed him a first-floor room in the back of the house, with a bed, a dresser, an end table and a rocker. Out the back window he could see the land behind the house, flat and empty.

"Will this do, Mr.—"

"Faulkner, ma'am," he said. "Just Faulkner, and yes, this will do fine. Would you like the two dollars now?"

"That would be nice," she said. "I do have to buy some supplies today."

Faulkner took two silver dollars from the pocket of his leather vest and handed them to her.

"Thank you, Mr. Faulkner. I'll leave you to get settled. Supper will be at five—that's about three hours from now."

"Yes, ma'am," he said. "I know what time it is."

"I'm sorry," she said. "I meant no offense."

"None taken. I just didn't want you to think me ignorant."

"I think you're anythin' but ignorant, Mr. Faulkner. I hear the unmistakable sound of an education in you."

"Guilty as charged, ma'am."

"I'll see you at dinner, then."

"Yes, ma'am."

"Oh," she said before leaving, "the hotels in town are not very good, but one of them has a bathhouse. I'd be obliged if you would avail yourself of their services before you get into that bed. I just put clean sheets on it."

"A bath was my very next stop, Mrs. Gentry."

"Well…see you at supper, then."

"Yes, ma'am."

CHAPTER THREE

Henry Tall Fellow had arranged to meet with Faulkner in Center. It wasn't Faulkner's choice. Their telegrams back and forth had resulted in Faulkner telling him that he had a job in Center. If talking was so urgent that it couldn't wait, then Tall Fellow could meet him there.

Tall Fellow was perfectly aware of what his friend's profession had been for the past twenty-two years. He didn't like to be around Faulkner when his friend was in work mode, but he needed his help badly.

It was past three when the town came into view. Tall Fellow paused before entering town. He'd passed a road sign a mile or so back that had had its population numbers crossed out and changed more than several times. Center did not sound like a town whose fortunes were on the rise, but that didn't matter to Tall Fellow. This was just a stop along the way, a place to meet with Faulkner and enlist his aid.

Whatever Faulkner had going on in Center, Tall Fellow had no part in it. His plan was to stand aside, let his friend complete his task, and then they'd get out of town and talk.

He gigged his pony into motion and headed for town.

FAULKNER CAME out of the hotel a hell of a lot cleaner than when he'd gone in. He'd slicked back his wet black hair with his hands after a shave and a haircut, and he had turned down an offer of Bay Rum. There was no point in him smelling pretty. He was not a pretty man, and what he had come to town to do was less than pretty.

Faulkner was looking for a man named Robert Cullen. Cullen had killed a woman and her two children down in New Mexico several months earlier. The husband and father, David Victor, had hired Pinkertons to track Cullen down, which they had done. They had tracked him to this little nothing town in Montana. After that, David Victor had needed a man with Faulkner's expertise to finish the job, and he was willing to pay well.

Faulkner's information was that Cullen was holed up in Center—doing what, he didn't know or care. Apparently, Cullen had come upon the Victor ranch and been shown hospitality, which he repaid by raping and murdering the mother, killing the two daughters and then robbing the house. Again, Faulkner did not know or care how Mr. Victor had come up with Cullen's name. He was being paid to do a job, and he was going to do it. Double-checking the facts was not part of it.

There were only two saloons in Center. Cullen had to be at one of them. Faulkner was armed with a complete description of the man, right down to a scar under his left eye. As long as he was still in Center, he would not be hard to find.

Faulkner never spent very much time in a town where he was going to do a job. He did not want people to get used to seeing him, and he certainly did not want anyone to be able to describe him later. Dealing with a livery man or a desk clerk at a hotel—in this case Mrs. Gentry—or a bartender was unavoidable, but beyond that he was able to keep to himself.

Now that he was clean and refreshed and knew he had a place to spend the night, he decided to take one quick look at the town. There was not much going on, and he was able to determine that they had a sheriff, but no deputies. He got most of his information by unobtrusively listening to other people's conversations. In this case there weren't many people available to him, but the people he did encounter were very talkative with each other. For the most part, they talked about getting out of Center and how useless the local lawman was.

It was getting on toward the time of day when the saloons would be busy in most towns. Center was in more trouble than even he had surmised upon riding in. He had not realized that it was virtually a ghost town. He felt bad for Mrs. Gentry and Billy being stuck here. It certainly would not be easy for the woman to sell her house. It was more likely she'd just have to pack up and leave it behind, if she truly wanted to leave.

Faulkner entered one saloon, which boasted four or five customers and a bored-looking bartender. None of the men fit the description of Robert Cullen. He moved on.

The second saloon was grandiosely called the Montana. It was even smaller and less patronized than the first one. About the only thing it had in common with the first was the bored-looking bartender.

There were two customers, one standing at the bar and the other seated. The standing man was portly and definitely not Robert Cullen. The other man sat with his hat on and his head down. Faulkner felt a familiar tickle in his stomach. It was not nerves, because he did not have any. It was that feeling that he'd found what he was looking for.

He looked at the bartender, who had obviously been at his job a long time, because he knew the look. The bartender leaned forward and said something to the standing man, who turned quickly, took one look at Faulkner and then left the saloon.

Faulkner walked to the bar.

"You know that fella?" he asked the bartender.

"I heard some boys call 'im Bob."

"Bob Cullen?"

"I don't know. All I ever heard was Bob."

"You better get out"

"Should I get the sheriff?"

"Just get out."

"Yessir."

"Get me a beer first."

"Yessir."

The bartender drew him a mug of beer, then hurried around the bar and out the batwing doors.

Faulkner picked up the beer and took it with him to the table.

CHAPTER FOUR

Faulkner sat down at the man's table and set his mug on it. The man looked up and the first thing Faulkner saw was the scar. The second was the haunted look in the man's red-rimmed eyes.

"Bob Cullen?"

Cullen frowned.

"Who're you?"

"That doesn't matter, but my name is Faulkner."

Cullen's eyes widened.

"I know that name."

"Then you know why I'm here."

"I—but you're a—hey, wait. I didn't mean—"

"You should've thought about what you didn't mean before you killed that woman and her daughters down in New Mexico."

"But you—who sent you?"

"The woman's husband," Faulkner said, "the girls' father."

"Look, I didn't mean...uh, I mean..."

Faulkner sipped his beer and regarded Cullen over its rim.

"Go ahead, tell me what you mean, Bob. I'm listening. We've got a little bit of time."

Bob Cullen sat back in his chair, shoulders slumped, looking defeated. An empty whiskey glass sat in front of him.

"It just got out of hand," he finally said.

"That's it?" Faulkner asked. "That's your defense?"

Cullen shrugged, lifted his arms and let them fall.

"That's all I've got," he said, "except to say that I ain't slept a night since it happened."

"That would be small consolation for the man I work for," Faulkner said. "I can't go back to him and say, 'The man who killed and raped your wife and killed your daughters can't sleep because of it.' That just won't work."

"I know," Cullen said. "I'm ready to go back. I'll give you my gun—"

"No."

"What?" Cullen looked confused.

"I'm not here to take you back, Cullen," Faulkner said. "If you know anything about me you know that's not what I do."

"B-but, I'm givin' up."

Faulkner shook his head slowly.

"Sorry." He pushed his chair back. "I'll wait outside."

"B-but—"

"If you go out the back I'll find you."

"There ain't no back way," Cullen said sullenly.

"A window, then," Faulkner said. "Whatever. It's a small town and you'll never make it out."

Cullen's eyes filled with tears, but men had cried in front of Faulkner before, and it didn't work.

"I'll be outside."

"You can't—"

"It's what I do, Bob."

Faulkner turned his back and headed for the door, alert for any movement behind him. It would have been better for both of them if Cullen had tried to shoot him in the back, but he made it to the batwings and then out.

Outside he stepped to the middle of the deserted street, turned and waited. He was prepared to find a lawman waiting for him out there, but that didn't happen. Apparently, the townspeople he'd eavesdropped on were right about the local sheriff.

He watched the batwing doors and just when he thought he might have to go back inside and do it there, Cullen appeared. The man stopped just inside and peered out over the doors. Obviously, he was hoping Faulkner would not be there.

Slowly Cullen opened the doors and stepped out. Faulkner didn't know if Cullen could handle a gun or not, but Faulkner wasn't a bushwhacker, and he wasn't the type to kill an unarmed man. He may have sold his gun for money, but he'd never killed a man who didn't have a fair try at killing him as well.

Cullen stepped outside, let the batwings swing shut behind him.

"Are you really gonna do this?" he asked.

Faulkner didn't answer.

"It's murder, you know."

Silence.

Cullen looked up and down the street, possibly seeking help. There was none.

"Damn you, Faulkner!" he shouted, and went for his gun.

Faulkner was not a fast-draw artist. He'd been outdrawn many times, but he shot straight, unlike other men in the same situation. It took a special talent to be able to draw and fire and hit what you were shooting at. Most men with fast moves had to fire two or three times before they hit their targets. Faulkner was not one of those men. He always hit what he shot at the first time.

His shot hit Cullen square in the chest. The man had cleared leather, but there was no danger that he might have outdrawn Faulkner. Instead, as he convulsively pulled the trigger, the shot discharged harmlessly into the boardwalk where he stood.

Cullen didn't keel right over. He sort of fell in pieces, folding in on himself, eventually ending up sprawled in the street.

Faulkner holstered his gun, walked to the fallen man, knelt and checked for a pulse. When he was satisfied Cullen was dead, he stood up and looked up and down the street. As far as he could see there had been no witnesses to the event, unless someone was peering out a window. If they were, they weren't coming forward.

Farther down the street he saw a man on a horse riding his way. He could tell from the man's seat who it was, so he stood his ground and waited for Henry Tall Fellow to reach him.

"How do you do that?" Tall Fellow asked, reining in his pony.

"Do what?"

"Your timing," the other man said. Tall Fellow was within a half hour of the time Faulkner had told him to meet him in Center.

"I have my life figured out to the minute."

"Remember me?" Tall Fellow asked. "I've been there when your life was totally out of control."

"Well, that's not the case now."

Tall Fellow looked down at the dead man.

"I take it your business here is done?"

"Oh, yeah."

Henry Tall Fellow stood in his stirrups and looked around. There was still nobody on the street.

"No law?"

"Not much to speak of, apparently," Faulkner said.

"Got a place to stay?"

"Yeah," Faulkner said. "You want a drink first, or a room?"

"Room first."

"Dismount and come with me, then," Faulkner said. "I know a lady and a boy who can use the business."

CHAPTER FIVE

Mrs. Gentry was very happy to have another boarder. When she walked Tall Fellow to his room Billy accompanied them, but the boy did not get up the courage to speak until they were actually in the room.

"Are you a real Indian?" he asked.

"Billy! Don't be rude," his mother chided.

"No, it's all right," Tall Fellow said. "He's curious. There's no harm in asking." He addressed Billy, who was staring up at him very solemnly. "My father was a Cherokee Indian, but my mother was a white woman."

"Wow! Was she kidnapped by the Indians?"

"No, she wasn't," Tall Fellow said. "My mother was the first woman Indian agent in the West, and that was how she met and fell in love with my father."

"You're really tall. Was your father tall? Was he a chief? Did he take scalps—"

"All right, now that's enough, young man," Mrs. Gentry said. "You still have plenty of chores to do, and I'm sure Mr. Tall Fellow wants to freshen up and take a bath."

"A bath, ma'am?" Tall Fellow asked.

"Yes," she said, "before you sleep on my nice clean sheets. Mr. Faulkner can show you where."

"Yes, ma'am."

"Supper's in one hour," she said. "If you miss it you'll have to eat in town. I wouldn't wish that on anyone."

"Yes, ma'am."

———

FAULKNER WAS WAITING for Tall Fellow when he came out of the house.

"You didn't tell me I'd have to take a bath to stay at this place," Tall Fellow said accusingly.

"Oh, yeah, I forgot about that," Faulkner said. "She has clean sheets. I'll show you where you can take one."

"Yeah, she told me you would."

"After that we can get a drink."

"She said supper's in an hour and we don't want to miss it," Tall Fellow said. "Apparently it ain't healthy to eat in town."

"I wouldn't think so."

They started walking toward town, having already put Tall Fellow's pony up at the livery.

"Ain't you worried about having to explain to the law why you killed that fella?"

"I'll deal with that if and when the law even shows up," Faulkner said.

Once again Faulkner waited outside, this time while Tall Fellow took his bath. He refused to allow a barber to cut his long locks, and he also eschewed the use of Bay Rum.

"I almost don't recognize you," Faulkner said when his friend came out.

"Shut up. I need a drink."

"We have time for one, and for a short talk before supper."

They went back to the Montana and saw that the body had been removed from the street out front. When they walked in only the bartender was there, behind the bar.

"You ain't here ta shoot nobody else, are ya?" he asked.

"I've done all the shooting I intend to for one day," Faulkner told him. "My friend and I want a beer."

The bartender eyed Tall Fellow critically. There was still some prejudice against serving Indians in saloons even in 1898, but in the end the bartender couldn't afford to turn away the business. He drew beers and Faulkner and Tall Fellow took them to a table.

"What's so almighty important that you had to meet me

here?" Faulkner asked. "You usually stay pretty far away from where I do my business."

Faulkner always found it odd that Tall Fellow disapproved of the way he made his living when their professions were so similar.

"I need your help and I didn't have time to wait," Tall Fellow said.

"Help with what?"

"Does the name Jack Sunday mean anything to you?"

Faulkner sat back in his chair.

"You're going to try for that bounty?"

"It's a lot of money."

"What is it? A thousand?"

"It's gone up," Tall Fellow said. "Twenty-five hundred for him, five hundred for each gang member."

"That is a lot of money," Faulkner said, "but men have tried to bring him in before."

"I know," Tall Fellow said. "Good men. Bryce Benteen, for one."

"He was a good man," Faulkner agreed.

"And Sunday killed him, fair and square, the way I hear it."

"That's how I heard it, too."

"If it was only Sunday, or only his men, I'd do it myself," Tall Fellow said, "but the combination is pretty deadly."

"So you want me to help you collect this bounty?"

"For half," Tall Fellow said. "I'll give you half."

"I don't want your money, Henry."

"It ain't even mine until we catch them."

"We'll catch them," Faulkner said.

"Then you'll do it?"

"I'll do it," Faulkner said, "but not for the money. You know that."

"Yes," Tall Fellow said. "I know that."

CHAPTER SIX

S upper was a quiet affair. The other two boarders did not seem to like eating with an Indian, but they kept their mouths shut. It may have been the fact that both Faulkner and Tall Fellow wore their guns to the table and were obviously friends.

Mrs. Gentry also did not seem to like the fact that the two men wore their guns, but remained silent about it. Still, the air was filled with tension for everyone but Faulkner and Tall Fellow, who thoroughly enjoyed the meal.

One person was completely oblivious to the tension, and that was Billy Gentry. He chattered on, asking both Faulkner and Tall Fellow questions, and when his mother objected, the two men assured her it was just fine.

"How's the lad going to learn if he doesn't ask questions?" Tall Fellow asked.

Mrs. Gentry was not happy, but she allowed her son to continue to voice his curiosity.

The other two boarders—a drummer and a traveling preacher—finished their meals first and left the table without availing themselves of Mrs. Gentry's dessert.

"That smells like apple pie, ma'am," Faulkner said.

"Would you like a slice?"

"A hunk would be more like it, if that's all right."

"That's fine, Mr. Faulkner. Mr. Tall Fellow?"

"The same for me, ma'am."

"Me, too," Billy said. "I wanna hunk, too."

"And what do you say, young man?"

"Aw, ma," Billy complained. "They didn't say it."

"I know, but I'm not their mother."

Billy looked as if he were going to resist until Faulkner said, "I'm afraid I forgot to say please, Mrs. Gentry."

He kicked Tall Fellow under the table.

"Oh, yeah, me too, ma'am... please."

Now all three adults were waiting for Billy to make up his mind.

"Please, Ma, can I have a hunk of pie?"

"Yes," Mrs. Gentry said, "you may all have a hunk of pie. Coffee, too, gents?"

"Yes, ma'am," Faulkner said, then added, "thank you."

"Yes, thank you," Tall Fellow said.

As she left the room Billy looked at Tall Fellow and asked, "How come you don't talk like an Indian?"

"My mother was a teacher," Tall Fellow said. "She taught me how to speak proper English."

Faulkner knew that Tall Fellow spoke properly until he was angered or provoked, and then his language became a little more like his father's. Although he was half white, it was the Indian part that drove Henry Tall Fellow, along with all its pride and anger.

"Wow," Billy said. "And what did your father teach you?"

"How to be a warrior."

"Wow!" Billy said again. "Can you teach me to be a warrior?"

"Billy!" his mother snapped as she entered carrying a tray.

"Mrs. Gentry, may I answer him?" Tall Fellow asked.

"Well..."

"Billy, first of all I won't be around long enough to teach you to be a warrior," Tall Fellow explained, "and second, there's no need for warriors anymore. What you have to do is mind your mama, learn your lessons, and grow up to be a good, hardworking man like your pa. Understand?"

"Yes, sir," Billy said unhappily.

Mrs. Gentry gave Tall Fellow a look that said, "Thank you," as she laid out the pie and coffee, along with a glass of milk for Billy.

But as she turned to go back into the kitchen, she heard Billy say something to Faulkner that really concerned her.

"Mr. Faulkner," he said, "it's all over town how you killed a man today, shot him in the street. Can you teach me to do that?"

CHAPTER SEVEN

ARKANSAS, 1875

F aulkner knew he needed Henry Tall Fellow, but that didn't mean he had to like the young half-breed.

Basically, he needed him because of his tracking abilities. The Eastern-educated Faulkner had a natural ability with a gun, but he knew nothing about tracking.

"We need some water," Faulkner said.

"I don't," Tall Fellow said.

"When I said we," Faulkner replied, "I meant me and the horses."

Tall Fellow looked up from the hard, dry ground and stared at Faulkner. The two young men had met in St. Joe, Missouri, and discovered they were after the same man, Tom Buckland. Since Buck-land was riding with his gang, they had decided to join forces, but they had been rubbing each other the wrong way since the beginning.

"There's a water hole just ahead."

"You know that for a fact?"

"I've been all over Arkansas and the territories, Faulkner," Tall Fellow said. "I know where all the water is."

Tall Fellow went down on one knee, dropping his horse's reins to the ground behind him. Faulkner backed his horse up, so the animal wouldn't cast a shadow where Tall Fellow was examining the ground. He'd only been advised about that once by the half-breed, but he was never a man who had to be told something more than once. It was one of the reasons he'd managed to go through four years of college in two and a half.

"What else do you know?" Faulkner asked.

"*1* know every inch of this land," Tall Fellow said, "and every town a man like Buckland can get help."

Tall Fellow stood up, walked away from his horse and stared at the ground.

"Do you know enough not to step on a rattler?" Faulkner asked.

"What?"

"Don't move. If you take a step back you'll step on it."

"You better not be kidding, Faulkner."

"It's kind of small," Faulkner said. "I never saw one like that before. It's not even two feet long."

Tall Fellow felt new sweat joining with the perspiration that was already dripping from his chin. It sounded as if Faulkner was describing a pygmy rattler, which, despite their size, were very deadly.

Tall Fellow had to look, and in doing so dragged his heel half an inch—just enough to startle the rattler. It started its death serenade and lifted its head, but before Tall Fellow could do anything, Faulkner drew and fired. The rattler's head flew off, and the body dropped to the ground. The rattle fell silent.

Tall Fellow turned quickly and scanned the ground for any more, then looked up at Faulkner, who was holstering his gun.

"Get in the habit of replacing the spent shells in your gun right away," he said, "before you holster it."

Faulkner stared at Tall Fellow, took his gun back out, ejected the spent shell and replaced it with a live one, then holstered it again. New to the West, he admitted to himself that he could learn a lot from Henry Tall Fellow, but he didn't have to like it.

"You're welcome," he said.

Tall Fellow walked to his horse. The pony was experienced and had not spooked at the sound of the rattler.

As he mounted up Tall Fellow muttered, "Nice shooting," just loud enough for Faulkner to hear it.

———

LATER THAT NIGHT THEY CAMPED, built a fire and made some coffee. They were traveling with dried beef jerky and nothing else. Tall Fellow had said they should travel light, and this was one of the first nights since they had left St. Joe a week ago that he was making coffee. Faulkner had almost gotten used to a cold camp.

"Wind's shifted," Tall Fellow explained, "and they're ahead of us. They won't smell the coffee."

"Why didn't we take the snake?" Faulkner said. "I understand you people eat them."

"'You people'?" Tall Fellow asked.

"I don't mean Indians," Faulkner lied, "I mean Westerners."

"If you're going to stay in the West you're gonna have to stop talking like that."

Faulkner bit off a piece of jerky and said, "You're probably right"

"What's an educated sonofabitch like you doing out here anyway?" Tall Fellow asked. "Weren't you being groomed for banking or politics or something?"

"Both," Faulkner said, impressed that Tall Fellow had been able to guess that.

"What happened?"

"I got disillusioned."

"Why?" Tall Fellow asked.

"They're all thieves," Faulkner said. "I figured if I'm going to deal with crooks I might as well come out here and make a living at it."

"Killing them?" Tall Fellow asked. "That's a living?"

"And what you do is different?"

"I track 'em and take them back for bounty," Tall Fellow said. "That's very different."

"Dead or alive?"

"Usually their choice."

"I don't see that it's so different."

"What do you feel when you kill a man, Faulkner?" Tall Fellow asked. "Or have you even killed one yet?"

Actually, he'd killed four since coming west. The first one was free, but he'd gotten paid for the next three, more each time. It just seemed like an easy way to make a living, and the men he'd killed had deserved it.

"I don't feel anything," he said.

"That's good," Tall Fellow said.

"Why do you say that?"

"If you're gonna kill men for a living," the bounty hunter said, "it's good not to feel anything—otherwise they'd haunt you."

"Haunt me?"

"In your sleep."

"I sleep fine," Faulkner said.

"Again," Tall Fellow said, "good for you."

"Where are we headed tomorrow?" Faulkner asked, changing the subject.

"Rock City is just ahead of us," Tall Fellow said. "I think Buckland is headed there."

"Any law?"

"None," Tall Fellow said. "This territory is covered by federal marshals out of Judge Parker's court in Fort Smith. And he ain't got nearly enough men to cover the area. We'll be on our own—especially if we have to go into the territories. We'll end up facing not only every kind of lowlife outlaw there is, but also some Indians."

"You're an Indian," Faulkner pointed out. "That should help us."

"I'm half white," Tall Fellow said. "That won't be any help at all."

"You haven't got any objection to killing Buck-land and his men, have you?" Faulkner asked.

"None," Tall Fellow said. "If that's what it takes. You got any objection to takin' the first watch?"

"None."

Tall Fellow rolled himself in his blanket and turned his back. Moments later he said over his shoulder, "Don't look directly into the fire. It'll destroy your night vision."

Just something else Faulkner would always remember.

CHAPTER EIGHT

Whe they rode into Rock City, Arkansas, they attracted very little attention, two skinny kids in their early twenties, one a half-breed and the other not much to look at. Faulkner's horse was a nondescript dun; Tall Fellow's horse was a useful mustang that wasn't much to look at.

"This is good," Tall Fellow said to Faulkner. "People aren't really looking at us."

"Jesus," Faulkner said, "people live here?"

The buildings were falling down, many of them had false fronts, and in some places where the buildings had fallen down, tents had been erected in the rubble.

"How long have you been out here, anyway?" Tall Fellow asked, meaning the West.

"More than a year."

Faulkner had killed his first man back east. It was only since he'd come west that he'd killed for money.

"You're gonna see a lot worse than this," Tall Fellow said. "You should try living on a reservation."

"That why you talk so well?" Faulkner asked. "You grew up on a reservation?"

"I was educated," Tall Fellow said. "Not college like you, but I had a mother who made sure I was educated."

"A white mother?"

"What of it?"

"Nothing," Faulkner said. "I was just asking."

They reined in their horses in front of the first saloon they came to, the Ruby Palace.

"Not much of a palace," Faulkner said as they dismounted.

"It doesn't have to be," replied Tall Fellow. "We just want a beer and some information."

They tied off their horses and entered the saloon. It was midday and the place was full. No music, a couple of tired-looking girls working the floor, no gaming tables.

"Are they going to answer our questions?" Faulkner asked.

"Why not?" Tall Fellow asked. "We're just a couple of harmless-looking kids."

Back then Tall Fellow was wearing his hair short, a worn hat jammed down on his head. He could pass for white if he had to, and in a saloon he usually had to. It was years later that he started wearing his hair long, with no hat.

They approached the bar and asked for two beers. The bartender eyed Tall Fellow suspiciously, but in the end he served them. It helped that Tall Fellow sounded educated.

"We're lookin' for some boys who rode with Tom Buckland," Tall Fellow said to the bartender.

"You law?"

"We look like law?" Faulkner asked.

"Ya look like a coupla snot-nosed kids gonna get themselves in trouble for askin' after the wrong people."

"That's our business," Tall Fellow said.

"If ya don't mind trouble, ya might try that table in the corner," the bartender said, jerking his chin in that direction. "I think a coupla those boys rode in with Buckland."

"Buckland ain't rode out yet?" Faulkner asked, adopting the bartender's speech pattern.

"He don't check in with me, but last I heard he was still in town."

"Much obliged."

Faulkner and Tall Fellow turned their backs to the bar, leaned on it and scanned the room. There were four men playing poker at the table the bartender had indicated.

"That was pretty good," Tall Fellow said grudgingly.

"Thanks. Sometimes it pays to say 'ain't.'"

"How do you want to play this?"

"I'm looking for Buckland," Faulkner said. "His men are of no interest to me."

"They mean money to me."

"Then you call it."

"We could split up," Tall Fellow said. "You take them, and I'll go look for Buckland."

"Like I said," Faulkner repeated, "these men mean nothing to me. Besides, do we know how many men Buckland has with him?"

"Not exactly," Tall Fellow said, "but certainly more than two."

"So taking these would just alert the others," Faulkner said.

"You make a good point," the half-breed bounty hunter said. "We should find Buckland and take him first."

"I'm going to kill him," Faulkner said. "That's my job."

"By the way," Tall Fellow asked, "who's paying you to kill him?"

"That's my business."

"All right, then." Tall Fellow turned and set down his half-finished beer. "Let's go and find him."

"You're not going to try to stop me from killing him, are you?" Faulkner asked.

"I've seen you shoot the head off a pygmy snake with a split-second draw," Tall Fellow said. "No, I won't try to stop you, but the bounty is mine."

"Agreed," Faulkner said. "I'm getting my pay."

Tall Fellow stared at Faulkner. He almost asked the killer how much he was getting, but decided against it. He didn't want to know if it was more than his bounty.

CHAPTER NINE

1898

When they left Center, Montana, Mrs. Gentry was not sorry to see them go. She could have used the money for their rooms had they stayed longer, but she did not like the impression they were making on Billy.

The night before, at the supper table, Faulkner had told Billy, "No, son, I can't teach you to shoot a man down. That you'll have to learn on your own as you get older—if there's even any need for it."

"You don't think there will be?" Billy asked.

"Billy, I think soon there won't be any need for me to carry guns."

The next day, as they rode out, Tall Fellow said, "Last night, what you said about there not being any need for guns?"

"Yeah?"

"You believe that?"

"We're approaching a new century, Henry," Faulkner said. "Yeah, I believe that. Oh, I think there'll be war, and guns to fight the wars with, but the days of a man walking around carrying a gun? Those days will pass."

"And what will that mean to men like us?"

"It'll mean we're old."

TALL FELLOW HAD ASCERTAINED that Jack Sunday and his boys were in Colorado.

"You ever hear of Ouray?" he asked. "Red Mountain?"

"Mining towns, weren't they?"

"Once upon a time," Tall Fellow said. "Might still be, for all I know."

"That where they're supposed to be?"

"Supposed to be headed that way. If we don't find them there, we can pick up their trail."

They rode a while in silence and then Tall Fellow asked, "Remember Buckland, Tom Buckland?"

"How could I forget?" Faulkner said. "First time we rode together. I learned a lot from you."

"You know," Tall Fellow said, "you really impressed me the day you shot the head off that pygmy rattler."

"Impressed myself, too," Faulkner said. "I was aiming for the fattest part of that snake."

Tall Fellow looked at Faulkner and said, "I think the head was the fattest part of that snake."

———

JACK SUNDAY LOOKED the rancher in the eye when he shot him. He watched the life go out of the man—or maybe that had already happened when he raped the man's wife and his twelve-year-old daughter in front of him. Yeah, maybe the life had already gone out of him.

He turned and looked at his five men.

"Don't just stand there," he said. "Go through the house and take anything of value."

One man was holding the sobbing wife by her arms, pulling them painfully behind her, and another man was holding the strangely quiet daughter around her waist, pulling her body tightly against his. The clothing of both females was in tatters.

"What about these women?" one of the men asked.

"Drop 'em," Sunday said. "We don't kill women."

The two men released the females. The wife crawled to her husband and draped herself over his body, sobbing uncontrollably. The daughter simply lay where she fell, unmoving.

"What about us?" asked the man who had been holding the wife. "We get to use the women?"

"No time," Sunday said.

"Can we take 'em with us?"

"What for?" Sunday asked. "There's plenty of whores for you where we're going. Now get goin'," he said. "Search the house, upstairs and down. We got to be on our way."

Another man came in from outside.

"We got the horses, boss."

"The ones I said?"

"Yeah, real good stock."

"Okay, get 'em ready to travel."

Sunday stared down at the crying woman and the catatonic daughter while his men ransacked the house. The daughter might have been worth taking with them, if she were any good anymore, but she seemed to have lost her mind. She was gonna be a pretty one when she got older, prettier even than her ma. But he didn't like that vacant look in her eyes.

Well, whatever happened to her, she'd been broken in.

His men came down with their arms full, carrying clothes and jewelry. One man had a chair.

"What the hell are we gonna do with that?" Sunday demanded.

"It looks real comfortable."

"You gonna carry that on your horse?"

"Sure, I can ride with it."

"Well, go ahead then, but I'm tellin' you now if it gets in the way it's gonna get left by the side of the road—"

"Okay."

"—along with you!"

CHAPTER TEN

F aulkner and Tall Fellow stopped in Denver. Faulkner had not bought a horse in Center. He hadn't wanted to stay in town any longer than he had to.

"This horse is stove in, Mister," Thatcher had told him. "You need a new one."

"I'll pick one up soon," he'd said to the livery man. "Thanks."

"I ain't just tryin' ta make a sale," Thatcher had answered. "I just don't wanna see you get stranded somewhere."

"I'm not riding alone, so that won't happen," Faulkner said, "but thanks." He paid the man more money than he asked for.

As he mounted up to meet Tall Fellow outside the man asked, "Hey, that feller you killed?"

"Yeah?"

"He deserve it?"

"Does it make a difference?"

"It does to me."

Faulkner nodded.

"Oh, yeah, he deserved it."

―――――

THEY STOPPED in Denver to refresh themselves and to get Faulkner a decent animal. They checked into the Hotel Metropole near the Broadway Theater on 18th Street and Broadway.

The desk clerk gave Tall Fellow a look, but apparently had instructions not to turn away any business. Each got his own room.

For the sake of convenience, they ate in the hotel restaurant. Luckily, it was one of the best in town. They ordered steaks and caught up on each other's lives since they'd last seen each other over a year earlier.

"You know," Tall Fellow said at one point, "we did this last time."

"Did what?"

"Talked, compared notes, caught up, and you know what?" Tall Fellow asked.

"What?"

"Nothing's changed."

"What did you expect to change, Henry?"

"I don't know, something," Tall Fellow said. "You know how old I am?"

"Forty-five moons?"

"Don't get smart," Tall Fellow said, "but yes, I'm forty-five years old. You know what that makes you?"

"Younger than you."

"Forty-four," Tall Fellow said, "for another few months."

"You remember my birthday?"

"Never mind."

"I don't remember yours."

"It's not important."

"I know. That's why I don't remember it."

"You know, I don't remember you having a sense of humor," Tall Fellow said. "You've always been a dour, dark man—especially in your youth."

"And I don't remember you being so sour on your life," Faulkner said. "Aren't you doing what you want to do?"

Tall Fellow hesitated before answering, played with his food.

"Maybe I'm not anymore...maybe. Are you?"

Faulkner shrugged.

"What else should I do?"

"How much longer can you do it?" Tall Fellow asked. "Back in Center you said it yourself. The day of the money gun is coming to an end."

"I didn't say it that way."

"It's what you meant."

"It's still a ways off," Faulkner said.

"Like how far? Six years? The twentieth century isn't going to have room for us, and we'll be fifty then."

"So?"

"Then what?"

"Then nothing."

"What does that mean?"

"It means nothing," Faulkner said again. "We'll be dead, and there'll be nothing."

"So we're gonna be dead in six years?"

"Maybe sooner," Faulkner said. "In fact, I might kill you myself if you keep this up."

"I'm just making conversation."

"Let's change the subject," Faulkner said. "What about dessert?"

———

FAULKNER DID NOT WANT to think about the future. Lately, he'd been thinking about the past, and that was enough of a waste of time. But at least he knew what had happened in the past. The future was a mystery, and rather than try to guess what was going to happen, he preferred to live it. He knew how old he was; he knew how outdated what he did for a living would probably become. He didn't need to be told those things.

They each had a piece of pie and then Tall Fellow suggested a walk to a saloon.

"Not me," Faulkner said. "I got a nice bed waiting in a real nice hotel room, and I'm going use it. I'll meet you for breakfast in the morning, and then I'll buy a horse and we can be on our way."

"Come on," Tall Fellow said, "one drink. It's early, too early to go to bed. Maybe we'll find some music and girls, or a card game."

"If I go to my room you're still going to go look for those things, aren't you?" Faulkner asked.

"Yes."

Faulkner sighed.

"That means by morning you'll probably be in jail, and by the time I find you and bail you out we'll be behind another day."

"See?" Tall Fellow said. "You have to come with me just to save me from myself."

"Or you could go to your room."

"I'll compromise," Tall Fellow said. "One drink."

"Someplace quiet?" Faulkner asked.

Tall Fellow frowned.

"You don't need a woman tonight, Henry. We have to get going early. Or if you really have to have one, tell the desk clerk. He can probably send one up to your room."

"I like to pick out my own."

"Fine, tell him to send up three and you can pick one."

"Come on," Tall Fellow said, standing up. "A walk to a saloon and a drink."

"No trouble?"

"I promise," Tall Fellow said. He put his hand up and added, "Honest injun."

CHAPTER ELEVEN

They walked only two blocks before finding a saloon that Faulkner thought would not offer as many opportunities for trouble as most. There was no music coming from inside, no one staggering around out front, and no loud voices. In addition, all the windows were in one piece.

"I pick this place," he said.

Across the street was a louder, brightly lit, raunchier-looking establishment that Tall Fellow pointed to.

"How about that one?"

"That would be the one if you were actively looking for trouble," Faulkner said. "This is the one for a quiet drink."

Tall Fellow didn't look happy, but didn't balk when Faulkner opened the door, and he followed his friend inside.

The green felt and leather inside still smelled new. Most of the men sitting at tables were wearing suits, and were probably lawyers and bankers.

At the bar stood a few common men, wearing normal work clothes that branded them less educated and not as well paid.

Faulkner and Tall Fellow walked to the bar and waved at the bartender.

"What'll ya have, boys?"

"Two beers," Faulkner said before Tall Fellow could order a whiskey. If there was one myth about Indians that Tall Fellow gave credence to, it was that they couldn't hold their firewater.

The bartender came back and set down the two beers.

"You boys are gonna get in trouble for wearin' them guns on the street," he pointed out.

"Is there an ordinance against it?" Faulkner asked.

"Not exactly, but this ain't the Old West anymore, ya know."

"Then I think we'll drink our beer and keep our guns, thanks," Tall Fellow said.

As the bartender went back to the other end of the bar, Tall Fellow shook his head and said, "See? I'll bet they wouldn't bother us about our guns across the street."

"Never mind," Faulkner said. "Drink your beer and let's get back to the hotel."

"This beer tastes like piss."

"When did you turn into such a complainer?"

"It comes with age," Tall Fellow said. "Don't tell me you ain't been complainin' more recently." He took a sip of beer. "You know, things bother me these days that never bothered me before."

"Well, sure," Faulkner said. "You been around as long as we have, something's bound to start bothering you."

Tall Fellow looked around.

"For instance, the way these fellas in their suits are lookin' at us, like we don't belong."

"They're looking at you, Indian," Faulkner said, "and we don't belong."

"Yeah, but they don't know that."

"I shouldn't have even let you sip that beer," Faulkner said. "You're spoiling for a fight. Come on, let's go."

"I ain't finished."

"You're finished." Faulkner took the mug out of his friend's hand. "It tastes like piss anyway. You said so yourself."

"Then let's go across the street and get a good one."

"Back to the hotel," Faulkner said.

He steered Tall Fellow outside and toward the hotel. He wasn't sure what was eating his friend—the way the men in the saloon had looked at him or his advancing age—but he figured if he could get him back to his room he could avoid trouble—for both of them.

AFTER HE DEPOSITED Tall Fellow in his room, Faulkner went to his own room. He removed his boots and his gun belt. He checked his poke and saw that he had enough for the hotel and for a horse. There was no need to go to the bank. He had money in several bank accounts, and actually had enough to retire if he wanted to—but retire to what? He could never be a storekeeper or a rancher. Neither was in him.

Tall Fellow had been right about one thing. It was too early to go to sleep. It wasn't even fully dark out yet. He lay down on the bed fully dressed, on his back, intending to close his eyes for a few minutes. Next thing he knew he was being awakened by a persistent knocking at his door, and when he opened his eyes it was pitch black.

He got off the bed and walked to the door and turned up the gas lamp on the wall next to it before opening it. There was a policeman in uniform standing in the hall.

"Can I help you?" Faulkner asked.

"Is your name Faulkner?"

"That's right."

"Do you know a man named Henry Tall Fellow?"

Damn it, Faulkner thought. He knew he should not have left Tall Fellow alone.

"What did he do?" Faulkner asked. "The last I saw of him he was in his room."

"Well, he ain't there no more," the policeman said. He was a broad-shouldered man in his forties, bouncing a nightstick in the palm of his hand while he talked.

"Where is he?"

"Jail," the policeman said. "He says the only person he knows in Denver is you."

"Let me get my hat and my boots and I'll be right with you."

CHAPTER TWELVE

Faulkner didn't like going out without a gun, but he was going to a police station, so strapping one on was not advisable. He had a small gun he used as a hideout, but he left that in the room, as well, just in case they decided to search him.

He accompanied the policeman down to the street where a cab was waiting.

"Nice of you to supply transportation," he said to the uniformed man.

"You're gonna have to pay when we get to the other end."

"Fine."

They both got into the cab, although Faulkner was tempted to tell the policeman to get his own. The man sat across from him, still bouncing the nightstick in his palm. Faulkner assumed he was supposed to be intimidated, but it wasn't happening.

He assumed Tall Fellow must have gone out again after he went back to his own room, and had gotten himself into trouble. Faulkner hoped he hadn't killed anybody.

When the cab stopped, Faulkner paid the driver and followed the policeman up a flight of stone steps into a three-story stone building.

"Wait here," the officer said when they got inside.

Faulkner stood right where he was and watched the policeman walk up to the front desk. He watched as the man spoke with another uniformed officer, this one with sergeant's stripes. The sergeant nodded, then waved at Faulkner to come forward.

"You're Faulkner?" he asked, giving him a hard stare.

"That's right."

"Got any identification?"

"No."

The sergeant stared at him.

"You'll have to take my word for it."

"Your friend got drunk and busted up a saloon," the sergeant said. "Will you stand his bail?"

"Yes."

"What about the damages?"

"They'll get paid." Faulkner would make Tall Fellow pay for it.

"Fine," the sergeant said. "Then I'll take your word that you're who you say you are."

"Believe me, Sergeant," Faulkner said, "nobody would want to claim to be me."

"Bail's a hundred dollars," the sergeant said.

"We'll send a bill to your hotel for the damages. You can pay it before you leave town tomorrow."

"Fine."

Faulkner paid the bail and asked for a receipt, just to be difficult. The sergeant handwrote one, then turned to another man and said, "Jensen, go get that Indian."

"Okay, Sarge."

The sergeant looked at Faulkner again.

"You should know better than to let your friend drink," he said. "Indians can't hold their liquor." He accompanied the words with another hard stare.

"He's only half Indian," Faulkner said, "but his white half can't hold it, either."

The sergeant thought that was funny and relaxed a bit. He told the policeman who had fetched Faulkner—and who was still standing by with his nightstick—that he could go.

After that, he gave Faulkner no more hard stares.

When Tall Fellow reached the front desk he saw Faulkner standing there waiting for him. He was still drunk, so his friend seemed to be wavering, but he was there.

"There he is," the sergeant said to Faulkner. "You want him?"

Faulkner eyed his friend critically.

"Do I have a choice?"

CHAPTER THIRTEEN

ROCK CITY, ARKANSAS, 1875

"Okay," Henry Tall Fellow said. "Let's leave these two jaspers be for now. Buckland is the big fish we're after."

"Agreed."

"Thanks," Tall Fellow said dryly.

"So should we split up and look for him?"

"You'd like that, wouldn't you?" Tall Fellow asked. "You could find him, take him and claim the bounty."

"I told you," Faulkner said, "I'm not after any bounty. I'm getting paid."

"Yeah, well, money's money."

"Not to me," Faulkner said. "I don't want any bounty money."

Tall Fellow looked at Faulkner, drawing himself up to his full height, from which he looked down on even the six-foot man next to him.

"You'll kill a man for money, but you look down your nose at me for collecting bounties?"

"I'm not looking down my nose at anybody," Faulkner said. "It's just not something I would choose to do."

Tall Fellow waited a few beats, then said, "I can see you and me are just never gonna get on, boy."

"Well, we won't have to after this is done."

Tall Fellow drained his beer mug and slapped the empty down on the bar loud enough to draw attention from the men standing around them. "Let's take a walk."

———

THE TWO MEN at the table who had ridden into town with Tom Buckland were Ralph and Vern. As Faulkner and Tall Fellow left the saloon, the two men playing cards with Ralph and Vern quit and left. It helped that they had lost all of their money.

Ralph and Vern split the winnings between them, even though one of them had won more than the other. That was the nature of their partnership. They shared everything fifty-fifty—which was not the way Tom Buckland operated. That was one of the reasons they were having second thoughts about joining up with him and the others. They had been discussing the subject before the two men had invited them to play poker, and now they took it up again as if they'd never been interrupted.

"And another thing," Vern said. "I don't mind robbin' a bank or two, but I draw the line at killin' for no reason."

"I'm with you there," Ralph agreed.

Vern regarded his partner from beneath the brim of his hat, which he customarily wore at a rakish angle.

"So how do we get away from him now?" he asked. "We've already pulled a few jobs with him. He ain't about to just let us walk away."

"We'll have to bide our time, wait for the right moment," Ralph said.

"It would be helpful if he'd catch a bullet on the next job."

"Yeah," Ralph agreed, "it would be."

They looked at each other, each wondering if the other would actually do it.

———

BACK OUT ON the main street of Rock City, Faulkner and Tall Fellow looked up and down, wondering where to start first. There was plenty of pedestrian traffic as well as a fair number of buggies and buckboards negotiating the street pitted with ruts and holes. Faulkner was starting to realize that Tall Fellow was more comfortable on the trail than he was in town. He'd noticed it when they had met back in St. Joseph, and again here. He didn't like being around a lot of people.

Tall Fellow had been invaluable in tracking Buckland and his gang across Kansas and nearly into Indian Territory. Faulkner thought that perhaps it was his turn to take the lead—if the half-breed bounty hunter was not too proud to follow.

"You got any idea what Tom Buckland looks like?" he asked the bounty hunter.

"Do you?"

"I've got a description."

"I've got a likeness on a poster."

Tall Fellow pulled the poster from his pocket and unfolded it. He handed it to Faulkner, who thought the drawing fit the description he'd been given.

"We should be able to spot him from this," he said, handing it back.

He had the feeling that the reason Tall Fellow didn't split up had nothing to do with the possibility that Faulkner might steal the bounty. He thought it had more to do with Tall Fellow not wanting to walk around town alone.

"Well," Faulkner said, "we might as well get started. How many saloons can there be in town? He's got to be in one of them. Failing that, we can check hotels."

"And whorehouses," Tall Fellow said. "My information is that he definitely likes whorehouses."

"Okay," Faulkner said, "maybe whorehouses before hotels."

"So," Tall Fellow said, "do you really think we should split up?"

"No," Faulkner said. "We might run into him while he's with other members of his gang. It's probably safer if we stay together."

If the suggestion relieved Tall Fellow, he didn't allow it to show. They started walking. Rock City was not a large town, and it wouldn't take long to walk from one end to the other.

"How much do you know about Buckland?" Faulkner asked.

"I know he rode with Bill Doolin's Wild Bunch for a while," Tall Fellow said. "Lately he's gone out on his own, put his own gang together, and started hitting banks. And I know he's either very brave or very stupid."

"How so?"

"Look where he's holed up," Tall Fellow said. "We ain't so far from Fort Smith, where Judge Parker sits on the bench. Buckland's thumbing his nose at him."

"Then Judge Parker will be real happy when you bring him in."

Tall Fellow didn't comment.

Faulkner knew that Buckland and his gang were hitting banks. He was being paid by a bank president to track and kill Buckland. The one bank teller Buckland had killed while robbing the bank had been the man's wife.

"What about the Wild Bunch?" Faulkner asked.

"What about them?"

"Ever tracked any of them?"

"I leave Bill Doolin and his men to Marshal Bill Tilghman," Tall Fellow said. "Those fellas have a history I don't want to get involved in."

"Have you met Tilghman?"

No," Tall Fellow said, "and I don't know that I want to. I don't think he likes bounty hunters very much." After a moment Tall Fellow added, "And he probably likes hired guns even less."

"Thanks for the warning."

———

THEY MADE a circuit of the town, stopping in three saloons. The decided it wasn't very smart to come out and ask bartenders if they had seen Buckland or any of his gang. Word might reach the outlaw before they did.

They did, however, ask one bartender the location of the whorehouses in town.

"You young fellas lookin' ta get yer ashes hauled, huh?" the man asked.

"Something like that," Faulkner said.

The man gave them two locations, and advised them on which whore to ask for at each.

"Guess you must go pretty often," Faulkner said.

"You kiddin'?" the man asked. "It's the only place I can get away from my wife."

―――

THEY FOUND Buckland at the second whorehouse. When they got in and talked with the madam, they pretended to be his men.

"We need to find our boss," Tall Fellow said. "Is he here?"

"He's been here for days," she said with distaste, "and he's tearin' through my girls. Two of them can't work for a week, and one of them left me. Can you get him out of here?"

Suddenly she seemed to realize she was talking to two of his men. Her hand went to her mouth and she said, "I'm sorry, I didn't mean—"

"Relax," Faulkner said. "We're not really his men."

She dropped her hand and looked at them with interest.

"Are you here to take him away?"

"Yes," Tall Fellow said.

"Not exactly," Faulkner said.

Tall Fellow looked at the woman and said, "I'm here to take him in; he is here to kill him."

"I don't care which one you do," she said, "as long as you get him out of here."

"What room is he in?" Tall Fellow asked.

"One," she said. "Top of the stairs."

"Any of his men up there?" Faulkner asked.

"No, just him and one of my girls, Elena. You'll try not to shoot her, won't you?"

"We'll do our best," Faulkner said.

"I mean," the woman said, "if you have to shoot her to get him I guess you could, but—"

"We won't shoot her," Tall Fellow assured her.

"Anyone else up there?" Faulkner asked.

"There are two more rooms in use," she said. "The other girls are in the parlor."

"Keep them there," Faulkner said. "And you stay there with them."

She went into the parlor and they could hear her telling the other girls that two men had come to take away Buckland. The girls cheered, but she shushed them.

"How do you want to do this?" Faulkner asked.

"Well," Tall Fellow said, "I want to take him, but you want

to kill him. I guess you should go in first. If he kills you, then I'll take him."

Faulkner didn't know if Tall Fellow thought he was being funny, but to him it sounded like a good plan.

"Okay then," he said, drawing his gun. "Let's do it."

CHAPTER FOURTEEN

1898

F aulkner tossed more bacon into the frying pan, then poured two more cups of coffee and reached across the fire to hand one to Tall Fellow.

They had left Denver early that morning, Tall Fellow in an evil mood because he was hungover and sore. Hungover because he had sneaked out after Faulkner left him in his room and gone to that other saloon. Once there he had ordered a bottle of whiskey and commenced drinking it. Three quarters of the way through, he had gotten into a fight with three locals who didn't like having an Indian in their place. By the time the police came, Tall Fellow had the three men out cold on the floor and had thrown a chair through the mirror behind the bar. The police had waded in with their nightsticks...which was the reason he was sore.

He didn't talk during their ride, and Faulkner did not try to get him to talk. Something was bothering his friend, and he was going to leave it to Tall Fellow to tell it when he was ready.

"Thanks," the bounty hunter said, accepting the coffee. He sipped it and said, "I'm sorry."

"For what?"

"I cost you money," he said. "I'll pay you back for the bail and the damages."

"Yeah, you will," Faulkner said. "As soon as we can get you to a bank."

"Don't worry," Tall Fellow said. "You'll get it."

"I'm not worried."

When the bacon was ready Faulkner doled it out and handed Tall Fellow a plate and a fork.

"Don't you want to know what happened?" the half-breed asked.

"I know what happened," Faulkner said. "The police told me what happened."

"Don't you want to know why?"

"That's up to you."

"So you're not going to ask?"

"You want me to ask?"

"No."

"Then I'm not," Faulkner said. "You'll tell me...if and when you're ready to."

They ate in silence, and then Tall Fellow said, "You've always been a good friend, Faulkner."

"Yeah, well... so have you, Indian."

They finished eating and had some more coffee. Then they rolled themselves up in their bedrolls.

"Maybe tomorrow," Tall Fellow said.

"What?"

"Maybe tomorrow I'll tell you."

"Go to sleep, Indian."

———

JACK SUNDAY REINED in his horse, but signaled to the rest of his men to keep going. He turned and watched the straggler. His name was Jerry Hobbs and he was struggling with that damned chair he'd taken from the ranch house.

When he reached Sunday he also reined in.

"Drop it," Sunday said.

"What?"

"Drop the damned chair."

"Aw, Jack—"

"Drop it or I'll drop you," Sunday said. "Your choice. You're slowin' us down."

Hobbs looked at the chair, which he was having trouble

balancing. It was upholstered with green and gold threads and he really liked it, but realistically speaking, when was he ever going to get a chance to sit in it?

And he sure didn't want to die over it.

He dropped it.

"Now catch up to everyone else, Hobbs."

"Right, boss."

Sunday looked down at the chair, lying on its side in the dirt. It reminded him of the ranch and what had gone on there. He allowed himself a moment to smile, then rode on to catch up with the others.

———

"WHAT MAKES you think we're even on their trail?" Faulkner asked.

"I have a friend says he saw Jack Sunday in Denver," Tall Fellow said. "And that he and his men were going to head south."

"South? Southeast? Southwest?"

"South," Tall Fellow said. "He's going to look for a place to hole up until the heat's off. Probably a small town. Maybe an old mining town."

"Sounds like a lot of guesswork to me."

"A lot of my work is guesswork, Faulkner. Don't worry. We'll come across something that tells us we're on the right track."

"Like what?"

"Knowing the reputation of Sunday and his gang," Tall Fellow said, "probably something like that."

He pointed into the distance, where black smoke curled up into the air.

"That's a wood fire," Faulkner said.

"And a big one."

"A house?"

Tall Fellow nodded.

"A house, a barn." He looked at his friend. "Maybe even a whole ranch."

They headed that way to take a look.

CHAPTER FIFTEEN

When Faulkner and Tall Fellow reached the fire they saw that they had been right. It was an entire ranch that was burning—house, barn, bunkhouse, corral. Men from a nearby town and some neighboring ranches were battling the inferno, but to no avail.

"Should we help them?" Tall Fellow asked.

"It's a lost cause, Indian," Faulkner said. "Let's find out if anyone knows how it happened."

They dismounted, walked over to where a potbellied man with a badge was standing. He was too old and fat to fight the fire, but that didn't keep him from barking orders.

"Looks like a lost cause," Tall Fellow commented.

The lawman looked at him, then at Faulkner, but didn't say anything.

"Anybody know how it started?" Faulkner asked.

"Not by accident, that's for sure," the lawman said. "We pulled Hank Foley and his family out. He'd been shot; his wife and daughter had been raped and killed."

"Daughter?" Faulkner asked.

"Twelve," the sheriff said. "It looks like her parents had been killed, but they left her alive. That didn't stop them from settin' the place on fire, though. The girl wouldn't leave her folks."

"Was she injured?"

"She was...slow," the lawman said. "Not right in the head, and bein' raped didn't help. No, she wasn't so injured she couldn't have got out." He looked at the two of them. "She just stayed with her folks and the smoke killed her even before the fire could get to her."

"Jesus," Faulkner said.

"What about the bunkhouse?" Tall Fellow asked.

"Empty. This family had fallen on hard times. They didn't have much, but that didn't keep them from being robbed and killed."

Tall Fellow was examining the ground. Even accounting for the men fighting the fire, he could see that there had been a gang there.

"Anybody see the gang that did it?"

The sheriff looked at Tall Fellow again.

"Folks over at the Emery place saw a bunch of riders go by. If they didn't have a bunch of hands over there with guns, they might've been the ones who got hit. So instead, they kept going until they got here. They also stole some stock out of the corral."

He paused to shout some more orders, but the men were starting to back off now. He turned and looked at Tall Fellow.

"Who you trackin', bounty hunter?"

"Jack Sunday and his gang," Tall Fellow said, not wondering how the lawman knew what he did for a living. "This looks and sounds like their work, right down to the stolen stock."

"Well then, you must be on the right track."

"I guess so."

Now the sheriff looked at Faulkner.

"You a bounty hunter, too?"

"No."

"Well, you ain't law."

"No."

"Then that'd make you a money gun."

Faulkner shrugged.

This time the lawman turned and faced them. His eyes were streaming. Could've been from the smoke, Faulkner thought. Or maybe not.

"Normally, I don't hold with bounty hunters or hired guns," he said, "but I'm tellin' you boys I wish you luck. Track them sonsofbitches and kill them all."

"You formin' a posse?" Tall Fellow asked.

"Yeah. I'm from over in Forsythe, a little ways from here. I ain't gonna get much more than some ranchers and merchants."

"If we stop to join you we'll fall behind," Tall Fellow said.

"I know that," the lawman said. "Just go, track 'em to hell if you have to—and Money Gun?"

"Yeah?"

"Put one in Jack Sunday's head for me, and for this family."

CHAPTER SIXTEEN

While the other men vainly fought the fire, trying to save whatever they could, Tall Fellow walked the grounds, examining the dirt for tracks. It was hard, because the gang had not only ridden their own horses, but had stolen stock as well. Tall Fellow had to try to separate the gang horses from the tracks the firefighters' horses made.

"How we doing?" Faulkner asked, coming up alongside him.

"I think I got them isolated," Tall Fellow said. "See there? The stock they stole are not shod. They're gonna leave an easy trail to follow."

"Good," Faulkner said, "let's follow it."

Tall Fellow looked over at the sheriff and the firefighters. The fire was going out, more by itself than from anything the men had done. The wood was beginning to smolder.

"Shouldn't have done that to the little girl," he said.

"Hey, Indian," Faulkner said. "Wasn't it you who taught me that you and I can't afford personal feelings in our business?"

"Yeah, but...a little girl, and she wasn't even right in the head." He looked at Faulkner. "That wasn't right, Faulkner. Did she even know what was happening to her?"

Faulkner slapped his friend on the back and said, "Track 'em, and we'll ask them."

They mounted up, took a last look at the tableau they were leaving behind, then rode off.

⸻

As THEY LEFT the ranch behind, the tracks became easier for Tall Fellow to see. He seemed to find particular characteristics for one of the shod horses and one of the unshod horses. Faulkner could tell the tracks of a horse with shoes from the ones without, but anything more individual than that escaped him. He remembered how impressed he'd been by Tall Fellow's skills the first time they'd met—not that he would have admitted it back then. They had both been much too full of themselves to admit anything like that—even though Tall Fellow did admit later that he was impressed with Faulkner's ability with a gun. Later in their friendship Tall Fellow said if they could have combined their talents, they would have been the perfect bounty hunter. Faulkner never really appreciated the observation.

"How far ahead?" Faulkner asked.

"Judging from the tracks and the fire, a day," Tall Fellow said. "Those boys were fighting that fire for a while, and it burned hot. They were too late to do any good when they got there."

"How'd they know about the little girl, then?"

Tall Fellow shrugged.

"Maybe the father lived long enough to drag her to safety. Or the mother. Who knows?"

Faulkner looked at the sky.

"Might as well camp here," he said. "You can't track them in the dark."

Tall Fellow looked up.

"I could with a better moon."

"The horses need rest, anyway," Faulkner said. "I'll build the fire." He handed Tall Fellow the reins of his horse. They may not have ridden together for a while, but they fell into their familiar roles. Faulkner made camp; Tall Fellow cared for the horses.

They sat around the fire, drank coffee and ate dried beef jerky. Some things never changed, Faulkner thought. Whenever they were tracking someone they traveled light, coffee and jerky really being the only necessities. With beef jerky they were able to make cold camps when they needed to.

"I'm gettin' old," Tall Fellow said.

"We're all getting old, Indian."

Apparently, his friend was ready to talk about what was bothering him. Faulkner allowed him to get to it in his own time.

"You know, there was a time I could have tracked these jaspers in the dark," Tall Fellow said. "But those times are past."

Faulkner didn't comment. There was something else coming.

"You remember the first time we rode together?" Tall Fellow asked.

"Tom Buckland."

"Yeah, Tom Buckland."

More silence.

"You remember the way you shot the head off that pygmy rattler?" Tall Fellow asked.

"Scared the shit out of you."

"That was some shot," the half-breed said. "Man, you could've shot the eye out of that snake, and I could see sign for miles."

"I remember." Faulkner thought he could still shoot the eye out of a rattler, but he kept quiet. This wasn't about him.

"*I* can't see so good anymore."

"What?"

Tall Fellow waved his hand in front of his face.

"My eyes. Not so good anymore."

"What are you saying?"

"I went to a doctor," Tall Fellow said. "Supposed to be pretty good one, too."

"And?"

"And...he says within five years I'll be totally blind."

"Well, crap," Faulkner said.

"Yeah," Tall Fellow said, "that was pretty much my reaction, too."

CHAPTER SEVENTEEN

ROCK CITY, ARKANSAS, 1875

Faulkner went up the stairs first, followed by Tall Fellow. Upstairs they could hear voices—a man yelling, a woman crying out in either pain or pleasure. When they reached the top they could tell that the voices were not coming from the room Tom Buckland was in.

They stepped to the door, taking up position on either side. Before they could move, a man came out of the room across from them, hitching up his pants and carrying his gun belt. He stopped short when he saw the two men standing there holding guns.

"What the hell?" he shouted, and inexplicably went for his gun.

"Damn it!" Faulkner felt he had no choice. The man was grabbing for his gun with bad intentions. Faulkner shot him dead center, driving him back into the room. At the same time, Tall Fellow kicked open the door of room one and ducked inside.

Faulkner followed him in, but all they saw was a skinny, naked girl on a bed.

"He went out the window," she yelled, pointing.

Neither man was distracted by her tiny breasts and bony hips, and they both rushed to the window.

"I'll go," Tall Fellow said.

"I'll take the front."

The second-floor window led to a low roof above an alley. Faulkner sprinted down the stairs, hoping he'd catch Buckland coming out of the alley.

Nobody got between Faulkner and the front door until he came charging out and ran into two middle-aged women carrying packages. He tried to avoid them, but while he did manage to miss running into then, he scattered their packages all over the street.

"That horrible, horrible place!" one of them shouted.

When Faulkner reached the alley it was empty.

"Tall Fellow!" he shouted.

Holding his gun ready, he entered the mouth of the alley, eyes and ears ready. There were a lot of possibilities. Buckland could have been hiding somewhere in the alley—there were doorways, crates and barrels—or he could have beaten Faulkner to the mouth of the alley. Maybe he didn't even come down the alley. Tall Fellow could have been chasing Buckland behind the buildings. Faulkner quickened his pace, ready for Buckland to jump out at him. It didn't happen. He reached the back of the alley and was now underneath the window.

The skinny whore leaned out the window. Faulkner suddenly noticed how pale her skin was, and how dark brown her nipples appeared. She was not an attractive girl.

"They went that way," she said, pointing.

Sure enough, Tall Fellow was chasing the outlaw behind the buildings.

"Where does that lead?" Faulkner asked.

"If you keep on goin' you'll get to the livery stable."

He waved with his left hand and began to run with his gun still held in his right. Tall Fellow would be in trouble if Buckland managed to get to some of his men.

———

RALPH AND VEIN left the saloon and started walking toward their hotel. They were across the street from the whorehouse when a man came bursting out, knocking packages from the hands of two women.

"Ain't that where Buckland is?" Ralph asked.

"That is where Buckland has been since we got here," Vern said.

"Wonder what's goin' on?" Ralph asked.

The man looked around, then turned and went into the alley next to the building.

"He's chasing somebody," Ralph said.

"Maybe he's going to solve our problem for us," Vern said.

"Where are the others?"

"I don't know," Vern said.

"Well…what do we do?" Ralph asked.

"As far as I'm concerned," Vern said, "we can just wait."

———

FAULKNER KEPT RUNNING, alert for the sound of shots he hoped he wouldn't hear. He wanted to catch up to Tall Fellow before any shooting started. He probably should have gone out the window right after the bounty hunter.

This was one of the reasons he had chosen a profession where he would be able to work alone. He always thought having a partner would be more trouble than it was worth. Here was a perfect example. Without Tall Fellow he would have been the one going out the window, and he'd be in pursuit of Tom Buckland.

Where was that goddamned Indian, anyhow?

CHAPTER EIGHTEEN

1898

When they woke the next morning, they had coffee in silence. Faulkner stole glances at his friend, as if now that he knew, maybe his eyes would look different, but they didn't.

"What about a second opinion?" Faulkner asked.

"Had one," Tall Fellow said. "Went to San Francisco to see a specialist. He confirmed what the other sawbones said. No hope. In five years my eyesight will be totally gone."

They fell silent again, until Tall Fellow said, "You know what good a blind tracker is?"

Faulkner shrugged. He knew that if he ever went blind he'd put his gun to his head and pull the trigger. Tall Fellow, being the same type of man he was, would probably do the same.

"I'll get the horses."

Faulkner kicked the fire to death, then stowed the coffeepot in his saddlebags. When Tall Fellow came over with the horses, they each saddled their own and mounted up.

"Looks like they're headed for the mountains," Tall Fellow said. "Might be wanting to hole up in a mining town like Red Mountain or Ouray."

"Well, you're on their trail," Faulkner said. "They're not going to get away."

"No," Tall Fellow said, "they're not."

———

"WHAT IS THIS PLACE?" Hobbs asked.

"It's called Ouray," Sunday said. "The mines here are playin' out some, but the town's hangin' on. It's a good place to stop over."

Ouray had never experienced a fire like the ones that had wiped out many other mining towns. This was the 1900s and there were families living there, unconvinced that the mines would play out completely. The railroad had almost come in once or twice, and there was still some hope that would happen, as well.

"There law here?" Hobbs asked.

"Far as I know," Sunday said. "We're here to lie low, though. Pass the word that any man starts trouble, I'll kill 'im. I want a good night's sleep and we all get out of here in the mornin', nice and peaceful."

"Gotcha, boss."

"That means you, too, Hobbs. Understand?"

"I said I gotcha, boss," Hobbs said, looking hurt.

"Just wanted to make sure."

They rode into town without the horses they had stolen. They were able to sell those along the way and make a pretty penny for them. Sunday figured he could keep his boys in check until morning. He'd let them loose on the next likely ranch they came to. He wanted to keep Ouray as a place he could go when he just needed to eat, drink and sleep. No trouble.

There had to be one place like that for a man like Jack Sunday to go, didn't there?

———

"HOW FAR IS HOORAY?" Faulkner asked.

"It's Ouray," Tall Fellow said. He pronounced it "yer-ray."

"Well, how far?"

"We could make it there tonight, if we have some luck."

At that moment luck did strike them, but it was bad. Faulkner's horse suddenly took a bad step and almost went down.

"Whoa!" Faulkner said, dropping to the ground immediately. He lifted the horse's front right leg, then dropped it. "This stupid sonofabitch stepped on something."

He was pissed not because he had become attached to the horse, but because he had just paid good money for the animal in Denver.

"What was that you said about luck?" he asked, looking up at Tall Fellow.

"There are some ranches up ahead," Tall Fellow said. "We might be able to pick up a mount there."

"I hate having to pay for another damn horse," Faulkner said.

Tall Fellow dismounted and took a look at the horse's hoof.

"It's bad, but not permanent," he said, dropping the hoof to the ground. It never got there. The animal kept it lifted. "I'll bet you could trade it and just throw in a little cash."

"I suppose so."

"Come on," Tall Fellow said. "We'll walk him so we don't do any more damage."

"So much for getting to hooray tonight," Faulkner said.

"Ouray," Tall Fellow corrected. "It's yer-ray."

"Yeah, yeah…"

––––––––

"THERE," Tall Fellow said an hour later. "A ranch, and a fairly good-sized one."

"It's not on fire," Faulkner said. "That's encouraging."

"Maybe they bypassed it because they'd already burned one down and killed the family that lived there. Maybe Jack Sunday just likes to do one of those a day."

"Might play havoc with a man's digestion, huh?"

"Not a man like Sunday."

"You talk like you know him."

"I just know the name," Tall Fellow said, "but I know him better now that I heard what he did to that little girl."

They started down the hill toward the ranch.

CHAPTER NINETEEN

As the men approached the ranch house they could see that the corral was full of horses. This was good news for Faulkner—as long as the owner was willing to part with one.

Their approach was noticed by several men who were milling about the house and barn. None of them were armed. As they reached the house one man broke away from the others and approached them. Faulkner noticed two or three men moving toward what appeared to be a bunk-house, and figured they wanted to be close to their guns, just in case. One man stepped into the barn and came out holding a rifle. Faulkner didn't feel threatened, though. He was sure it was just a precaution on their part.

"Afternoon," the man said. "Help ya?"

"I hope so," Faulkner said. "My horse went lame. I was hoping I could buy one from you—maybe trade."

"Well, we got plenty of horses," the man said. "What's wrong with yours?"

"Looks like a stone bruise," Tall Fellow said.

The man nodded. "My name's Christian," he said, with no indication of whether it was first or last. "I'm foreman here."

"You got the authority to sell?" Faulkner asked.

"I do," Christian said. "I'll have my man look at your horse while you look over our stock and pick out one you like. Then we can talk price."

Christian waved and another man came over.

"Unsaddle this man's horse and check the animal out. He may be using it to trade as partial payment for a new mount."

"Okay, Chris."

The other man led the horse toward the barn.

"Let's go over to the corral."

The three of them walked over, Tall Fellow still leading his own horse. When they reached the corral, he tied the horse's reins to it.

"Good-looking stock," Faulkner said.

"We pride ourselves on raising good horses," Christian said.

"Mind if I go in?"

"Go ahead, pick yerself out a good one."

"Henry?" Faulkner was always careful not to call Tall Fellow by his Indian name in front of others.

The two men opened the corral gate, entered and closed it behind them. They walked among the horses.

"See," Tall Fellow said right away, "this is what I'll miss when I'm totally blind."

"What's that?"

Tall Fellow pointed to the ground. All Faulkner saw was a jumble of tracks, hoof-print atop hoof-print.

"I don't see it."

Tall Fellow stooped and pointed.

"There."

Now Faulkner saw it.

"Is that the track we've been following?"

"One of them," Tall Fellow said. "These fellas bought the horse from Jack Sunday."

"What do we do now?" Faulkner said.

"There's no brand on the horses," Tall Fellow said. "Probably because the guy had no ranch hands. Maybe he was going to hire some and brand the stock, but it wasn't done."

"So we can't prove these are stolen horses."

"No."

"Well," Faulkner said, "I need a horse, and you need to catch up to Jack Sunday. Let's just buy a horse and keep moving."

"I wonder if these men—this man, Christian—knew they were stolen? Or is he just trying to impress his boss with a corral full of horses when he gets back?"

"Doesn't matter to us, Indian," Faulkner said. "Once we

catch Sunday we can send a telegram, if you want, tell that sheriff where he can find these horses. Let him determine if they're stolen, and then take legal action."

Tall Fellow thought a moment, then said, "Why not? We've already lost enough time."

"Then help me pick out a horse and let's get back on the trail."

They did not choose one of the best horses in the corral because Faulkner did not want to pay top dollar.

"You always scrimp on your horses," Tall Fellow complained. "That's why you go through so many."

"I just need four legs and a back to sit on," Faulkner said. "Hey, maybe if we tell them we know they're stolen we can buy even cheaper."

"Never mind," Tall Fellow said. "We're not taking the best, but let's not take the worst."

They decided on a six-year-old mare who looked like she'd have a good wind.

They pointed out the horse to Christian, who nodded.

"Not bad," he said. "Not one of the best, but not bad. Eddie tells me your horse is pretty sound except for the stone bruise. I think we can come to a fair price."

They talked a while and Faulkner paid what Tall Fellow would later say was not a fair price.

"It was worth it to me not to have to dicker," Faulkner would say. "I hate dickering."

"You would've made a horrible horse trader."

"Thank God."

"I'll need my bridle," Faulkner told Christian, who sent a man to the stable to fetch it. He slipped the bridle over the mare's head and led her from the corral. Eddie took her to the barn to saddle her while Faulkner and Christian closed the deal.

"You fellas got time for a drink?"

"We've got to get on our way," Faulkner said.

"Who you trackin'?"

Faulkner and Tall Fellow exchanged a look. "Who says we're tracking anybody?'

"You just got the look."

Faulkner glanced around. The men who had gone to the bunkhouse had strapped on guns. Several other men had retrieved their rifles. He had the feeling if Christian thought they'd figured out that the horses were stolen, they would be in trouble.

"We just have to keep moving," Faulkner said.

He knew the remark gave the impression that they were being tracked, not doing the tracking, but that seemed best at the moment. He got a look of approval from Tall Fellow that only he was able to read.

Eddie brought the horse back out, saddled and ready to travel. He handed the reins to Faulkner.

"There ya go," he said.

Faulkner wanted to check his saddlebags, but decided not to do it in front of them. Besides, there wasn't much of value in them to be stolen— an extra shirt, a backup gun, a coffeepot. If they wanted any of those things, they were welcome to them.

They both mounted up and started their ride out, turning to exchange a wave with Christian.

"A lot of guns for a ranch," Tall Fellow said.

"An odd ranch," Faulkner said. "They buy stolen horses and claim to have raised them."

"I wonder if there even is an owner," Tall Fellow said. "That Christian shows a little more authority than a foreman should."

"Even more reason to have a lawman come back and check this place out," Faulkner said. "Maybe from the next town?"

"Don't know how much law there is between here and Ouray," Tall Fellow said. "But we can send a telegram. Maybe a federal marshal."

"Let's move a little faster before they change their minds," Faulkner suggested, and they both gigged their horses into a canter, then a trot, and then a full run.

CHAPTER TWENTY

The extra stop to buy a horse kept them from reaching the town of Ouray that day. They actually camped at the base of the San Juan Mountains, with intentions of continuing in the morning.

Once they started up the mountain, it would be difficult to find tracks on the hard ground. They had to hope that Sunday and his gang had, indeed, continued on to Ouray and not taken a detour somewhere along the way.

Faulkner would have bet a lot that his friend could track a mouse through a snowstorm. But with his announcement about his eyes, they would probably have to depend a little more on luck than they usually did.

"We better stand watch in case they decide to double back this way," Tall Fellow said.

"You figure they're expecting a posse?" Faulkner asked.

"I'm hoping they're going over this mountain to avoid one," the half-breed said. "A posse of an overweight sheriff and a bunch of store clerks is not going to track a gang over a mountain."

Faulkner poured a cup of coffee for Tall Fellow and handed it to him, then one for himself.

"That was good," Tall Fellow said.

"What?"

"You didn't mention my eyes."

"It's not for me to mention," Faulkner said. "They worked pretty good in that corral back there."

"Yeah, some days they work just fine. Other days...and at night...I never know what it's going to be like."

"I can stand the first watch," Faulkner said.

"That might be best," Tall Fellow said. "It will be darkest then. You will see better than me."

———

IN OURAY JACK Sunday met in a saloon with Hobbs and a few of the other men. Of the twelve men who rode with him, four were present. These were his core four, as the others came and went— sometimes killed in action, other times killed by him in a fit of rage.

"I've decided where we are goin' from here," he said to the men.

"Where's that, Jack?" Eddie Hall asked.

"Gunman's Crossing."

They all exchanged a glance.

"Have any of you been there?"

The men shook his head.

"Have you been there, Jack?" Hobbs asked.

"No," Sunday said, "but I'm lookin' forward to it. If it's everything we hear it is, it'll be a place for us to rest for a bit."

"I thought that's why we were here," Hobbs said.

"Here?" Sunday asked. "There's one damn saloon here, and no whorehouse. And not a decent restaurant. No, Gunman's Crossing is where we'll be able to get back—"

He stopped short.

"Get back what, Jack?" Hobbs asked.

"That's all," Jack Sunday said. "We'll be leavin' at first light. Tell the other men."

The four exchanged glances once again.

"Get out!" Sunday shouted.

Other patrons looked over as the four men stood and left Sunday to sit alone.

Jack Sunday needed to get back the fire he usually felt in his belly, the edge he usually lived on. Gunman's Crossing—a notorious, legendary home for outlaws. But part of the story of

Gunman's Crossing was that anyone wishing to stay there had to pay for the right.

Sunday was going to have to come up with a pretty good score between Ouray and Gunman's Crossing in order to raise the money. One last score before taking a restful leave from the robbing and stealing and killing that defined Jack Sunday's life.

CHAPTER TWENTY-ONE

In the morning Henry Tall Fellow woke Faulkner and handed him a cup of coffee.

"No more after this," he said. "The fire is already out."

"Just as well. We should get going."

Faulkner rolled out of his bedroll and got to his feet.

"Can I ask you something?" Tall Fellow asked.

"Sure."

"How are you are hired?" Tall Fellow asked.

"What do you mean?"

"How do people know what you do?" Tall Fellow asked. "How do they know where to find you?"

"Word of mouth," Faulkner said.

"So whoever it is hired you to kill Jack Sunday just tracked you down, person by person, until he found you?"

"Exactly."

"It sounds…painstaking."

"If someone wants to hire my services bad enough," Faulkner said, "they find me."

They saddled their horses, climbed aboard and headed up the mountain.

———

THE SAN JUAN MOUNTAINS were beautiful, but the same could not be said for Ouray. Mining towns did not aspire to beauty, but to functionality. In its time Ouray had functioned just fine. Someday they might see prosperity again. At the moment the town was hanging on, trying not to go the way of most mining towns. That was because, for the most part, it was not inhabited by the transients who were attracted to most mining towns—the gamblers, the merchants, the thieves, pimps and whores—who knew in their hearts that their stay was temporary, until the next big strike was hit.

Ouray was inhabited by miners, merchants and their families, whose intent was to stay and to grow with the town.

However, when Faulkner and Tall Fellow rode in, all they saw was a mining town on the verge of death. Later, in their absence, it would rise again as new minerals were discovered in the mines. For now, the rutted, muddy streets were empty, and the smell of panic and despair hung in the air.

They rode up to the saloon, dismounted and tied their horses to a rickety post.

"Gone," Tall Fellow said.

"The town?" Faulkner asked, thinking his friend was advancing an opinion.

"Sunday and his men," Tall Fellow said. "They wouldn't stay here more than a day. There's nothing here for them."

"Well," Faulkner said, "if they were here, this is the place to find it out. Why would they come here and not go to the saloon?"

"Agreed."

They approached the ramshackle building that housed the saloon and entered. Inside it was empty due to the early hour. What miners were left were hard at work. A bored-looking bartender stood up straight as they entered, maybe just in anticipation of having something to do.

"Help you gents?"

"Two beers and some information," Faulkner said.

"I got both for ya," the barman said. He drew the two beers and laid them on the scarred, pitted bar in front of them. "There's your beer. What's this information you need?"

"We're tracking about ten or twelve men led by an outlaw named Jack Sunday," Tall Fellow said.

"Well, let's see…"

"This is a yes or no question, my friend," Tall Fellow said, cutting him off. "Were they here or weren't they?"

"There was a bunch of fellers in here yesterday, and I do believe I heard one of them be called Jack. So I guess the answer's...yes."

"And where are they now?"

"That I don't know," the bartender said. "They left town this mornin'." He shrugged. "Could be anywhere by now."

Faulkner sipped the beer, then turned his head and spit it out onto the floor.

"I think I know why they left."

"Yeah, I know. Ain't very good. Yer better off with whiskey."

Faulkner did not want Tall Fellow to get started drinking whiskey, so he said, "No, that's okay. We have to be on our way."

"You gonna follow them fellers?"

"We are," Faulkner said.

"Bounty hunter?"

Tall Fellow asked, "Why?"

"Well, seems to me a bounty hunter might be willing to pay for a little...information?"

"What kind of information?" Tall Fellow asked.

The bartender hesitated.

Tall Fellow took a dollar out of his pocket and placed it on the bar.

"That's all?"

"Until I hear the information," Tall Fellow said, "I won't know what it's worth, will I?"

The man picked up the dollar and put it in his own pocket.

"Them fellers had a conversation last night about where they was goin' from here. That worth more?"

Tall Fellow put another dollar on the bar. The bartender picked it up and put it in the same pocket as the other one.

"They mentioned Gunman's Crossing."

Faulkner and Tall Fellow exchanged a look.

"But there ain't such a place for real, is there?" the bartender asked.

Tall Fellow put five one-dollar pieces on the bar and he and Faulkner walked out.

"What do you think?" Tall Fellow asked when they reached the horses.

"Why not?" Faulkner asked. "It's as good a place as any for them to go to lie low for a while."

"Yeah, but we don't want Jack Sunday lying low," Tall Fellow said. "I want him in a cell, and you want him dead."

"I guess that means we're going to Gunman's Crossing."

"You ever been there before?"

"No," Faulkner said. "You?"

"No. You believe there actually is a place called Gunman's Crossing?" the bounty hunter asked.

"If there is," Faulkner said, "a man would have to be crazy to go there."

"And two men would have to be even crazier to follow ten or twelve there," Tall Fellow added.

"You got any idea where it is?" Faulkner asked.

"I got an idea."

"Can we take a shortcut, maybe get there ahead of them?"

"From here?" Tall Fellow shook his head. "We're just gonna have to take their trail from here. No way we can get ahead of them."

"We're gonna be braced as soon as we ride in," Faulkner said. "We're going to need a story."

Tall Fellow mounted up and said, "We got time to come up with one, don't we?"

CHAPTER TWENTY-TWO

1875

Faulkner ran virtually the length of Rock City before he reached the livery stable. When he got there it was quiet, no movement at all. He crept closer, gun ready, wondering what trouble that Indian had gotten himself into.

He had two ways to go, the front or back of the stable. He could see people walking by out front, so he turned and walked toward the back. Behind the building he found a horse trough, a corral, and an unconscious Henry Tall Fellow.

He rushed to the bounty hunter's side, still alert for a trap. With his gun in his right hand, he reached out with his left to find a pulse while continuing to look around. Nobody jumped out at him or took a shot, and at that point the half-breed groaned.

"Hey, Tall Fellow?" Faulkner said, shaking the man. "What happened?"

Tall Fellow rolled onto his side and squinted up at Faulkner.

"I don't know. Everything just went dark."

"You hurt?"

"I don't know."

"Sit up." Faulkner reached out his left hand to help Tall Fellow into a seated position. "Check out your parts."

Tall Fellow wriggled his arms and legs, found them sound and working.

"I don't seem to be wounded, but I have a helluva headache." He felt the back of his head. "Ow."

"Bump?"

"Not yet. Kinda pulpy."

"Yeah, you'll get a bump. Can you get up?"

"Yeah."

Again, Faulkner gave him his left hand, this time pulling him to his feet. Tall Fellow started looking around.

"Try the trough," Faulkner said.

"Huh?"

Faulkner pointed.

Tall Fellow searched the ground a little longer, then walked to the trough and plunged his hand in. Moments later he came out with his gun.

"How'd you know?" he asked Faulkner.

"It's what I would have done."

"And would you also have let me live?"

"No," Faulkner said. "If it was me I would have killed you while you were lying on the ground."

"I guess I'm lucky it wasn't you."

"You'll have to clean and dry that gun," Faulkner said. "My bet is Buckland is gathering up his men."

"I guess the element of surprise is gone," Tall Fellow said.

Faulkner, finally satisfied that nobody was going to start shooting at them, holstered his weapon.

"We better get back to our hotel," he said. "We're going to need more guns."

"Let's do this quick," Tall Fellow said. "They may come after us, or they may leave town. We better be ready for both."

They headed for their hotel.

———

WHEN RALPH and Vern saw Tom Buckland they both cursed softly.

"Where you runnin' to, Tom?" Ralph asked.

"Coupla bounty hunters just tried for me at the whorehouse," Buckland said. "We're gonna need the rest of the boys to take care of them."

"You sure they were bounty hunters?" Vern asked.

"Bounty hunters, lawmen, it don't make no difference," Buckland said. "We gotta get rid of them."

"Why don't we leave town?" Ralph asked.

"Because I ain't ready ta leave town," Buckland said. "I cold-cocked one of 'em but he ain't gonna stay out forever."

"Why didn't you kill 'im?" Ralph asked.

"Because his partner was on my tail," Buckland said. "Where are the rest of the boys?"

"One of the saloons, I guess," Vern said.

"Well, you two split up and find 'em," Buckland said.

"Where are you gonna be?" Vern asked.

"I'm gettin' my rifle," Buckland said. "Get the rest of the boys and meet me in front of the rooming house."

"Okay," Ralph said, exchanging a look and a nod with Vern.

"Okay," Vern said.

When they got back to their hotel, Faulkner went to his room for his rifle, then came back down the hall to Tall Fellow's room.

"Dry that gun out?" he asked.

"Later," Tall Fellow said, holding up another handgun. "I've got an extra one." He holstered it and grabbed his rifle. "Let's find those sonsofbitches."

As Faulkner and Tall Fellow came down the stairs, two armed men walked through the front door into the lobby. They immediately covered them with their rifles.

"Hold up," Vern said, putting his hands in the air. "We're just here to warn you."

"About what?" Tall Fellow asked.

"Buckland and about six of his men will be at a rooming house at the north end of town," Ralph said.

Both Faulkner and Tall Fellow recognized these two from the saloon. The bartender had pointed them out as two of Buckland's men.

"And why aren't you two going to be there with them?" Faulkner asked.

"We don't want to be part of any killing," Ralph said.

"You're two of Buckland's men, aren't you?" Tall Fellow asked.

"We want out," Vern said.

"That's right," Ralph said.

"We ought to take you in right now," Tall Fellow said.

"You can do that," Ralph said, "but you'll probably miss the others."

"And Buckland's the one you really want," Vern said. "There's more money on his head than the rest of us combined."

"You're better off lettin' us go and goin' after them," Vern said.

Tall Fellow looked at Faulkner, who said, "I'm after Buckland, remember? You can take these guys to the jail and turn them over to the sheriff. Collect your reward."

"While you go and face Buckland and the rest?" Tall Fellow asked. "Get yourself killed? How could I live with myself if that happened?"

Faulkner looked at Ralph and Vern.

"I guess you boys lucked out," he said. "Get out of town and don't let us see you again—ever."

"Don't worry," Vern said. "You won't."

"We're goin' straight," Ralph said. "There's too much killin' involved in stealin'."

CHAPTER TWENTY-THREE

1898

"We fell farther behind than we thought," Tall Fellow said, studying the ground.

Faulkner looked down from his horse. He never bothered to dismount for two reasons. One, he never saw what Tall Fellow saw, and two, he didn't want his friend to think he didn't trust his eyes.

"How'd we do that?"

"We didn't," Tall Fellow said, climbing back into the saddle. "I may have misread the sign."

"The bartender in Ouray only put us a few hours behind."

"Well," Tall Fellow said, "somehow it's gotten stretched to about half a day."

"Still not bad," Faulkner said. "If we start pushing we can catch up."

"That's part of the problem," the bounty hunter said. "It looks like they're pushing."

"In a hurry to get to Gunman's Crossing."

"I was hoping we might have a chance to catch them before they got there."

"We'll just have to go back to the original plan," Faulkner said. "Track them there and take them there."

Tall Fellow sat still in his saddle.

"What is it?" Faulkner asked.

"Doesn't it occur to you that I might get you killed?" his friend asked.

"That's occurred to me quite a bit over the years," Faulkner said.

"But I mean now…especially now."

"Sure, it occurred to me," Faulkner said, "but you asked me for my help. What was I supposed to do?"

"But I wasn't fair to you, Faulkner," Tall Fellow said. "I didn't tell you everything. I didn't tell you about my eyes."

"Well, now I know," Faulkner said, "and the longer we sit here talking, the farther behind we're getting."

"I just wanted to tell you, if you want to pull out now, there's no hard feelings."

"I'm not pulling out."

"I just wanted to give you the chance."

"Well, you did," Faulkner said. "Thanks."

"You're welcome."

Faulkner pointed ahead of them and said, "Gunman's Crossing."

"Yep," Tall Fellow said. "Gunman's Crossing."

Late in the day they came to a town called Milner. It was a fair-sized town, visible from miles away, and as they got closer they decided they'd stop there for the night.

"Might as well," Faulkner said. "It's here, so is dusk, and we could use some coffee."

Tall Fellow didn't argue.

But as they entered Milner something felt wrong. People on the streets pointed at them and got off the streets. They didn't walk, they ran. And there was something in the air, something tangible, real, not a feeling.

"Burning," Faulkner said.

"Yeah, something was definitely burning around here," Tall Fellow agreed.

And then they saw it. The other buildings were all intact, some older than others, some very recently erected. Milner seemed to be a town on the rise—only it didn't have a bank anymore, because somebody had not only burned it down, they'd obviously blown it up.

"Oh, hell," Faulkner said as a group of men wearing badges and carrying rifles appeared ahead of them.

CHAPTER TWENTY-FOUR

"They look mad," Tall Fellow said.

"If we go for our guns there's going to be a blood-bath," Faulkner said.

"So what do we do? Turn and run?"

"Then they'd start shooting for sure," Faulkner sad. "We're going to have to talk to them."

"Okay," the bounty hunter said, "but about what? What are they mad at us for?"

"We're about to find out."

Faulkner and Tall Fellow stood their ground and waited as the group approached. They became aware of people behind curtains and windows, staring out, watching. And the street had cleared. There was only the two of them, plus the eight or ten lawmen approaching.

As the group came closer Faulkner spotted one man in the front and decided to key in on him. He looked the most comfortable wearing the tin star.

Remembering Tall Fellow's eyes he said, "Thickset fella in the front, looks like the sheriff."

"I got him," Tall Fellow said. "The rest look like a posse, not used to wearing the star."

"I think Sunday and his gang hit the bank," Faulkner said, "and these boys want to take it out on us."

"That ain't fair," Tall Fellow said.

"Let's see if we can convince *them* of that."

———

SHERIFF EVAN TUCKER eyed the two strangers like they were his salvation—and maybe they were. The town fathers were up in arms. They wanted his badge and his head—not necessarily in that order—because of the gang who had robbed the bank, taking every cent in the vault while blowing up the building, killing two people in the process.

All he had to do was convince everyone that these two strangers were part of the gang. If he could at least put two of the gang in jail—or in the ground—it might save his job. All he had to do was convince these part-time deputies—who had all been deputized after the fact—to go along with him.

Holding his shotgun tightly in his hands, Tucker stopped his makeshift posse in front of the two men and glared up at them. He didn't know who they really were, but it didn't matter. As far as he was concerned, they were part of the gang. If he could convince himself, he could convince anyone.

———

"YOU BOYS GOT a lot of nerve comin' back here!" the sheriff said to Faulkner and Tall Fellow.

"We don't know what you're talking about, Sheriff," Faulkner said. "We just got to town."

"A little too late to split the booty with your partners, eh?" the man said.

"Booty?" Tall Fellow asked. "What booty?"

"Look at 'em," the sheriff said. "Actin' like they're all innocent."

"Uh, Sheriff," one man said. "Maybe they are innocent."

"What are ya talkin' about, Lew?" the sheriff said. "Don't you think it's a coincidence that two strangers ride into town right after a bunch of 'em rob the bank? These fellas obviously got here too late to help their buddies."

"Uh, yeah," the man called Lew said, "and that would make 'em innocent, Sheriff."

"It don't make 'em innocent," the sheriff argued. "It makes 'em part of the gang that got here too late to help their buddies —but they know where they are!"

A few of the other deputies liked that logic and started nodding in agreement.

"Sheriff, if we were part of a gang who just robbed your bank, and we were too late to be in on it, wouldn't we be pretty stupid to ride into town? Especially since we can see the bank's been hit."

"Then that's what you are," the lawman said. "Stupid."

Faulkner looked at Lew, pointed to him.

"You sound like a smart man, Mister," he said. "You don't believe that, do you?"

"It don't matter what he believes," the sheriff said. "He's a goddamn storekeeper. I'm the law around here."

"Sheriff," Tall Fellow said, "you've got to be a pretty piss-poor lawman if all you can do after your bank is robbed is accuse two innocent men. Why didn't you stop them when they were robbing it?"

"That's what a lot of folks are wondering," Lew said.

"And if they're gone, and you've got this posse, why aren't you on their trail?" Faulkner tossed in.

"We were headin' out when you rode in," the sheriff said. "Now that we got you, you can tell us where they're headed."

"We've got no idea, Sheriff," Faulkner said, "because we're not part of the gang. As a matter of fact, if it was who we think it was, we've been trailing them for some time."

"Who do you think it was?" Lew asked.

"The Jack Sunday gang," Tall Fellow said.

"You fellas ain't lawmen," the sheriff said.

"No, we ain't," Tall Fellow said.

"Bounty hunters?" Lew asked.

"I said you were a smart man," Faulkner said. "That's it exactly."

"Sheriff," Lew said, "at least these two fellas are tellin' who robbed the bank."

"Course they are, damn it!" the sheriff snapped. "Because they were supposed to be in on it."

"Nobody believes that, Sheriff," Tall Fellow said.

"You're just trying to save face at our expense," Faulkner said, "and we ain't about to let you do that."

"Whataya gonna do about it?" the lawman asked. "Yer outgunned, Mister."

"By you and a bunch of storekeepers?" Faulkner asked. "I don't think so, Sheriff."

"These men are duly appointed deputies."

Faulkner ignored the sheriff and addressed the other men.

"How many of you boys want to die because your sheriff is trying to save face? And his job?"

The men muttered among themselves, exchanging glances.

"Mister," Lew said, "maybe if you told us your names it'd help."

"I'm nobody," Tall Fellow replied, "but maybe you heard of my partner, here...His name's Faulkner."

Faulkner didn't know if any of the deputies recognized his name, but he could see by the look on the sheriff's face that he did.

"Wait a minute," one of the men said. He was standing at the back of the group of deputies, and pushed his way to the front. "I know who this fella is. He ain't no bounty hunter. He's a money gun."

"You're right," Lew said. "I know that name, too, and he ain't never been a bank robber that I know of."

"So what?" the sheriff said. "He's a hired killer. That makes him better than the bank robbers? I say we take him, anyway."

"You've got no wanted posters on me, Sheriff," Faulkner said. "I don't want to go up against the law, but I'm not about to let you take me down for something I didn't do."

"Me, neither."

"You a money gun too, Mister?" Lew asked.

"He is a bounty hunter," Faulkner said. "His name's Henry Tall Fellow, and he brings most of his bounties in dead."

"And you're after the bounty on Jack Sunday's head?" Lew asked.

"That's right."

"Seems to me we'll be doing your lawman's job for him," Faulkner said. "Killing Jack Sunday and his boys, and bringing back your money."

"That sounds good to me, boys," Lew said. "I don't aim to go against these fellas with a gun."

"You're yella, Lew," the sheriff said.

"And where were you when your town's bank was being robbed, Sheriff?" Tall Fellow asked. "Under your desk?"

The harsh words pushed the sheriff into action. He started

to bring the shotgun around, but he found himself staring down the barrel of Faulkner's gun. The sheriff had left Faulkner no choice but to draw, despite the fact that the movement might have also pushed some of the other men into action—but it didn't. They were all stunned by the speed with which Faulkner had produced his gun.

"He coulda killed you, Sheriff," Lew said. "He coulda killed you easy."

"I told you I didn't want to go against you, Sheriff, but you're not leaving me much choice," Faulkner said. "It's your play."

CHAPTER TWENTY-FIVE

Faulkner knew he was facing a man with a badge, but he wasn't willing to be pushed. All he and Tall Fellow had done was ride into town, and this clown with a tin star on his chest was trying to save his job by blaming them for the bank robbery. He could count the times he'd drawn on a lawman on one hand, and he had only killed one over the years —a bad one. This one wasn't bad, really, just desperate and stupid. But Faulkner was ready to not only draw on this one, but to kill him if he had to. It was the man's own choice.

―――

HENRY TALL FELLOW had never killed a lawman, but he was ready to back his friend's play. He didn't care if only the sheriff drew, or if all nine of the men in front of them drew (he had counted). He had been angry ever since the day his eyes had been diagnosed. So far all he'd done about it was get drunk and start fights, like in Denver. Maybe today was the day he took out his anger on someone and killed him. This idiot with a badge was asking for it.

―――

SHERIFF EVAN TUCKER knew he'd bitten off more than he could chew. How was he supposed to know that one of the strangers riding into town was a famous gunman and killer, accompanied by a bounty hunter? He stared up at the two men on horseback and knew that even if he got lucky and killed one of them, the other one would kill him. He had no doubt that they would target him before anyone else in the group. It was what he would do, kill the leader first.

And there was no guarantee that any of the other men with him would even make a move.

Jesus Christ, he thought, it's just a fucking job!

"SO GO AHEAD, SHERIFF," Faulkner said. "Make a decision."

Both Faulkner and Tall Fellow thought that the lawman could probably use a way out, but neither one was in the mood to give it to him. The moron had put his foot in his mouth; let him swallow it or spit it out.

Well," Sheriff Evan Tucker said, "maybe I made a mistake."

"Maybe you did," Faulkner said.

"Put your guns up, boys," the lawman said. "These men ain't part of the gang."

Faulkner and Tall Fellow saw all of the men roll their eyes. They had never raised their guns.

"Sheriff," Lew said, "if these two men are trackin' the Sunday gang I don't think you need any of us anymore."

"Maybe you're right, Lew."

"You should probably just ride along with them."

The sheriff turned and looked at Lew as if he were crazy.

"That's okay, Sheriff," Tall Fellow said. "We usually work better with just the two of us."

"You men go on back to your businesses," Sheriff Tucker said. "Drop your badges off at my office later."

He didn't have to tell them twice. Three of the men took their badges off right away and handed them to him.

"Sorry about this," Lew said to Faulkner and Tall Fellow as the other men drifted away. He stepped closer and said, "My name's Lew Hilton. I'm a member of the town council."

"When did the Sunday gang hit?" Faulkner asked.

"Late yesterday," Lew said. "The first we knew of what was happening was when the bank blew up."

"How many killed?" Tall Fellow asked.

"Two," Lew said. "A teller and a woman who was making a deposit."

"How many were there?" Faulkner asked.

Lew looked at Sheriff Tucker.

"Ten, twelve," the lawman said.

"You get a shot off?" Tall Fellow asked, already knowing the answer.

"Uh, no," the sheriff said. "I was, uh, in my office...workin'."

Asleep was more like it, Faulkner thought.

"You boys want to come over to the saloon I'll stand you to a drink," Lew Hilton said. "Make up for the...mistake."

"We don't have time," Tall Fellow said. "We've been tracking these boys for a long time now."

"Where you figure they're headed?" Lew asked.

Faulkner knew that Tall Fellow—who was, after all, after the bounty—would never answer a question like that.

"Don't know," he said.

"We're tracking them," Tall Fellow said.

"Well," Lew said, "you need any supplies before you leave?"

"Some," Faulkner said.

"Come on over to the general store and I'll get you a good price on what you need."

"That going to be okay with the owner?" Faulkner asked.

"No problem," Lew Hilton said. "That's me."

CHAPTER TWENTY-SIX

L ew Hilton not only gave them supplies at a cheap price but poured them each a shot of whiskey to cut the dust. They declined a second drink and packed the supplies they'd purchased into their saddlebags. They would have liked to stop for a hot meal, but that would only put them farther behind Sunday and his gang. They were acting on the assumption that the bartender in Ouray had heard right and the outlaws were on their way to Gunman's Crossing, but there was always the chance that they weren't. There was always the chance they might catch up to them in the open somewhere.

Saddlebags filled with bullets, coffee, bacon, beans and cele-bratory cigars that the man had thrown in free—"To light up when the job is done"—they mounted up in front of the general store. Hilton and the sheriff watched them from the boardwalk in front of the store. Then, suddenly, a group of men closed in on them from all sides. These were men with guns, no badges, and bad intentions.

"What's going on?" Sheriff Tucker demanded.

Faulkner and Tall Fellow might have been able to gig their horses and ride through the group, but not without shots being fired. They exchanged a glance that said, "We thought we were done with this," and waited.

"We heard you caught two of the gang that robbed the bank," one man called out.

"That was a mistake," Lew Hilton shouted back, doing the

sheriff's job. "These men are not part of the gang. They're trackin' the gang."

"They said that?" a second man called.

"And you believed 'em?" a third added

"Yes," Hilton said, "the sheriff and I believe them."

"So you're just gonna let 'em ride out, Sheriff?" someone shouted.

"That's right," the sheriff said. "When they catch up to the gang they'll recover whatever money they can and bring it back here."

Faulkner, getting tired of being accused, wasn't so sure he would do that. Once they caught up to the gang, who was to say where recovered money came from?

"I think we ought ta keep 'em here and question 'em some more," someone said.

"Nice friendly little town you got here, Mr. Hilton," Faulkner said.

Hilton moved closer to Faulkner.

"They're good people," he replied. "They're just scared and upset. Many of them lost their life's savings in the robbery."

"All the more reason they should let us go and get it back," Tall Fellow said.

"You have to get these people to move, Mr. Hilton," Faulkner said. "We don't want to have to shoot our way out of this town."

"Just let me talk to them," Hilton said, stepping away to address what was becoming a mob. If any more men joined in, there would be far too many for Faulkner and Tall Fellow to successfully shoot their way out.

"People, people," Hilton shouted, raising his hands. "Nothing will be accomplished by detaining these two men except to let the gang get farther away."

"That's what you say!" somebody said.

"The sheriff and I have determined that these two men are who they say they are."

"The sheriff's an idiot!"

"And you're no lawman!"

Different voices were joining in now.

"I say we go ahead and lynch 'em!"

Suddenly it got quiet, as if the statement had shocked everyone into silence.

Faulkner drew his rifle from its scabbard and Tall Fellow followed.

"We're not about to sit here and let anyone hang us for something we had no part of," Faulkner called out. "You men outnumber us, but how many of you have ever killed a man?"

There was no answer.

"And how many of you are willing to die so the others can hang us?" Tall Fellow asked.

Again, there was no answer.

Tall Fellow levered a round into the chamber of his rifle, and this time it was Faulkner who followed.

"Make a move," Tall Fellow said, "or make a path."

There was plenty of tension in the air as each member of the mob examined his own conscience, and courage, and stupidity. One by one they began to move aside, until suddenly there was a path.

"Good thinking," Faulkner said. "Tall Fellow, you go ahead. I'll bring up the rear."

Tall Fellow started down the path and Faulkner followed, but turned in his saddle so he could keep a watch on the crowd in case somebody got brave.

Nobody did.

CHAPTER TWENTY-SEVEN

"What the hell is wrong with people?" Henry Tall Fellow asked.

They were camped, hours later, with a pan of beans on the fire, cups of coffee in their hands.

"They're either stupid or scared," Faulkner said, calmly.

"I think we just ran into a town full of people who are both."

Tall Fellow shook his head and sipped his coffee.

"You know," he said, "two other men would've just started shooting and taught them a lesson."

"You're probably right."

"In fact," the bounty hunter went on, "there was a time we would've taught them a lesson."

"The townspeople don't make me as mad as the sheriff," Faulkner said. "How does someone who is that much of a moron wind up wearing a badge?"

"Probably because nobody else wanted it."

"That's a job I'd never want," Faulkner said. "I don't know of a more thankless job than town sheriff or marshal. You see those folks who were backing him? None of them ever would've lifted a gun against us."

"Yeah, but that mob later. Somebody there would've started shooting if you hadn't talked them out of it. You're good with words, Faulkner."

The beans were ready and Faulkner dished them out, handing a plate to Tall Fellow.

"But you know," Tall Fellow continued with a mouthful, "I really wanted to shoot somebody today."

"I know."

"You knew?" Tall Fellow asked. "How?"

"I can feel it in you, Henry," Faulkner said. He rarely—if ever—called his friend by his first name. "You're angry, and unless you get it under control, somebody's going to pay for it."

Tall Fellow chewed, washed his food down with coffee, then held the cup out to Faulkner.

"I've got a right to be angry," he said, as Faulkner handed the cup back.

"I know you do," the money gun said.

After a moment Tall Fellow added, "But I guess somebody else shouldn't have to pay for it."

Another moment of silence went by and then Faulkner asked, "Yeah, but who should?"

CHAPTER TWENTY-EIGHT

1875

Ralph and Vern had delivered Tom Buckland's message to his men before they went to the hotel to find Faulkner and Henry Tall Fellow. Everything was set for them all to shoot it out with each other while Ralph and Vern left town.

Naturally, they hoped that the two bounty hunters would come out on top, but even if Buckland survived, they would be long gone. And they were going to find themselves a small town that nobody had ever heard of, where he'd never find them.

———

FAULKNER AND TALL Fellow knew that Ralph and Vern had to have their own reasons for warning them, but they didn't care. Faulkner's job was to kill Buckland, and the bounty on these two men—if there was one—was of little interest to Tall Fellow.

They were both interested in Buckland first, and anyone else second.

———

BUCKLAND WAITED in front of the rooming house for his men to arrive, which they did, mostly two at a time. Before long he was standing there with seven men. The only two missing were Ralph and Vern.

"What happened to them?" one of the other men asked.

"It don't really matter," Buckland said. "They were never really part of the gang anyway, were they?"

"They never did join in on any of the fun," another man said —and by fun he meant raping and killing.

"So what's goin' on?" a third man asked.

"Bounty hunter," Buckland said. "Almost caught me with my pants down at the whorehouse."

"We lightin' out?"

"No, we ain't lightin' out," Buckland said. "You better all check yer guns and make sure they're workin'. We're gonna kill us some bounty hunters."

"Anybody we know?" a man asked.

"No," Buckland said. "From what I saw, it's a coupla kids tryin' to make a name for themselves."

"Too bad," one of the gang said. "I'd like to kill me a famous bounty hunter."

"Well," Buckland said, "we'll kill us these two, and then find you a famous one to kill. How's that?"

The other man grinned, showing tobacco-stained teeth, and said, "I like the sound of that!"

———

AS INEXPERIENCED AS THEY WERE—RELATIVELY speaking—the thing Faulkner and Tall Fellow had in their favor at that time was their youth. As impetuous as it made them, it also made them fearless.

However, that didn't mean they were going to go rushing in without having a look first.

"How many?" Faulkner asked.

"I count nine."

"That's what I get. Spot Buckland?"

"On the porch," Tall Fellow said. "He has the demeanor I've seen on the old chiefs."

"You're comparing Tom Buckland to a chief?"

"No," Tall Fellow said, "obviously not. I just meant the way the others are staying together it's obvious he's in charge."

"Oh...I can see that."

"Also," Tall Fellow said, "I've seen him once before."

"Fine," Faulkner said. "How do you want to do this?"

"If we go walking in there they'll just start shooting."

"How about the local law?"

"We might lose them."

They were standing alongside a building, their backs to the wall. Faulkner peered around the corner. "No horses," he said. "It doesn't look like they're going anywhere." He turned back and looked at Tall Fellow. "I think they're waiting for us."

"No," Tall Fellow said. "They don't know we know where they are."

"Unless those other two sent us into a trap?"

Tall Fellow thought a moment, then said, "No, I believed them. They wanted to get away from Buckland. They're hoping they can get away while we are all shooting at each other."

"Okay, that makes sense to me. You got any suggestions?"

"I've got one."

"And?"

"We let them come find us."

CHAPTER TWENTY-NINE

1898

J ack Sunday and his gang rode into Gunman's Crossing as if they were entering a church.

"There ain't no law here at all?" Hobbs asked.

"None," Sunday said. "The only law here is what you're wearin' on your hip."

They kept riding until they reached a livery stable.

"I didn't see no bank," a man named Harry Wells observed.

"Why would there be a bank here?" Sunday asked. "Somebody would just rob it."

Hobbs laughed and added, "Every damn day!"

They all laughed then, until Sunday shut them up.

"This is like any other town, minus the bank and a lawman wearin' a star," he told them, "but I'll kill the first man I hear talkin' about what we do, understand? We took a nice chunk of money out of that last bank. Anybody in this town hears about it, they'll try to take it away from us."

"But...we're all the same here, ain't we?" Hobbs asked.

"If by that you mean we're all thieves and killers," Sunday said, "the answer is yes—and remember that. Any man here would just as soon kill ya as look at ya."

"What about us?" a Mexican named Soul asked. Sunday found the man's name ironic, because he doubted that Soul had one.

"Whataya mean?" Sunday asked.

"Can we kill anyone, *jefe?*"

"You can kill or rape anybody you want," Sunday said. "Just don't expect me to back you up. You can back each other up, but every man here is responsible for his own life. You wanna back each other up, that's fine. Just don't come runnin' to me to pull your bacon out of the fire if you fuck up."

"What if one or more of us wants to leave?" Danny Barker asked.

Barker was the only college-educated member of the gang. He had come west after school, looking for adventure, and Sunday found him to have less conscience than any man he'd ever met. At twenty-three he had a lot of killing ahead of him. It was too bad he'd come along this late in the century, though. Sunday wished he'd had Barker around ten or twenty years ago.

"Any man wants to leave can go ahead and do it," Sunday said.

"With our share?"

"No," Sunday said. "We divvy up after we leave here together. If you leave, you leave with what you have in your pocket."

"That ain't fair," Hobbs said.

Sunday stared at him.

"You wanna take that up with me now, Hobbs?"

Hobbs hesitated, looked around to see if he had any supporters, then said, "No."

"Anybody else?" Sunday asked, just to make sure.

The men all looked at each other, then said, "No," or shook their heads.

"Good. Let's get our horses taken care of. Then it's up to all of you to find your own rooms. You wanna do that in a hotel, a boarding house, a saloon or a whorehouse, I don't care."

"If we're all on our own," Barker asked, "how will we know when you're ready to leave?"

"Don't worry," Sunday said. "I'll let you know when it's time to leave."

CHAPTER THIRTY

Tall Fellow became morose nearly every night when they camped. He was okay during the day, unless he got very quiet. That was when Faulkner knew he was starting to stew, so he'd start up a conversation to try to distract his friend from his thoughts.

Sometimes, though, like this afternoon, Tall Fellow felt the need to talk, and Faulkner obliged him.

"You know, they say Hickok's eyes were failing him when he was killed," the bounty hunter said.

"I heard that," Faulkner said. "I never did hear that it had anything to do with him getting killed, though."

"No," Tall Fellow said, "but what do you think his life would've been like if he hadn't been killed that day in Deadwood? He was a scout, a gunman, a gambler...what good would he have been at any of that without his eyes?"

"I guess he would've gotten himself killed sooner or later, then."

Tall Fellow paused for a while, then said, "Reckon that's what I'll do, then. Keep tracking and hunting until I get myself killed."

Faulkner took a moment to think before answering, "I guess that's what I would do, too, Indian."

"There is no sense in going out the way Doc Holliday did," Tall Fellow said. "Flat on his back in bed in a nursing home."

Faulkner shuddered at the thought of dying that way.

"What about—" he started to ask, then thought better of it.

"What about what?" Tall Fellow asked. "Go ahead, Faulkner. You're the only friend I've got. If you can't say it, nobody can."

"I was just going to ask, what about eyeglasses?"

"I talked to a doctor about that," Tall Fellow replied. "He said it might help for a while, but my eyes will continue to get worse and I'd have to keep changing the glasses."

Once again Faulkner considered the prospect of losing his own eyesight. For a man in his profession, if he didn't take his own life at that time, someone else was sure to do it for him. He wondered how brave he would be in that situation. Few things frightened Faulkner after all these years. In his youth it had been ignorance that kept him from feeling fear. Now it was experience. But to go blind?

"Can we talk about something else, Indian?" he asked.

"Sure, Faulkner," Tall Fellow said, "sure...remember that day, years ago, in Rock City? The Buckland gang..."

———

ROCK CITY, ARKANSAS, 1875

The young bounty hunter and young hired killer withdrew and went back to the center of town.

"We can choose our own battleground," Tall Fellow told Faulkner as they stood in front of their hotel.

"Is that what you learned from your elders?" Faulkner asked.

"Don't scoff," Tall Fellow said. "I learned a lot sitting at the feet of those men."

"I wasn't scoffing," Faulkner said seriously. "I was just wondering."

"Oh... well, yeah, that's what I learned."

"Think we should bring the local law into this?" Faulkner asked.

"I don't know if we have time," Tall Fellow said. "Those fellas are going to come looking for us pretty quick."

"As long as they don't decide to run for it," Faulkner said.

"I think we tweaked Buckland's ego, don't you?" Tall Fellow asked. "He isn't going to run. He's going to want to teach us a lesson."

Faulkner decided to bow to Tall Fellow's experience in this matter. They may have been the same age, but Tall Fellow had grown up out here. That gave him the edge in decision making, as far as Faulkner was concerned.

On the other side, Henry Tall Fellow was glad that Faulkner did not feel the need to make all the decisions all the time. He hadn't liked the Easterner when they first met, but the money gun was beginning to grow on him—starting back at the moment when he'd shot the head off that pygmy rattler.

"So, where do we make our stand?" Faulkner asked.

Tall Fellow went into the hotel lobby and came out with two straight-backed wooden chairs. He set them down and turned to Faulkner.

"Right here."

———

BUCKLAND CAME DOWN off the boardinghouse porch and eyed each of his men.

"I want these two jaspers dead, you got that?" he said.

They all nodded and one of them said, "We got that, boss, but..."

"But what?"

"What about the sheriff?"

"If he gets in the way," Buckland said, "kill him, too."

The men all liked that, and almost cheered. It wasn't often they got the okay to kill a lawman.

"But don't get yourselves distracted by a shiny little tin target," Buckland warned. "I want them two bounty hunters dead first!"

"Okay, boss."

"Let's go, then," Buckland said. "They're in town somewhere."

"What if they left town?" one of the men asked.

"With the price on my head?" Buckland asked. "They're not going anywhere. They're in town and they won't be hard to find."

CHAPTER THIRTY-ONE

Tom Buckland's prediction was very true. Faulkner and Tall Fellow were not hard to find. They were still seated in front of the hotel when they spotted Buckland and his boys coming down the street and were, in turn, spotted.

"Here they come," Tall Fellow said.

"A lot of them," Faulkner said.

"We knew that."

"Well," Faulkner said, "there are two fewer then there might have been."

They both stood up.

"I'll take across the street," Tall Fellow said.

"Two against nine?" Faulkner asked. "Are we ready for that?"

"I don't know," Tall Fellow said. "Are we?"

"I guess we're about to find out."

Tall Fellow nodded, stepped off the boardwalk and walked across the street.

Faulkner stepped down into the street and waited. Buckland saw one man moving across the street and the other standing just in front of the hotel.

"Hobbs," Buckland said, "take three men and kill the one across the street. The rest of you are with me. We're takin' that one." He pointed.

They all drew their guns and quickened their pace.

———

FAULKNER SAW that Buckland was in the group of men moving toward him.

"Lucky me," he said to himself. "I'm going to get to collect my fee."

He started toward the men.

———

THE STREETS WERE EMPTY. Word got around fast when something like this was going to happen.

Get off the streets.

Get behind locked doors.

But watch from your window.

And if the word had gotten to the sheriff, he was staying inside, just like everyone else.

As Buckland and his men got closer, Faulkner wasted no time. He drew his gun and fired.

———

AS FAULKNER FIRED, Tall Fellow drew and did the same. Neither man was able to take a look at the other. Each was on his own.

CHAPTER THIRTY-TWO

1898

"There it is," Faulkner said.

"Gunman's Crossing," Tall Fellow said, shaking his head. "It does exist."

"A town with no law," Faulkner said. "You'd think it would be in a state of perpetual chaos."

"Maybe it is," Tall Fellow said. "We just can't hear it from here. Let's get a little closer."

"Hang on a minute," Faulkner said, putting out a hand to stop his friend. "Let's not be in such a hurry."

"What's on your mind?"

"There's a chance one or both of us might be recognized in that town. We've put away a lot of men, some of whom might have gotten out and come here."

"I've put away a lot of men," Tall Fellow corrected him. "You've put a lot of men in the ground."

"Whatever," Faulkner said. "The point is, we ride in there together and we're going to attract attention."

"You've got a point," Tall Fellow admitted. "Okay, I'll ride in first, you follow me in a few hours."

"I was thinking more like a day apart," Faulkner said, "just to be sure."

"Okay, then you follow me first thing tomorrow morning."

"No, I was thinking you'd follow me first thing in the morning."

"Why should you go first?"

"Because if you go first you're liable to get killed before I get there."

"Are you saying I don't know how to do my job?" Tall Fellow demanded.

"I'm saying you've been making some bad decisions lately. Like in Denver—and by the way, you still haven't paid me back for bailing you out."

"Don't worry," Tall Fellow said. "You'll get your money."

"I don't want my money," Faulkner said. "I want to go into town first. You let me do that and I'll call that debt square."

Tall Fellow stared at his friend for a few moments.

"You're not going to do anything until I get there?" he asked finally.

"Just scout the place out, make sure Sunday is there," Faulkner said.

"You won't try to take him to complete your own job?"

"I won't fire a shot until you get there. I'm not out to steal your bounty, Tall Fellow. Don't tell me that after all these years I still have to convince you of that fact?"

"No," Tall Fellow said. "No, you don't. I'm sorry, Faulkner. Like you said, I've been making some bad decisions lately. And you're right, I'd probably ride on down there, have a few drinks and go after the whole gang alone. I hate this damned Indian blood!"

"You liar. You're proud of your Indian blood. You're just saying what you think I want to hear."

"Fine," Tall Fellow said. "You go first. I'll ride in tomorrow and we'll find each other. You can tell me what you found out, if he's there or not."

"He's there," Faulkner said, "with his whole gang and the money they stole from that bank. I think we both know that."

"Well, get going, before I change my mind," Tall Fellow said. "I'll make a cold camp and follow you tomorrow."

He put out his hand and they shook.

"Good luck," Tall Fellow said. "I think you'll need it to stay alive in that town until I can get there and save your ass —again!"

THERE WERE three hotels in Gunman's Crossing, two rooming houses, five saloons, and three whorehouses. Jack Sunday picked out one of the hotels for himself, then told all his men to find someplace else to stay.

"I don't want any of you around me while we're here," he told them.

Hobbs looked hurt and said, "We can't even have a drink together?"

"What did I say, Hobbs?"

"Okay, okay," Hobbs said. "We'll all stay away from you while we're here. Is it okay if we have a drink with each other?"

"Hobbs, I don't care if you fuck each other," Sunday said, "Just stay...away...from...me."

Sunday went into his hotel, leaving his men standing outside.

"Whataya think that's about?" one of the men asked Hobbs.

"How the fuck should I know?" Hobbs asked. "Ya know what? Stay away from me, too!"

CHAPTER THIRTY-THREE

Faulkner rode into Gunman's Crossing the way he rode into any town. He was usually looking for somebody, so it didn't take much acting.

But he wasn't going to go looking for anybody just yet. The normal thing to do would be to put his horse up at the livery and find himself a hotel room. He ignored the looks he got from men on the street, figuring they all had prices on their heads. There were no women in sight on the street.

At the livery he handed his horse over to a shifty-looking gent who made him pay two dollars first.

"That horse better be here when I come for him," Faulkner said, "or I'll shove that two dollars up your ass. You got that?"

The man tried to match stares with Faulkner, but finally had to look away.

"Yeah, sure, I got it."

Faulkner figured this was the best way to act in this town. He didn't want to get tabbed as a soft guy. Better to be known as a hard man.

He left the livery, carrying his rifle and saddlebags. On his way to a hotel he ignored stares from men he passed on the street. He figured he'd first have to stand up to their stares before any of them actually stepped up to try to intimidate him. That would come later, and he'd be ready. He was sure that every man in that town was on the run, or had a price on his head. If he had to kill any to make his point, he wouldn't lose any sleep over it.

He. really didn't have any fear of being recognized. He had never worn a badge in his life, and his reputation as a money gun certainly entitled him to be in a place like Gunman's Crossing, since popular opinion of such a man usually lumped him in with outlaws, thieves and indiscriminate killers.

On the other hand, while lawmen lumped bounty hunters in with killers, killers lumped bounty men in with lawman. If Tall Fellow was recognized, someone might try to kill him. It was for that reason Faulkner did not want his friend riding into town first, and not that he was afraid Tall Fellow would get drunk and make a mistake.

Although that was certainly a possibility in Tall Fellow's present state.

Faulkner stopped in the first hotel he came to. It really didn't matter to him where he stayed, so the state of the accommodations didn't concern him. It suited him that the building was standing.

"Got a room?" he asked the clerk.

"Who wants ta know?" the tall, skinny clerk asked.

"I do," Faulkner said. "I'm tired and in no mood for games. If you don't want my money, say so. I'll be on my way. If you just want to give me a hard time I'll just put a bullet in you, and still be on my way."

"Okay, okay," the man said. "Don't get offended." He opened the register book and said, "Sign in."

"You're kidding, right?"

The man withdrew the book, turned, picked a key off the wall and handed it to Faulkner.

"Room seven, upstairs," he said. "Enjoy your stay."

Faulkner took the key and, without another word, went up the stairs.

———

OUTSIDE OF TOWN Tall Fellow made his cold camp and chewed on some tough beef jerky. He hated like hell to admit that Faulkner was right. He probably would have gotten himself killed if he'd gone into town on his own. Maybe he'd been trying to do that ever since the doctor had told him about his failing eyesight.

He walked to his saddlebags, reached in and touched the bottle of whiskey he had there. Touched the smooth surface of the bottle, but finally left it where it was. Instead, he grabbed his canteen and washed the tough, dry meat down with a swig of water.

He sat down with his back up against his saddle. It wasn't even dark yet. Sitting here doing nothing, waiting for morning, was going to be tough. He was not the kind of man who did well sitting or standing still. Maybe there was some way he could sneak into town without being seen.

He thought about the whiskey bottle in his saddlebags, then shook his head and tried to think about something else. There was something about the Jack Sunday gang that Faulkner didn't know. He wondered what his friend would say when he finally told him what that was.

He sat and stared straight ahead, his mind drifting back almost twenty-five years, as it had been doing a lot lately...

CHAPTER THIRTY-FOUR

ROCK CITY, 1875

During the relatively short time he'd been in the West, Faulkner had not been involved in many shootouts of this kind. Mostly he'd killed men one on one, usually facing them to give them an equal break—even when they didn't deserve one.

There was nothing equal about this situation. Of the nine men approaching them, five were heading for him, while four made their way toward Tall Fellow. Faulkner, still with something of the Easterner in him, marveled at how they would simply come walking up the street toward him.

His first shot struck one man in the chest, spinning him and dumping him onto the ground. The others began firing back at him and he had to dive for cover as lead zipped over his head. He heard it strike the front of the hotel, shattering glass.

From behind a horse trough, he fired several times, hoping to hit Buckland with at least one of those shots. He saw another man stagger and fall, but Buckland himself had broken off and gone for cover.

Suddenly, the shooting stopped, even from across the street. Everybody had to be reloading and he took the opportunity to do the same.

ACROSS THE STREET Tall Fellow had held his own in the first volley, putting two men down before he was also forced to reload. Both he and Faulkner had decided not to use their rifles. They realized they were much better shots with their pistols.

Tall Fellow had taken cover behind a couple of barrels, and as he reloaded he realized there was no shooting anymore, not even from across the street. He hoped Faulkner had been able to avoid getting killed, because if he was alone, he was in a lot of trouble.

———

BUCKLAND THOUGHT the two bounty hunters were crazy. Faced with nine armed men, most men would have broken and ran. Not these two. They stood their ground and only went for cover when they had to.

Buckland reloaded, then looked over at the two men he had left on his side of the street. They had all taken cover behind a buckboard.

"Pin him down," he told them. "I'm going around behind the hotel. I'm gonna come at him from the lobby."

The two men waved, then started shooting. Buckland ran down a nearby alley.

———

ACROSS THE STREET Tall Fellow raised his head and drew fire, thus locating the three men who were trying to kill him. He knew that if they all just remained where they were, this could go on all day. Most likely they'd try to close in on him, so he decided to try to change his position.

On his side of the street were several businesses, all of which had closed their doors just before the shooting started. It didn't much matter, though, because all the lead flying about had taken care of most of the glass in their windows. Tall Fellow chose one of those windows and decided it was his goal.

He raised his gun, fired twice and then started running for the window. He heard the shooting behind him, felt hot lead whizzing by him like angry bees, and then leaped...

Faulkner watched Tall Fellow jump through the broken

window of the hardware store. It was a good move, to get off the street. It was probably something he should do himself, as soon as Buck-land and his men stopped to reload again. Luckily, they weren't smart enough to stagger their shots, so that one could reload while the others continued to fire.

He sat on his butt with his back to the trough, waiting for the shooting to stop, then realized that they were shooting without any hope of hitting him. It dawned on him that they were just trying to pin him down. The only reason for that was that somebody was trying to flank him, or trying to get around behind him.

It would be a good idea if he changed position, as Tall Fellow had done.

The question was, where to go?

———

BUCKLAND MADE his way to the back of the hotel. He found the rear door locked, but it could not stand against him. He kicked it open and went inside, moving down a hallway that took him to a curtained doorway. As he rushed through it, he found himself behind the desk.

The clerk turned, saw him and said, "What the hell—" but never finished. Buckland clubbed him to the floor, then came around the desk and headed for the door.

———

TALL FELLOW WENT through the window and just kept on going. He went through a door in the back and found himself in a storeroom. There were tools all around him—picks, shovels, axes. He grabbed an axe that reminded him of a tomahawk his father once had, and shoved the handle into his trousers. He didn't know if the outlaws would pursue him into the hardware store or not. If he knew, he could wait for them, but he would rather be on the move. Staying still was not easy for him. There was no back door, but there was a rear window. He moved to it and peered out to see if anyone was waiting for him. He could still hear shooting from out front. Could it be possible they hadn't see him run through that window? That they thought they had him pinned down?

He picked up a wooden stool from nearby, used it to knocked the glass out of the back window, and climbed out.

CHAPTER THIRTY-FIVE

Faulkner had an idea. It was daring, but he didn't think the outlaws would believe it. He couldn't stay where he was, not if someone was working his way to him from behind. Once he got into a crossfire, he was as good as dead.

He needed to wait until they were reloading. When the last shot came, even before the echo faded, he was on his feet and running...toward them!

THE TWO OUTLAWS began to reload, quickly ejecting their spent shells and thumbing in the live ones. Once they were loaded they stood up, prepared to fire again, but what they saw stunned both of them. The bounty hunter was running at them, was almost on their position, and started to fire.

TOM BUCKLAND CAME RUNNING out the front door of the hotel, expecting to see Faulkner's back as a nice big target. Instead, he saw the man running away from him, toward his two men, who were standing there, gaping. As Buckland watched, the man gunned down his two men. Buckland stole a look across the street, saw the rest of his men rushing through a window to the hardware store. He didn't know what the dumb bastards were doing, but that left him and the one bounty hunter on the street. He stepped down off the boardwalk.

———

FAULKNER CAME around the buckboard and checked the two fallen men. They were dead. He hoped they had a nice-sized bounty between them for Tall Fellow to collect.

He turned to see a lone man coming toward him from the direction of the hotel.

Tom Buckland.

Faulkner stepped out from behind the buckboard.

———

TALL FELLOW WAS GOING out the back window when he heard them coming in the front. He stopped, climbed back in and waited, his gun in his hand. As they came rushing through the door into the storeroom, he opened fire. His first volley caught one of them in the chest, knocking him to the floor. As he fired at the second man his gun suddenly jammed.

"Oops," the outlaw said, grinning. He raised his gun slowly and pointed it at Tall Fellow, who quickly drew the small hand axe from his belt and threw it.

———

FAULKNER AND BUCKLAND moved toward each other.

"What's your name, kid?" Buckland asked.

"Faulkner."

"Bounty hunter?"

"No."

"Then what are you doin' here?"

"I came to kill you."

"Why? What did I ever do to you?"

"Nothing," Faulkner said. "Until I took this job I never heard of you."

"What job?"

"I told you," Faulkner said. "I'm here to kill you."

Suddenly, Buckland started to laugh.

"You're for hire?" he asked, laughing harder. "A hired killer?"

"There are lots of names for what I am, I guess."

"And your friend?"

"He's not my friend," Faulkner said, "but he is a bounty hunter. I'll kill you, and he'll collect the bounty."

"And you'll get paid."

"Yes."

"By whom?"

Faulkner shook his head.

"You get to know that someone hired me to kill you," Faulkner said. "You don't get to know who. Just know that someone hates you enough to want you dead."

"All right, then, Money Gun," Buckland said, holstering his gun, "let's see who the better man is, you or me."

"I'd rather see who the smarter man is," Faulkner said.

He didn't holster his gun, as Buckland expected him to do. Instead, he raised it and shot the man in the chest.

———

TALL FELLOW CAME out of the hardware store in time to watch the confrontation between Buckland and Faulkner. He, too, expected Faulkner to holster his gun and engage in a fair fight. He was shocked when Faulkner simply shot the man dead.

By the time he reached them Faulkner was standing over the dead Buckland.

"You can collect your bounty now, Tall Fellow."

"You just shot him," the bounty hunter said.

Faulkner looked at him.

"That's my job."

"But... he was willing to fight it out with you fair."

Faulkner ejected the spent shell from his gun, replaced it with a live one, and then holstered the gun.

"I didn't grow up here, Tall Fellow," he said. "I don't have to follow your ridiculous code of the West. It was my job to kill him and he made it easy."

"So any way you can get it done is good?"

"You got it."

Tall Fellow looked around him at the bodies in the street.

"Is this all of them?" Faulkner asked.

"Two more in that hardware store."

"Bounties are all yours," Faulkner said.

"You leaving town?"

"My job's done. I'm going right to the livery to get on my horse and ride out. Got a job in Denver."

"Sure you don't want a share of the bounty on the rest of these fellas?" Tall Fellow asked. "You earned it."

"All yours, Tall Fellow."

He walked away.

"See you somewhere down the trail."

Faulkner waved without looking back.

CHAPTER THIRTY-SIX

1898

J ack Sunday picked the Lucky Ace Saloon to spend his time in. If any of the other men showed up, he chased them out. The Ace was now his place.

He also chose the restaurant right across from his hotel to eat all his meals. He had steak for every meal when he could get it.

Faulkner didn't know about the steak. He only knew which saloon and which restaurant Sunday was patronizing. It had been easy to find Sunday, since they were staying at the same hotel.

Faulkner had been standing out in front of the hotel, pondering his next move, when Jack Sunday came walking out. Question answered. He didn't look at the man, but when Sunday started walking, so did Faulkner.

By late afternoon, Sunday had eaten twice at the small restaurant and stopped into the Lucky Ace three times. He had not yet stopped at any of the whorehouses.

Also, he was obviously staying away from the other members of his gang, since he'd chased several of them out of the Ace.

Since Faulkner did not want Sunday to catch on to him, he chose a different saloon and a different restaurant. He decided to go ahead and remain in the same hotel.

Later that evening, Faulkner—satisfied that Sunday would be at the Lucky Ace for a while—went to the Happy Thief Saloon. He liked the name. It was obviously somebody's idea of irony. That required a brain. Somebody in Gunman's Crossing was more than a mindless thief and murderer.

He stood at the bar in the Thief and nursed a beer. He just had to kill time until Tall Fellow rode into town the next morning, and then they'd have to figure out how they were going to take Sunday. Sunday staying away from his own gang members might even make it easy. The gang leader obviously felt safe enough in Gunman's Crossing to not have to keep his gang around him. Still, they were in town, so when Faulkner and Tall Fellow made their move against him, they still might have to deal with the rest of the gang.

An argument broke out at a corner table and Faulkner turned to look. There was a poker game going on. Two of the players were members of Sunday's gang. They were two of the four he had identified by watching Sunday.

They were apparently being accused of working together to take money from the other three men. Faulkner watched with interest. If the argument escalated into violence and they got themselves killed, Sunday would have two fewer men. He stood there, rooting for guns to be drawn, but it didn't happen. Instead, Sunday's two men stormed out of the place without their money.

Faulkner turned back to the bar and ordered another beer. He was still nursing that one when a woman sidled up next to him. She stood there a few moments before he turned his head and looked at her. Definitely not a saloon girl. And she wasn't drinking. There was only one other explanation. He looked straight ahead again.

"You own this place?" he asked.

"Good guess."

She was blond, about thirty-five, attractive but not beautiful. There was a confidence about her, though, that made her striking. She attracted attention, and she was standing next to him, which meant he'd attract attention.

"You're new in town," she said.

"Good guess on your part. Can I help you with something?"

"You can if you are who I think you are."

"And who do you think I am?"

"A man who hires out his gun."

"Just any man who hires out his gun?" he asked. "That would be an amazingly good guess."

"Faulkner," she said. "Your name is Faulkner."

He looked at her.

"We can talk in my office."

CHAPTER THIRTY-SEVEN

They went into a small office and she seated herself behind a small, pitted desk.

"What can I do for you, Miss…"

"My name is Gena Miller," she said. "Mrs. I'm a widow."

"Sorry to hear it."

"Don't be. My husband was a sonofabitch. When he died two years ago, it was the best thing that ever happened to me."

"Okay. What can I do for you, Mrs. Miller?"

"You can do what you do best."

"What I do best is kill people," Faulkner said. "Just so there's no mistake."

"Oh, I understand," she said. "I am the only woman in Gunman's Crossing who owns a business. Do you know what that means?"

"That you inherited it from your husband when he died?"

"That I got it from my husband after I killed him," she said.

"That was what I assumed you meant when you said he died."

"You're a smart man," she said. "What's a smart man like you doing in Gunman's Crossing?"

"I came across it by mistake," he said. "I never really believed it existed, so I decided to have a look."

"What do you think?"

"I like your place."

"Seems to me a man like you would find more enjoyment at the Lucky Ace. Gambling girls…"

"Excuse me, Mrs. Miller, but you don't know what kind of man I am."

"You're undoubtedly right," she said. "I apologize. Why don't we get back to business?"

"You wanted me to do what I do best."

"Yes," she said, "I need you to kill a man."

"Just one?"

"Yes."

"Any reason why you can't do it yourself?"

"Five."

"And what are they?"

"Five bodyguards."

"Ah. Tell me something."

"What?"

"What would you have done if you hadn't seen me tonight?"

"I would have kept waiting for the right man to come through the door."

Faulkner fell silent.

"I mean, after all, you are just passing through, right?"

"That's right."

"So there's no reason you can't work for me."

"Not until I find one."

"Is that how you do business?" she asked. "You look for a reason not to do a job?"

"As a matter of fact," Faulkner said, "it is. I don't kill for no reason."

"I thought your reason would be you're being paid."

"That's what my reason would be once I take the job," he said.

"So will you take the job?"

"I need a lot more information," he said.

"Perhaps I can give you that information over a meal?" she asked.

"That sounds like a good idea," he said. "I could use a good meal."

"Good." She stood up. "I have a nice dining room upstairs, and a good cook in my employ. Why don't you wait at the bar until I get things ready?"

"All right."

She walked to the door and opened it.

"I won't be long. Steak all right?"

"Steak will be fine."

He left the office and went back to the bar.

———

"SHE MAKE YOU A GOOD OFFER?" the bartender asked, as he set a beer in front of Faulkner.

"I'm sorry?"

"Did she make you a good offer for your gun?"

"What makes you think she tried to buy my gun?" Faulkner asked.

"She's been waitin' for the right man for months," the bartender said. He was in his forties, very fit, with short dark hair and a well-cared-for mustache.

"And what makes you think it's me?"

The man smiled.

"Because I'm the one who told her you were here."

CHAPTER THIRTY-EIGHT

The bartender's name was Zack Lawrence.

"I saw you kill a man in Abilene a few years back," he said. "I recognized you as soon as you walked in, knew you were the man she's been lookin' for."

Faulkner studied the man for a moment.

"You're in love with her."

"That doesn't matter."

"Why don't you do what she wants done?" Faulkner asked.

"I'm no gunman," Zack said. "I'm just a bartender."

"So who does she want killed?"

"That's for her to tell you."

Faulkner looked around.

"Does everyone here know who I am now?"

"No," Zack said, "not unless they recognized you on their own. But would it matter? You're safe here. As far as I know, you've never worn a badge in your life."

"No, I haven't."

"Lawmen, or ex-lawmen, or even ex-bounty hunters, they'd have a problem here. Not you. After all, you've probably killed more men than anybody else in this town."

"You're probably right."

"So have you accepted her offer?"

"I haven't heard the whole offer yet," Faulkner said. "She's going to make it over a steak."

"Ah..."

"Tell me about her husband."

"Thornton Miller."

Faulkner's eyebrows went up.

"Yep, that Thornton Miller."

"There's only one that I know of. I didn't make the connection."

"No reason you would. Miller is a common name."

"What happened to Miller?"

"He came here, started this place. He had put his guns down, thinking he'd be safe here."

"And he wasn't."

"Somebody shot him in the back."

"Any idea who?"

"Nobody cares," Zack said. "There's no law here. So, Gena took over the place. She's the only woman running a business in town, except for two of the whorehouses."

"Two?"

"One of them is owned and run by a man."

"Seems to me the kind of men who live here," Faulkner said, "wouldn't take kindly to having a woman own a business. I mean, a real business, not a whorehouse."

"You've got that right. Whoever she wants you to kill, she wants you to do it before they kill her."

"But you won't tell me that."

"No," he said, shaking his head. "That's up to her."

"Okay," Faulkner said. "So I guess I'll just have another beer."

"Comin' up."

———

FAULKNER WAS STILL WORKING on that beer when Zack came over and said, "Stairway in the back. Takes you right up to the dining room."

"Should I take my beer?"

"Naw, that's okay," Zack said. "You'll have a fresh one up there."

Faulkner looked at the stairway in the back, and then back at Zack.

"Oh, don't worry," Zack said. "There's nobody up there but her."

Faulkner hesitated.

"I know you've been shot at a lot of times," the bartender said, "but it ain't gonna happen here. She needs you."

Faulkner was thinking that this woman had shot her own husband—a one-time famed gunman—in the back. What was to stop her from doing it to him?

Well, for one thing, there was no apparent reason for her to do that.

And he did really want a steak.

"Okay," he said.

He walked to the back of the room and up the stairway. The room at the top was well lit, which was encouraging. If it had been dark at the top of the stairs, he would not have gone.

When he got to the top he saw a table set up in a small dining room. Just the one table, with Gena Miller sitting at it.

"Thanks for coming," she said. "Your steak is getting cold."

———

"HOW'S THE STEAK?" she asked, fifteen minutes later.

"Excellent," he said.

"And the vegetables?"

"Very good," he assured her. "You do have a good cook working for you."

"Yes, I do. More wine?"

"Please."

The table was small enough that all she had to do was lean over and pour.

"You're very educated," she said.

"There are different kinds of educations."

"I meant you sound college-educated."

"Along time ago," he said, "back east."

"Yes, me, too. Where?"

"Just...east."

She smiled and said, "Me, too."

"And your husband?"

"Oh no," she said. "Thornton was a Westerner, through and through."

He nodded.

"You know that name, don't you?" she asked. "Thornton Miller?"

"Yes, I do."

"But you weren't surprised when I said it," she commented. "Who had the big mouth? Zack?"

"Yes."

"I should fire him."

"Somehow I don't think you will."

"No," she said, "I probably couldn't run this place without him."

"Mrs. Miller—"

"Gena," she said. "Please call me Gena."

"Gena," Faulkner said, "can we get to the person you want me to kill? The one with the five bodyguards?"

"Of course," she said. "His name is Gary Blaine. He owns the Lucky Ace."

"Uh-huh."

"And a few other businesses in town."

"Including a whorehouse?"

"How did you know that?"

"Lucky guess. Is the reason you want him dead that he's your competitor?"

"No," she said. "I don't care about competition. There's plenty to go around for all of us, that's what I think."

"But he doesn't feel the same?"

"Not at all," she said. "He wants to own it all. In a town of snakes and crooks and killers, he's the worst."

"I see."

"Or he was," she added, "until you got here."

CHAPTER THIRTY-NINE

"He wants me dead."

"Then why doesn't he just kill you?" Faulkner asked. "Or have you killed?"

"Even though this town is filled with killers," she said, "there aren't that many who want to kill a woman."

"Especially not Thornton Miller's widow."

"You're right. My husband had a lot of friends here," she said.

"But none who want to bother trying to find out who killed him, right?"

She sat back.

"Anyone trying to find out would be acting like a lawman," she said. "These men would rather be caught dead than act like a lawman."

"But they idolized your husband."

"Some of them did," she said. "If they found out I killed him…"

"They might forget you're a woman."

"Yes."

"Then why doesn't Blaine just let the word out?" Faulkner asked.

"He doesn't know," she said. "Nobody does."

"Not even Zack?"

"He suspects, but he doesn't know."

"So why did you tell me?"

"It gives you something on me," she said. "It tells you I'm serious."

"How do you know I wasn't hired to come here and kill you?"

"If that's the case I wouldn't be able to stop you. You could do it right now and you'd probably get away with it. You might have to kill Zack, too, but you'd get away."

"Well, lucky for you that's not the case, then," he said.

"So...will you do it?" she asked. "I mean, while you're here you might as well make some money. What's the going rate for money guns these days?"

"It goes up," he told her, "per bodyguard."

———

GARY BLAINE WALKED UP to Jack Sunday, who was sitting alone at a table with a bottle of whiskey.

"Mind if I join you?"

Sunday looked up at him.

"Depends on who you are."

"I own this place," Blaine said.

"And why should that mean anything to me?"

"I can arrange for everything you have in here to be free."

Sunday sat back.

"Have a seat, Mr. Blaine." Blaine waved to a passing saloon girl and told her to bring a fresh bottle.

———

"I'LL HAVE to check Gary Blaine out first," Faulkner said. "I can let you know by tomorrow night."

"You're an odd sort of gun for hire, Mr. Faulkner," she said. "I thought once we agreed on the money, that would be it."

"It's not all about the money for me," he told her. "The steak helped, but there are still other considerations."

"Oh, I see," she said. "The bodyguards. You want to take a look at the setup. I can understand that."

"Good," he said. "Then I assume there's a dessert that goes with this fine meal?"

"Oh, yes," she said with a smile, "there is definitely dessert."

CHAPTER FORTY

"Let me get this straight," Jack Sunday said to Blaine. "You want me to kill a woman?"

"Yes."

"This town is full of killers."

"Not like you," Blaine said. "They have...scruples."

"And I don't?"

"I've followed your career, Mr. Sunday," Blaine said. "You're the man I've been waiting for."

"And why would I do this?"

"For money."

"What makes you think I need the money?"

"Everybody needs money," Gary Blaine said.

Sunday poured himself another shot of whiskey and said, "I've got money."

"Well," Blaine said, "maybe I can sweeten the pot."

"With what?"

"The woman I want killed is Thornton Miller's widow," Blaine said. "That mean anything to you?"

Sunday sat up straight.

"I'd like it better if it was Miller himself."

"Can't help you there," Blaine said. "Somebody beat you to it."

"I didn't hear."

"He was shot in the back."

"By whom?"

"Nobody knows for sure."

"But you have an idea?"

"Yeah."

Sunday waited, then said, "Her? You think she back-shot her own husband?"

"Yes."

"Why would she?"

"He hung up his guns, but not his violent nature," Blaine said.

"Huh?"

"He used to beat her up," Blaine said. "She got tired of it."

"So whoever killed him didn't claim his rep."

"Right."

Sunday thought it over.

"A man would've done it and announced it to everyone," he said. I agree.

"Okay, so she did it," Sunday said. "How does that help me? I kill her, I don't get credit for him."

"Are you tired of what you've been doing, Jack?" Blaine asked.

Sunday stared at his drink.

"I been doing it for a long time."

"Gunman's Crossing would be a good place to settle down," Blaine said. "You could have the Happy Thief if you killed Gena Miller. And the money I'll pay you. And the satisfaction of knowing you killed Thornton Miller's wife—the person who killed him."

Sunday had another drink. Was he tired of doing what he'd been doing for so many years? He knew he was tired of the men he had to use, to ride with. That was why he didn't want any of them to come near him while they were here.

"I tell you what," Blaine said. "Think it over and let me know. There's no rush. Meanwhile, whatever you want here—whiskey, women, food—it's on the house. Both here and at the whorehouse I also own."

"You own a whorehouse?"

The light in Jack Sunday's eyes told Gary Blaine he may have just hit upon his real route to recruiting the man.

Faulkner finished his delicious apple pie and coffee and Gena walked him down the stairs to a back door.

"I don't think anyone should see us together anymore," she said, and he agreed.

At the door she said, "Just come into the saloon tomorrow and stand at the bar if you're going to do the job."

"And if I'm not going to do the job?" he asked. "Where do I stand then?"

"No offense, Faulkner," she said, "but if you're not going to do the job, then don't even come back into my place."

"Hey—" he said as she pushed him out the door.

"In fact," she added, "don't even stay in this town."

She slammed the door and left him standing out behind the building. He found an alley and took it back to Gunman's Crossing's main street.

He didn't even know why he had entertained her offer. He wasn't in town looking for more work; he was in town to help Tall Fellow collect his bounty on Jack Sunday.

But the steak dinner had been good.

———

TALL FELLOW STARED up at the sky, lying on his back next to the fire he had decided to go ahead and build. He needed the warmth, and he wasn't cooking bacon or making coffee or anything that could be smelled from miles away.

He had played back the whole Tom Buckland affair in his head over and over during this hunt for Jack Sunday. After it had all been over and Faulkner had left, he'd gone back to collect the bodies for the bounties, and one had been missing. One man had not been dead, and he had gotten away. It had taken Tall Fellow many years to find out who that man was. It was like an unfinished part of his history that he had to track down that final man. It connected his life then to his life now.

He had never, over the years, during all the times they had worked together, told Faulkner what had happened. He didn't know why. Maybe it never seemed important, but it was important to him now.

He wondered what Faulkner would think about the young man who'd been part of the Tom Buckland gang growing up to be Jack Sunday, who now had a gang of his own.

CHAPTER FORTY-ONE

Faulkner went directly back to his hotel and turned in. He could have gone to the Lucky Ace to check on Jack Sunday but decided there was no need. Sunday was in town and wasn't going anywhere soon. The only reason to even come to Gunman's Crossing was to lie low for a while. Or to kill somebody.

Tall Fellow rose in the morning, kicked dirt on the fire until it was out, then mounted up and rode into Gunman's Crossing. He was pleased to see that his arrival went without much notice. The men walking the streets didn't care who he was, unless they saw the glint of the sun on a badge.

He also breathed a sigh of relief when he came within sight of one of the hotels and saw Faulkner very casually sitting out front.

Good. He was still alive.

Jack Sunday woke that morning, rolled over and looked at the girl in the bed next to him. She had looked a lot better last night when he was drunk. And, of course, when she was free.

He got out of the bed and walked to the window so he could look down at the town. What more perfect place could there be to settle down than a town with no law? The only other question he had to answer was, did he want to settle down and give up the life he was leading?

If he could put together the right gang it would be different, but they were approaching a new century, and he couldn't find dependable men anymore. It wasn't like when he started riding with Tom Buckland all those years ago. Back then every man in the gang was good—or was that like being drunk the night before when he picked out this whore? Maybe the older he got and the further away he got from those days, the better the memories became. Actually, Tom Buckland was a good leader, but he was far from perfect. He was a good planner, but he wasn't very smart.

Sunday considered himself a good planner and a smart man. He was so smart, in fact, that he couldn't stand to hold a conversation with any of his men that didn't have to do with robbing or lolling.

So now he had an opportunity to settle down, have his own place in Gunman's Crossing, with no law to bother him, and he'd only have to talk to people if he wanted to. And the price seemed small enough.

All he had to do was kill a woman he didn't know—and he'd done that enough times before.

———

FAULKNER WATCHED Tall Fellow ride past, on his way toward the livery. He decided to wait where he was for the bounty hunter to come back. He didn't know where Sunday was at the moment, but it was a good bet he was either still in his room or across the street at the restaurant he favored. If he wasn't in one if those locations, then it would probably be a whorehouse. From what he had learned about the town, there were three.

He thought some more about the previous night's offer from the widow of Thornton Miller. Miller was about ten years older than Faulkner— or he would have been if he were still alive. When Faulkner first came west, Miller already had a reputation as a gunman. It had been so many years since he'd heard anything new about him, though, that he'd just assumed the man was dead. Well, he was dead, but only two years in the ground. Faulkner would have liked to meet Miller, but that wasn't possible. But he had been given the chance to help the man's widow. And where was the harm in picking up some money once he was finished with his favor for Tall Fellow?

It took fifteen minutes for Tall Fellow to come walking back up the street, carrying his saddlebags and rifle. It would make sense for him to stop, since this was the first hotel he'd come to.

Faulkner deliberately did not look at his friend as he mounted the boardwalk.

"Excuse me," Tall Fellow said.

Faulkner looked up.

"You staying in this hotel?"

"I am."

"Is it any good?"

"Beds are better than the ground."

"Sounds good to me."

"The clerk's probably going to ask you to sign the register."

"Thanks for the warning."

Tall Fellow went inside to get a room, and Faulkner remained where he was.

Another fifteen minutes later Tall Fellow came out, stopped, and made a production out of rolling a cigarette.

"Where is Sunday?" he asked, without looking at Faulkner.

"He's actually staying in this hotel," Faulkner said. "He's either inside or in that restaurant across the street." He also told him about the likelihood that Sunday might be in a whorehouse if he wasn't in one of those places.

"The only other place he favors is the Lucky Ace saloon."

"And do you favor that saloon?"

"*I* do my drinking at the Happy Thief."

"And his men?"

"All over town, but they apparently have orders to stay away from him."

"That's good for us."

"Saloons aren't open yet," Faulkner said. "Get yourself something to eat across the street."

"Where are you going to be?"

"Right here."

"See you in a while."

Tall Fellow stepped down and Faulkner watched him walk across the street and enter the restaurant. Suddenly he realized he was hungry. Should have told Tall Fellow he'd be going to get something to eat himself. Now he'd have to sit until Tall Fellow was finished. It was just as well. Tall Fellow had spent the night on the ground in a cold camp. It was only fair.

CHAPTER FORTY-TWO

Sunday left the whorehouse and headed back toward his hotel, then crossed the street and entered the restaurant. He'd seen the man seated in front of the hotel, but didn't give him any more thought than he gave the other diners around him. He grabbed a table in the back and called the waiter over.

"Steak and eggs, sir?"

"And coffee."

"Comin' up."

Sunday was going to eat a leisurely breakfast, and by the time he was done he was going to come to a decision about whether or not to kill the woman for Gary Blaine. However, if he was going to do it, Blaine was going to have to understand that Jack Sunday didn't work for anybody. If he did it, he intended to come out the other end as Blaine's partner—whether the man liked it or not.

When Faulkner saw Sunday coming down the street he remained still. He couldn't afford to give any indication that he recognized him, or that his appearance meant anything to him. If Sunday entered the hotel he'd keep his eyes straight ahead, as he had with Tall Fellow. Instead, Sunday headed across the street to the restaurant and went inside. Now it was up to Tall Fellow to maintain his composure with his meal ticket right in front of him.

As Jack Sunday entered, Tall Fellow recognized him, not

only from his posters, but from almost twenty-five years ago. He was bigger, heavier, older, but Tall Fellow could still see the young man he had shot all that time ago. Too bad he had not shot him twice.

When Sunday's steak came, he took a bite and his eyes moved around the room until they came to a stop on one man. As he chewed he tried to place him. He couldn't, and it bothered him. He knew him from somewhere. It would come to him, eventually.

When Jack Sunday's eyes came to a stop on him, Tall Fellow could almost physically feel them. He was eating steak and eggs of his own, and kept his head down and his eyes on his plate. He was tempted to try to take Sunday then and there, but there were too many other people in the place— most of them wearing guns. Besides, he and Faulkner had each agreed not to try to take the man alone.

He kept eating his breakfast, wondering—if Sunday had not already recognized him—how long it would take him to do so.

Tall Fellow finished eating first, paid his bill and walked out. He didn't look in Sunday's direction at all, but felt the man's eyes on him every step of the way.

He crossed over to the hotel, stepped up on the walk and stopped.

"We need to talk."

"The Happy Thief, as soon as it opens."

Tall Fellow went inside. Faulkner stood up and went in search of his own breakfast.

Jack Sunday watched the man walk out of the restaurant, even more convinced that he knew him. And it was more than just having seen a poster, or maybe being in the same jail cell some time.

This was a face from his past, and he was going to place it before the day was out.

Tall Fellow was already at the bar when Faulkner walked into the Happy Thief. He joined him there, but left some room between them.

The bartender was not Zack, and Faulkner didn't know him, so he just ordered a beer without any other comments. He was just hoping that Gena would not put in an appearance. He wasn't ready with an answer for her yet.

As the bartender moved away Faulkner looked around and

saw that he and Tall Fellow were the first two customers, so he moved closer so they could talk.

"He recognized me," Tall Fellow said.

"What? What are you talking about?"

"There's something I didn't tell you."

"About what?"

"Jack Sunday. We've met before."

"You and him?"

"All three of us."

"What the hell are you talking about, Indian?" Faulkner demanded.

"The Buckland gang," Tall Fellow said. "All those years ago? We got them all but one."

"One?"

"Sunday," Tall Fellow said. "He got away. I put a bullet in him, but he got away."

"You never told me one got away."

Tall Fellow shrugged.

"Didn't seem important."

"And you're choosing to tell me now?"

"There's no danger of him knowing you," Tall Fellow said. "You and him never came face to face back then."

"So how do you know he recognized you?"

"I could feel it. I don't think he placed me, but he knows he's seen me before."

"We may have to move fast, then, before he does place you," Faulkner said. "He's keeping away from his men. Doesn't seem to want to socialize with them."

"So maybe we can take him in the Lucky Ace?" Tall Fellow asked. "If he's on his own. Is there anybody else likely to take a hand?"

"Doesn't seem so," Faulkner said. "I think everybody here fights their own battles."

"Is there any bad news?"

"Maybe. I got a job offer."

"What? I think I need to hear about this."

"I'll tell you." He gave Tall Fellow the story of Thornton Miller's widow and her problem. And their problem.

"Since this fella Blaine has a bunch of bodyguards, the Lucky Ace may not be the place to take Sunday."

"So we can figure out a better place," Tall Fellow said. "For now, tell me...you going to take this job?"

CHAPTER FORTY-THREE

"You're getting your money," Faulkner said to Tall Fellow. "Why shouldn't I get mine?"

"*I* told you I'd share the bounty with you."

"No," Faulkner said, "I don't want your money. I want my own."

"So you're going to go up against these five bodyguards to kill this man? Has this woman got a hold over you already?"

"It's not the woman, Tall Fellow," Faulkner said.

"Ah," Tall Fellow said, "it's the legend. The Thornton legend."

"Look, I haven't made my mind up yet," Faulkner said. "I may not do it. I'll check the guy out today and make up my mind."

"Okay," Tall Fellow said.

"Okay what?"

"Okay, you came all this way to help me out," the bounty hunter said. "If you decide to take that job, I'll back you."

"I'm not asking you to do that."

"I know it," Tall Fellow said. "I'm offering. After all, if I let you go against five bodyguards alone, I'll probably never hear the end of it."

"What makes you think I'd come out of that alive?" Faulkner asked.

"Are you kidding?" Tall Fellow asked. "They would be outnumbered."

The batwing doors opened and several men came walking in.

"We have to get out of here before we attract attention," Faulkner said. "And I don't want to run into Gena Miller yet."

They turned and headed for the door.

"Want to walk out separately?" Faulkner asked.

"What the hell," Tall Fellow said. "If anybody wants to come after us, let them come."

They walked through the batwing doors together.

————

JACK SUNDAY WALKED into the Lucky Ace and went right to the bar.

"Tell your boss I'm here."

The bartender stared into Sunday's eyes and decided not to tell him he didn't know who he was. He'd just tell his boss "some guy" wanted to see him.

"Sure thing."

The barman left the bar and walked to the office in the back, went inside. Moments later Gary Blaine came out with him.

"Eddie," he said to the bartender as they reached the bar, "get me and my friend a beer, will you?"

"Sure thing, boss."

"Good morning, Jack."

"I made up my mind," Sunday said.

"Good," Blaine said. "I was hoping it wouldn't take you long."

As Eddie put two beers on the bar, Blaine picked one up and handed it to Jack Sunday, then picked the other one up for himself.

"Let's drink to it."

"Not so fast," Sunday said. "We still got some negotiatin' to do."

"Fine," Blaine said. "We can do that over a beer, can't we?"

Sunday stared at Blaine for a few moments, then said, "Why?" and drank his beer down, spilling much of it over his chin and onto his chest.

CHAPTER FORTY-FOUR

Faulkner took Tall Fellow over to the Lucky Ace and they peered in one of the front windows.

"Who's that sitting with Sunday?" Tall Fellow asked. "He's too well-dressed to be one of his men."

"I'm pretty sure that's Gary Blaine."

"The man you're supposed to kill?"

"That's right."

Tall Fellow looked at Faulkner.

"They're just sitting there, Faulkner, waiting for us."

Faulkner kept looking through the window, moving his gaze around the room.

"We can just walk in and take them," Tall Fellow said.

"No," Faulkner said.

"Why not?"

"Gena said he has five bodyguards." Faulkner looked at Tall Fellow. "Where are they?"

"Maybe she was lying to you," Tall Fellow suggested.

"Why? To make the job sound harder so I wouldn't take it?"

"Doesn't make sense."

"No, it doesn't." Faulkner looked around. "Let's get away from here before we're spotted. We'll have to figure this out."

BLAINE AND SUNDAY had taken their drinks—a second beer for Sunday—to a back table, where Sunday laid it out for the other man.

Blaine started to laugh.

"What's so funny?"

"You want to be my partner?" Blaine asked.

"That's right."

"I'm not looking for a partner, Mr. Sunday," Blaine said. "I'm looking for an employee."

"I'm not anybody's employee," Sunday said. "You want that woman dead, it's gonna be on my terms. Otherwise, I can just go about my business."

"I offered you money and her business," Blaine said. "That's not good enough for you?"

"I got money," Sunday said. "And I ain't interested in owning a saloon."

Blaine had a feeling.

"What kind of business would you like to own?"

Sunday smiled.

"Now we're negotiatin'."

As Faulkner and Tall Fellow turned to leave the saloon, two men stepped out of the alley next to it, their guns in their hands and pointed at them.

"Can we help you fellas?" one of them asked.

"Actually," Faulkner said, "we've been drinking over at the Happy Thief and were wondering if we should change to the Lucky Ace."

"Any suggestions?" Tall Fellow added.

"Yep," the other man said, "I got a suggestion. Stand still and don't move while my partner relieves you of your guns."

"Now why would we want to do that?" Faulkner asked. "And why would you want our guns?"

"Because we got our guns out, and you don't," the first man said.

"You try to take my gun," Faulkner said, "and we're really going to answer a question I've been asking myself for a long time."

"Oh yeah?" the second man asked. "What question's that?"

"Whether or not I can successfully draw against an already drawn gun," Faulkner said. "What do you think, Tall Fellow?"

"I'd put my money on you, Faulkner."

Now, they didn't expect the two men to recognize Tall Fellow's name, but were hoping that Faulkner's name would ring a bell—and, apparently, it did.

"You're Faulkner?" the second man asked.

"That's right."

"Listen," the second man said, "our boss owns this place. I think he'd like to buy you a drink."

"You think so?" Faulkner asked. "What about my friend here?"

"We don't know him," the first man said.

"He can go," the second one added.

"The first thing that has to go is your guns," Faulkner said. "Why don't you boys just put them up? We don't want anybody getting hurt…accidentally, do we?"

The two men exchanged a glance, then shrugged and holstered their guns.

"You going inside for a drink?" Tall Fellow asked.

"Why not?" Faulkner asked. "A free drink's a free drink, right?"

Tall Fellow looked at the two bodyguards— both in their thirties and similarly dressed in black—and said, "I'll pass."

"You ain't invited," the first man said.

Tall Fellow stared at him.

"We'll see each other again," he told both of the men. "I don't like having a gun pulled on me for no reason."

"We had a reason," the first one said. "It's our job."

"I'll see you later, Faulkner," Tall Fellow said.

"I'll come over to the Happy Thief when I'm finished here."

"Who is that guy?" the first man asked.

"Somebody I met here in town," Faulkner said.

"I don't like him," the second man said.

"Seems like the feeling is mutual," Faulkner said. "Should we go inside? It would be rude to keep your boss waiting."

"Oh, he don't know you're comin'," the first man said. "But trust me, he's gonna want to buy you a drink."

"Like I said," Faulkner replied, "a free drink is a free drink."

CHAPTER FORTY-FIVE

Faulkner entered the saloon ahead of the two bodyguards. He'd managed to get Tall Fellow out of harm's way, and he had a good idea of why the bodyguards thought their boss would want to buy him a drink.

As they approached the table, both Gary Blaine and Jack Sunday looked up at them, wondering why they were being interrupted.

"What's going on, boys?" Blaine asked his two men.

"This here fella was lookin' in the window, boss," the first man said. "When we braced him he said his name was Faulkner."

"We thought you might wanna talk to him," the other man said.

"The Faulkner?" Blaine asked. "The Money Gun?"

"I'm the only Faulkner I know of."

"Faulkner," the man said, "my name's Gary Blaine. This is my...associate, Jack Sunday."

"Can't say either name rings a bell," Faulkner said. "Sorry."

"No reason why mine should," Blaine said.

Sunday scowled at Faulkner.

"What's a hired gun doin' in Gunman's Crossing?" he asked.

"The name of the town just had a certain ring to it," Faulkner said. "Thought I'd check it out."

"You wanted anywhere?" Sunday asked.

"Not that I know of."

"Most of the men in this town are," the outlaw said.

Faulkner looked at Sunday and said, "I'll bet that makes their mothers very proud."

Blaine started to laugh. Sunday didn't think it was so funny, and he started to get up.

"You know, Jack," Blaine said, "I think we can finish our business a little later. I really think Mr. Faulkner and I should have a talk."

Sunday looked at Blaine, then at Faulkner. This was Faulkner's first close-up look at Sunday. He and Blaine obviously came from two ends of the spectrum. Although they were about the same age—mid-forties, which made them contemporaries of Faulkner—Blaine was well-dressed and obviously educated, while Jack Sunday was obviously uneducated, and barely civilized.

"Got no use for a hired gun, anyway," he said. "I'm gonna get some fresh air."

"You do that, Jack."

Sunday gave Faulkner another hard stare, then left the saloon.

"Why don't you boys stand by the bar," Blaine said to his bodyguards. "Have a drink."

"Sure, boss."

"Have a seat, Mr. Faulkner," Blaine invited. "Can I get you a drink?"

"A beer would be fine."

He made a signal to the bartender, who brought over one beer. The man was obviously well trained. Faulkner had not seen anything in Blaine's signal that made him think of beer.

"You shouldn't push him, you know," Blaine said.

"Push whom?"

"Sunday."

"*I* wasn't aware I was."

"Saying you didn't recognize his name," Blaine said. "He thinks he's left quite a mark on the West."

"Sorry to disappoint him," Faulkner said.

"You honestly don't know who he is?"

"I'm not a bounty hunter."

"No," Blaine said, "of course not. Your profession is much more... precise than that."

"Your boys said you might want to buy me a drink," Faulkner said. "What would the reason for that be?"

"First, why were you lookin' in my window?" Blaine asked.

"Trying to figure out if I should drink here instead of the Happy Thief."

"Well, the answer to that is very simple," Blaine said. "Have you been to the Thief?"

"Yes," Faulkner said.

"And?"

"I have to admit your beer is better."

"Everything is better over here, Mr. Faulkner."

"Just Faulkner."

"Tell me, Faulkner, have you met the owner of the Thief?"

Now here he had to decide whether or not a lie would come back to bite him.

"A woman claiming to be Thornton Miller's widow? I met her."

"Oh, she doesn't claim to be Miller's widow," Blaine said. "She is Miller's widow."

"Interesting."

"I'll tell you something else you may find interesting," Blaine said. "I've got a proposition for you."

"Let's hear it."

"First I have a question for you," Blaine said, "and I'm afraid your life may depend on the answer."

Faulkner turned his head. The two bodyguards had their guns out again, as did the bartender. More signals he did not catch. Apparently, Blaine's men were a well-trained bunch.

"Looks to me like I better think over this answer very carefully."

"It's just one question," Blaine said. "The answer should be fairly simple. And I have to warn you, I'm pretty good at knowing when I'm being lied to."

"Okay, then," Faulkner said, "before my beer gets warm maybe you can ask it."

Blaine laughed.

"I like a man who gets right to the point."

"The point being?"

"Have you been hired by Gena Miller to kill me?" Gary Blaine asked.

Faulkner stared the man right in the eyes and said without hesitation, "Mr. Blaine, I can safely say that I have definitely not been hired to kill you."

CHAPTER FORTY-SIX

"What about Jack Sunday?"

"What about him?"

"You're not here to kill him, are you?"

"I told you," Faulkner lied. "I have no idea who he is."

Blaine leaned back in his chair and regarded Faulkner across the table.

"I could use a man like you in my operation, Faulkner," he said.

"What operation is that, Mr. Blaine?"

"Gary, please," Blaine said. "Just call me Gary. I'm talking about this saloon and various other businesses in town."

Faulkner turned to look at the men at the bar, who still had their guns out.

"Looks to me like you've got plenty of help."

Blaine waved his hand and the men holstered their guns. The bartender stowed his behind the bar.

"I can use a good man," Blaine said. "Somebody I can depend on."

It was Faulkner's turn to sit back. He was trying to get a look around the saloon without seeming obvious. If there were more bodyguards hidden, he wanted to find out where.

"I don't consider Gunman's Crossing an ideal spot to settle down," he said.

"Who's askin' you to settle down?" Blaine asked. "I'm only askin' you to work for me for a while."

"How long is a while?"

"Until you get tired," Blaine said. "I would pay you very well."

"I was planning on leaving tomorrow," Faulkner said.

"Why don't you think it over?" Blaine said. "Give me an answer in the morning."

"It would help if I could talk to some of your men," Faulkner said. "You know, find out what kind of boss you are?"

"It was Kirk and Ben who brought you in here," Blaine said. "Talk to them."

"That it?" Faulkner asked. "You only have two bodyguards right now?"

Blaine smiled and said, "They're the two you can talk to. Let's just leave it at that."

Men were starting to enter the saloon and belly up to the bar.

"Looks like it might start to get busy in here," Faulkner said.

"It's busy every day," Blaine said. "Look, I'll make sure Kirk and Ben are available to you—in here, or outside. Your choice."

"I'll let you know," Faulkner said. "I'm not real impressed with them."

"Why not?"

"They had me dead to rights outside," Faulkner said, "and they let me talk them into holstering their guns."

"Maybe they were influenced by your reputation," Blaine suggested.

"Well, if I wasn't impressed with them before, that's certainly not going to do it."

Faulkner stood up, made a show of pushing in his chair, and then looked around. The Lucky Ace was certainly larger and better outfitted than the Happy Thief.

"Impressive place you have here," he said, looking around.

"I made sure it was," Blaine said. "Think over my offer, Faulkner. You know where to reach me."

Faulkner found Tall Fellow standing at the bar in the Happy Thief.

"So?"

"Behind the walls," Faulkner said. "You can barely see the cutouts in the wall, but he's got bodyguards behind the walls."

"Cutouts big enough to see through, or shoot through?"

"Both."

"So you can't take him in the saloon."

"Doubtful."

"You'll have to find out how he uses them when he leaves the saloon."

"He offered me a job, told me I could talk to two of his men —those two who drew down on us—before I make up my mind."

"Maybe you can get the information out of them, then. Just get them talking."

"That's what I was thinking," Faulkner said.

"What about Sunday?"

"He left when we started talking."

"So if we take him today, is that going to ruin your shot at this fella Blaine?"

Faulkner rubbed his jaw.

"I don't know...maybe we can take them both in the same day."

"How do we do that?"

"I don't know," Faulkner said. "Let's have a beer and figure it out."

CHAPTER FORTY-SEVEN

"The key may be talking to his men," Tall Fellow said over a beer. "They might say something...helpful."

"I don't want to interfere with you taking Sunday," Faulkner said. "I'm supposed to be helping you out with that, not making it harder."

"I'll need your help with his gang," Tall Fellow said, "if they try to get involved. If he's staying away from them, I should be able to take him alone."

"It would be good if we could both make our move at the same time."

"That only works if Sunday really is isolated from his men, and if you can do the same with Blaine and his bodyguards."

The Happy Thief was starting to do a brisk business when suddenly the door to the office opened and Gena Miller came out.

"That the boss?" Tall Fellow asked.

"That's her."

"Handsome woman."

"Got nothing to do with it."

"I was just saying."

"I'll introduce you."

Gena came over to where they were standing and smiled at Faulkner.

"Do we have to go into my office for this?" she asked.

"I don't think so," he said. "I'll take the job."

"Thank you. Did we discuss money?"

"We did not," Faulkner said.

"Are you reasonable?"

"I'm high," Faulkner said. "Very high."

"My husband left me well situated," she said. "I don't think that will be a problem."

"Gena, this is Henry Tall Fellow," Faulkner said. "If anyone asks, he and I just met today."

"But you didn't?"

"No," Faulkner said. "We came here together."

"Hello, Mr. Tall Fellow."

"Ma'am."

"Are you in the same business as your friend?"

"No, ma'am," Tall Fellow said. "I'm a bounty hunter."

"And you're here working?"

"I am."

"I won't ask who it is you're hunting," she said. "It's none of my business." She switched her gaze to Faulkner. "When will you do it?"

"Soon."

"Then I suppose I should pay you?"

"Half," he said. "Half when I'm done."

"Then we do have to go to my office. Mr. Tall Fellow? Will you come with us?"

"No, ma'am," Tall Fellow said. "I have some work to do."

"Wait for me," Faulkner told him.

"If I wait," the bounty hunter said, "I'm going to have another drink."

"Okay," Faulkner said, "but no firewater. Just a beer."

"I'll see to it you're not charged," Gena told Tall Fellow.

"There you go," Tall Fellow said with a rare smile. "That's a good reason for me to wait."

Gena signaled to the bartender, who drew Tall Fellow another beer and set it down in front of him. Apparently, something in her signal meant there should be no charge. Faulkner wondered what kind of code this was that saloon owners had with bartenders.

"Shall we go?" she asked him.

"Lead the way."

In the office they took up their former positions, she behind the desk, and he seated across from her.

"Have you seen Blaine?" she asked.

"Seen and met."

"Really. Did he try to hire you?"

"He did," Faulkner said.

"To do what?"

"He didn't say yet," Faulkner said. "Just said he could use a man like me."

"Thinking about his offer?" she asked.

"That's what I told him," he said, "but I have another offer already."

She took a strongbox out from beneath her desk, set it on top and opened it.

"How much?" she asked.

He told her how much half would be. She flinched, but counted out the money and handed it across to him.

"Will that do it?"

"One more thing," he said.

"What's that?"

"One more dinner before I leave town."

She smiled and said, "I think that can be arranged."

CHAPTER FORTY-EIGHT

Jack Sunday didn't like leaving Gary Blaine to talk with Faulkner. They still had not settled the question of a partnership for him to kill the woman. Now if Blaine hired Faulkner, Sunday would be on the outside looking in. Suddenly, he wanted to be on the inside.

He was walking down the street toward his hotel when he saw Hobbs and a couple of the men coming toward him. When they spotted him they abruptly changed direction and crossed the street. Good, they were keeping to the agreement and staying away from him.

"I'm tellin' you," Hobbs said, as he and his *corn-padres* entered the Lucky Ace, "if somebody would just take care of Sunday we'd be a lot better off."

"Then who would plan the jobs?" one of the men asked him.

"And whose gang would it be?"

"Me," Hobbs said, "and mine."

"You?"

"What's the matter with me as leader?" Hobbs demanded angrily.

"Hobbs, the only way you're gonna get the others to accept you as leader is to kill Jack Sunday yerself. You man enough to do that?"

"Sure I am," Hobbs replied without thinking.

The other man grinned and said, "That I gotta see."

"Shut up," Hobbs said. "Let's get some beer."

———

WHEN FAULKNER CAME out of the office, Tall Fellow was still nursing his beer—if it was the same beer.

"Ask him," Tall Fellow said, pointing at the bartender. "Same one."

The barman nodded.

"You get paid?" Tall Fellow asked.

"Yup."

"Okay," Tall Fellow said. "Why don't you go and talk to those two bodyguards."

"What are you going to do?"

"I'm going to locate Jack Sunday."

"Don't try to take him."

"I know I can take him," Tall Fellow said, "but I won't make a move until you're ready with your man."

"Okay," Faulkner said. "Suppose we meet back here in two hours. We should both have some useful information by then."

"Okay," Tall Fellow said. "Two hours. If one of us isn't here by then, he's in trouble."

"Don't," Faulkner said, "get into trouble."

"I never get into trouble on purpose," Tall Fellow pointed out.

"Just remember Denver."

"That was different!"

"I'm just saying…"

———

FAULKNER WALKED over to the Lucky Ace and entered. He scanned the walls, saw the two openings that were large enough for a rifle barrel to poke out. He'd been in saloons in the old days when men armed with shotguns sat on a raised platform out in the open where everyone could see them. This was supposed to act as a deterrent, but it also gave the man the opportunity to act quickly in the event of trouble.

Blaine had his men hidden—at least, some of them. The two men who had drawn their guns on Faulkner and Tall Fellow were standing at the bar, talking with the bartender. Blaine himself was nowhere in sight. Faulkner remembered that Gena had told him Blaine had five bodyguards. He wondered if that included the bartender, or if he was still missing one.

He approached the two men at the bar. He noticed that while the saloon was full, the patrons gave the two bodyguards plenty of room.

"Here comes the Money Gun," one of them said.

"Money Gun," the other man said, chuckling. "We got the drop on 'im pretty good, didn't we?"

"We sure did."

"Your boss says you fellas will talk to me," Faulkner said, ignoring their jibes.

"About what?"

"About him," Faulkner said.

"Yeah, well, he said we could tell you some stuff."

"Which of you is Kirk, and which is Ben?" Faulkner asked. "Are you allowed to tell me that?"

"I'm Kirk," the tall, thin one said.

"I'm Ben."

"Bartender," Faulkner said, "I'll take a beer."

Kirk and Ben were already holding beer mugs.

"Comin' up," the man said. When he set the mug down he said, "Boss says it's on the house."

"Thanks."

"What's on yer mind?" Kirk asked.

"What kind of boss is Blaine?"

The two men exchanged a glance. The bartender ducked his head and walked away.

"That bad?"

"Look," Ben said, "our job is to keep him alive. We don't have to like the guy."

"Hey," Kirk said warningly.

"What the hell," Ben said. "If he offered this guy a job he deserves ta know."

"Also," Faulkner said, "if you scare me off I can't replace one of you."

"You ain't gonna replace one of us," Kirk said. "The boss needs you for...other things."

"Things that suit your... talents."

"He needs me to kill somebody?"

"He didn't tell you?" Kirk asked.

"Well, I haven't agreed to work for him yet."

"Better get the whole picture," Ben warned.

"And what would that be?"

The two men exchanged a glance, then looked around. There was no one within earshot.

"Come on," Faulkner said. "It's just us guys."

"Let's just say," Ben replied, "he's probably wonderin' if you've ever killed a woman."

CHAPTER FORTY-NINE

"He wants me to kill a woman?"

"Probably," Kirk said.

"He's been talkin' to Jack Sunday about doin' it," Ben said, "but the minute we heard who you were we knew he'd wanna talk to you."

"Do you know who the woman is?"

"Let's just say," Ben answered, "it's a competitor."

"We're getting off the trail here," Faulkner said, not surprised that if Gena wanted Blaine killed, he'd want her killed, too. "Does he pay well?"

Kirk snorted.

"If he does we don't get it."

"What about the way he treats you?"

"Like dirt," Ben said. "Like we're beneath him."

"And does he have others working for him?"

Kirk leaned in.

"He's real skittish about gettin' killed," he said. "He's got five bodyguards."

"I see the rifle slots in the wall," Faulkner said.

"You got good eyes."

"What does he do when he goes out?"

"Takes two of us with him," Kirk said, "and the others are on the rooftops. He doesn't go anywhere at least two of us can't see him."

"So then I guess I wouldn't be one of his bodyguards," Faulkner said.

"Oh, no," Kirk said, "you'd be his pet killer."

"Almost sounds to me like you boys wouldn't be too upset if he got killed."

The two men leaned back against the bar.

"We ain't sayin' that," Kirk said.

"We ain't sayin' that at all," Ben said.

Suddenly, it was as if the two of them thought they'd said too much.

"Don't worry," Faulkner said, putting his beer mug down on the bar. "This is all just between us."

"'Preciate that, Faulkner," Kirk said.

"We're sorry about razzin' ya," Ben said.

"No problem," Faulkner said. "Listen, do the other body-guards feel the way you do?"

"Pretty much," Ben said.

"Then I guess there's no point in me talking to them. I'd get the same response."

"Probably," Ben said.

"So, you gonna take the job?" Kirk asked.

"I haven't decided yet," Faulkner said, "but you boys have given me something to think about."

As he turned to walk out, Kirk asked, "Hey, have you ever killed a woman?"

Faulkner didn't answer.

———

TALL FELLOW WENT to the hotel he, Faulkner and Sunday were sharing. He knew what room Sunday was in, and crept down the hall to put his ear to the door. He thought he heard the man moving around in there, but couldn't be sure. He went back downstairs to the front desk, held out a dollar to the clerk.

"What's that fer?" He'd been dozing, and Tall Fellow thought the smell of the dollar had woken him up.

"The answer to a few questions."

"One dollar buys one question," the man said.

"Four bits per question," Tall Fellow countered.

The man thought a moment, then grabbed the dollar and said, "Yer on. You got two comin', so far."

After Faulkner left the saloon, Ben and Kirk turned to lean on the bar. The bartender came over.

"You boys plan on goin' up against him?" he asked them.

"Hell, no," Kirk said. "For the money Blaine pays us, I ain't goin' up against a man with Faulkner's rep."

"Me, either," Ben said. "That man is a stone killer. You can see it in his eyes."

"So what are you gonna do if he is here for Blaine?" the barman asked.

"I don't know about you, Eddie," Ben said to the bartender, "but if he comes after Blaine I plan to get out of the way."

"Me, too," Kirk said, "and I recommend you do the same thing."

"What about Vin and Jimmy," the bartender said, "behind the false walls?"

"They can make up their own minds if and when the time comes," Kirk said.

"You boys don't have any desire to go after a man with a rep? Maybe get one of your own?"

"Go back to pouring drinks, Eddie," Kirk told the bartender. "You're startin' ta talk crazy."

CHAPTER FIFTY

F aulkner didn't need two hours. He'd gotten what he needed. Five bodyguards or not, if Blaine had men working for him who didn't care if he lived or died, then he was vulnerable.

He'd noticed three other men in the saloon he recognized. Well, two, actually. They were the two he'd seen arguing at the poker table in the Ace the previous night. He assumed that the third man with them was also one of Sunday's men. It seemed pretty clear that while Sunday didn't want them around him, the men were sticking together. Less chance of someone throwing down on them that way. Maybe there had been more of the men in the saloon the night before.

If Jack Sunday's men were watching each other's backs, then nobody was watching his.

He was pretty sure Tall Fellow was going to find out the same thing.

By the time Tall Fellow got back to the Happy Thief, Faulkner was already there. As he approached the bar Faulkner held a beer out to him.

"You expected me this early?"

"I think we both got what we wanted."

"You first," Tall Fellow said.

Faulkner told him what he had learned from the two Blaine bodyguards. He also told him he had seen three of Sunday's men in the Ace.

"I guess now we know why he said he needed to hire you," Tall Fellow said, "somebody he could count on."

"What about you?"

"Sunday's in his room. He splits his time between three or four places."

"His hotel, the restaurant across the street..." Faulkner started.

"...the Lucky Ace, and one of the whorehouses," Tall Fellow finished.

"So all you've got to do," Faulkner said, "is stay away from the Ace, and catch him in one of the other three places."

"What about you?" Tall Fellow asked. "Can you wait until Blaine decides to leave his saloon?"

"I don't think so," Faulkner said. "I don't want to be in Gunman's Crossing very much longer, now that some people know who I am. The word is bound to circulate."

"So what? You don't have any law in your background. Why will anyone care?"

"Somebody will want to make a try for my rep," Faulkner said. "It always happens. The sooner I get out of this town, the better."

"Then why not get out without doing the job?" the bounty hunter asked. "We'll take Sunday and leave."

"I already took the job," Faulkner said. "I already took half the money. There's no going back."

"Okay, then. What's the timing going to be?"

"I think I can convince Kirk and Ben to take a walk," Faulkner said. "Should take me about twenty minutes."

"I can keep Sunday in sight until then," Tall Fellow said. "Twenty minutes from when we leave here, right?"

"Better make it half an hour, just to be on the safe side."

"Okay," Tall Fellow said. "Thirty minutes."

Tall Fellow looked ready to leave.

"Before we go," Faulkner said, putting his hand out to stop his friend, "tell me one thing."

"What's that?"

"This thing with Sunday—it's not about the bounty for you, is it?"

Tall Fellow hesitated, then said, "The money on Jack Sunday is big. It seems fitting to me that I bring him in, collect the money, and then try to do something about my eyes."

"I thought you said nothing could be done."

"There's a doctor in New York," Tall Fellow said. "He's real expensive. I heard that maybe he could do something."

"Why didn't you tell me this before?"

"I didn't want to appear foolish," Tall Fellow said. "Not in your eyes. You're the only man I respect, Faulkner."

"All right," Faulkner said. "Let's make damn sure you get Sunday, then."

"How do we do that?"

"We'll take him together."

"I take them alive if I can, Faulkner," Tall Fellow reminded him. "You take them dead."

"Your bounty," Faulkner said to his friend, "your call."

CHAPTER FIFTY-ONE

Gary Blaine thought that all his problems were solved. He'd made a grave error in approaching Jack Sunday, but Faulkner was going to help him correct it. First, the hired gun was going to get rid of Gena Miller for him. She'd been a thorn in his side since her husband had been killed. Privately, Blaine suspected that Gena herself had shot Thornton Miller in the back. That alone made her much more dangerous than anyone had ever thought.

Then, after he got rid of Gena, Faulkner would take care of Jack Sunday. Killing the man was the only way to get out from under his demands of a partnership. Blaine didn't know who the man thought he was, but he was certainly not going to be a partner, even in the most minor sense. No, all that Jack Sunday was going to get for his trouble was...death.

Faulkner would see to that.

Faulkner would be the first man in Blaine's employ that he could really count on. Little by little he'd get rid of the other idiots. He was sure he could convert Faulkner from a top-notch money gun into a first-rate bodyguard. All it would take was money.

———

GENA MILLER THOUGHT that all her problems were solved. Of course, the only problem she had was Gary Blaine. Not only was he her main competitor—plus the little fact that he wanted her dead—but she knew he suspected that she had killed Thornton. If she were a man she would have bragged that she'd killed the great Thornton Miller. But she was a woman, and she didn't want anyone to know about it. There was no macho in her killing of her husband, just a desire to get rid of an abusive man.

She'd gotten rid of one man in her life herself. It would take Faulkner to get rid of the other one.

———

TALL FELLOW COULD SEE in Faulkner's eyes that the man did not think him foolish, nor did he pity him. All he saw was friendship, and he was willing to accept that from Faulkner.

His eyes were his problem, and he'd try to get them taken care of on his own. But he didn't mind accepting Faulkner's help with Jack Sunday.

"Indian," Faulkner said, as they left the Happy Thief, "the only way this is going to work is to put him down. For good."

"I thought you said it was my call," Tall Fellow said, stopping right outside the batwing doors. "Wasn't that you a minute ago? 'Your bounty, your call?' Remember that?"

"I do remember it, and I said it," Faulkner replied. "But I've been thinking it over. We put Sunday down, then go right to the Lucky Ace and take care of Blaine."

"I have one problem with this," Tall Fellow said.

"What's that?"

"I'm your friend and I'll back your play," Tall Fellow said, "but I won't kill a man in cold blood. That's your profession, and I don't judge you for it. Maybe I did back in the beginning, but not anymore. We've been through too much together for me to judge you."

"I appreciate that, and I'll accept whatever form your help comes in."

"Then we can proceed."

They stepped down off the boardwalk and crossed the street.

———

SUNDAY LEFT the hotel and headed for the whorehouse owned by Gary Blaine. He needed to release some of his tension and anger before he talked to Blaine again. If the man was trying to edge him out already—before they'd even come to an agreement—he was going to be sorry. But Sunday needed to be coolheaded and calm when he confronted the man.

That meant a big blonde with wide hips and gigantic tits was going to get the ride of her life.

When Faulkner and Tall Fellow reached the hotel, the bounty hunter said to the money gun, "Give the man a dollar."

"What for?"

"Because I don't have any left."

"No, what's the dollar for?"

"Oh, that's so he'll answer some questions."

Faulkner looked at the clerk, the same man who had checked him in.

"Oh," Faulkner said, "I think he'll answer some questions without getting paid, won't you, friend?"

CHAPTER FIFTY-TWO

B efore going into his saloon—which was close to packed at the moment—Blaine checked on the men behind the false walls.

He asked each of them, "Do you know what Jack Sunday looks like?"

They answered in turn, yes.

"You better damn know him on sight, you sonofabitch," Blaine said to each man. "And keep him in your sights if he walks into my place. You got it?"

They both said they did.

"If anything goes wrong I'll have your hides."

They nodded.

"And did you see the man I was sitting with today?" he asked, as an afterthought.

They said they did.

"His name is Faulkner. Yeah, I can see you've heard of him. Keep him in your sights, too, if he comes in. I don't want to take any chances."

They said they would. Then, as Blaine walked away, they each wondered what he'd look like with a bullet in his back.

———

"SEE?" Faulkner said. "I told you he'd answer questions without getting paid."

"I had an arrangement with him," Tall Fellow said. "Four bits a question."

"I saved you money through a little intimidation," Faulkner said.

"*I* don't like scaring people."

"Tall Fellow, you're half Indian," Faulkner told him. "You automatically scare people."

They walked to the end of town where Blaine had his whorehouse situated. Sunday was not at his hotel, not in the restaurant and not at the saloon. This was the only other place he could be— unless he had suddenly broken his pattern.

"This remind you of anything?" Faulkner asked.

"Yeah," Tall Fellow said. "Buckland."

"If that other fella hadn't come out of the room across the hall, and assumed we were law, we would have had Buckland easy."

"Figures Sunday would like whorehouses," Tall Fellow said. "He learned from Buckland."

———

SUNDAY WAS GIVING the whore a thorough going-over. When he was finished with her, she'd never be the same. She was a big girl, though, and she was giving as good as she got. Sunday remembered Buckland used to do this with smaller women, but he didn't like small women. When he smacked a woman he liked to feel meat, and it was the same when he fucked one. And when he was doing both at the same time, it was doubly important.

The gal yelped and yowled whether he hit her or porked her. He had the feeling she liked both just fine.

———

HOBBS WALKED over to where the two bodyguards were standing at the bar.

"Afternoon, Kirk."

"Hobbs. This is Ben. Hobbs came in with the Sunday gang."

"Sunday?" Ben asked. "I never see you with him. He's always here alone.

"That's how he wants it," Hobbs said. "Can't associate with the likes of us."

"Hmm," Ben said.

"What?" Kirk asked.

"Maybe Hobbs here should tell his boss about the money gun."

"What's this?"

"Fella named Faulkner rode into town yesterday."

"I know that name," Hobbs said.

"Well," Ben said, "he don't usually come into a town to say howdy. He's usually after somebody."

"And you think he may be after Sunday?" Hobbs asked.

"Well," Ben sad, "he did ride in real soon after you fellas did. Might want to warn your boss about it."

"Right now my boss is probably beatin' the shit out of a whore," Hobbs said. "And remember I said he don't wanna associate with us? Well, he likes it even less when he's interrupted while he's tearin' up some whore."

"I hope he ain't tearin' up Becky," Kirk said. "I like Becky."

"That fat-assed blonde?" Ben asked.

"She's got a fine ass," Kirk said.

And he, Ben and Hobbs started talking about all the women they'd known with fine asses on them.

———

FAULKNER AND TALL FELLOW entered the whorehouse to be greeted by the madam, a busty woman in her fifties with pasty skin.

"This the whorehouse owned by Gary Blaine?" Faulkner asked.

"It is," she said, then added, "don't tell me he sent you fellas over for a free poke, too?"

"No, ma'am," Faulkner said. "We're not interested in a poke right now."

"That's a bold-faced lie," she said. "Men are always interested in a poke. It's all they think about."

"Okay," Faulkner said, "let me rephrase it. While we're interested, and we have the wherewithal, we just don't have the time."

"Oh," she said. "Then what—"

"He sent someone else over for a free one?" Tall Fellow asked.

"He did."

"Where is he now?"

"In the room all that yellin' and cryin' is comin' from." Faulkner looked at Tall Fellow. "Inside or out?"

"I'll take the inside."

"Good luck," Faulkner said, and hurried outside.

CHAPTER FIFTY-THREE

T all Fellow went up the stairs and followed the sound of the woman's voice to a room. Having learned from previous experience, he opened the door to the room right across the hall. A tall, gangly young man was putting it to a Chinese whore from behind, and they both stopped to stare at him.

"Sorry," Tall Fellow said. "Just wanted to tell you not to come running out of this room no matter what you hear."

"Mister," the boy said, "I ain't about to take my dick outta this here whore until I'm done."

Tall Fellow looked at the woman. She was small and fragile-looking, with slanted eyes and very black hair that was a mess from having been pulled.

"Good lad," he said, and closed the door.

———

OUTSIDE, Faulkner worked his way around to the back of the building. Above him he could see a row of windows. He hoped Sunday was in one of those rooms. If he was in a room across the hall, with no window, Tall Fellow was on his own. He settled down to wait.

———

TALL FELLOW MOVED to the door, drew his gun and then kicked the door open. The sight of a big naked butt greeted him, pale except for the redness on each cheek from somebody slapping there.

Sunday was also naked, but he didn't hesitate. As soon as the door crashed open, he went for his gun, hanging on the bedpost. The girl screamed, got up to her knees, and ended up right between Tall Fellow and Sunday.

Tall Fellow hesitated.

Sunday didn't.

One shot.

———

FAULKNER HEARD THE SINGLE SHOT, was tempted to run back into the building, but he stood his ground and was rewarded for it. A half-dressed Jack Sunday appeared in the window, then dropped down to the ground. He landed like a cat, pants and gun belt in one hand and gun in the other.

"You're quick, Jack," Faulkner said. "But not quick enough."

Sunday stared at Faulkner with hatred.

"This how you're gonna take my partnership from me?" he asked.

"Partnership?"

"Me and Blaine was gonna be partners, until you showed up."

"This has got nothing to do with a partnership," Faulkner said. "There's a price on your head, and we tracked you here to get it."

"A bounty hunter? I never heard you were a bounty hunter, Faulkner."

"I helping a friend who, by the way, better be alive up there."

"Stupid whore got in the way," Sunday said. "She caught the bullet. Your man is all right and should be down here any minute, so I got no time to waste. Don't suppose you'd give me a fair chance?"

"Not what I'm about, Jack."

"Too bad."

"Don't—" Faulkner said, but it was too late. The man was

grabbing for his gun. Faulkner fired once, put Jack Sunday down for good with the single shot.

Tall Fellow came running from the alley and stopped when he saw Sunday on the ground.

"He gave me no choice, Indian," Faulkner sad.

"I believe you," Tall Fellow said. "Dead money spends just as well as live money."

"Think anyone heard those shots?"

"Just two? Spaced out like that? Even if somebody did they don't care, as long as nobody's shooting at them."

"We need to move fast," Faulkner said. "What do we do with him?"

Tall Fellow spotted a bunch of crates and said, "Let's put him behind there for now. He'll keep until we get back."

They lifted the dead outlaw and dumped him behind the crates, then tossed his pants and gun belt after him. Faulkner picked up the dead man's gun and tucked it into his belt.

"Just in case," he said. "Now let's get over to the Lucky Ace."

CHAPTER FIFTY-FOUR

They walked through town toward the Lucky Ace. Nobody was on the street in Gunman's Crossing.

"You know," Faulkner said to Tall Fellow, "this business of having no law around might not be too bad. This town is actually pretty quiet."

"I know," Tall Fellow said. "I expected more shootouts in the streets."

When they reached the Lucky Ace they paused. Briefly, Faulkner described to Tall Fellow where the slots for the guns were.

"My guess is the walls are false, and probably thin. Don't be afraid to shoot through them."

"Got it."

"You take the one on the right," he continued. "I'U take the left."

"Right, I've got the right."

"And watch the bartender," Faulkner said. "He's got a gun under the bar."

"Don't they all?"

"He might be the fifth bodyguard."

"I got that, too."

"I'll do the talking."

"Be my guest."

Together, they walked through the batwing doors.

Blaine saw Faulkner enter with Tall Fellow, whom he didn't know.

Kirk and Ben saw them enter, knowing both men instantly.

The bartender saw them, moved to stand in front of his gun.

The two men behind the false walls saw Faulkner and raised their rifles. They didn't have time to do much else.

Faulkner drew his gun and the extra gun, while Tall Fellow produced his. They both shots holes in the walls while patrons in the place sat stunned.

"This is private business," Faulkner shouted. "Anybody interested in taking a hand?"

Men exchanged glances, but nobody was even willing to stand up. This was an interruption in their evening they hoped would not last long.

Faulkner looked at Kirk and Ben.

"Go for your guns or take a walk."

"We're walkin'," Kirk said without hesitation. He walked and Ben walked right out the door behind him.

Faulkner looked at the bartender.

"Pull that hogleg or get away from it."

The bartender hesitated, then backed away, showing his hands.

Faulkner looked over at the three of Jack Sunday's men. They were all watching the action with interest.

"You boys should know that Jack Sunday is dead," Faulkner said. "We're claiming the bounty on his head."

The three men stared at Faulkner, and then one man stood up, showing his hands.

"That suits us, Mister," Hobbs said. "We was lookin' for a new leader, anyway."

"You better get moving, then," Faulkner said.

"Yes, sir," Hobbs waved at the other two men, "we're movin'. We're gonna gather up the rest of the gang and head out."

"That's a good idea," Faulkner said. "Anybody still in town after we're finished here is fair game."

Faulkner looked over at Gary Blaine, who was standing at his table, watching them.

"What's going on, Faulkner?" Blaine demanded. "What the hell?"

"I'm turning down your offer of employment, Blaine," Faulkner said.

"You're dead," Blaine said. "You hear me, Faulkner? Dead."

"No," Faulkner said, "I'm afraid you are."

He shot him once.

CHAPTER FIFTY-FIVE

Early the next morning Faulkner met Tall Fellow at the livery stable. The bounty hunter had already tied Jack Sunday to the back of his horse. The rest of Sunday's men had left town as quickly as Hobbs had been able to collect them.

Faulkner had collected the rest of his money from Gena Miller over supper. She'd offered him more, but he didn't want to get tangled up with a woman who would kill her own husband. You just couldn't trust a woman who would do that.

"You ready to go?" Tall Fellow asked.

"As soon as I saddle up."

Nobody in town had made a fuss over them killing Jack Sunday and Gary Blaine, or the two bodyguards who had been behind the walls. There really was a mind-your-own-business policy in Gunman's Crossing that worked to their definite advantage.

Tall Fellow waited outside the livery for Faulkner, who eventually saddled his horse and walked it out.

"Where you headed, Faulkner?" Tall Fellow asked.

"With you," Faulkner said.

"I've just got to get to a town with some law, a telegraph and a bank, and I can collect my money."

"You gonna have enough for that doctor in New York?" Faulkner asked.

Tall Fellow shrugged.

"Who knows? If not, I'll just have to track down a few more bounties."

"Maybe not." Faulkner held out an envelope.

"What's that?"

"The money I got paid for killing Blaine," Faulkner said. "I charged her double."

"That's your money."

"I'm throwing it in with yours, Indian," Faulkner said to his friend. "And if you don't mind, I'll just go along with you to New York to see that doctor."

Tall Fellow looked at him.

"I don't know what to say."

"Just take the money, bounty hunter."

Tall Fellow took the envelope.

"You're footing the expenses, though," Faulkner told him.

Tall Fellow grinned and said, "I wouldn't have it any other way, Money Gun. Thanks."

TRAPP'S MOUNTAIN

"TAKE OUT YOUR PISTOL!"

"No," Train gasped. "You'll kill me."

"I'm gonna kill you anyway, scum!" Trapp shouted. "Take it out!"

"Why are you doing this?" Train said desperately. "She was just a squaw."

"Maybe," Trapp said, removing the pistol from his belt, "but she was *my* squaw."

"Who are you?"

"Trapp," John Henry said, "the man who killed you. Now take out your pistol and die like a man, or get down on your knees and die like a coward. Your choice."

To his credit—and Trapp's relief—Train reacted angrily.

"Damn you!" the young man called, and drew his pistol...

PROLOGUE

GREEN RIVER, 1846

John Henry Trapp came down from the Green River country with killing on his mind.

Trapp was thirty-nine years old at that point of his life, and was coming off the happiest year of his life. The reason for that had been White Dove. He had found the Crow squaw hurt and frozen a year ago, and had taken her back to his hut with him. He'd nursed her back to health, and since then they had been living together.

Until a week ago.

He had gone downriver to set some new traps and check the old ones. He'd been gone two days, and when he returned, his hut was gone, burned to the ground. Everything he owned that he hadn't had with him had burned with it.

In the rubble he found White Dove—what was left of her. He had picked up her charred, scorched body in his arms and carried her away from the hut. He spent hours digging in the hard ground until he had a deep enough grave and then laid her in it and covered her up. After that he mounted up and started tracking the men who had killed her.

Their trail led him down from the mountain.

He had no way of knowing that he would not see that mountain again for twenty-five years.

HUNTSVILLE PRISON, TEXAS, 1871

When John Henry Trapp walked through the front gates of Huntsville Prison—*out*, not in—the first thing he did was look at the sky.

It looked different.

It looked different from the piece of sky he'd been able to see from the window of his cell. It looked cleaner, bigger...freer.

But it still didn't look like the sky he could see from the Rockies.

For the first five years he'd been in jail, all he could think of was White Dove.

After ten years he found that he'd forgotten what

White Dove looked like—but he had never forgotten that Rocky Mountain sky.

Now that he was out, there was nothing he wanted more than to see it again.

He was wearing clothes they had given him, had five dollars in his pocket that they had given him. There was a horse waiting for him—not much of a horse, but then they'd given him *that*, too.

All he had that was his was his old Sharps. A guard, a man who loved guns, had taken care of it for him, kept it in good working order, and had given it back to him. The guard, a man named Connors, had started working there the same time Trapp had been brought there, and had promised to care for the weapon.

To Trapp's surprise, he had kept his promise. It was the only decent thing that had happened to Trapp in the last twenty-five years.

"You're getting out," Connors said to him as he handed him the Sharps. "I'll be here until I die. Ain't much I can do about that."

"You could leave, too," Trapp said.

"And go where?"

"To the mountains."

"You go to your mountain, Trapp," Connors said, shaking his head. "Don't stop for nothing until you get there, ya hear?"

"I hear."

They shook hands.

That was when Trapp went outside and looked up at the sky.

Now he walked to the flea-bitten nag they had given him and mounted up. That was okay.

He was pretty flea-bitten himself. He was sixty-four years old.

Part One

BACK TO THE WORLD

CHAPTER ONE

F ry rode into Littlesworth, Texas, hungry enough to eat a bear.

He stabled his horse and went directly to the saloon. He'd find himself a hotel room after he saw to the inner man.

He entered the Lucky Star Saloon, approached the bar, and immediately helped himself to one of the hardboiled eggs that were piled up in a bowl. Next to the bowl was a sign that said FREE.

"Hey!" the bartender said.

Fry looked at the man, still holding an egg in his left hand.

"What?"

"Those are for paying customers."

Fry looked at the sign to see if he'd read it correctly.

"Don't that say free?"

"It does," the bartender said, "but it means free with a drink."

"Why don't it say free with a drink then?"

The bartender, a rangy man with big shoulders and hands, leaned forward and said, "Are you lookin' for trouble, son?"

Fry was twenty-five, but he knew he had to live with looking younger, and sometimes getting treated that way.

"No, sir," Fry said, "I'm looking for a drink to go with this egg."

"What'll you have?"

"Beer."

"Comin' up."

Fry rolled the egg on the bar top while waiting for his beer, then began to peel it. When the bartender set his beer down in front of him, he took a bite of the egg and washed it down with a deep swallow of beer.

"You payin' for the beer?" the bartender asked.

"Of course I'm paying," Fry said, digging into his pocket. "What do I look like, a deadbeat?"

The bartender didn't comment. He just kept looking at Fry until a coin hit the bar top. It bounced once and the bartender caught it with a quick, practiced motion.

"One drink," he told Fry, "one egg."

As the man turned away, Fry made a face at him and quickly snatched another egg, pushing it into his vest pocket. He picked up his beer then and walked to a table at the rear of the room. It was early and there were only three or four other people in the place. The gaming tables were covered, and there were not yet any women working the place.

Fry had enough money for another beer, one night in the hotel, and then he had to pick between a meal or a woman.

For a man who had been on the trail as long as he had, it was a difficult choice.

––––––

WHEN TRAPP RODE into Littlesworth that afternoon, he attracted attention. He had always attracted attention wherever he went because he was such a big man. Now he still had the height he'd always had, but there was a lot less meat on his bones. When he'd gone into prison, he'd had huge shoulders, a deep chest, hard biceps, and thighs like tree trunks. Although he was far from emaciated, he was still only a shadow of the strapping young man he'd once been. Add to that that he was riding a half dead horse and wearing ill-fitting clothes, and he would have been a curiosity anywhere he went.

He rode to the livery and the liveryman cast a critical eye over him and the horse.

"What do you want me to do with him?" the man asked. "Bury him?"

"Just give him some feed," Trapp said.

"A waste of good feed, if you ask me."

"I didn't," Trapp said, fixing the man with a hard stare.

The man met Trapp's eyes for only a moment, then he swallowed and looked away.

"Jest makin' a comment, is all," he muttered, walking the horse inside the livery.

Trapp turned and walked toward the center of town. This was the first town he'd been in since being released from prison that morning. It was a small town, but to Trapp it seemed to bustle with activity. That was because he was still used to the mountains, where if you ran across one other person over the course of a month it was a lot—unless, of course, you went to rendezvous. That was what Trapp missed the most, the mountain man rendezvous, but they were gone even before he went to jail.

As uncomfortable as he was being out among people, he kept his back stiff and walked purposefully, as if he knew exactly where he was going. In point of fact, he had no idea *where* he was going or what he was going to do until he saw the saloon.

He hadn't had a beer in twenty-five years.

———

FRY WAS LOOKING over the saloon girls, trying to decide if any of them was worth more than a meal, when the big man entered the saloon. Fry noticed him right away. He noticed the ill fit of his clothes, the prison pallor of his face. He thought that this man must have been a monster ten or twenty years ago, but he still wouldn't want to tangle with him now.

He also noticed the old buffalo gun the man carried, a Sharps. Although old, the gun looked to be in excellent condition. Fry was impressed by guns, and by the men who took good care of them.

He watched as the big man walked to the bar.

———

"WHAT CAN I GET YOU?" the bartender asked.

"A beer," Trapp said, setting the Sharps down and leaning it against the bar.

Trapp's eyes wandered to the bowl of hardboiled eggs, and the sign.

"These eggs are free?" he asked.

The man set the beer down and said, "You get one with your drink."

"Much obliged," Trapp said, taking one.

He took out the five dollars they'd given him at the prison and set it on the bar. The bartender took it and made change.

"You just out?" the bartender asked.

Trapp took a moment to savor the first sip of beer as it went down and then said, "Why do you ask?"

"Oh, it's just that we get a lot of prisoners in here when they're released, and they usually pay with five dollars and look about as pale as you."

"I ain't a prisoner anymore."

"No," the bartender said, "of course you ain't."

Trapp picked up one of the eggs and hefted it.

"How do you eat this thing?"

"Ain't you ever seen a hardboiled egg before?"

"No."

The only eggs Trapp had ever had were broken and mixed up. "Scrambled" somebody at rendezvous had once called them. There weren't many chickens in the mountains and the meals he usually had were either game meat or wild vegetables.

"You peel it," the bartender said.

Trapp frowned and said, "How?"

One of the saloon girls had been standing at the bar to Trapp's right a ways, and had heard the conversation. She moved closer to Trapp and he looked at her. She was the first woman he'd seen in twenty-five years.

She had dark hair, and a smooth complexion beneath her makeup. The scent of her tickled his nose and he started to feel somewhat foolish in her presence—especially since she'd heard him talking about the egg.

"Can I help you?" she asked.

"Well—" he said.

"Watch," she said. She took the egg and rolled it on the bar a few times, then held it up to show him that the shell was cracked. After that she started to peel it for him, until the shell was completely removed.

She held it out to him and said, "Now you can eat it like this or put salt on it."

"Thank you," he said, taking it.

"Don't mention it," she said, giving him a dazzling smile. He couldn't guess her age. He was well out of practice for that, and anyway the makeup was making it harder. He knew that she was a helluva lot younger than he was.

Hell, everybody was.

It was funny how inside he felt the same as ever, the same as when he'd been in the mountains. In prison, age didn't matter all that much either. This was the first time he fully realized that he was an *old man*. This pretty gal was helping him not because she was attracted to him, but because he was *old*.

He took a bite of the egg and chewed thoughtfully. The white tasted okay, but the yellow was too dry for him. He washed it down with a swallow of beer.

He turned his head to look around the saloon. It wasn't large, and all the tables had somebody sitting at them. He saw the woman walking around the room, talking to the men, smiling at them, and there were two other women as well. Looking at the three of them, he was able to see that the pretty woman who had spoken to him was the oldest of the three, although she wasn't the prettiest.

He bit the egg again and sipped the beer. He was nursing both because he didn't want to go through his money too fast. He hadn't yet decided whether he would buy some new clothes, or some black powder for the Sharps. Connors had given him some, but he needed more. There was also the problem of where to sleep. He'd gotten used to sleeping on a cot in prison. He didn't know now if he would prefer to sleep outside, or get a hotel room.

He didn't think he'd ever *been* in a hotel room before.

Suddenly, he thought of the wealthy father of one of the two men he'd killed. The man had not been able to get him executed, but he'd done the next best thing. He'd had Trapp sent to a prison far away from his beloved mountains, so that he wouldn't even be able to see them from a cell window.

For a long time, Trapp thought he would surely die in prison.

For some of the time he was there, he *wanted* very badly to die.

After a while that all faded away, along with White Dove's face, and the faces of the men he'd killed for killing *her*.

The funny thing was, he could still see the father's face, although he'd seen the man in court only once or twice.

He used to plan how he would gain revenge against the man when he got out, but now that he *was* out, he realized that the man must have been dead a long time. Twenty-five years ago he was as old as Trapp was now.

So now that he was out, there was not even revenge to look forward to.

All he had to look forward to was getting back to his mountains. To do that, he needed money to outfit himself for the trip.

He posed a question to himself.

How does a sixty-four-year-old man make money?

CHAPTER TWO

F ry was not the only one to notice Trapp when he entered.

Wes Gardner and Bob Stanley sat together at a table, watching the big man at the bar.

"He just got out," Gardner said.

"That means he's got five dollars in his pocket," Stanley said.

"Minus what he paid for that beer."

Stanley looked at Gardner and said, "We'd better get to him before he drinks up the rest of our money."

Gardner and Stanley lived in Littlesworth for a reason. One of the ways they made their money was to roll the cons who came out of Huntsville for the five dollars they were given. There were other, larger towns in the area, but Littlesworth had no real law.

"He don't look like much," Stanley said. "Why don't we just scare it out of him?"

Gardner grinned and both men stood up. They were both in their thirties, Gardner tall and rangy, Stanley shorter and stocky. The tall ex-con at the bar looked frail and old to them, one of the easier targets in recent months.

They walked to the bar and took up a position on either side of him.

FRY SAW the two men rise and stand to either side of the old ex-con. They looked like a couple of vultures circling in for the kill. They must have known what Fry knew, that the man had just gotten out of prison.

What could they want from him?

What could they think he had?

Trapp felt the men on either side of him.

"Just get out, old man?" the man on his left asked.

Trapp turned his head slightly to look at Wes Gardner, and then to his right to eye Bob Stanley.

"Yep."

"Bet that beer tastes right good," the man on his right said.

"Good enough."

"Old fella like yourself, though," Gardner said, "shouldn't have more than one of those. Not when you just got out of jail. You're not used to that stuff."

Trapp stared straight ahead and said, "Make your point."

"We want to help you," Gardner said.

"Yeah," Stanley said, "we'll just take the rest of that five dollars off of you so you won't be tempted to have another."

"All right," Trapp said, "you've said your piece. Now move on."

Gardner and Stanley exchanged a glance and they both decided that the old fella must have been hard of hearing. He just didn't know what they were saying.

"Look, old timer," Wes Gardner said, "hand over the money and you won't get hurt."

Trapp looked Gardner—the man on his left—in the eye and said, "Move on, friend, or you will."

Gardner's eyebrows went up in surprise and he looked past Trapp at Stanley.

"Look, Grandpa—" Stanley said.

For some reason the word "Grandpa" ticked Trapp off. In prison everyone did the same work, and was the same age. Now that he was out, he wasn't about to start answering to "Grandpa," no matter how old he was.

He swung his elbow back so that it slammed into Stanley's gut, cutting him off in midsentence. As he did so, Gardner started to swing his fist and Trapp reached up and caught it in one of his huge hands. The years fell away from him as he squeezed. Wes Gardner's face screwed itself up in pain as the bones in his hand began to rub together. Trapp continued to squeeze until he had driven the man to his knees, and then released him. Gardner immediately cradled his hand to his body and began to rock back and forth.

Trapp turned to look at the other man, Stanley, and was in time to see the man straighten up and reach for his gun. He grabbed for the Sharps, but already knew that he would be too late. He was going to die in a little saloon in a small town the very same day he got out of jail after twenty-five years.

As his hand closed over the barrel of the Sharps, he heard a shot. He felt no impact and looked in surprise at Bob Stanley, who had been driven against the bar by the force of a bullet, and now slumped to the floor.

He looked at the rest of the room and saw a man standing up by a table with his gun out.

"You looked like you could use a little help," the man said, holstering his gun.

"More than a little," Trapp said. "Thanks."

"Behind you!" a woman shouted.

Trapp turned and saw that Gardner, the man on his knees, was trying to draw his gun left-handed. He swung the Sharps back and caught the man on the butt of the jaw with the butt of his rifle. Something cracked, and Gardner slumped to the floor, unconscious or dead.

Trapp turned around and saw the woman who had shouted. She was the same one who had helped him with the hardboiled egg.

"Thank you, too," Trapp said.

"Don't mention it," she said, folding her arms beneath her firm breasts.

The man who had shot Bob Stanley came over and checked the man over.

"He's dead," he announced, straightening up.

Trapp leaned over the other man and examined him. Apparently, the meeting of the butt-of-the-jaw with the butt-of-the-Sharps had resulted in a broken neck.

"This one, too," Trapp said. He looked at the woman and said, "You live here. What kind of trouble are we in?"

"Not much," she said. "These two, Gardner and Stanley, are no great loss and I'm witness that they started the trouble."

"What about the law?" Fry asked.

"What law?" she asked. "We got a sort of unofficial sheriff, but I wouldn't worry about him."

The bartender spoke up then.

"Somebody go and get Ben! This mess has to be cleaned up."

"Ben?" Fry said to the woman.

"Ben Frost. He's our unofficial sheriff."

"What's an unofficial sheriff do?" Fry asked.

"Cleans up," she said. She looked at Trapp and said, "You handle yourself pretty good for..."

"For an old man?" Trapp finished for her.

"I didn't mean—"

"That's all right, ma'am," Trapp said. "I appreciate your help here."

"My name is Annie," the woman said. "Annie Bennett." She extended her hand and Trapp took it after a moment's hesitation.

"John Henry Trapp, ma'am," he said, awkwardly.

"Glad to meet you, John Henry."

"Uh, if anyone cares," Fry said, "my name is Fry."

"Mr. Fry," Annie said, shaking hands with the younger man.

"I'm indebted to you, Mr. Fry," Trapp said, extending his hand.

Fry looked at the big hand and said, "If you don't mind, I've seen what you can do with that hand."

Trapp frowned, then withdrew the hand and grinned.

"Never to my friends," he said.

"While we're waiting for Ben to come over and make noises," Annie said, "why don't I buy the both of you a drink?"

"Sounds good to me," Fry said.

"I *would* like another beer," Trapp said.

Annie took hold of his arm and turned him back toward the bar. For a moment he felt one of her firm breasts pressed firmly against his arm.

Suddenly, he didn't feel sixty-four at all.

CHAPTER THREE

Ben Frost had an exaggerated idea of his own importance.

Frost, a man in his early thirties, had become the unofficial lawman of Littlesworth by default. After the elected sheriff had been killed two years earlier, no one else wanted the job. People in trouble began to go to Frost, because he knew how to handle trouble. Over the past two years he had "kept the peace" without benefit of a badge. What that amounted to was breaking up fights, jailing drunks, shooting wild dogs, and having the scene cleaned up after a serious altercation—like the one that had just taken place in the Lucky Star Saloon.

When Frost walked into the saloon, he did so with a flourish. He paused just inside the doorway for as long as it took the batwing doors behind him to stop swinging. He felt that this was ample time for everyone in the place to look at him.

"What happened here, Ed?" he said, speaking to the bartender.

He hadn't bothered to look down at the two bodies.

The bartender came out from behind the bar and approached Frost, explaining to him what had happened.

"Is he telling it like it happened?" Fry asked Annie Bennett.

"I'd say so," she answered. "Ed's a pain in the neck, but he wouldn't have any reason to lie."

While Ed was talking to Ben Frost, Fry helped himself to another hardboiled egg and put a second in the other pocket of his vest. Trapp had decided that he didn't like hardboiled eggs, and settled for working on the second beer. He wanted the excitement to be over so he could go and find a hole he could sit in and continue to plan his future.

"What are you doing to do?" Annie asked.

"Do?" Trapp asked.

"After this is all over."

"I...I'm not sure," Trapp said.

"Well, let's discuss the immediate future," Annie said. "Do you have a place to stay?"

"A place to stay?" Trapp repeated. He looked past Annie at Fry and the younger man simply shrugged his shoulders.

"Yes, a place to sleep? I mean, you did just get out of prison today, didn't you?"

"Yes, I did."

"So you'll need a place to sleep. I mean, you don't have much money, right?"

"No, not much."

"Then you do need someplace to sleep."

"I...yes, I do."

"All right," she said, smiling. She put her hand on his arm and said, "Come back after we close and meet me. All right?"

Trapp looked at Fry again, who nodded this time.

"A—all right."

"I'll talk to Ben."

She pushed away from the bar and went over to where the bartender was talking with Ben Frost.

Fry moved closer to Trapp.

"I wish she had made me that offer."

"What offer?" Trapp asked.

"She's giving herself to you, man."

"Giving herself?"

"Wake up, John Henry Trapp," Fry said. "She's gonna share her bed with you tonight."

Trapp stared at Fry for a moment, then looked at himself in the mirror behind the bar.

He looked at Fry again and said, "Why?"

Fry smiled, shrugged, and said, "I guess she likes older men."

Trapp looked into the mirror again and touched his face.

"I need a shave."

Fry slapped him on the back and said, "Now you're thinking straight."

Fry looked at Frost, Ed, and Annie having their conversation and said, "You know, if this guy doesn't have a badge, we don't have to talk to him."

Trapp looked at Fry and said, "You're right."

The conversation at the door ended. Ed the bartender hurried around behind the bar and Ben Frost walked very slowly over to where Trapp and Fry stood. The two bodies were still on the floor, where they'd fallen.

Frost looked around the room and said, "Tanner, get some boys and drag these poor bastards out of here."

"Sure, Ben," one of the men said. He got up and left the saloon.

Frost looked at Trapp and Fry.

"I believe I have all the pertinent facts in this case," Frost said officiously.

"What case?" Fry asked. "These two clowns tried to rob Trapp, here, and then tried to kill him."

"I have that information."

"Well, good," Fry said. "What else can we do for you, then?"

"I just wanted to tell your friend here," Frost said, "Trapp, is it?"

"That's right."

"I know a lot of fellas come out of prison with a grudge against the world, but—"

"I don't have any grudge," Trapp said.

"How long were you in?" Frost asked.

Trapp lifted the beer mug and took a drink.

"Look," Frost said, "I'm the law—"

"Show me your badge," Fry said.

"Hey—" Frost said.

"Show *me* your badge," Trapp said.

Frost looked at them both and then said irritably, "I don't have a badge."

"Then stop wasting our time," Trapp said. "Just clean up the mess."

Frost opened his mouth to speak but couldn't think of anything to say. The fact that Trapp had spoken in a low voice and no one else in the saloon had heard him made it easier for Frost to back down.

"Why don't we finish these at a table," Fry suggested.

"Sure," Trapp said. He picked up his beer and his Sharps and followed Fry back to his table.

"Too bad you had to be bothered with this your first day out," Fry said.

"It wasn't too bad," Trapp said. "It could have been worse, if not for you."

"I just happen to like fair fights."

"What did you say your name was?"

"Fry," Fry said.

"Just Fry?"

"I don't much like my first name," Fry said, "so I don't use it."

"Oh."

"Where are you from, John Henry?"

"The mountains," Trapp said. "The Rockies."

Fry's eyebrows went up and he said, "A mountain man?"

Trapp nodded and said, "I guess."

"Well," Fry said, sitting back and looking at Trapp through new eyes, "a real mountain man. What the hell did you do to get put into Huntsville Prison, so far from the mountains?"

Trapp put his beer down and stared across at Fry.

"You saved my life," Trapp said, "so I'll tell you what I wouldn't tell that make-believe lawman. I was in Huntsville Prison because I killed two men twenty-five years ago."

Fry whistled.

"Twenty-five years in Huntsville?"

Trapp nodded, and then told Fry the story, of White Dove, the men who killed her, the father of one of the killers and his influence, and his twenty-five years in prison...

CHAPTER FOUR

1846

John Henry Trapp was a patient man.

He knew that as long as he stayed on the trail of the men who had killed White Dove and burned his home to the ground, he would find them. He was especially confident because they did not appear to be running. It was very probable that they did not even know that they were being hunted.

Two weeks after he'd begun his hunt, he rode into the settlement called Pike's Landing. It was mostly tents and shacks, but it boasted a trading post that served liquor and beer. It also boasted a whorehouse with three women available.

Trapp dismounted and began to examine all the horses outside the trading post. One of the horses he was tracking had a chip in a shoe, which left a very distinctive track.

He tried the mounts in front of the trading post first, then moved over to the tent that housed the whores. There were three horses out front and he patiently lifted their hind hooves for his inspection.

The third horse had the chip in the shoe.

"Hey, there!"

Trapp turned and looked at the man who had called out and was now approaching. The man looked vaguely familiar to him.

He was tall and slender, with an angular face that made it hard to guess his age, which was thirty.

"Can I help you?" the man asked.

"Is this your horse?" he asked, pointing to the animal with the offending horseshoe.

"No, it's not, but—"

"Then you can't help me."

The man frowned a moment and then said, "Don't I know you?"

Trapp studied the man for a moment before recognizing him.

"Is your name Pardee?" Trapp asked.

"That's right," Pardee said, "Nathan Pardee. You're John Trapp, aren't you?"

"I am."

"We met at the last Green River rendezvous."

"That was a few years ago."

"Yes, it was. What brings you here?"

"I'm hunting."

"Not much buffalo around here."

"I'm not hunting buffalo," Trapp said.

"Not much beaver, either—"

"I said hunting, not trapping."

Pardee frowned.

"Trapp—"

"Do you know who owns this horse?"

"I do," Pardee said.

"Who?"

"You're not hunting the owner of this horse, are you?"

"I am."

"No, Trapp," Pardee said, "let me tell you something. The man who owns this horse is connected with the Great Missouri Fur Company. Do you know who owns that company?"

"No."

"Sam Train."

"So?"

"You've never heard of Sam Train?"

"Can't say I have. Who is he?"

"A rich man," Pardee said, "a very rich man. He owns things, Trapp, and he owns people—important people."

"And he owns this horse?" Trapp asked, tossing a thumb at the animal.

"No, no," Pardee said, "his *son* owns this horse."

"His son?"

"Dan Train."

"He's riding with someone."

"Yeah, Toady Mcfarren, a real bad one. I don't know what your beef is, Trapp—"

"They killed my squaw and burned my home," Trapp said. "What would you do?"

Pardee let some air out of his mouth noisily and said, "I don't know, Trapp. I'm sorry, but I feel I've got to warn you—"

"You already have," Trapp said, cutting him off. "I thank you for that. Are they inside?"

"As far as I know."

Trapp nodded and turned to approach the tent. At that moment the flap was thrown open and a man and a woman appeared. The man was dressed, the woman was wearing something filmy that showed off large, overripe breasts. The man's arm was around her, his left hand cupping one of her breasts.

"That's Train," Pardee said, and moved out of the line of fire.

Train came out of the tent with the woman and was followed by a second man, who had to be Toady Mcfarren. Trapp could see how the man got his name. He was huge, and had a face like a toad. There was no woman with him. Trapp took notice of the fact that Mcfarren had two Kentucky pistols tucked into his belt. Trapp had a similar pistol in his belt, and was carrying his Sharps. Because of the woman, Trapp couldn't be sure what Train was carrying.

When Dan Train looked up from the woman's breasts, he saw John Henry Trapp standing by his horse.

"This your horse?" Trapp asked.

Train took his arm from the woman's waist and she backed away, bumping into Toady Mcfarren before slipping back into the tent.

"It is," Train said. "What's it to you?"

Train appeared to be about twenty-two, and having heard who his father was, Trapp was sure the young man had more than his fair share of arrogance. Behind him the man called Toady moved to his left, so that he was no longer directly behind Train. Toady was so ugly it was hard to guess his age, but Trapp was willing to bet on late thirties.

With the woman gone, Trapp could see the ornate, silver encrusted handle of Train's Kentucky pistol.

"You've got a chipped shoe."

"Is that right?"

"Yes," Trapp said. "It led me right to you."

Train frowned.

"You've been looking for me?"

"That's right," Trapp said. "For two weeks."

"Whoa!" Train said, smiling. "You must want to see me real bad."

"I do," Trapp said. "You have no idea how bad—but I'm about to tell you."

"Go ahead, friend," Train said. "Whatever you want, I can afford it."

"Two weeks back you burned down a hut and killed a squaw. You probably raped her, too. Remember?"

Train frowned. White Dove was probably of so little conse-quence to him that he *was* having trouble remembering her.

Toady knew, though.

"Danny!" he shouted, immediately going for his pistol. He had it out of his belt when Trapp raised the Sharps and fired. The ball struck Toady right in the center of his ugly face, oblit-erating his nose, driving

through and taking out the back of his head. A woman chose that unfortunate moment to move the flap aside to see what was happening, and she was splattered with blood and brain matter for her trouble. She screamed and withdrew.

Train turned to look back just as Toady was falling. The man toppled forward and Train had to move aside to avoid being hit.

The young man stared at Trapp in horror and said, "You killed him!"

"That I did, son," Trapp said, "and you're next."

"Wait, wait—" Train shouted, his eyes wild, tears streaming down his face.

"Take out your pistol," Trapp said.

"No, no," Train gasped, "you'll kill me."

"I'm gonna kill you anyway, scum!" Trapp shouted. "Take it out!"

"Why are you doing this?" Train shouted desperately. "It was just a squaw."

"Maybe," Trapp said, removing his pistol from his belt, "but she was *my* squaw."

"Jesus, no," Trapp said. "I have money, I can pay you"

"Not enough," Trapp said, "not nearly enough."

"Who are you?"

"Trapp," John Henry Trapp said, "the man who killed you. Now take out your pistol and die like a man, or get on your knees and die like a coward. Your choice."

To his credit—and to Trapp's relief—the young man reacted angrily.

"Damn you!" he shouted, and drew his pistol. Trapp waited until he had it cocked before he shot the young man in the chest. The ball drove him back a few steps and he fell through the flap into the tent, out of sight. From inside there were numerous screams, and three women came running out in several stages of dress—or undress.

Trapp turned as Pardee came running over.

"Trapp," he said, "you'd better mount up and start running."

"I ain't running," Trapp said. "I didn't do anything wrong."

Pardee shook his head and said, "Tell that to Sam Train's money."

CHAPTER FIVE

1871

"And?" Fry asked.

"And I went to jail for twenty-five years," Trapp said.

"Sam Train's money?" Fry said.

"His money, and his influence," Trapp said.

"But he didn't have enough of either to get you sentenced to death."

Trapped swirled the last of the beer at the bottom of his mug and said, "Maybe he should have."

"Why do you say that?"

Trapp shrugged.

"I don't know the first thing about this, Kid."

"About what?"

"About this world," Trapp said. "I've been inside for a long time, Fry. Things have come and gone and changed and I've stayed the same—except for one thing."

"What's that?"

"I've aged, and I don't know the first thing about being old."

"Well," Fry said, "you didn't look so old when you were handling those two yahoos. Did you feel old?"

"Well...no—"

"Then who says you have to *be* old if you don't want to be?"

"What do you mean?"

"I mean to hell with the fact that you're...how old are you?"

"Sixty-four."

"Sixty-four?" Fry said, surprised. "Hell, you don't look that old."

"Thanks," Trapp said wryly.

"You've got a perfect opportunity tonight to find out how old you really are."

Trapp frowned, then said, "Oh, you mean the woman, Annie—"

"If you go home with that woman tonight," Fry said, "and nothing happens, then you'll know how old you truly are."

"I don't know," Trapp said. "You don't think she was serious, do you?"

"Oh, I sure do," Fry said. "I saw the look on her face while you were handling those two."

"Maybe she just feels sorry for me—"

"Sure, and maybe you remind her of her father," Fry said. "It doesn't matter *why*, Trapp!"

Trapp looked around, found Annie, and watched her for a few moments. She seemed to feel that he was looking at her and she caught his eye and smiled. He felt a tingle below his belt.

"You're only as old as you feel," Trapp said.

"That's the way to think, Trapp," Fry said.

"Yeah," Trapp said, looking at the twenty-five-year-old man sitting across from him. He smiled and said, "What the hell could a young whippersnapper know about it?"

"Nothing," Fry said, "nothing at all."

———

"WHERE ARE YOU STAYING TONIGHT?" Trapp asked Fry.

"I have no idea," Fry said. "I thought one of these nice young ladies would take me under their wing—and their covers."

"Do you have any money?"

"Not much," Fry said. "Enough for a room or a girl."

"Wait a minute—" Trapp said.

"What?"

"I don't have enough money to pay this woman, Annie—" Trapp began.

Fry shook his head and waved his hands.

"From the sound of her invitation, Trapp, I don't think you'll have to worry about that."

"No?"

"No."

"Well then here," Trapp said, taking out some of the money, "take some of it—"

"No, no," Fry said, pushing it away, "I don't need your money."

"Take it—"

"You need it," Fry said, "don't you?"

"I need more than this," Trapp said, "so don't worry about it."

"Where are you headed, Trapp?" Fry asked, leaving the money on the table. "I mean tomorrow, after you leave here. Where do you want to go?"

Trapp looked past Fry, but Fry knew that he wasn't looking at anything *behind* him, he was looking at something *beyond* him.

"I want to go back to my mountain, Kid," Trapp said. "Back where I belong."

"That's a long ride," Fry said. "You'll need to get outfitted."

"Don't I know it," Trapp said.

"We'll see what we can do about that starting tomorrow," Fry said.

"We?"

"Sure," Fry said. "I was in San Francisco once, and I heard that the Chinese feel that when you save someone's life you become responsible for it."

"And you saved mine?"

"Well," Fry said, "I helped out...but seriously, I don't have anyplace special to go. Why don't I just help you get back to your mountain?"

"Why?" Trapp asked.

"Why not?" Fry asked.

Trapp studied Fry for a few moments and then said, "You ever been to the mountains?"

"Not me," Fry said. "I'm a flatlands man."

"All right," Trapp said.

"All right what?"

"All right, you can come to my mountain."

CHAPTER SIX

When Trapp woke up the next morning, he wasn't sure where he was. It was the first time in twenty-five years that he had not awakened in a cell on a cot. Once he had resolved that he was *not* in a cell, and that he was in a real bed and not on a cot, he had to deal with the other thing.

There was someone in bed with him.

He rolled over and looked down at the naked young woman in bed with him—or rather, it was *he* who was in bed with *her*.

He looked under the sheet and saw that he, too, was naked. His first urge was to get out of bed quickly, but he checked that. He took a moment to think about what had happened last night, and it all came back to him...

He had met Annie Bennett after the saloon closed and had followed her to her room, above the general store. When they entered, she closed the door and turned to him, discarding her wrap.

"I find you interesting," she said, "and attractive."

"I'm a lot older than you," he said.

"I know that," she said, "but I've had younger men. I've had men younger than me, and men older."

"Have you ever been with a man my age?"

"No," she said, "but I'd like to be with you."

"I just got out of jail."

"I know that, too," she said. "Men who get out of jail are usually looking for a woman before anything else."

"Young men," he said.

She shook her head and moved closer to him, toying with the buttons of his clothes.

"They could have given you better clothes."

He laughed and said, "A better horse, too. I, uh, need a bath."

"I have a bathtub," she told him, unbuttoning his shirt...

By God, he thought now, they had taken a bath together and he had put his hands on her firm, *slippery* young flesh. She had put her hands on *him*, and to his delight—and *hers*—he had reacted.

They had moved to the bed and made love, and he had been able to satisfy her—he *thought* he had satisfied her—no, he *felt* that he had satisfied her.

In his younger days, whenever he'd had sex with a woman— before White Dove—he had never worried about satisfying his partner. Sex was something that came rarely in the mountains, and when it did, a man enjoyed it. He didn't worry about whether or not the woman was enjoying it.

When he and Annie had started to make love, he'd found that old attitude coming back. Once he'd realized that he *could* still have sex, he decided to enjoy it. It was Annie Bennett who had slowed him down and had shown him how sex could be when *both* participants were enjoying themselves.

They had made love not once but twice during the night. She had awakened him during the night and he had been *sure* that he wouldn't be able to do it again, but she had been equally sure that he could—and then proceeded to prove it.

He had never been with a woman like her before—but then, when could he have ever met a woman like her twenty-five years ago in the mountains?

She rolled over at this point and opened her eyes.

"Want to run?" he asked.

She smiled and said, "Was that your first reaction?"

"I didn't know where I was," he said, "and then I didn't *believe* where I was."

"Well, trust me," she said, "you're here."

She stretched, causing the sheet to fall away from her bare

breasts. It was the first time he had seen them in daylight, and they were as beautiful as they had been the night before.

She reached a hand out to him and ran it over his torso, then down below.

"Oh, no—" he said.

"Oh, yes," she said. "You have the constitution of a horse, mountain man...and the resemblance," she continued, moving her hand beneath the sheet and between his legs, "does not stop there..."

———

THE NIGHT BEFORE, Trapp had agreed to meet Fry for breakfast.

"We'll figure out how to pay for it then," Fry had said. Trapp wasn't worried about that. He had enough money for a couple of breakfasts, but that was about all.

He met Fry in front of a small cafe that Annie had recommended to them.

"Well," Fry said, "you don't look any the worse for wear. How did it go?"

Trapp hesitated, then grinned and said, "Surprisingly well."

"Me, too," Fry said. "One of the gals you left behind succumbed to my charms and was even willing to waive her usual fee. I have money to buy my own breakfast."

"Well then, let's eat," Trapp said. "For the first time in years, I'm starved."

Fry patted him on the back and said, "Welcome back to the world."

Part Two

TRAPP AND THE KID

CHAPTER SEVEN

Over breakfast they discussed money—or their lack of it.

"I have an idea, if you're interested," Fry said.

"What is it?"

"Well, those two ne'er-do-wells that we, uh, got rid of yesterday might have some paper on them."

"Paper?"

"Posters."

"You mean they might be wanted?"

"And there could be a reward."

"How do we check on that?" Trapp asked. The possibility sounded interesting. He didn't need a *lot* of money to get outfitted for his trip back to his mountain.

"Well, we could check with that fella Frost, the unofficial sheriff," Fry said, "or we could send a telegram to the closest town that has a real sheriff."

"I don't really want to talk to Frost again," Trapp said. "The man's attitude just didn't impress me."

"I agree."

"What's the closest town?"

"Portsville," Fry said.

"Can you send a message from this town?"

"I'll check and see if they have a telegraph office," Fry said. "You wouldn't know much about the telegraph, would you." It was more a statement than a question.

"I heard something about it while I was in prison," Trapp said. "Usually, when a new prisoner comes in, the other convicts pry the news of the world out of him. Being in prison is actually very educational."

"I'll learn all I can outside of the prison walls, if that's all right with you."

"I insist on it."

"There's just one thing," Fry said.

"What?"

"When I send the telegram, I'd like to do it in your name."

"Why?"

"My name might be...recognized."

Trapp stared at Fry for a moment and then said, "As what?"

"Well...I have a little bit of a reputation in some places."

"As what?" Trapp asked again.

"You should know this if we're going to travel together."

"Know what?"

"Some people call me 'Kid Fry.'"

"Why?"

"I, uh, am pretty good with a gun."

"You mean...like Paul Fountain?"

Fry looked surprised and said, "You know Paul Fountain?"

"He served five years with me," Trapp said. "He got out about three years ago."

"Well," Fry said, impressed in spite of himself, "I don't have the kind of reputation that Fountain has—"

"Well," Trapp said, "you're still young. You have time. How many men have *you* killed?"

Fry frowned.

"I'm sorry," Trapp said, "I shouldn't have said that, but I didn't like Paul Fountain at all, and I don't like the idea that you might be like him—or want to be."

"What was he like?"

"He was, and probably still is, a vicious animal. *He's* the one who should have been in there for twenty-five years, not me."

Trapp's vehemence was such that Fry wondered how much it must have wounded him to be in prison with a man like Fountain, and watch him walk out after only five years.

"I'm not like him, Trapp," Fry said. "It's important to me that you believe that."

"Are you wanted by the law?"

"No."

"Then I don't see why we can't travel together."

"I have to warn you," Fry said, "I get tested sometimes—by one man, or more."

"I'll back you."

Fry's eyes went to Trapp's Sharps, which was leaning against the table.

"What?" Trapp said. "Is something wrong with my gun?"

"Well, it's a little old," Fry said. "Don't you own a handgun?"

"I used to own a Kentucky pistol," Trapp said. "I don't know what happened to it after I went to prison."

"Have you ever seen one of these?" Fry asked, taking his six-gun from his holster and laying it on the table.

"Only in prison," Trapp said, not touching the gun. "The guards wore them...and Fountain talked about them...all the time."

"Pick it up," Fry said.

"No, thanks," Trapp said. "I'll stick with my Sharps. It suits my needs."

"You're not in the mountains now, Trapp," Fry said, "and you're not in the 1840s anymore. Everyone is carrying one of these now, and half of the people who do are anxious to prove they can use them."

"Like you?"

Fry stared at Trapp for a few moments, then sighed, took the gun off the table, and slid it back into his holster.

"You told me about your past," he said to Trapp, "so it's only fair that I tell you about mine..."

CHAPTER EIGHT

1865

Wendell Fry was born in New York City.

He was an orphan, living in homes until he ran away at sixteen and started living in the streets. By the time he was nineteen he had been a member of a street gang called the Blind Cats for three years.

The gang lived in the basement of a rundown building in the area called Five Points, and was constantly at war with other gangs. In the three years he'd been a member, however, he had not killed anyone. He knew of other gang members who had, but the opportunity had never presented itself to him.

He always kept himself ready, though. He practiced constantly with an old Walker Colt he had stolen from a man in a restaurant. He used to go out to a field every chance he got to practice firing, but inside the city he always practiced moves without actually loading the gun.

He got so he could hit what he was shooting at almost every time.

Practicing with the gun got him interested in reading about the Old West—newspaper articles, dime novels, whatever he could get his hands on, and he finally decided that he would leave New York and go west.

He stole enough money for his train tickets and went first to Chicago, and then from there to Denver. He got off the train with the Walker Colt stuck in his belt, and walked right into trouble.

He didn't have enough money for a hotel and was walking around looking for a place to stay when he bumped into someone on the street—a man, walking with two other men.

The man got upset and called him street trash.

"How dare you touch me, you street trash," the man had shouted.

All three men were wearing guns and they fanned out in front of him. His heart was pounding. He had read about such confrontations in the dime novels, but had never expected to become involved in one—not right off the damned train.

"Look, I'm sorry—" he started.

"Look, Cole," one of the other men said, "he's got a gun."

"What are you doing with a gun, street trash?" the man called Cole asked.

Fry looked down at the gun in his belt and said, "It's my gun."

"What's your name, trash?" Cole asked.

"Fry," Fry answered, "Wendell Fry."

"Wendell?" one of the other men asked in disbelief. "Wendell?"

"That's my name," Fry said, grudgingly.

"And that's your gun, street trash," Cole said. "Let's see you go for it."

"What?"

"Your gun, son," one of the others said. "Draw it."

"Why?"

"Because if you don't," Cole said, "I'll kill you where you stand."

"I don't understand—" Fry began, but he saw all three men reach for their firearms and grabbed for his own.

Fry brought his out and cocked the hammer and pulled the trigger as quickly as he could. When he was done firing, all three men lay on the ground, dead.

———

1871

"One of the men I killed was named Clay Cole," Fry said.

"You killed Clay Cole?" Trapp said.

"And two other men," Fry said. "You've heard of Clay Cole?"

Trapp nodded and said, "In prison. You hear of most every lawbreaker with a reputation in prison."

From what Trapp had heard in jail, Clay Cole had been considered extremely fast and deadly with a gun—and Fry had killed him *and* two others.

"Well, I haven't broken any laws that I know of,"

Fry said, "but a Denver newspaper came out the following day calling me 'Kid Fry,' and the name stuck. No matter where I went, it stuck."

"Why didn't you go back to New York?"

"It never occurred to me," Fry said. "I mean, I was young then, and I was flattered by all the attention I was getting. Hell, some storekeepers even gave me some free clothes, and one shop gave me a holster. *This* holster that I'm still wearing."

"What did you do?"

"I stayed in Denver for about two weeks after that, and then some yahoo with a gun wanted to try me. I couldn't get out of it."

"And you killed him, too?"

Fry nodded.

"I left Denver the next day, but that name and the reputation that goes with it has been following ever since."

They sat in silence for a moment, then Trapp said, "All right."

"All right, what?"

"You can send the telegram in my name."

"Thanks."

They finished their breakfast, called the waiter over, and each paid for his own.

"This is all I have left," Fry said, showing Trapp a dollar.

"I have two."

"We'd better send a short telegram," Fry said. "They charge by the word."

They got up and walked outside, but before they stepped into the street to cross, Fry put his hand on Trapp's arm to stop him.

"What?" Trapp asked.

Fry hesitated a moment, then said, "Wendell."

During the telling of the story he had refrained from mentioning his first name. He had simply said that Cole and his two friends had made fun of it.

"What?"

"My name," Fry said, "my first name. That's it. Wendell."

"Wendell," Trapp repeated. "Well, that's not so bad, Wendell."

"Maybe not," Fry said, "but now that I've told you, will you do me a favor?"

"What's that?"

"Don't ever call me that."

CHAPTER NINE

T rapp and Fry went to the telegraph office, where Fry composed as brief a message as possible to the sheriff of Portsville, Texas. As an afterthought he added the two words *Immediate response*. He thought it would be worth the extra cost.

Trapp waited outside, and when Fry came out he asked, "All done?"

"Now all we have to do is wait for an answer."

"Wait where?" Trapp asked. "We don't have a hotel room—"

"I told the clerk that I'd check back every hour. Until then I guess we'll just have to find something to do."

"Like what?"

"Well," Fry said, "if we're going to travel together, why don't we each show the other what we can do."

"About what?"

Fry touched his gun and said, "With this. I want to see how well you shoot, and show you how well I shoot."

Trapp started to look around and Fry said, "Let's get our horses and ride outside of town—but let's stop at the saloon first."

"What for?"

"Empty whiskey bottles."

AFTER THEY HAD POUNDED on the saloon door and collected some empty bottles from the annoyed owner, they walked to the livery stable. They each carried a sack with empty bottles, which clinked together noisily with every step.

Fry's horse was a handsome steeldust, and when Trapp saw it, he hesitated about pointing out the rundown mare he'd been given at the prison.

"Which one's yours?" Fry asked.

"Well," Trapp said, "you have to remember she's not really mine."

"All right."

"She was given to me when I got out."

"Okay."

"I wouldn't have—"

"Which one is it, Trapp!"

"That one," Trapp said, pointing.

Fry looked at the animal he was pointing at and made a face as if he'd stepped into a pile of horseshit—while barefoot!

"That one?"

"Yes."

"You actually rode that animal here?"

"I did."

Fry looked at Trapp and said, "I can see we're going to need more money than I thought. We've *got* to get you a new horse."

"How can we do that with no money?"

"Well, if those two yahoos were wanted, we'll have money."

"Waiting for us in Portsville."

"Right."

"But we still have to get there."

Fry looked at the horse again and then said, "Do you think she'd make it?"

"She got me here," Trapp pointed out.

"Let's see how she reacts to a short ride," Fry said. "Let's go shoot."

They saddled up, mounted up, then rode out of town. Once or twice Trapp had to shout at Fry to slow down, because he could feel his mount staggering as it tried to keep up.

"This is far enough," Fry said, dismounting.

Trapp got down and grounded the reins. He didn't think the animal had the energy to run off anyway.

They were standing among some low foliage and flat

ground. Fry paced off twenty yards and set three whiskey bottles on the ground, then returned to stand next to Trapp.

"All right," he said, "I'll go first."

Before Trapp could reply, Fry drew and fired three times, shattering all three bottles in quick succession.

"I don't suppose that had anything to do with luck, did it?" Trapp asked.

"Nope," Fry said. He ejected the empty shells and reloaded, then returned the handgun to his holster.

"You can't do that with your Sharps," Fry said, folding his arms across his chest.

"Maybe not," Trapp said.

This time he picked up one bottle and paced off one hundred yards. He walked back to stand next to Fry, raised the Sharps, and fired. It was the first time he had fired the weapon—any weapon—in twenty-five years, but it was like falling off a log. The ball traveled straight and true and shattered the glass bottle.

"Your pistol couldn't have done that."

Fry squinted, then looked at Trapp and said, "I don't suppose *that* had anything to do with luck?"

"After twenty-five years?" Trapp said.

Fry squinted again then said, "Shit, I couldn't even *see* the bottle."

"I just caught a glint of sunlight off of it," Trapp said.

"Can you do that every time?"

"I could twenty-five years ago," Trapp said.

"Well," Fry said, "this demonstration is good enough for me. I'm willing to travel with you and have you back any play I make. I can promise you the same."

Trapp stuck out his hand and said, "That's good enough for me, Kid."

"Well, let's get back to town and see if we can't scare up some money."

———

WHEN THEY GOT BACK to town, Trapp's mount was about to keel over. They handed their mounts over to the liveryman again, who demanded payment for the day. They dug into their meager finances and paid.

"Still think this one should be shot," the liveryman said, leading both horses into the stable. There was no doubt about which horse he was referring to.

"We're gonna have to get out of town by tomorrow morning," Fry said. "We can't afford to stay here one more day."

"If there's no reward, then what do we do?" Trapp asked.

"Let's not worry about that until the time comes," Fry said.

"Well, what do you usually do when you need money?" Trapp asked, persisting.

Fry hesitated before replying.

"I work," he finally said.

"Doing what?"

Fry stared at Trapp and let his hand come to rest on his gun in a very suggestive manner.

"Oh."

"I don't like to do it, Trapp," Fry said, "and I don't unless I have to. It's all I have to offer anyone in the way of talent."

"I understand."

Trapp had very little in the way of talent himself to be able to criticize young Fry.

They took a turn around town, getting further acquainted, and then headed for the telegraph office. Once again Trapp waited outside, and Fry returned in a matter of seconds.

"We're in luck."

"We are?"

Fry nodded.

"It's not big money, mind you, but they were each wanted to the tune of one hundred dollars."

"That's two hundred dollars!" Trapp said, his eyes wide. "How can you say it's not a lot?"

Fry put his hand on Trapp's shoulder and said, "The dollar simply doesn't buy what it did twenty-five years ago, Trapp."

CHAPTER TEN

Trapp and Fry rode into Portsville in the late afternoon of the following day.

They were riding double on Fry's horse.

When they reached the livery, they dismounted and handed the horse over to the curious liveryman.

"My friend's horse died a few miles outside of town," Fry explained.

"What about his saddle?" the man asked.

"It wasn't much of a saddle," Trapp said.

"I got some real nice saddles for sale."

"Have you got any used ones?" Trapp asked.

"Sure, but—"

"I might be back later to take a look," Trapp said.

"How about a horse?"

"That, too."

"I'll be here."

As they walked away from the livery, Fry said, "Why a used saddle?"

"I don't need a brand-new one, Fry," Trapp said. "A used one will do. Besides, if what you said about money is true, we'll have to use it carefully."

"Good point," Fry said, "although…"

"Although what?"

"Well, there is *another* way to make money."

"How?"

"Well, there are times when I've made money playing poker," Fry said.

"Are you good?" Trapp asked.

"Well, more lucky than good," Fry said, then added, "Uh, when I'm lucky, that is."

"Well, if we come across a game," Trapp said, "maybe I should play."

"You played poker in the mountains?"

"Not in the mountains," Trapp said, "in prison—and I became pretty good at it."

"Are you lucky?"

"I'll tell you what the man who taught me how to play told me," Trapp said. "When you're good, you don't need luck."

They were walking down the main street when Trapp started to veer off toward a hotel. Fry put his hand on his elbow, stopping him.

"Let's go and talk to the sheriff first and get our money."

Before leaving Littlesworth they had gone to see Frost, the "unofficial" sheriff, and had him write a note verifying the fact that they had killed the two wanted men, Wes Gardner and Bob Stanley.

They found the sheriff's office and knocked before entering.

The man behind the desk wore a sheriff's star on his chest. He was about fifty years old, with gray hair and a gray mustache.

"Sheriff?"

"That's right," the man said. "Sheriff Fulton. What can I do for you?"

They had decided that Trapp would be the spokesman.

"I sent you a telegram, sheriff, about two men named Gardner and Stanley?"

"Oh, yes, the reward," Fulton said. "Do you have verification?"

"Right here."

He handed over the note from Frost.

"What's an 'unofficial' sheriff?" Fulton asked.

"The town doesn't have a real sheriff, so this fella is a sort of acting sheriff."

The sheriff frowned at the note, then said, "Well, I suppose it's all right. There's not that much money involved anyway."

"Two hundred dollars," Fry said.

"I know," the sheriff said, "but the dollar doesn't buy what it used to."

The sheriff sat down and filled out a chit for two hundred dollars.

"Here, take this to the bank," he said, handing it to Trapp. "They'll give you the money."

"Thanks, Sheriff."

"I hope you don't mind me saying so, but you're a very unlikely looking bounty hunter."

"I'm not—"

"Let's go, Trapp," Fry said, interrupting him.

"Who are you?" Fulton asked.

"I'm his partner," Fry said. "Thanks very much, Sheriff."

Fry opened the door and ushered Trapp out of the office.

"What did you do that for?" Trapp asked. "Now he thinks we're bounty hunters."

"Let him," Fry said. "At least he won't be asking any questions about us."

"Like your name?"

"Right."

They went directly to the bank and Trapp received the money from the teller.

"Let's get a hotel room," Fry said after leaving the bank, "and you can give me my half there, and not out on the street."

"Good idea."

They got one room with two beds, and Trapp registered, keeping Fry's name out of the book.

Up in the hotel room Fry dropped his saddlebags on one of the beds and sat down. Trapp counted out a hundred dollars and handed it to him.

"The first thing we'll have to do is get you a horse," Fry said. "It won't be an expensive one, but it'll be better than that bag of bones you had before."

"Right."

"You go and get the horse and rig, and I'll get the supplies we'll need to travel."

"We can do that tomorrow, Fry."

"What's wrong with tonight?"

"What you said about poker before has me interested. Let's go over to a saloon and see if there's a game."

"Are you sure you can win?"

"If I start to lose, I can always quit. Besides, I'd like to play just once in a game outside of prison walls."

"All right," Fry said, "I can use a beer anyway."

———

THEY LEFT the hotel and went directly across the street to the Iron Horse Saloon. It was after dinnertime, so the saloon was doing a brisk business.

"Two beers," Fry said to the bartender.

He and Trapp both looked the room over. It was larger than the saloon in Littlesworth had been. Consequently it had more tables, more games, and more women working the floor.

"This reminds me," Fry said.

"Of what?"

"Did you say goodbye to Annie?"

"No, I didn't," Trapp said.

"Well, it probably doesn't matter," Fry said. "As long as you both got what you wanted from each other."

Trapp didn't reply.

"Did you?"

"I suppose so," Trapp said. "She satisfied her curiosity."

"And you?"

Trapp shrugged.

"I didn't want anything from her to begin with, so I guess I'm satisfied with what I *did* get."

Fry raised his eyebrows and said, "I'd be satisfied with that, too."

The bartender brought their beers over and Fry drank half of his down quickly. Trapp settled for a few sips.

"I've gone too long without this," he explained to Fry. "I want everyone I have to last."

They drank their beer and studied the room. There were two house-run poker games going on, but Trapp wanted no part of those.

"The man who taught me the game warned me about house run games," Trapp said. "The odds are always on the house's side."

"Well, there's a game over there that's not house run," Fry said.

There was a table toward the back with four people playing

poker. They were playing with paper money, so the stakes were decent for Trapp and Fry's purposes.

"All we need to do is maybe double our money," Trapp said. "That game looks like just the place to do that. Shouldn't take more than a few hours to win it."

"Or lose what you've got."

"This is not a prison, Fry," Trapp reminded him. "I can get up and walk out any time I want to."

————

ONE OF THE men at the poker table looked up and saw Trapp approaching.

"Looks like we've reeled one in, boys," Dan Smith said to the other three men.

"It's about time," one of the other men said. "I'm getting tired of passing the same money back and forth over and over again."

"Let's hope he's got enough to make it worth our while," Smith, the leader of the four, said.

The four men moved from town to town with their "private" poker game, playing until a stranger came over and asked to join them. When that happened the four of them proceeded to clean the stranger out, then leave town before anyone could figure out their game.

Smith watched this old codger approach the table and felt that they could play him all week and he'd never be the wiser.

————

FRY LEANED against the bar and said to the bartender, "Let me have another one."

"Sure thing."

The bartender brought the beer over and Fry asked, "What do you know about that poker game?"

"Which one?"

"That table toward the rear."

The bartender squinted and said, "I don't know nothing about it."

"You don't know those men?"

"Nope," the bartender said. "They all came in together about an hour ago and started playing cards."

"Together? They all know each other?"

"Far as I can tell, they ride together."

Fry thanked the bartender, and decided to keep a close eye on the poker game.

CHAPTER ELEVEN

"You fellas mind if I sit in?" Trapp asked.

"Sure, old timer," one of them said. "Pull up a chair."

Trapp knew that he would hear himself called that a lot, but he didn't think he'd ever get used to it. Inside, he was still thirty-nine.

He pulled a chair out and sat down.

"What are the stakes?"

"It's a small game," the same man said, "a dollar and two. Dealer's choice, no limits on the raises."

Trapp knew *that* turned a lot of small stakes games into larger ones.

They played for an hour, usually either five card stud or draw, and Trapp won a little bit.

"What's say we raise the limit a little?" one of the men asked. "I'm gettin' sort of bored."

There was a general nodding of heads at the table and Trapp said, "Why not?"

"Five and ten?"

"Sure," Trapp said, and the others nodded.

FRY MOVED CLOSER, trying to see everyone's hands—not the cards they were holding, but their *hands*. He was no expert, but if there was any cheating going on, he couldn't spot it. Besides, Trapp was winning.

Over the course of the next hour Trapp doubled his money and Fry was beginning to wish that the older man would quit. Even though he couldn't see anything going on, he had a feeling that *something* was.

At one point Trapp rose and walked over to the bar, where Fry was standing.

"How are you doing?" Fry asked.

"I'm up," Trapp said.

"Ready to quit?"

"Not yet."

"I think you should know—"

"Not now," Trapp said, "I want to speak to the bartender."

Trapp moved down the bar, spoke briefly with the barkeep, then came away with a beer and went back to the table to play cards.

———

DURING THE THIRD hour a big hand started to develop.

They were playing draw poker, and right off the deal there were two raisers. One of the men, named Borden, opened, the man named Dan Smith raised, and Trapp raised. Borden saw the two raises, then Smith reraised Trapp, who called.

Fry moved closer still, trying to see what Trapp was holding. He could see that Trapp was holding two pair, Kings high. He wasn't sure how strong such a hand was in the face of two other bettors.

"How many cards?" the dealer, a man named Coleman, asked.

"One," Borden said.

"Two," Dan Smith said.

"I'll play these," Trapp said, and Fry frowned. He felt that Trapp should have at least taken one card.

Fry did not see the smile that briefly touched Dan Smith's mouth.

"It's up to you, Borden," Coleman said.

"Well, why don't we raise things up a little?" Borden asked. "I bet twenty. Any objections?"

"Not from me," Dan Smith said. "You fellas?"

No one else complained, including Trapp.

"Well, in that case," Smith said, "I'll call the twenty and raise forty."

The man to his left, Styles, said, 'I'm out."

"I call the sixty," Trapp said, "and raise forty."

The dealer, Coleman, dropped out.

"You fellas must have some hands," Borden said. "I call the eighty to me, and raise a hundred."

"Call the hundred, and raise a hundred," Smith said.

Trapp counted out the money he had on the table and he was short forty dollars to call.

He looked at Fry and called him over.

"Let me have your hundred."

Fry stared at him and said, "Are you sure?"

"Let me have it."

Fry wondered if he'd read Trapp's cards wrong. Maybe he had *three* Kings and not just two. That would give him a full house.

Fry took out his hundred and handed it to Trapp.

"I call the two hundred to me," he said, "and raise another sixty."

That tapped him out—*and* Fry.

Fry saw some sort of eye contact between Smith and Borden, and the man called Borden said, "Well, I guess I'm out. You fellas look strong."

Now he knew something was going on, and Trapp was caught right in the middle of it—with all their money.

"Well, old timer," Smith said, "that just leaves me and you."

"I guess so," Trapp said.

Smith looked down at his money, counting it, then picked it up.

"Call the sixty and raise another sixty."

"I don't have another sixty," Trapp said. "I have no money left."

"I can't help that," Smith said. "Call or fold."

By now a crowd had gathered around the table, and all eyes were on Trapp.

"All right," he said. He reached for his Sharps, which was leaning against the table.

"Easy," Smith said as Trapp swung the gun up.

"This here's a Sharps Old Reliable," he said, setting the big gun down on the table, "in mint condition. It will cover the bet."

Smith's eyes widened when he saw the gun. He was in his forties, but he looked as if he recognized the gun for what it was. He ran his hand over the barrel, and then a crafty glint came into his eye.

"It's an old gun," he said. "I don't know if it will cover the entire amount."

"It covers it," Trapp said.

"That's what you say."

Trapp looked at Fry.

"What have you got?"

"Are you sure about this?" Fry asked.

Trapp simply stared at Fry.

"All right," Trapp said. He unbuttoned his shirt and slipped out a small ivory-handled derringer. "This should make up the difference."

He put the two shot weapon down on the table and there was a murmur of assent from the crowd. They knew that the bet was now well covered. Smith couldn't back out, not with the crowd on Trapp's side.

"All right," Smith said, "the bet's covered." He smiled and fanned his cards out on the table. "Four aces," he said, and the crowd caught their collective breath. "Sorry, old timer."

"Hold it," Trapp said as Smith reached for the pot. Trapp fanned his cards on the table as well and said, "Straight flush, to the King. All black."

The crowd caught their breath again.

"What?" Smith said, shocked. He looked at Coleman, his gaze accusing.

"I swear, I didn't—" Coleman started to say, but he stopped himself before he could admit to cheating.

The most shocked man in the room was Fry. He *knew* Trapp didn't have *anything* like that in his hand.

"The pot's mine, young fella," Trapp said. "Sorry. Game's over."

"Now wait a minute—" Smith said.

Trapp didn't pick the Sharps up, he just swiveled it around on the table so that the barrel was pointing at Smith.

"You got a problem, Mr. Smith?"

Smith looked from the barrel to Trapp and back to the barrel again.

"N—no, no problem," he said. He pushed his chair back viciously and barked at the others, "Let's go."

On the way out he grabbed Coleman by the scruff of the neck and the other man said, "But I swear, Dan, I never—"

Trapp picked up the derringer and handed it back to Fry. The crowd began to move away and Fry sat down next to Trapp.

"I saw your hand," Fry said. "You had Kings over, no better."

"That's what they dealt me," Trapp said, making a neat pile out of the money.

"You mean you *knew* you were being cheated?"

"From the moment I sat down and saw the first deal," Trapp said.

"But how?"

"I was taught to recognize a crooked deal, and a crooked game," he said.

"And you obviously learned that lesson well," Fry said, "but...how the hell did you get that straight flush?"

"When I talked to the bartender," Trapp said. "I told him that they were cheating, and I wanted to teach them a lesson. I asked for some cards from an identical deck, and slipped them in on the last hand."

"I never saw that."

"They didn't either," Trapp said. "Nobody was supposed to."

"But you had all spades," Fry said, pursuing it further. "What would have happened if one of the same cards had shown up in his hand?"

"Cheaters have a fondness for aces," Trapp said. "That's why I made the straight to the King."

"But if it had—"

"If it had," Trapp said, cutting him off, "you would have had to back me." He smiled and handed Fry a stack of money. "Here's your half."

Fry took the money and said, "There must be five hundred dollars here."

"Six hundred and ten," Trapp said.

"You know," Fry said, "you've got to tell me more about this fella who taught you how to play poker."

"That's a story for another time," Trapp said, standing up. "Come on, I'll buy you a drink and then I'm going to turn in. Tomorrow we head for my mountain."

CHAPTER TWELVE

After they had a beer together, Trapp announced once again that he was turning in.

"How about you?"

"Well," Fry said, "I've got money in my pocket and it really isn't that late, is it?"

"Maybe not for you," Trapp said. "Maybe it's time—at least for tonight—that I started to act my age."

Trapp looked at Fry, but Fry was looking past Trapp at one of the saloon girls, a young woman with an impressive bosom and a bee-stung mouth.

"I'll leave you to act yours," Trapp said, turning to leave.

He stepped through the batwing doors and stopped for a moment outside. It was dark and it took him a moment to acquire night vision. When he could see, he stepped into the street and started across to the hotel.

He heard the first shot and turned quickly, bringing the Sharps up into position. The flash from the second shot showed him where the shooter was, and he fired his Sharps immediately. The ball struck the shooter in the midsection and continued on through, punching a considerably larger exit hole.

There was another shot, which apparently came from a rooftop. It struck the ground inches from Trapp's left foot. Trapp turned and ran, looking for cover from which he could reload and return fire.

———

AFTER THE FIRST SHOT, everyone in the saloon fell silent. With the sound of the second shot, Fry moved immediately, running outside. He saw Trapp standing in the street, and saw the dirt in front of Trapp kicked up by a bullet.

Trapp turned and ran and Fry pulled out his gun. He ran into the street, looking up at the rooftops. A second shot was fired at Trapp, and Fry fired at the muzzle flash. The man cried out. The gun hit the ground just a second before he did.

Trapp had reloaded and now saw Fry moving toward him.

"What's going on?" Fry demanded.

"I don't know," Trapp said. "All of a sudden I was being shot at. Luckily, they're lousy shots."

"Maybe that's because they're poker players, and not gunmen?" Fry suggested.

"That thought had occurred to me," Trapp said.

"Well," Fry said, "there was four, and now there are two."

"Maybe the other two aren't in on this," Trapp said.

"We can sit right here until some law shows up," Fry said, "or we can try to find out."

"What do you suggest?"

"Well, I've never liked depending on someone else to save my bacon."

"I thought this was my bacon we're trying to save," Trapp said.

"Let's just say we're both in the same frying pan, at the moment."

"Then let's get out," Trapp said. "You go left, I'll go right."

"Ready," Fry said.

"Now!"

They both moved, and as they did, several hurried shots were fired.

Trapp went down to one knee and fired his Sharps one more time. The ball struck home, and the firing from his side stopped.

Fry threw himself into the street, rolled over twice, and then fired, silencing the firing from his side.

Both men stood up just as a man wearing a badge ran up on them, followed by two other men. They all had their guns drawn.

"What the hell is going on here?" the sheriff demanded.

———

TRAPP AND FRY left the sheriff's office after having explained the evening's happenings to him. Their story was backed up by several witnesses from the saloon, including the bartender.

"All right," Sheriff Roy Macklin said, "I buy what you're selling me, but that doesn't mean I don't want the two of you out of my town by tomorrow morning."

"All we need is time to stock up on supplies," Trapp said, "and then we'll be gone."

As they started to leave, the fortyish sheriff called out, "Hey, friend."

They both turned.

"You," Macklin said, pointing his finger at Fry. "Don't I know you?"

"I don't think so," Fry said.

"What's your name?"

Before Fry could answer, Trapp said, "Trapp."

"No, not your name," Macklin said, "him."

"I told you his name," Trapp said. "Trapp."

The sheriff frowned.

"He's my son," Trapp said, and opened the door for Fry.

On the street Fry said, "Your son?"

"Do you want to go back in and tell him your real name?"

"No, Daddy."

"I'm gonna do what I set out to do," Trapp said. "Turn in."

"I'm going back to the saloon," Fry said. "I'll be in later."

"Don't come in too late, sonny," Trapp said.

"Yes, Poppa."

———

TRAPP WENT to the hotel room, stripped to the waist, and lay down on the bed. He thought about the way he'd felt when he spread those cards on the table—knowing that *he* had slipped the entire hand into the game in plain sight of a saloon full of people.

He hadn't felt *that* alive in years—not even when he was having sex with Annie Bennett.

He thought back to the man who had taught him how to do that—and that made him think back to certain other parts of the past twenty-five years.

Part Three

INSIDE

CHAPTER THIRTEEN

After the thirty-nine-year-old John Henry Trapp had gone through the ignominy of being shaved, shorn, bathed, and dressed, he was escorted to the warden's office before he was even shown to his cell.

The guard walked him into the warden's office and the man behind the desk stood up.

"All right, guard," the warden said. "You can go."

"Warden," the guard said, "he's a killer—"

"You can go," the warden said again.

The guard backed out and closed the door.

"Sit down, Mr. Trapp—or can I call you John?"

"Trapp."

"All right, Trapp," the warden said. "My name is Warden Bellows."

Trapp didn't respond, and he didn't sit.

"The reason you're here is because I want to warn you about a few things," Bellows said.

"Like what?"

"Well, basically I wanted to warn you that a fella your size is liable to run into some trouble right at the beginning of your term."

"You mean there's trouble in here?" Trapp said. "I would never have guessed."

"The cons in here are going to want to try you out right away," Bellows said.

"I can take care of myself."

"I'm sure you can," the warden said, "but I have to tell you that I wouldn't take very kindly to having you *kill* anyone while you're here."

"Is it all right if I break a few bones?" Trapp asked sarcastically.

"You can do anything you have to do to protect yourself and earn yourself some respect," Bellows said, "but I do not want you to kill anyone."

"I see," Trapp said. "Is that all?"

"Just so long as you know the rules."

"All of the rules were explained to me while they were dousing me with buckets of water."

"I mean my rules."

"Your rules," Trapp said. "Right, don't kill anyone."

"Right."

"I understand."

"Good," the warden said. "Guard!"

The guard came in quickly, as if he expected to find something wrong.

"You can take Mr. Trapp to his cell."

The guard looked from Trapp to Bellows, wondering if they were keeping something from him, then said to Trapp, "Come on."

Trapp went out into the hall. At that time he didn't know how soon the warden's warning would be put to the test.

———

TRAPP WAS PUT into a cell with three other men, two bank robbers and a kidnapper.

"I didn't kidnap anyone," Jerry Heald said when he introduced himself to Trapp.

"Of course not," Sid Green said, "and Walter and I didn't rob any banks."

"Of course not," Walter Pierce said.

"What are you here for?" Green asked.

"For killing two men."

"But you didn't do it, right?" Green asked.

"Wrong," Trapp said. "I did it."

"Well, well," Green said, "somebody who's in here for something he *did* do."

Sid Green and Walter Pierce were both in their thirties. They had each been there for four years, with one more to go on their sentence.

Jerry Heald was in his late twenties. He'd been there for three years and had seven left on his sentence.

"I don't belong here," he complained. "I'll be an old man when I get out."

"I'm older now than you'll be when you get out," Trapp said, "and I'm here for twenty-five years."

"You can take some of that off for good behavior," Green said.

"No," Trapp said, "I can't."

He knew that the father of one of the men he killed would use his influence to make sure that never happened. In fact, he wouldn't have been surprised if the man tried to have him killed while he was in here.

"You're a bad one, huh?" Green asked, misunderstanding.

"As long as I'm left alone," Trapp said, "I'll be fine."

"Well, somebody your size," Green said, "I doubt that will happen. They'll be trying you out as early as today, you can be sure of that."

"Who will?"

"The ones who run this place."

"The guards?"

"No, not the guards," Green said derisively. "They work here, but they don't run the place. I mean cons like Big Teddy Speck and his people, Billy Kirk and his crew. There are several different groups fighting for control in here."

"And which group are you a member of?" Trapp asked.

"Some of us stay outside the group and watch our step, Trapp," Green said. "You, on the other hand, because of your size, will first be tested, and then courted."

"Courted?"

"Sure," Green said, "all of the groups will want you on their side—especially when they find out what you're in here for."

"Like I said," Trapp said, "all I want is to be left alone."

"Well, *we'll* leave you alone," Green said, "but I can't say that others will."

Trapp sat down on an empty lower bunk and said, "That will do for a start."

———

THE NEXT DAY after breakfast the prisoners were allowed outside for a short time, an exercise period.

Trapp's three cellmates moved to one side of the yard, away from the others. Trapp wandered the yard alone. Studying the other prisoners, he could see what Green had been talking about. There were some people, like himself and his cellmates, who were off to themselves, but for the most part the prisoners gathered in groups, and in the center of the group was the leader, being kept safe from harm.

Trapp was watching one such group, because the man in the center interested him. He was not as tall as Trapp, but he *was* the biggest man Trapp had ever seen. He looked almost as wide as he was tall, and yet he was not fat.

He wondered if this was the "Big" Teddy Speck whom Sidney Green had mentioned.

He became aware of a movement behind him and turned just in time to avoid being stabbed in the back. He grabbed the man by the wrist and twisted. The weapon fell to the ground and he saw that it was a knife fashioned from a spoon.

The man, six feet and in good shape, glared at him and tried to pull his hand free.

"Hey, fella," the man said, "no hard feelings, huh? I was just doing a job."

"Sure," Trapp said, "no hard feelings."

Trapp slid his grip up the man's arm to the elbow, then grasped the man's wrist with his other hand and promptly broke his forearm like a dried twig.

The man screamed and sank to the ground when Trapp released him. The man apparently had some friends, and two other men charged Trapp. The big man pivoted and lifted his foot, actually planting it into one man's face as he charged him. The man fell back, his nose squashed flat, his face covered with blood.

The third man threw a punch, which Trapp allowed to land. The blow had little effect as it struck his cheek, and then he hit the man. The blow snapped his head back and the man sank to the ground, unconscious.

By this time several guards had rushed forward, and two of them took hold of Trapp's arms. The big man did not resist.

"Take him to the warden," a third guard said. He turned to some prisoners and said, "Pick these men up and take them to the infirmary."

Trapp was escorted across the yard and he knew that he was the center of attention. As he walked past his cellmates, he saw Green smile and nod to him, as if telling him that he had done well.

————

HE WAS STANDING in front of the warden's desk, waiting for the man to speak to him.

Finally, Bellows looked up from reading a report.

"You broke one man's arm, another's nose, and a third's jaw," he said.

Trapp smiled at the warden and said, "Satisfied? None of them are dead."

"No," the warden said, shaking his head, "nobody's dead —yet."

CHAPTER FOURTEEN

The next day he was approached by two men in the yard.

"Big Teddy wants to talk to you."

"Good," Trapp said, "I want to talk to him."

He followed the two men over to the group that surrounded Big Teddy.

"Let him through," Teddy Speck said.

Up close, Trapp could see that Teddy Speck was a few years younger than himself. He was surprised to find that the man was under six feet tall.

"Your name is Trapp?"

"That's right."

"You're in for murder, aren't you?"

"Right again."

"Did you do it?"

"I did," Trapp said, "and I'd do it again."

Teddy Speck smiled.

"I can use a man like you."

"I'm not interested."

"Don't be so hasty, Trapp," Speck said. "If you join me, there will be a lot of privileges."

"I'm only interested in one privilege."

"I have the power to grant it."

"All I want is to be left alone."

Speck stared at Trapp for a few moments, then said, "Have

you had other offers already?"

"You're the first I've spoken to," Trapp said, "but I'll tell others the same as I've told you—leave me alone."

"That's not possible," Speck said. "You're too valuable to walk the fence like your cellmates. If you are not on my side, you are against me."

"I'm not your enemy."

"I could break your back now," Speck said. He straightened to his full height of possibly five-ten. With his bulk he was an imposing figure.

"If you had that much nerve," Trapp said, "you wouldn't be hiding behind all these men."

Teddy Speck surprised Trapp and smiled.

"You haven't been here long enough, Trapp. You don't know that I'm a target, just like Billy Kirk and a few others. We run this place. We say who is neutral and who isn't—and you, my friend, just don't qualify."

Trapp turned to walk away and found his path blocked. He waited, staring at the man standing directly in front of him.

"Let him go," Teddy Speck spoke finally. To Trapp he said, "Think about my offer, Trapp. I can get you anything—food, drink...women?"

Trapp turned and said, "Can you get me released?"

"If I could do that," Speck said, "would I still be here?"

"You heard the man," Trapp said to the men blocking his path. "Let me pass."

They opened a path for him and he used it.

"Think about it, Trapp," Speck called out. "Give me your answer tomorrow."

———

THAT AFTERNOON BILLY KIRK made his move.

"Come on, Trapp," a guard said, unlocking the door to Trapp's cell. "Somebody wants to see you."

"Who?" Trapp asked.

"You'll see."

The guard opened the door and Trapp walked out. He waited while the guard locked the door again and said, "This way. Walk ahead of me."

After they had gone a hundred yards or so, Trapp said, "This isn't the way to the warden's office."

"We're not going to see the warden."

"Then who?"

They reached another block of cells and there was one with the door wide open.

"In there," the guard said.

"I don't understand."

"The man who wants to see you is in there."

Trapp looked at the open door, then walked toward it. There was a convict standing on either side of it, but they made no move to stop him.

"Come in, Trapp," a voice said from inside.

Trapp entered and saw a man sitting in an overstuffed easy chair. The wall bunks had been folded up to give him more room. Obviously, he shared the cell with no one.

As Trapp entered, the man stood up. He was in his early forties, slim, dark-haired, and when he spoke, it was obvious that he was educated.

"I'm Billy Kirk."

Now Trapp understood. Kirk was about to make his offer, as Speck had made his.

"I saw what happened in the yard yesterday," Kirk said.

"Everyone did."

"I'd like you to work for me."

"I don't think so."

"You haven't heard my offer yet."

"I don't have to," Trapp said. "I bet it will sound just like Teddy Speck's offer."

"Ah, Teddy," Kirk said. "He got to you first, did he?"

"That's right."

"Then you're working for him?"

"No, I'm not."

Kirk looked happy.

"Then you're available to work for me."

"No, I'm not."

Kirk frowned.

"Who are you working for then. Simmons? Taylor? They can't offer you what Speck and I can."

"I'm working for myself, Kirk," Trapp said. "I want to be left alone."

"Look, Trapp, a man of your abilities—"

Trapp held up his hand to stop Kirk.

"I've heard this from Speck. You are both going to have to accept the fact that I want to be left alone. I don't want to work for either of you."

"We can't do that," Kirk said. "You're a potential weapon—"

"Only for myself," Trapp said. "I'm sorry, Kirk, but you and Speck will have to wage your struggle for control without me."

Trapp turned and the two men outside moved to block his path.

"Make them move," Trapp said.

"Think about it, Trapp," Kirk said. "You'll see that you have to make a choice, one way or another."

Trapp didn't answer. He saw one of the men watching Kirk behind him, and then the two men suddenly moved out of his way.

Trapp found the guard several cells away and said, "I'd like to go back to my cell now."

The guard looked at Trapp, surprised, then said, "This way, then."

———

ON THE WAY back to his cell, the guard asked Trapp, "So which one you gonna work for?"

"Neither."

"Was I you," the guard went on, as if he hadn't heard Trapp's reply, "I'd work for Big Teddy. He and Kirk are in here for a long time, but I think in the long run Big Teddy is gonna be in total charge soon."

"How soon?"

"A year, maybe two."

"That long?"

"Hey, it takes a while to gain control. Hell, they're in for another ten each, at least," the guard said. "How long are you in for?"

"Twenty-five."

The guard's eyes widened and after a moment he said, "Shit, by then you should own the place."

CHAPTER FIFTEEN

1851

Five years later Trapp was still being left alone, by Big
Teddy and his people, by Billy Kirk and his people, by
everyone—even the guards.

He went his own way, had his own routine. During the first
four months he was in Huntsville he broke two jaws, four arms,
and three legs.

Nobody was killed, and the warden was happy—relatively.

1857

Eleven years. Big Teddy and Billy Kirk were gone. Big Teddy
finally caught it in the back with a spoon/knife by one of his
own men. Billy Kirk was released. Nobody ever knew if Kirk
had Big Teddy killed or not. It could have been anyone with the
right price.

After Teddy and Kirk had left, their people floundered
around for a while, looking for a new leader. Some of them even
approached Trapp about being a leader, but he refused.

Over the first eleven years Trapp went through nine different
cellmates. They had all been released, allowed to return to their
worlds while he remained inside, away from his.

Trapp had accepted his fate early. He didn't sit in a corner pounding his head against a wall like some of the newcomers did. He didn't pick fights with the other convicts, testing death every day. He did fantasize about revenge, but that faded. The only man he could have revenge against would be dead by the time he got out.

He wondered how long after the man's death his influence would last. May he'd get out a year or two early, if the man died early enough.

And maybe not.

———

1861

Fifteen years.

Trapp had his beard and long hair back. Nobody bothered telling him to cut it anymore, not even the new young warden.

He didn't feel any older, although he knew he looked older than when he had first arrived. Age didn't mean anything inside. Everybody was the same age—inside it was *strength* that made the difference, and there was no one in Huntsville who wanted to match strength with Trapp.

He made no friends, not once in fifteen years. His cellmates were just that, people he shared a cell with, and they soon came to accept that. They did, however, benefit from that fact, because no one wanted to tangle with Trapp's cellmates. Even though they weren't his friends, it still wasn't known how he would take it.

For fifteen years Trapp got what he wanted."

He was left alone.

During the sixteenth year, John Welcome arrived at Huntsville.

Welcome was a notorious gambler and lady's man, and for a while the others wondered which of those avocations had gotten him to Huntsville.

Welcome didn't talk to anyone, not even his cellmates. He was a private man, maybe even more private than Trapp.

The gambler was in his early forties and the others eventually learned that he was serving seven to ten for killing a man over a woman—after he had cleaned the man out in a poker game.

Everyone in Huntsville was waiting for Trapp and Welcome to come face to face.

They managed to avoid each other for two years.

————

1864

The door to the warden's office opened and John Welcome stepped out. "Trapp, isn't it?" he said.

That's right."

"I'm John Welcome."

"I know."

"I understand you've been here a long time."

"That's right."

"I've been here two years, and I don't know anyone I can talk to."

"So?"

"So maybe we can talk."

"Why me?"

"Why not?"

They stared at each other for a few moments.

"Maybe," Trapp said, and stepped into the warden's office.

Warden Bill Blair had taken over three years ago. He was young, about thirty, when he took the job. His hair was always cut, he never looked as if he needed a shave, he always wore a tie, and he never went anywhere inside without at least four guards.

He was the wrong man in the wrong job.

"Sit down, Trapp."

"I'll stand."

Blair frowned.

"You pretty much go your own way, don't you, Trapp?"

"Yeah."

"Everyone in here respects you," Blair said. "The inmates, the guards…everyone."

"So?"

Blair set back in his chair and said, "I want you to be a trustee."

Trustees were convicts who were given certain privileges as long as they performed certain functions for the warden. The other convicts did not look kindly on trustees. They felt that they were spies.

"No thanks."

"I know that the inmates don't like trustees," Blair said, "but you and I could change that."

"How?"

"If you took the job, the others would think differently about trustees, simply because you were one," the warden explained. "What do you think?"

"I still think the same thing," Trapp said. "No thanks."

"Trapp—"

"I'd like to go back to my cell now."

Blair leaned forward and stared at Trapp.

"You're disappointing me, Trapp."

"You're ruining my day," Trapp said. "I'd like to go back to my cell."

Blair assumed what he must have thought was a menacing look, but to Trapp he just looked ridiculous.

"You think you own this place, Trapp," the warden said. "You're wrong."

"I don't own anything, Warden," Trapp said, "and I don't want to. All I've ever wanted is to be left alone."

"Well, you've been left alone, my friend, for fifteen years," Blair said, "but you've got another ten to do. Think about it."

Trapp didn't respond.

"Guard!" Blair yelled. When the guard came in, the warden said, "Take Mr. Trapp back to his cell."

"Yes, sir."

In the hall Trapp said, "Take me to John Welcome's cell."

"What?"

"The gambler, Welcome."

"Aw, come on, Trapp," the guard said, "I got to take you to your cell."

"You will," Trapp said, "after you take me to John Welcome's."

Welcome looked up as Trapp appeared in the doorway of his cell.

"You fellas want to excuse us?" he asked his cellmates.

"Sure," one of them said, and all three of them filed out past Trapp—gingerly.

Trapp stepped into the cell. Welcome sat on his bunk with a deck of cards.

"What can I do for you?" he asked.

"You said you wanted to talk."

Welcome stared at Trapp for a long moment, then said, "So sit down and talk."

Trapp hesitated and then sat.

"You ever play cards?" Welcome asked.

"Some."

"Poker?"

"Some."

"You any good?"

"No."

"Why not?"

Trapp shrugged.

"Not smart enough, I guess."

"Nah," Welcome said, "you're smart enough. Maybe you don't concentrate enough." Welcome showed Trapp an ace, then passed a hand over it and seemed to change it to a King.

"How did you do that?"

"I concentrated," Welcome said, "and you didn't. Now, watch again."

Welcome did it again, and Trapp still didn't see a thing.

"You're still not concentrating," Welcome said. "I can teach you to concentrate, if you'll let me."

Trapp hesitated a moment, then shrugged and said, "Why not?"

"Watch," Welcome said.

"Before you start," Trapp said, "what did the warden want you for?"

"He asked me to become a trustee."

"Yeah, me too."

"What did you tell him?"

"I told him to forget it."

"Yeah, me too. Are you watching now?"

"Yeah, I'm watching."

"Well, *don't* watch…concentrate!"

CHAPTER SIXTEEN

1866

"You know," John Welcome said to Trapp, "for a man with hands the size of yours you really picked this up quickly."

"Quickly?" Trapp repeated. "It's been two years, John."

"I know," Welcome said, "but it took me four. You're a natural, and it's amazing with hams like that for hands."

"It wouldn't have taken so long if we'd been able to be cellmates," Trapp said.

"Ah, the warden would never allow that."

"Well, he may not be warden much longer," Trapp said.

"What have you heard?"

"Some of the guards say that he's being replaced soon," Trapp said.

"It couldn't happen to a nicer guy," Welcome said. "Come on, let me see you deal seconds again."

For the first time in years, Trapp had a man he could call his friend. It was an odd alliance, an educated gambler and a man from the mountains, and the other convicts wondered about it.

From the point of view of Trapp and Welcome, it was simple. They were each the only person the other had met who didn't claim he was innocent.

Trapp freely admitted that he'd killed two men with good reason, and would do it again.

Welcome's contention was that he killed in self-defense, saving not only his own life but the life of the woman involved as well.

They were the only ones who weren't constantly trying to find someone who would believe they were innocent.

Trapp dealt out a hand of five-card draw, deliberately giving Welcome three aces and himself nothing. Welcome drew two cards, and he drew three. Welcome did not improve, and Trapp introduced some foreign cards into his hand and ended up with a straight flush to the King.

"That was excellent," Welcome said, his tone admiring, "truly excellent."

"Did you see it?"

"Well, of course I saw it," Welcome said. "Any professional gambler would have seen it, but it was still excellent. I just wouldn't try it on any professionals for a while."

"Hell," Trapp said, "I probably won't have any use for this skill at all, ever."

"You never know, Trapp," Welcome said wisely. "You just never can tell."

———

1871

"Well," John Welcome said.

"Yeah," Trapp replied, "well."

"I guess it never dawned on us that you'd be getting out before I did," Welcome said.

"I never thought you'd serve your full sentence," Trapp said, looking around his cell.

"And you?"

He looked at Welcome.

"Hell, I always knew I'd serve mine out," Trapp said. He was still looking around.

"What are you looking for?" the gambler asked him.

"I don't know," Trapp said, looking bewildered. "I honestly don't know. It just seems that after twenty-five years there should be something that I'd want to take with me."

"Here."

"What's this?"

Welcome handed Trapp a well-used deck of cards.

"Take that with you, to remember me by."

Trapp took the cards, looked at them for a moment, and then tucked them into his shirt pocket.

"Well," he said, "I'm all packed."

"Better get going before they change their mind," Welcome said.

Trapp started toward the open cell door then stopped.

"What is it?" Welcome asked.

"I don't know," Trapp said. "I just got this feeling...that I don't know who I am, or where I'm going."

"You're Trapp," Welcome said, "and you're going to your mountain." Welcome moved next to him and put his hand on the bigger man's shoulder. "Don't ever let anyone get between you and it, Trapp...not anyone!"

"What are you gonna do when you get out in a year?" Trapp asked.

"I don't know," Welcome said. "I haven't been inside as long as you. Things won't have changed as much."

"I know," Trapp said. "It's not the world I left out there."

"No, it's not," Welcome said. He squeezed his friend's shoulder hard and spoke urgently, hoarsely. "Just go to your mountain, Trapp. From what you've told me, it won't have changed."

"I hope not," Trapp said. "That's what I'm holding on to, John. If it's changed..."

John Welcome heard something in John Trapp's voice that he had never heard before. He wasn't sure, but it might have been...fear?

"If it's changed," Welcome said, "you'll find something else to hold on to."

Trapp didn't reply for a moment and then he said, "What about you?"

"Me?" Welcome said. "I hold on to a deck of cards. Cards don't change, Trapp—like mountains."

Trapp found himself fervently hoping that John Welcome was right—on both counts.

———

TRAPP CAME BACK to the present, sitting up in his bed. He went to the window and opened it, letting in the cool air. He could hear the voices and music from the saloon across the street.

What would he do, he wondered, if somehow the mountains had changed?

What would he hold on to then?

CHAPTER SEVENTEEN

The next morning Trapp and Fry had breakfast and then went looking for a horse.

"We've got enough money now to get you a decent horse," Fry said.

"That's all I need," Trapp said, "a decent mount to get me to the mountains."

"You know," Fry said as they continued to walk toward the livery, "with the money we've—the money *you* won—we could get ourselves a couple of real nice ponies—mustangs, maybe."

"You can spend a lot of your money on a horse if you want to," Trapp said. "I'll just take a decent, competent animal and save my money for something else."

"Like what?"

"I don't know," Trapp said, "but I feel a little better about being out of prison and in a strange world now that I have some money in my pocket."

"That's called security."

"I guess so," Trapp said. "Don't you want a little security in your life?"

"I don't know," Fry said. "I think I'm a little young for that —if you don't mind my saying so."

"Go ahead and say it."

"I'm just afraid I'll lose my edge."

"Your edge?"

"Yeah, you know, I'll relax too much and some young buck

—*younger* buck—will come along and put me down. When you're a walking target, Trapp, you've got to keep alert at all times."

"Stay in the mountains with me," Trapp said. "You can't get into trouble there."

Fry gave Trapp a surprised look and said, "Look who's talking."

Trapp opened his mouth to reply, then realized he had nothing to say to that. Fry was absolutely right.

"End of advice," he said as they reached the livery.

They went out back with the liveryman, who showed them some expensive horses. Trapp finally picked out an aged gelding who looked as if he still had some good miles in him and bartered the man down to fifty dollars. He also gave him five dollars for one of the used saddles he had.

"You drive a hard bargain," the liveryman said, counting his money.

"Sure," Trapp said, saddling his animal.

"What about you, young fella?" the liveryman asked Fry. "You looking for a new horse?"

Fry eyed a healthy-looking young mustang that the man had in his corral, but then shook his head and said, "No, the animal I've got is good enough."

"You sure?"

"I'm sure," Fry said.

"Suit yourself," the man said, then tried another tack. "You fellas traveling far? I can offer you a good deal on a pack animal."

"No thanks," Trapp said. "We'll travel light."

Fry proceeded to saddle his horse and then he and Trapp rode to the general store.

"Why travel light?" Fry asked when they reached there. "With a pack horse we wouldn't have to stop along the way for more supplies."

"I would just feel slowed down by a pack animal," Trapp said. "If we use our supplies sparingly, we'll get where we're going a lot faster, even with a few stops for more supplies."

Fry shrugged and said, "It's your trip, you call the shots."

They went inside and bought enough supplies to split evenly between them so that they'd each be carrying a fair-sized sack tied to their saddles.

Outside, as they mounted up, Fry said, "Maybe there's one other thing we should buy."

"Like what?"

Fry inclined his head to indicate the gun shop across the street.

"How about a handgun?"

"I don't think so."

"One would have come in handy last night," Fry reminded him.

"Maybe," Trapp said, "but I'll stick with the Sharps."

"Nobody says you have to give up the Sharps," Fry said. "I'm just saying—"

"I don't think so," Trapp said again. He didn't know exactly why he was refusing so firmly, unless it was a way of resisting progress. He wouldn't be able to do that for very long, because he *was* now living in a world that had progressed a long way since 1846.

He had seen only two small towns since leaving Huntsville. He knew that there was a lot more he was going to see that was going to surprise him, and perhaps even shock him.

The present would thrust itself upon him soon enough, but at the moment he just wanted to get his trek to his mountain under way, just him, his horse, and his Sharps, the way it used to be in the mountains.

"Are we ready to go?" Fry asked.

He looked at Fry, a young man who may or may not have been what he claimed to be. So far Fry had done nothing to make Trapp think ill, or different of him.

Many times in the mountains he had gone hunting with friends, or people who were simply partners. He wondered about them, and if any of them would still be around when he reached his destination.

For now, Fry was both friend and partner, coming along for the ride.

It struck Trapp that this was going to be a long way to go just to come along for the ride.

"Yeah," he said, "we're ready, Fry."

During the trip he'd find out more about Fry, and Fry would find out more about him. When they reached the mountains, they *might* be friends—good friends, with no reservations on either side. That remained to be seen.

———

FRY LOOKED at Trapp riding alongside him and wondered about him. He certainly didn't act like a man over sixty should act. After all those years in Huntsville, he was still an imposing figure, still had pretty good reflexes, and—if Annie Bennett was any indication—was still attractive to women more than half his age.

Fry was curious about Trapp, but it was more than curiosity that drove him to join Trapp on his trek to his mountain.

Much more.

Maybe, at some point, he'd even tell Trapp the truth about that.

CHAPTER EIGHTEEN

Keller was angry.

He was in Littlesworth, a nothing, dustbowl of a town in a godforsaken section of Texas, and nothing but a job could have brought him there.

He'd arrived at the gates of Huntsville Prison only to find out that John Henry Trapp, through some clerical error, had been released two days early.

He'd been forced at that point to put his hunter's skills to work.

Very often in his business Keller put himself in his quarry's position, trying to figure out what the other man would do.

He decided that if he was John Henry Trapp, getting out of prison after twenty-five years, he'd want to stay away from large towns for the time being. That meant heading west, to Littlesworth, which was where he was now.

It only took some conversation making in the saloon for him to find out that he was right. Trapp had been there, and had been involved in an altercation during which he had killed two men.

When Keller first took the job, he'd been assured that he was going after an old man. These did not sound like the actions of an old man.

He took a moment to recall his initial meeting with Sam Train at his home in Denver...

———

KELLER WALKED UP to the door of the big house and made use of the large brass knocker. He waited a few moments and was about to knock again when he heard the lock click and the door opened.

"Can I help you?" a well-dressed, balding man asked.

"Mr. Train?" Keller asked.

"No, sir," the man answered politely. "I am not Mr. Train. May I ask who you are and what your business is?"

"My name is Keller, and Mr. Train knows my business."

"Ah, yes, Mr. Keller," the man said, "we have been expecting you."

"Good," Keller said.

"Come in, please."

Keller entered and waited while the butler closed the door.

"This way, sir," the butler said, and led Keller down a long hall to a pair of glass French doors. The house was impressive, but Keller was not impressed with it or with the wealth that had built or bought it. Keller was not impressed by material things, he was only impressed by men—very *few* men.

The butler opened the doors and stepped in, then to the side.

"Mr. Keller, sir."

Keller was not yet in the room and he thought he heard a voice, but could not be sure. Apparently the butler had heard it, for he responded.

"Yes, sir," the man said, and then to Keller. "Please, come in."

Keller entered the room and found it oppressively hot. He immediately removed his jacket, revealing the gun he wore under his arm in a shoulder rig. It was his city gun, and he wore it when he was in Denver, or San Francisco, or New York, or anywhere a gun on the hip attracted undue attention.

"Sit down, Mr. Keller," he heard a whispery voice say. He looked around for the speaker and recoiled in shock that he immediately covered.

The man who had spoken was old—no, not old, *ancient!* He sat in a wheelchair with one blanket over his legs and another over his shoulders. His hair was the whitest Keller had ever seen, like snow, but it was thin and beneath it he could see a gleaming pink scalp.

The flesh of the man's face, instead of being wrinkled, was smooth and pink. The only wrinkles on the face were beneath the man's bloodless bottom lip, where there used to be a chin.

Keller would have guessed eighty, but even that might have been generous.

"Please," Sam Train said, "you must come closer or you will not hear me."

As it was, Keller didn't hear him, but he reacted to the crooking, skeletal finger of one of the old man's hands.

Keller moved closer and sat in a well stuffed chair.

"Oliver," Train said, "some brandy."

"Yes, sir."

Oliver—the butler—went to a sideboard and poured a glass snifter of brandy. He carried it over and handed it to Keller.

"None for you?" Keller asked Train.

"I would not be able to get it down," Train said.

Keller made a face and hid it behind the snifter.

"Would you like a cigar?" Train asked.

"Yes."

"Oliver?"

Oliver brought over a box of cigars and Keller took one. He passed it beneath his nose, enjoying the scent, and then lit it by a flame Oliver held. He took one puff and was sorry he had accepted. It was hot enough in there without smoking.

"Oliver," Train said, "the stones."

"Yes, sir."

Keller watched Oliver walk to a tub filled with water. He used a small pot to scoop some up and Keller could hear the ice clinking against the metal. Oliver then walked over to the pit and poured it in. The water struck a group of heated stones, and the result was a huge cloud of steam. The result was that the heat became even more oppressive.

"I apologize for the heat," Train said, "but I have very little blood left. Without it I would surely freeze to death."

"I understand."

"Remove your shirt if you must."

"If we get down to business," Keller said, opening his collar, "I won't be here that long." He took out a handkerchief and mopped the beads of sweat from his face and neck. He couldn't

do anything about the rivulets of perspiration that were trick-
ling down his back.

"Very well," Train said. "I want you to kill a man."

Keller looked at Oliver.

"Oliver can hear anything we say."

"Killing is my business, Mr. Train," Keller said. "You knew
that when you sent for me."

"Yes," Train said, "but I want you to kill an old man. Have
you any qualms about that?"

Keller shrugged. "None."

"This man has just about finished a twenty-five-year prison
term in Huntsville Prison. He's getting out in a week."

"And you want me to kill him?" Keller asked. "Hasn't he
been through enough?"

"No," Train said, "he has not. Twenty-five years ago he killed
my son. I was not able to have him executed, but I *was* able to
use my influence to get him sentenced to twenty-five years in
prison."

"Why not have him killed in prison?" Keller asked.

"I considered it," Train said. "In fact, I had it tried twice, to
no avail. I was about to have it done a third time when I realized that would be letting him off easy."

"So you decided to let him serve his entire sentence, and
then have him killed."

"P-precisely," Train said.

It was clear that the old man was tiring.

"I—I'm sure he thinks I'm dead," Train said, "but I refuse to
die until he does. He won't be—be expecting someone like
you—"

The old man stopped speaking and Oliver moved to his side.
Train waved a hand and Oliver leaned over to hear what he had
to say.

When he straightened up, Oliver said to Keller, "Do you
accept?"

Keller looked at Train, who seemed semiconscious, and said,
"Yes, with one condition."

"What condition?"

"I want to be paid in advance."

"Impossible," Oliver said.

"It's the only way I'll take the job," Keller said. He looked at

Train and said, "No offense, Mr. Train, but you could die and I won't get paid."

"How do we know you won't take the money and not do the job?" Oliver asked.

Keller gave Oliver a hard stare, and the butler began to fidget.

"I'm sure Mr. Train checked me out before sending for me," Keller said. "I've never failed to carry out a job."

"I—I didn't mean—" Oliver said, but he stopped when the old man raised a hand like a claw and pulled on his sleeve. Oliver bent over so Train could say something in his ear, and then straightened.

"Mr. Train accepts your condition."

"I want to be paid in cash."

Oliver looked at Train, who dropped his chin. He had either nodded, or nodded off.

"Come with me," Oliver said. "I will give you what you need."

Keller rose and started to say something to Train, but Oliver stopped him.

"He won't hear you."

They went outside and Oliver closed the doors behind them.

"How old is he?"

"Eighty-nine."

"He looks older."

―――――

THE BUTLER PAID Keller in cash, twenty-five thousand dollars, described John Henry Trapp, and supplied the mountain man's background.

He had been told that Trapp was about sixty-four, and had not expected any trouble. This should have been the easiest money he had ever made. He had been instructed to make sure that Trapp knew that Sam Train had sent him to kill him before he actually did it.

Because of the early release, and the story he'd heard about Trapp in Littlesworth, he was starting to think that the old mountain man might be more of a challenge than he'd thought. From what Oliver had told him, the mountain man had been formidable twenty-five years ago.

That was all right with Keller. His anger had faded and had been replaced by the old excitement that usually rose up when he began a hunt. He'd follow Trapp all the way to the Green River country if he had to, and kill him there.

Yes, that would be poetic justice. Kill him just when he reached his precious mountains.

Sam Train would like that.

If he lived long enough to find out about it.

Part Four

THE JOURNEY BEGINS

CHAPTER NINETEEN

John Henry Trapp had never seen land as flat as the Staked Plains of Texas.

And hot? Jesus, it was hot enough to fry bacon on his head, if he'd been bald. Hell, as far as he was concerned, it was even too hot to eat.

Though Fry didn't think so. Even when they stopped at midday to camp, Fry would take out the frying pan, build a fire, and fry up some bacon to go with the coffee. Trapp couldn't drink the coffee. The cold water they had put into their canteens a few miles back at the water hole had gone tepid already, but at least it quenched his thirst.

"How can you drink that?" he said to Fry, who was having his second cup of coffee.

"I like coffee," Fry said. "No, it's even worse than that. I *love* coffee. I've got to have my coffee."

"Your outsides are burning up in this sun, and now you want to burn up your insides as well?"

"Don't worry about it, Trapp," Fry said. "Here, have a slice of bacon."

"I don't know how you can eat that either," Trapp said.

"It's cooled off now," Fry said, putting the bacon into his mouth.

Trapp made a face and looked away. Something caught his eyes and he put down his canteen.

"What is it?" Fry asked.

"Have you had much experience with Indians?"

"Some," Fry said. "I've known a few, but they weren't plains Indians."

Fry looked where Trapp was looking and saw riders coming toward them. They were off a ways, but it was clear that they were Indians.

"What about you?" he asked.

"I've had experience with some of the mountain Indians," he said. "The Blackfeet, the Crow, the Shawnee. I don't know anything about these plains Indians."

"Comanches," Fry said.

"You can tell from here?"

"No, but that's what I hear they got around here, Comanches."

"Have you ever been to this part of Texas before?" Trapp asked.

"No."

"Are we near any towns?"

"I think there's a fort near here, Fort...McAdams, or something like that."

"Which way?" Trapp asked.

"I asked around in Littlesworth," Fry said. "The fort should be about ten miles east of here."

"It's out of our way," Trapp said, "but maybe we should head for it. We could pick up some supplies and ask about the Indians in the area."

Fry looked again at the approaching Indians, who were still too small to make out clearly, and then started kicking out the fire.

"Let's go, Trapp," Fry said.

"I'm with you," Trapp said. He stood up and then grabbed his back and staggered.

"What's wrong?" Fry asked

"Nothing," Trapp said. He rubbed the pain away from his lower back. Between sitting in the saddle and sitting on the hard ground, his back was killing him. "I just haven't spent this much time in the saddle in a lot of years."

They broke camp and saddled up, then took one more look back at the Indians.

"You think we can beat them to the fort?" Trapp asked.

Fry looked at Trapp and smiled.

"If you don't fall apart on me, old timer."

"I'll give you old timer," Trapp said. "Set the pace, you young whelp."

"You know," Fry said, "it's a good thing you ain't riding that fly bait you were riding when we met."

"If I was," Trapp said, "we wouldn't have to worry about *me* falling apart."

"All right," Fry said, "we'd better ride before we're up to our knees in Indians."

They started riding east, and Trapp hoped that the information Fry had gotten about Fort McAdams was right.

———

"THEY STOPPED."

Trapp turned and looked. Sure enough, the Indians, who" had slowly been cutting into the gap between them, had suddenly stopped.

"Why?" Trapp wondered aloud.

There was a small rise ahead of them and Fry said, "Maybe they know something we don't know."

"Like what?" Trapp said.

"Let's keep going."

They rode up the rise, and as they topped it, they saw that fort.

"Like that," Fry said.

"Fort McAdams," Trapp said.

"We made it."

"Maybe…" Trapp said.

"What do you mean, maybe?"

"Well, even after we go in," Trapp said, looking behind him, "we've still got to come out again."

With that sobering thought between them they started for the front gates.

———

THEY WERE ADMITTED to the fort and rode through it to the settlement behind it.

Fort McAdams settlement was larger than either of the towns Trapp had seen since he was released from Huntsville

Prison. It was larger, and it was busier. The streets were teaming with people and wagons, and

they had to stop once or twice as they rode down the main street toward the livery stable.

"Crowded, eh?" Fry asked.

"Yeah," Trapp said. He felt uneasy and he wondered if it showed.

"I was in San Francisco once," Fry said. "This is like one street in San Francisco."

"Is that right?" Trapp asked. "I don't think I'll be visiting San Francisco in the near future."

"Are you all right?" Fry asked.

"Yeah," Trapp said. "I'm just not used to being around this many people, that's all."

"Relax," Fry said. "People are people, whether there are five, fifty, or five hundred."

"Once a year," Trapp said, "in the mountains we would have a rendezvous."

"Rendezvous?"

"Yeah," Trapp said. "All of the trappers and hunters would get together with the buyers from the East, sell their skins, have contests—"

"Contests? What kind of contests?"

"Sharpshooting, wrestling, different things. We would do business and have fun."

"What's your point?"

"That's the only time I've ever been someplace where there were more than five or six people in one place at one time. Just that one time each year—and the last rendezvous took place five years before I went to prison."

"Just take it easy, Trapp," Fry said.

"I will," Trapp said. "I'll take it easy."

Trapp's heart was pounding and he felt closed in, but he fought the feelings of confinement away.

They reached the livery and gave their horses over to the liveryman.

"How many hotels are there in town?" Fry asked the liveryman.

"Two," the man said proudly. "We just opened the second one."

"Really?" Fry asked. "That's great. Which one would that be?"

"McAdams' House," the man said.

"McAdams' House?" Fry repeated. "That's a clever name for a hotel. What was the first hotel called?"

The liveryman grinned, showing gaps where teeth used to be, and said, "Hotel."

Fry looked at Trapp and said, "What do you say we try McAdams' House?"

Trapp didn't relish the walk back to the hotel, through the crowded streets, but what he wanted most now was to get into a hotel room, where he'd have enough space to breathe.

"Sure," he said. "Let's go."

He held his breath while they walked from the livery to the hotel. Beside him Fry was talking, but Trapp didn't hear a word he was saying. He came face-to-face with two men at one point and froze, but the look on his face made the two men go around him.

"Come on, Trapp," Fry said, putting his hand on his arm.

They reached McAdams' House and went inside, and Trapp released the breath he was holding.

"I'll get a room," Fry said.

"Two," Trapp said, his chest aching, "get two. I'll pay."

"I can pay for my own room, Trapp," Fry said. "I'll get two."

Fry got the two rooms and they went upstairs.

"You want to get something to eat?" Fry asked outside Trapp's room.

"In a little while," Trapp said. "Just give me...a little while."

"Sure, Trapp, sure," Fry said. "I'll come by for you later, eh?"

"Sure," Trapp said, "later."

Trapp went inside, shut the door behind him, and threw his saddlebags on the bed. He set the Sharps down and walked to the window. Outside on the street, people were still walking back and forth, civilians and soldiers; wagons were still going both ways. It was about three in the afternoon. He wondered how long it would be before the people began to thin out, before he dared to step outside of this room.

He sat on the bed. How the hell was he going to get along if being around people scared him. That's right, it *scared* him, and it choked him, and if he couldn't get over that...

Well, he didn't *have* to get over it. Once he got back to his mountain, he wouldn't have to worry about being around people.

They'd spend the one night here, buy some supplies, get some advice about the Indians, and then be on their way.

He lay back on the bed, enjoying the softness beneath him. He was warning himself about getting used to that when he drifted off to sleep.

———

WENDELL FRY LAY BACK on his bed and thought about Trapp. Being around people was really unnerving the older man. Fry could understand it. Even in Huntsville, Trapp probably wasn't as crowded as he had been walking on the street from the livery to here. For a man who was used to the space he had in the mountains, this many people would have to be scary.

Fry himself, he liked people. He liked the big cities, like San Francisco, even though he rarely got to them. The more the merrier, he thought, especially when some of the people were pretty ladies—*available* pretty ladies.

He thought about this new friendship with John Henry Trapp. The two of them were as alike as night and day. There was more than years between them. They had different likes and dislikes, and the only thing they had in common was…what?

They didn't have *anything* in common. Even their reasons for riding to Trapp's mountain were different.

Trapp was riding *to* something.

Fry was riding *away* from something.

CHAPTER TWENTY

Trapp woke a few minutes before Fry knocked on his door. In those few minutes he spoke harshly to himself about his problem. It was something he could live with, he told himself. People are people, Fry had said, and he was exactly right.

He could put up with it for one day.

When Fry knocked on the door, Trapp opened it.

"Are you all right?" Fry asked.

"Sure, Kid," Trapp said, "I'm fine."

"You want to go and get a drink, and then something to eat?"

"Yeah," Trapp said, "a drink sounds good."

"Okay," Fry said. "Let's get a drink, something to eat, and then we'll talk to someone about the Indians."

"And we can get going in the morning," Trapp said.

"Sure," Fry said, "we'll get going in the morning."

Trapp picked up his Sharps, stepped out into the hall, and pulled the door shut.

———

NICK BODINE THOUGHT a lot of himself.

He thought he was a great lover of women, and a great man with a gun. Not a *good* man with a gun, but a *great* man. He *knew* he was great with women, he had proven that over and over again, but he still had to prove to people that he was great with a gun.

Bodine had been looking for months for the opportunity to do that, and then it rode right into Fort McAdams, right down the center of the main street.

"You know who that is?" he asked the two men who were standing on the street with him. They had just come out of the saloon.

"Who?" Tom Masters asked.

"That one, riding in."

"The old guy?"

"No, stupid," Bodine said, "the guy with him."

"The young guy."

"Yeah, the young guy, genius," Bodine said. "You know who that is?"

"No, I don't know who it is."

"I seen him down in New Mexico, a couple of years ago," Bodine said. He looked at the other man, Sam Gorman. "You know who he is?"

"No, Nick," Gorman said with a shrug, "I don't know who he is."

"That's Kid Fry."

"Who?" Gorman asked.

"Oh yeah," Masters said, "I heard of him. He's supposed to be pretty good with a gun."

"Pretty good?" Bodine said. "Shit, I saw him take two men at one time. *Two!* That takes more than a man who's *pretty* good."

"All right, Nick, all right," Masters said, "so he's great with a gun."

"That's right," Bodine said, "he's great, but I'm better."

"Sure you are, Nick," Masters said.

"No, I mean it," Bodine said. "I'm better, and I'm gonna prove it."

"When, Nick?"

"Today," Bodine said. "We don't know how long he's gonna be here, so I'll do it today...I'll do it later today."

"Hey, Nick," Gorman said.

"What?"

"If you was in New Mexico and saw him take two men, how come you didn't take him then?"

Bodine looked at Gorman and said, "Why don't you shut up?"

———

TRAPP AND FRY walked into the Lucky Spur Saloon and approached the bar.

"What can I get for you gents?" the bartender asked.

"Beer," Fry said. He looked at Trapp, who nodded and said, "Two beers."

"Coming up."

Trapp turned and looked the room over. It was a big saloon, and it was doing good business. During the walk over he'd allowed himself to breathe slowly, and now he felt as if he could actually stand being among this many people. As long as he knew they were leaving tomorrow, he could stand it.

"Here you go, gents," the bartender said. "Nice and cold, the way it's supposed to be."

"Thanks," Fry said.

Trapp turned and picked up his beer.

"Your friend here looks like he just came down from the mountains," the bartender said good-naturedly.

"He came down a long time ago," Fry said. "Now he's looking to go back up again."

"Well, enjoy the beer, gents. If you need more, just let me know."

"Thanks."

Fry looked the room over and saw a couple of poker games going. It was still too early for the house tables to be open.

"You feel like some poker, Trapp?"

"Not tonight, Kid," Trapp said. "You can try your hand, though."

"Maybe later," Fry said. One of the saloon girls came by and ran her hand over Fry's chest, and then kept going. "Maybe I'll try some of that later, too, but first we got to get something to eat."

"Yeah," Trapp said, "yeah, I am kind of hungry." He was surprised to find that he was hungry. Also, the knot in his stomach was gone.

They drank their beers and then Fry asked the bartender where a good place to eat was.

"There's a small restaurant just down the street; it's run by a woman named Maria. They've got great food there, just great."

"Okay, we'll try it," Fry said. "Thanks."

"You fellas passing through?"

"Yeah, we got herded this way by some Indians," Fry said.

"The Comanches," the man said knowingly. "Quanah Parker's braves."

"Quanah Parker?"

"Yeah. He's half white and he's their leader. How do you like that?"

"Half white, eh?"

"Yeah," the bartender said, "I even hear he's got blue eyes."

"A blue-eyed Indian."

"If you had a run-in with him, you'd better talk to the commanding officer at the fort, Major Fisher."

"Major Fisher," Fry said. "All right, we'll do that, but first we'll eat, huh?"

"Sure," the bartender said, "you've got to take care of the inner man first, right?"

"You're so right," Fry said.

"Let's go and eat," Trapp said. He was getting hungrier by the minute. "I'm starved."

"You wouldn't be so starved," Fry said, "if you had eaten some of my bacon."

———

THEY WALKED down the street to Maria's, unaware of the fact that they were being watched by three men across the street.

"Where are they going?" Gorman asked.

"They just got to town, where would you be going?" Bodine asked.

"I'd be looking for a whore," Gorman said.

"You're a damned animal," Bodine said. "They're looking for someplace to eat, probably Maria's."

Bodine and his friends had been in Fort McAdams for a month, and had eaten in Maria's many times.

"At least he'll have a good meal under his belt when I kill him," Bodine said.

CHAPTER TWENTY-ONE

"Well, at least we found out something," Fry said after they had ordered from a heavyset woman in her late forties. They assumed that she was Maria.

"Like what?"

"Quanah Parker," Fry said.

"The blue-eyed Comanche," Trapp said. "I've never seen an Indian with blue eyes."

"Neither have I. You curious?"

"Not enough to go out looking for him," Trapp said fervently. "After we eat we'd better go and talk to that major..."

"Fisher," Fry said. "I agree."

"Maybe we can get an escort part of the way."

"I doubt that," Fry said. "They've got enough to do out here besides escorting a couple of civilians, but we might be able to get some advice."

The woman came back with a pot of coffee and two cups.

"Your steaks will be ready in a moment," she told them.

"Don't forget," Fry said. "Rare."

"I won't forget."

It was actually early for dinner, but the small restaurant was full. Luckily, there was enough room between tables that Trapp didn't feel too crowded.

"How are you doing?" Fry asked.

"I'm all right," Trapp said. "It just takes some getting used to, you know?"

"How many men did you share your cell with in Huntsville?"

"Three others," Trapp said, "sometimes two."

"It must have been cramped."

"It was," Trapp said, "but there were only four of us at the most. It wasn't bad."

"I'll take your word for it," Fry said.

"Never been inside?"

Fry looked at Trapp for a moment before answering.

"Once or twice, for a night, when I was younger and thought that courage came out of a whiskey bottle, but never for any length of time."

"Good," Trapp said.

The woman returned bearing two huge plates. On each was a big slab of steak, a bunch of boiled potatoes, and some vegetables.

"I'll bring out some rolls."

"Thank you," Fry said.

As the woman left, Trapp said, "You've got to be the politest sonofabitch I ever met. You 'thank you' to everybody for everything."

"You stay out of trouble that way," Fry said. "Nobody can ever question your tone."

"Have you had trouble with that?"

Fry put his elbows on the table.

"About the same time I learned that courage doesn't come in a whiskey bottle I learned that if somebody wants to start a fight with you, it's real hard to do when you're being polite."

"You seemed to have learned a lot for one so young."

"Tm not that young," Fry said. "I'm twenty-five, but I feel older."

"That's funny," Trapp said.

"Why?"

"I'm sixty-four and I feel younger."

"Maybe we can meet halfway somewhere."

"No," Trapp said, "don't give away any of your youth. Enjoy every minute of it, because you never know when someone is going to try and take it away from you."

"I live with that, Trapp," Fry said. "Any minute some fella

who fancies himself with a gun could come through that door and try for me. At least when they put you away, you stayed alive. My way, I could end up dead very young."

"Sometimes I wished I *was* dead," Trapp said, "but then I realized that no matter where you are or what you're doing, life is precious. So I hung on, and I beat the bastards."

"Here's to beating the bastards," Fry said, holding up his coffee cup.

"Beating the bastards," Trapp said.

———

KELLER HATED THE STAKED PLAINS. He'd spent some time there over the years, and liked it less and less each time. This time, however, he regarded it as a rainbow, and at the end of it maybe there was a pot of gold. Although he'd gotten his money already, he wouldn't feel that it was truly his until he did what he was paid to do—kill John Henry Trapp.

Two days, at the most he was two days behind them. It didn't seem so much when you thought of it in days rather than hours. Two days sounded like a lot less than forty-eight hours.

Two days.

———

"WHY DON'T we just go in and tell him to come out onto the street?" Sam Gorman asked.

"Quiet," Bodine said.

"I mean, instead of standing out here waiting for him. Are we even gonna do it when they come out?"

"Shut up, Gorman," Bodine said.

Gorman gave Bodine a wounded look, but fell silent.

"What about it, Nick?" Masters asked.

"I want to watch them for a while," Bodine said. "Maybe they'll split up."

"Come on," Masters said, "an old man with an old buffalo gun can't be that much trouble."

"We'll watch them and wait, Tom," Bodine said, "unless you want to go in there yourself and make a try for Kid Fry yourself."

"Not me, Nick," Masters said. "I'll back your play, but I got no hankerin' to go up against him myself."

"Smart," Bodine said, "real smart. You just back my play, Tom, and everything will turn out fine."

———

FROM WHERE FRY WAS SITTING, he could look out the front window.

"We've got some company," he said to Trapp.

"Who?"

Trapp was sitting with his back to the door and started to turn around.

"Don't turn," Fry said, arresting the movement. "Three jaspers, standing across the street."

"What makes you call them company?"

"They followed us here from the saloon."

Trapp frowned, chewing on a potato.

"For what?"

"If I had to guess," Fry said, "I'd say they were looking for trouble."

"Do we look like we've got something worth taking?" Trapp asked.

"Well, we do have some money on us, thanks to you, but that's not what they're after."

"What *are* they after?"

"Me, I'd say," Fry said. "One of them might have recognized me."

Trapp frowned again and stopped chewing.

"I thought you said you had a *little* bit of a reputation."

"I do," Fry said, "but that doesn't mean I couldn't have been in the same place at the same time with somebody, and they remember."

"So what do we do?"

"Nothing," Fry said. "We finish eating and go and talk to the army."

"What about them?"

"They'll watch and wait for a while," Fry said.

"How do you know?"

"It's what I'd do."

"You think they're as smart as you are?"

"God," Fry said, "I hope not."

CHAPTER TWENTY-TWO

After they had finished eating, they complimented the woman—who was indeed Maria—and left the restaurant, heading for the fort.

"Are they still there?" Trapp asked.

"Still there," Fry said, "but I doubt that they'll follow us into the fort."

As it turned out, he was correct. As they passed through the gates into the fort, the three men behind them stopped and simply watched.

"I told you," Fry said, "they'll watch and wait. They might even wait and see if we split up."

"In that case," Trapp said, "we won't."

"Well," Fry said thoughtfully, "we can talk about that later."

———

"THEY WENT INTO THE FORT!" Sam Gorman said.

"I can see, Sam," Bodine said.

"What do we do now?" Masters asked.

"What the hell are they going into the fort for?" Gorman said.

"Maybe they had a run-in with some Indians," Bodine said. "If that's the case, they'll just talk to the commander and come right back out."

"And we'll be waiting?" Gorman asked.

"Waiting and watching."

"Shit," Gorman said, "I'm getting damned tired of waiting."

"If you're so tired of waiting, then you can move on, Sam," Bodine said. "If you're staying with me, then just try keeping your trap shut for a change."

"Jeez, Nick, you don't have to—sure I'm staying—I was just—"

Masters closed his hand over Gorman's elbow to attract his attention and then shook his head to shut him up.

It worked.

———

"AND YOUR NAME IS?" the lieutenant asked.

Trapp had presented himself at the commanding officer's office, and Lieutenant Avery had introduced himself as the major's aide.

"My name is Trapp, and we'd like to talk to the major about some Indians."

"What Indians?"

"That's what we'd like to talk to him about," Trapp said. "We're not quite sure what Indians."

"Wait here, please," the young lieutenant said. "I'll see if the major has time to see you."

"Thank you," Trapp said, thinking about what Fry had told him about being polite.

As they had reached the commanding officer's office, Fry had suggested that maybe he should stay outside.

"You know, Kid," Trapp said, "we're going to have to have another talk about this reputation of yours."

"Sure," Fry said, "maybe when we get to your mountain, huh, Trapp?"

"We'll see."

Trapp waited a few minutes and then the lieutenant came back out.

"The major will see you now."

As Trapp stepped into the room the major, a white bearded, white-haired man stood up and stared at him curiously. Trapp made a mental note to buy some new clothes later. He was still wearing what the people at Huntsville had given him, and up to now it hadn't made much difference. It was time for a change, though.

"Major," he said, approaching the desk and shaking hands, "thank you for seeing me."

"My aide said something about Indians," the major said. The man's handshake was not that of a leader, Trapp thought. It was too limp. "Have you had some dealings with Quanah Parker?"

"Well, sir, my partner and I aren't quite sure who we encountered," Trapp said. "We were—well, *stalked*, I suppose is the word, as far as this fort—"

"How close to the fort did they follow?"

"That rise just south of the gate? They followed us to that point—"

"It would have to be Quanah's men, then," the major said. "They're the only ones with the nerve to get that close."

"Major, we were wondering if you might not have some suggestions as to how we might, ah, avoid them when we leave come morning."

"Avoid them?" the major said. "There's only one way to do that, sir."

"And what's that?"

"*Don't* leave."

Trapp laughed shortly and said, "We can't do that, sir. We have to leave."

"Then you'll just have to outrun them, mister," the major said, "although if they want you bad enough they'll ride all day until they ride you down. It's either that or wait until our next supply train comes in. You can leave with them."

"When will that be?"

"About a month or so."

"You're not being very encouraging, Major."

"I'm sorry," the major said, "but I'd rather tell you the truth than coddle you with some story."

"I see," Trapp said. "I appreciate that. I don't suppose you'd be able to, uh, supply us with some kind of escort—"

"Impossible, unless you're carrying supplies for the government, or have women and children who are in danger?"

"Neither one, I'm afraid," Trapp said.

"Then I guess we don't have much else to discuss, sir. Good day."

"Yeah," Trapp said, forgetting about being polite, "it was nice talking to you, too."

———

OUTSIDE FRY SAID, "SO? WHAT HAPPENED?"

"Nothing," Trapp said. "He says we either stay here or take our chances out there, trying to outrun them."

"Not much of a choice," Fry said.

"Kid, you can stay here and wait for the supply train, and then leave with them."

"And you?"

"Me? I've been away from my mountains too long as it is," Trapp said. "I'll be leaving in the morning."

"Well, I'll be leaving with you, then," Fry said.

"Maybe we won't even meet up with them again," Trapp said.

"There's always that possibility," Fry said.

They started walking toward the back gate.

"Our friends are probably still out there waiting for us," Fry said. "Don't pay them any mind."

"What if they—"

"They won't," Fry said. "It isn't time yet."

They walked out the back gate and sure enough the three men were standing off to one side, watching them. Trapp didn't turn his head, but he could see them out of the corner of his eye.

"There's another possibility," Fry said.

"What's that?"

They began to walk through town, and the three men fell in behind them.

"Maybe there are some others in the same predicament as we are. Maybe they want to leave town, but don't dare."

"So?"

"So, if there are enough of them we could all leave together," Fry said. "A small show of force might persuade the Indians to leave us be."

"I guess that is a possibility," Trapp said, but his tone clearly showed that he wasn't in favor of it.

Fry looked at Trapp and said, "So what's wrong with that?"

"I don't know," Trapp said. "Maybe old habits die hard, but I never used to make it a rule to travel with strangers. You never knew what they really wanted."

"Well, we'll have to decide where the least risk is," Fry said. "Let's talk about it over another beer."

"Another beer sounds good."

―――――

"WHERE ARE THEY GOING NOW?" Tom Masters said.

"Looks like they're headed for the saloon again," Bodine said.

"Good," Gorman said, "I could use a beer."

Bodine looked at Gorman and said, "I can hardly believe it."

"What?" Gorman asked. "What did I do now?"

"Something I would never have expected of you, Sammy," Bodine said.

"What?"

"You came up with an idea."

"I did?" Gorman said, sounding pleased with himself—then he frowned, looked at Masters and Bodine, and said, "What is it?"

CHAPTER TWENTY-THREE

Trapp and Fry got themselves a beer and found a table against the wall for themselves. Fry sat with his back to the wall, something Trapp noticed that he always did.

"Why do you always sit like that?" he asked.

"Like what?"

"With your back to the wall?"

Fry sipped his beer and put it down.

"So no one can ever come up behind me."

"Do you expect that?"

"Why else would I sit this way?"

"It must be a terrible way to live," Trapp said, "always expecting someone to sneak behind you and put a bullet in you."

"I don't *always* expect it," Fry said, "but it could happen. Why take chances, right?"

"Oh, right," Trapp said. He wondered why he suddenly developed an itch between his shoulder blades.

Suddenly, he wondered if the old man, Sam Train, was still alive. And if he was, would he just forget about Trapp? That was unlikely. If he was still alive, he probably knew the exact date that Trapp was getting out of Huntsville.

Maybe Trapp should also start sitting with his back to the wall.

"What's on your mind?" Fry asked.

Trapp told him.

"How old would this Train be by now?"

Trapp shrugged.

"In his eighties, I guess, maybe ninety."

"Probably too old and senile to care that you were getting out," Fry offered.

"Maybe."

"Where did he live?"

"Denver."

"I guess we could check it out by telegraph," Fry said, "if you're interested."

Trapp didn't answer.

"If he is alive, you think he'd send someone after you?"

Again, Trapp shrugged.

"I'm sure he tried to have me killed inside a few times," Trapp said. "Why not outside?"

"The way to do it would be to hire someone to kill you," Fry said. "A gunman."

"Like you?"

Fry stared at Trapp.

"Is that what you think?" he asked. "That I'm here to kill you?"

Fry seemed genuinely offended, and Trapp was sorry for what he'd said.

"No, I only meant—"

"I may have a reputation with a gun, Trapp," Fry went on heatedly, "but I've never been a hired killer. That's not my style."

"All right," Trapp said. "I'm sorry. I believe you."

"I hope you do."

"I do. Okay?"

"Okay," Fry muttered, but Trapp could tell the younger man wasn't just going to forget it.

They sat and nursed their beers in silence, each alone with his own thoughts, and Fry finally broke the silence.

"You know them fellas that were following us?"

"Yeah?"

"One of them's been at the bar for a while, watching us."

Trapp started to turn but stopped himself.

"Just watching?"

"That's all."

"Maybe we should go over and have a talk with him."

"Maybe," Fry said. "I tell you what—why don't you get up and get us another couple of beers."

"Me? I'm no hand with a gun, Fry."

"I don't want you to shoot him," Fry said. "Fact of the matter is, you're pretty scary looking, Trapp. Let's see how he reacts."

Trapp stared at Fry, mulling over the remark that he was "scary" looking, and then said, "Well, all right.

He stood up and started walking to the bar.

There were a lot of men at the bar and at first he didn't know which one was watching them, but it didn't take a genius to figure it out. Almost everyone watched Trapp, because even as thin as he had become in prison, he was still of imposing height. But one fella, medium height and sort of weasely looking, suddenly developed a bad case of nerves. His eyes darted around the room, he licked his lips, and he started to sweat.

Trapp altered his course and walked right toward the man. The man didn't know whether to bolt and run or stand his ground. Finally he turned to face the bar, put his elbows on it, and hunched his shoulders.

Trapp reached the bar, elbowed his way between the nervous man and another man, and told the bartender, "Two beers."

"Comin' up."

While he waited, Trapp looked at the man on his right through the mirror, and then at the nervous man on the left. The man was fighting to keep his eyes down on his drink, but finally he raised them and looked into the mirror. He saw Trapp looking at him and for a moment Trapp thought he *was* going to run. Hastily, the man lowered his eyes and kept them there.

The bartender came with the two beers. Trapp thanked him, picked them up, and turned to walk away. The move startled the nervous man and he jerked, his arm knocking one of the beers from Trapp's hand. Some of the beer went on Trapp, but most of it went on the nervous man, who leaped back from the bar as if he'd been scalded.

"Hey—" Trapp said.

"I'm sorry!" the man said quickly. He shook his hands, trying to shake the wet beer from them. "Hey, my fault," he went on, "I—I'm just clumsy. I'll—I'll buy you another one."

He signaled the bartender, who put another beer on the bar for Trapp. Trapp picked it up and looked at the other man hard.

"Thanks," he finally said.

"Hey, no problem," the man said, the front of his shirt soaked with beer. "My fault, right?"

"If I was you," Trapp said, "I'd be careful—*real* careful."

"Huh? Oh, sure," the man said. It was clear he didn't quite know exactly what Trapp was talking about. "Sure thing, mister."

Trapp took the beers and walked back to the table.

"Nice performance," Fry said. "Spilling the beer on him was real smart."

"That was his fault," Trapp said, "not mine. That's one very nervous man."

"Yeah," Fry said, "and he's heading for the door like a scared rabbit."

Trapp turned just in time to see the man scurry out the door.

"Now what?" he asked Fry.

"Now we wait," Fry said. "We just wait."

———

OUTSIDE, Sam Gorman hurried over to where Nick Bodine and Tom Masters were standing.

"What happened to you?" Masters asked. "You look white as a ghost."

"You're all wet," Bodine said. "What is that?"

"Beer," Gorman said. "That big fella spilled it all over me."

"On purpose?" Bodine asked.

"Well of course on purpose," Gorman said. "He knows, Bodine."

"Knows what?"

"That I was watching him!" Gorman said. "Why else would he spill beer on me?"

"Maybe you did it," Bodine said. "Maybe you got scared and spilled it all over yourself."

"You're damned right I'm scared," Gorman said. "You don't know how big that sonofabuck is until he's standing right next to you!"

"And what about Kid Fry?" Bodine asked.

"He just stayed at his table and watched."

"Yeah," Bodine said, nodding. "He sent the big fella over to scare you."

"Well, he did."

"Did he talk to you?"

"Yeah," Gorman said, his eyes widening. "He said if he was me, he'd be real careful."

"Sure," Bodine said again, nodding.

"Well?" Gorman asked.

"Well what?" Bodine said.

"Are we?"

"Are we what?"

Exasperated, Gorman said, "Are we gonna be careful?"

"Oh, yeah," Bodine said thoughtfully, "we're gonna be real careful, just like the man said."

"What are we gonna do, Nick?" Masters asked.

Bodine looked at Masters and said, "Come on, we're going in."

———

"WHAT IF IT'S THEM?" Trapp asked.

"Them...what?" Fry asked.

"What if it's them that Sam Train sent to kill me?" Trapp asked.

"No sense in wondering about that until we find out whether or not Train is still alive, is there?" Fry asked. "They might just be after me."

"Well then, let's find out."

"I doubt the telegraph office will be open at this time," Fry said. "We'll just have to wait until morning to check that out. We'll do it just before we leave."

"We'll have to wait for an answer," Trapp reminded him.

Fry shrugged and said, "You're calling the shots, Trapp. Do we wait for an answer, or get moving?"

Trapp didn't hesitate.

"We'll wait," he said, even though he didn't relish spending another day in Fort McAdams. "We might as well find out one way or the other."

Fry looked past Trapp at that point, to the entrance, and said, "We may find out even sooner than we thought."

CHAPTER TWENTY-FOUR

"Steady," Fry said to Trapp. "Let's wait until they make their intentions clear."

"We could be dead by then," Trapp said urgently.

"Easy," Fry said. "I can kill any two of them before they clear leather."

"You're sure of that?"

Fry took his eyes off the three men who had entered the saloon just long enough to fire Trapp a confident look when he said, "Oh, yes."

Fry looked again at the three men and asked Trapp, "Can you handle the other one?"

Trapp hesitated just a moment before saying, "Sure."

"Nice and easy now, just slide your chair sideways a bit and put your hand on your Sharps."

The Sharps was leaning against the table, with Trapp's body between it and the three men. He slid his chair around as Fry had said and placed his hand on the barrel of the gun. From his new position he could see the three of them.

"No matter what position they take up," Fry said, "you take the one on your left. Got it?"

"I've got it."

"Don't move until they do."

"Right."

Trapp was nervous. He'd killed men before—even before he

killed Sam Train's son—but he'd never had to do it under these conditions.

The three men fanned out, and it was clear that the two on the ends were taking their cue from the one in the center. Fry studied the man, but was sure he didn't know him from anywhere.

The others in the saloon gradually became aware that something was developing, and conversation died down to a low hum.

"You're Kid Fry," the man in the center finally said.

"So?" Fry said.

"I hear you're pretty good with a gun."

"So," Fry said again.

"I'm here to find out."

"Just you, or all three?" Fry asked.

"Just me."

"Then tell your friends to leave."

"You've got a friend," the man said. "They'll stay just to keep an eye on him."

"My friend's a harmless old man, mister."

Trapp gave Fry a quick look of annoyance, but then went back to watching the man on his left. His hand on the barrel of his Sharps was slick with perspiration.

"Stand up, Fry," the man said.

"What's your name?" Fry asked.

"What's that matter?"

"Come on," Fry said, "you know you want all these people to know your name. Why else would you be doing this than to build yourself a reputation? Besides, I don't like killing a man without knowing his name."

"You sure you're gonna kill me?"

"Son," Fry said, even though the other man was at least five years older than he was, "I'm not only gonna kill you, I'm gonna kill one of your friends, and *my* friend is gonna take care of the other one."

Trapp's man was the one who had spilled the beer, and the mountain man could see that he had gone beyond nervous all the way to scared. He was so scared he didn't know whether to watch his leaders, Fry, or Trapp, and his eyes were bouncing around in his head as he tried to watch all three.

"My name's Nick Bodine, Fry," Bodine said, "and you're a dead man. Stand up."

"I'll sit," Fry said. "You go ahead and make your move—or turn around, walk out, and keep on living."

A flicker of doubt crossed Bodine's face, but he pushed it away—Fry could *see* him doing it—and the man went for his gun.

Fry drew from his seated position and shot Bodine in the chest.

As Bodine drew, so did his friend on the right. Fry fired again, catching the man in the belly.

Trapp snatched his Sharps up, laid it across his lap, and pulled the trigger. The ball hit the nervous man in the chest before the man could decide to draw.

Fry stood up now and walked over to check the three bodies. When he was sure they were dead, he ejected the spent shells from his gun and replaced them with live ones. That done, he holstered his gun. Trapp took the hint and hurriedly took up his powder horn to reload.

Fry looked at the bartender and asked, "You got a sheriff in this town?"

"Sure do," the man said, "Sheriff Del Keeper. He's a good man."

"Is he an understanding man?"

"He'll listen," the bartender said, "but he's gonna make his own mind up."

Fry looked at Trapp and was about to say something when the door to the saloon opened and a man with a badge walked in. Behind him were two soldiers holding rifles. They must have been passing by and been commandeered by the lawman.

Sheriff Del Keeper had his gun out, and looked as if he knew how to use it.

"What the hell—" he said, looking down at the bodies. He looked up at Fry then, who slowly lifted his hand away from his gun.

"This can be explained, Sheriff," Fry said.

"Good," Keeper said. "Why don't we go over to my office and see if we can't work on it?"

CHAPTER TWENTY-FIVE

"Did you have to be so truthful?" Fry asked.

"Excuse me," Trapp said, "but somehow, over the past twenty-five years, I've gotten into the habit of not lying to the law."

"What were you, some kind of model prisoner?"

"As a matter of fact—"

"All right, all right, never mind."

The bone of contention between them was the fact that when the sheriff had asked Trapp where they'd come from, he had answered honestly. Now the sheriff would probably check back with Littlesworth and Portsville and would find out that they had been involved with killings in each place.

"*We* know that it's just coincidence," Fry said, "but how do you think it's going to look to a lawman?"

"We can't help it if we attract trouble," Trapp said.

"That's all we have attracted since you got out of prison, and since we met."

"Well, this one obviously wasn't my fault," Trapp said. "They were after you!"

"And those two in Littlesworth?" Fry asked.

"They were ragging me, but you invited yourself into that one."

"And Portsville?"

"Some sore losers at poker," Trapp said.

"And we were partners by then, so I had to take a hand and save your ass."

"I was doing fine."

"Yeah, with that one-shot Sharps."

"It didn't do too badly tonight," Trapp said. "Maybe I saved *your* ass."

"Yeah," Fry said, "maybe."

Fry had been resting his face between the bars that were separating his cell from Trapp's. He looked at Trapp curiously now.

"Hey, how you holding up?"

Trapp looked up at the bars, then the ceiling, and finally the window. It was almost daylight, and they'd been there all night. Trapp had not been able to sleep. He was afraid he'd wake up and find himself back at Huntsville Prison.

"Well, I'm not real *happy* with my room, but I guess I'm holding up okay."

"It's not gonna work in our favor if the sheriff finds out you just got out of Huntsville," Fry said. He frowned at Trapp and asked, "You didn't tell him that, did you?"

"No," Trapp said.

"Well," Fry said, "luckily since we been traveling you've gotten rid of that prison pallor, so maybe he won't guess."

At that point, the door to the sheriff's office opened and the lawman came through. He had the keys in his hand and unlocked each of their cells in turn.

"Come out front when you get yourselves together," he said, and went back to his office.

Trapp and Fry picked up their shirts and left the cells. They followed the sheriff into the office.

Sheriff Del Keeper had Fry's gun and Trapp's Sharps on top of his desk. The sheriff had seated himself behind his desk and was rolling a cigarette. He was in his forties, with slate gray hair and a bushy mustache. He was starting to go thick around the middle, but still looked like a man who enjoyed the authority he held, and was confident in his ability to handle it.

"I checked you boys out."

"And?" Fry said.

"You've had quite a string of bad luck—or has it been good luck? Three shootings in three weeks, and not a scratch on either of you."

"We didn't start any of them, Sheriff," Trapp said.

"Oh, don't worry," Keeper said. "I got the stories from Littlesworth and Portsville. You fellas just seem to attract trouble, don't you?"

Neither Trapp nor Fry answered.

"All right," Keeper said. "Pick up your iron and go and attract it somewhere else."

"What does that mean?" Fry asked.

"I want you out of Fort McAdams."

"We only came here to get away from some Indians," Fry said.

"Well, I wouldn't wish you two on many people, but maybe your brand of luck can do some damage to Quanah Parker."

"We have to send a telegraph message before we leave, Sheriff," Fry said.

"And we have to wait for an answer."

"How long will that take?" Keeper asked.

"We're hoping only one extra day," Fry said. "We're eager to get going, Sheriff, even if it means trying to outrun Quanah and his boys."

"All right," Keeper said, rubbing his jaw, "I guess we can stand you for one more day—but stay out of trouble."

"That's always our intention, Sheriff," Trapp said, picking up his Sharps.

"That's a beautiful weapon, Trapp," the sheriff said. "It looks well cared for."

"It has been."

"It made a hole in that fella you could have driven a wagon through."

"That was the chance that fella took," Fry said, buckling his gunbelt on.

Keeper stood up, straightening to his height of better than six feet.

"I know your reputation, Fry."

Trapp looked at Fry, who didn't comment.

"Don't look to add to it here."

"Killing those three men wouldn't add to anyone's reputation, Sheriff," Fry said, adjusting his gunbelt so that it sat just right. "In fact, it was the other way around."

"Did you know those three, Sheriff?" Trapp asked.

"Yes," Keeper said. "They'd been here about a month now. Hadn't caused any trouble—until now."

"Well, I'm sorry to have been the cause of it," Fry said.

"A hazard in your profession, eh?"

"My profession?" Fry asked. "You don't know what my profession is, Sheriff. You might assume, but you don't know."

"No," Keeper admitted, "maybe I don't. All right, Mr. Fry, Mr. Trapp. I hope the accommodations were to your liking."

"My compliments," Fry said wryly. "Is the telegraph office open this early?"

"Not for a couple of hours."

"And the restaurant, Maria's?"

Keeper shook his head.

"Not for another hour."

"Well," Fry said, "I guess we'll just have to wait for our breakfast."

"I'm sorry to release you so early," Keeper said. "Another hour and I would have served you breakfast in your cells."

"That's all right, Sheriff," Trapp said. "We'd just as soon fetch it ourselves."

"Good morning, Sheriff," Fry said.

Keeper nodded and watched Trapp and Fry walk out.

On the boardwalk in front of the office, Trapp paused and took a deep breath.

"Okay?" Fry asked.

"*Now* I am, yes," Trapp said.

"Hungry?"

"Starved."

"Why don't we go to the hotel and change into fresh clothes," Fry said, "and then go to breakfast."

"I don't have any fresh clothes," Trapp reminded him.

"Yeah," Fry said, wrinkling his nose, "I've been meaning to talk to you about that, Trapp."

CHAPTER TWENTY-SIX

They returned to the hotel so that Fry could change into fresh clothes.

Maria's was among the earliest of the businesses to open. They went there and had breakfast while waiting for the telegraph office and the general store to open.

"We'll get you a pair of jeans and some shirts at the general store," Fry said, "and then we'll try the telegraph office."

"Let's try the telegraph office first," Trapp said, "and while waiting for the answer we can look for the new clothing."

"Sure, okay," Fry said. "That makes sense."

They finished their leisurely breakfast and found the telegraph office open.

"Sam Train, right?" Fry asked.

"That's right."

Fry composed the telegram and read it to Trapp.

"Who are we sending it to?" Trapp asked.

That stumped Fry for a moment, but then he said, "I might as well send it to the Denver Police Department. I'll just say that I heard that Sam Train had been killed, and we'll see what happens."

Trapp waited outside while Fry sent the telegram, and endured the unpleasant looks that passing women gave him. He was going to have to get some new clothes.

Fry came out and said, "All right, it's sent. If Train was, or is, the big shot you said he was, we should get a prompt reply."

A woman walked by and gave Trapp a long, disapproving look.

"Let's get you those new clothes," Fry said.

"Good idea."

They went to the general store and bought the largest sized shirts and jeans they had.

"What about a hat?" the clerk asked.

"Up to now you could use the sun on your face," Fry said. "Maybe now it's time for a hat."

"What kind?" Trapp asked.

"I have several different kinds," the clerk said.

Trapp looked at the hats and didn't like any of them. He finally settled on the same flat crowned Stetson that Fry wore, only one less fancy. Fry's had a band of silver around the crown. Trapp took one that was plain.

They went back to the hotel with the clothes and Fry said, "Time for a bath."

"A what?"

Fry laughed and said, "A bath."

"Is that really necessary?" Trapp asked.

"It is as long as we're here," Fry said.

"We're only going to be here another day."

"If you're going to put on new clothes, you should take a bath."

Trapp didn't like the idea—that was obvious.

"Didn't you take baths in the mountains?"

"Sure, every so often."

"How often?"

"Eight, maybe nine times."

"A month?"

"A month!" Trapp said, shaking his head. "Eight or nine times a *year*"

"Yeah, well," Fry said, "I take a few more than that. I really think this is a must."

Fry went to the clerk and asked where the bathhouse was. When he had directions, he went back to Trapp.

"Come on," he said, "I'll protect you."

"From what?"

"From the big bad water."

"I don't need to be led by the hand," Trapp said.

"All right," Fry said. He told Trapp where the bathhouse was. "I won't have to come back and check on you, will I?"

"I'll take a bath," Trapp said, "but this one's going to last a while."

"Fine," Fry said, smiling.

Trapp went around behind the desk and down a long hallway to where the bathtubs were. There were three, and they were all available.

"Can I help you?" a man asked. He was a small, wiry man in his late fifties.

"I...want to take a bath."

"Hot or cold?"

"Hot?" Trapp said. Anytime he'd taken a bath in the mountains it had always been in a spring, or a lake. In prison when they bathed, it was with cold water. He had never had a hot bath, not even with Annie Bennett.

"Yeah, hot or cold?" the man said. "You got a choice."

"If I have a choice," Trapp said, "I'll take a hot one."

"Okay," the man said. "Get undressed and grab some soap and a towel. I'll fill the tub."

When the tub was filled, the man left and Trapp tested the water with his toe. It was scalding, but if he was going to take his first hot bath, he wanted to take it while the water was *very* hot. He forced himself to submerge completely, and after a few moments his entire body felt...soothed.

He hadn't felt this good in years.

———

FRY WAS WAITING in the lobby and just when he thought something might have happened—could Trapp have drowned? —Trapp came walking out. He was dressed in his new clothes, and he was *clean*.

"What happened?" Fry asked.

"What do you mean?"

"You were in there a long time."

Trapp looked embarrassed.

"Well, if I was going to take a bath, I wanted to do it right."

"You old fraud," Fry said, grinning. "You enjoyed it, didn't you?"

"Well...I've never had a *hot* bath before," Trapp said. "It was...relaxing."

"A bath and some new clothes make all the difference," Fry said. "You look...different. One more thing would make the picture perfect."

"What's that?"

"A shave and a haircut."

Trapp poked Fry in the chest with a rigid forefinger and said, "Don't push your luck."

They went outside and the first women who walked past nodded at them pleasantly.

"See?" Fry said. "Now you look more human."

"What did I look like before?"

Fry shrugged and said, "A mountain man."

"Well," Trapp said, "I sure wouldn't want to look like one of them, would I?"

CHAPTER TWENTY-SEVEN

For the rest of the morning and all of the afternoon, they awaited a reply to the telegram. They passed the time by getting two chairs from inside the hotel and sitting on the boardwalk outside.

"Sitting in front of the telegraph office would be pushing it, just a little," Fry said.

"This is all right," Trapp said. Td rather be sitting here than trying to walk around. How can you stand being among this many people?"

"Well, I grew up around a lot of people, you know. I can understand your feelings, though."

Trapp fell silent and stayed that way.

"What's it like in the mountains?" Fry asked.

"It's quiet," Trapp said. "God, sometimes it's so quiet that all you can *hear* is the wind." Trapp's eyes became vague, as if he wasn't looking at anything in particular—or at something only he could see. "Sometimes the wind is all you hear for days, for weeks—unless it's an animal. You know, I've gone as long as six months without seeing another living soul."

"How could *you* stand that?" Fry said. "I need to see people every day."

"Wait," Trapp said. "Wait until you get to my mountain. You'll see what I mean. The air is like nothing you've ever breathed. The snow caps are like...like what pearls probably look like." Trapp looked at Fry and said, "I've never seen pearls, but they couldn't possibly be any more beautiful."

"I don't know," Fry said. "I've never seen pearls either."

"And the water," Trapp went on. "So clear, so damned cold that it brings every inch of your body to life."

Trapp put his head back and closed his eyes. Fry was about to do the same when he saw Sheriff Keeper coming their way.

"Here comes the law," he said.

Trapp opened his eyes and said, "Now what?"

They watched while the lawman drew closer.

"Taking it easy, I see," Keeper said, reaching them.

"Just doing what we said we'd do, Sheriff," Fry said, "staying out of trouble."

"I just got a telegram from Denver," the sheriff said. He took a piece of paper out of his pocket and read from it. "Sam Train alive and well. Please investigate threat." There was more, but that was all Keeper read to them.

"Why did you get that message?" Trapp asked.

"What threat?" Fry asked.

"That's what Denver wants to know," Keeper said. "It seems this Sam Train is a very important man in Denver, and has been for a long, long time. Why would you, Mr. Fry, write to the Denver Police and ask if he was dead?"

Fry shrugged and said, "Curiosity."

"And that's all?"

"That's it."

"There was no threat here?"

"Why would I threaten the man?" Fry asked. "I don't even know him."

"Then why would you be concerned about his health?"

"I told you," Fry said, "curiosity."

"Let me tell you something, Fry," Keeper said, putting his boot up on the boardwalk and leaning on his knee, "if you heard anything about a threat, or a planned attempt on Sam Train's life, Denver would really like to hear about it."

"I don't know anything, Sheriff Keeper," Fry said. "I swear I don't." He raised his right hand to give the oath strength.

"All right," Keeper said, straightening up. "I had an obligation to ask. I'll respond to Denver and tell them they have nothing to worry about."

Trapp watched the sheriff walk away and said, "I wish I could say the same for us."

"Why do you say that?"

"If he sends a telegram to Denver and mentions *my* name," Trapp said, "then if Train wasn't on my trail already he will be—mine and yours."

———

THE SHERIFF WENT to the telegraph office and composed a short message:

CHIEF COLE, DENVER POLICE,
QUESTIONED FRY AND TRAPP. NO CAUSE FOR ALARM.
SHERIFF KEEPER

Satisfied that he had discharged his obligation to a fellow lawman, Keeper left and headed for the saloon.

———

KELLER WAS FURIOUS.

Just when he knew he was closing in on John Henry Trapp, his horse stepped on a stone and bruised its hoof. Now he was camped out in the middle of nowhere with very few options. He could stay where he was and wait for the damned thing to heal, or he could start walking toward Fort McAdams.

He was furious at the horse for stepping on a stone he could have just as easily missed.

He was furious at Sam Train for hiring him in the first place.

He was furious at John Henry Trapp for not dying in prison.

He was furious at himself for not being able to turn down the job, and for having his own code of ethics. When he took a job he never let anything keep him from doing it—even if it meant walking a full day to get to Fort McAdams.

As far as his options were concerned, if some Comanches happened to show up, he had one other.

He could die.

He could have ridden the horse until he was dead lame, but he decided against that. If he *did* run into some Indians, he could mount up and push the animal until he dropped.

Hopefully that wouldn't happen until they reached the safety of the fort.

Angrily he kicked out his campfire and packed his supplies.

Somebody was going to pay for this, and when he caught up to him, that someone would be John Henry Trapp.

Who else was there he could take it out on?

———

"WHAT IS IT, OLIVER?" Sam Train asked.

The butler eased into the bedroom and moved to Train's bedside.

"I didn't want to wake you, sir," Oliver said.

"How could you wake me?" Train asked. "I'm never asleep. I *can't* sleep anymore. What is it?"

"We just had a visit from a policeman," Oliver said. "He was sent by the chief of police."

"So?"

"It seems the police had an inquiry about you, sir."

"And?"

"Someone wanted to know if you were still...er, alive."

Sam Train snorted.

"If you call this living. Who wanted to know?"

"The request came from a man named Fry, from Fort McAdams, in Texas."

"And?"

"The Denver Police routed the reply to the sheriff of Fort McAdams, and asked him to check it out."

Train closed his eyes and for a moment Oliver thought he had fallen asleep...or...

"Am I going to have to drag this out of you, Oliver?"

"No, sir," Oliver said. "When the sheriff replied, he mentioned two names. He said he had questioned Fry...and Trapp."

"Trapp!" Train said. His reaction was so violent that he began to cough.

"Sir—"

"I'm all right, damn it. Have we heard from Keller?"

"No, sir."

"Well, when we do, tell him that Trapp was asking about

me. Now that Trapp knows I'm alive, he'll probably assume that I've sent someone after him. Keller should know that."

"Yes, sir."

"Damn the man!" Train said. "I wish I could see him myself when Keller kills him. I wish I could see it with my own eyes."

"You know that's impossible, sir."

"I know it, you jackass!" Train said. "I just hope I'm still alive when it happens, so I can hear about it. Now, get me out of this damned bed!"

CHAPTER TWENTY-EIGHT

Trapp and Fry debated leaving immediately—now that they had their answer—or waiting until morning.

"Neither one of us is an Indian fighter," Fry said. "I don't mind admitting I don't know when we'd have a better chance of getting by Quanah, now or in the morning."

"Maybe we should find someone to ask," Trapp said.

"That's not a bad idea, Trapp."

They went to the saloon and found the same bartender on duty. They ordered a beer each, and when he set their drinks down in front of them, they asked if he had a minute.

"Sure," he said, wiping his hands on a rag. "What can I do for you?"

"We need to speak to someone who has experience with the Indians."

"What kind of experience?" the man asked. "Living with them? Fighting them?"

"Fighting them, I guess."

"Ah, but a man who lived with them, he'd know them even better."

"Well, who would you suggest?"

"If you want to talk to someone who's lived with them, talk to Jerry Blake. If you want to talk to someone who's fought them, go and see Sergeant Caleb Nichols, at the fort."

Fry looked at Trapp and said, "I guess it wouldn't do any harm to see both of them."

"Why don't you talk to Blake, and I'll go and see Sergeant Nichols."

"All right," Fry said. "I'll meet you back here."

"Right."

Trapp drained his beer, and left the saloon.

"So tell me," Fry said, "where I can find Jerry Blake..."

———

TRAPP WENT to the fort and asked a soldier where he could find Sergeant Caleb Nichols.

"He's out on patrol right now," Private Rufus McKay replied. "Is this something personal?"

"Well, I understand he's had some experience fighting Indians."

"Oh, yes sir, he sure has—years of it. He's the most experienced Indian fighter in the outfit."

"Do you know when he'll be back?"

"He'll be back in time for mess," McKay said. "I can tell him you was asking for him."

"I'd appreciate it," Trapp said. "Tell him if he comes over to the saloon, John Trapp would like to buy him a drink."

"I can safely say he'll be there, sir," McKay said. "Ol' Caleb ain't one to turn down a free drink."

Trapp nodded and said, "Thanks for your help."

———

THE ONE THING the bartender had not told Fry was that Jerry Blake, as well as being a man who had lived with the Indians, was also Fort McAdams's town drunk.

Fry found Blake passed out in the livery. He shook him a few times but it was to no avail. The man did not stir. Fry knew a surefire way to wake up a drunk, and he decided to use it.

He grabbed Blake, a frail man who weighed hardly anything, by the back of the shirt and the back of the belt, and carried him out behind the livery to a horse trough. Once there he unceremoniously dropped the man into the water.

Blake sank like a stone and for a moment Fry thought he wouldn't surface, but finally there he was, sputtering and coughing.

"What the hell—" Blake shouted. He sat up straight, looked around, wiped his face with his hand, then smelled the hand. "It's water!" he said, sounding alarmed.

"It sure is, Blake," Fry said.

"How did I get here?"

"I dropped you in."

"What in the sam hill for?"

"To wake you up."

"Why?"

"To talk to you."

"You woke me to talk?" Blake demanded. "Jesus, if you woke me, the least you could do is buy me a drink."

"Maybe after we talk."

A crafty look came into the waterlogged man's eye and he said, "I talk better with one under my belt."

"I don't think you've *ever* had *one* under your belt in your life, Blake," Fry said. "Let's get you out of that water before you catch your death of cold, and we'll see if we can come to some kind of an arrangement."

Fry gave the man his hand and hauled him out of the water.

———

WHEN TRAPP RETURNED to the saloon, he saw Fry sitting at a back table—back to the wall, as always—sitting across from a man who was soaking wet from head to toe. The man didn't seem to mind, though, because Fry was dangling a glass of whiskey in front of him.

"Is this Jerry Blake?" Trapp asked, approaching the table.

"This is Jerry Blake," Fry said. "He's agreed to talk to us, for a price."

"And that price is?" Trapp asked, sitting down.

"A drink."

Trapp eyed the man and asked, "How the hell did he get so wet?"

"That's a long story," Fry said. "Let's just say he took some persuading."

"Can I have—" Blake said, reaching for the drink.

"No, Jerry," Fry said, pulling the drink away, "remember what our deal was. You can smell, but you can't touch."

"Jesus," Blake said, and he put his hands down at his sides.

Fry passed the shot glass beneath the man's nose and Blake breathed in deeply.

"AH right," Fry said, removing the glass, "what we want to know is this: We have to leave town and we'd like to avoid meeting up with any of Quanah Parker's boys. How do we do that, by leaving tonight, or in the morning?"

"Is that what this is about?"

"That's it."

Blake looked at the drink mournfully and asked, "Do I still get the drink if you don't like the answer?"

"As long as you *do* answer, you get the drink," Fry said.

"Then you're shit out of luck," Blake said, "because you ain't gonna get by Quanah either way."

"Why not?"

"Because Quanah sees everybody who goes into this fort, and who comes out. He ain't gonna let you two get through, not without trying to stop you."

"Why not?"

"It just ain't his way," Blake said. "Quanah regards this as his land. He ain't just gonna let the white man come and go as he pleases—especially two white men comin' from this fort."

"What do we do then?"

"When you leave you ride like the devil's on your tail —'cause he's gonna be."

Trapp and Fry exchanged glances.

"See, I knew you wasn't going to like the answer. Can 1 have the drink now?"

Without looking at Blake, Fry held the drink out. Blake grabbed it without spilling a drop and drank it down in one swift motion.

"This is not encouraging at all," Fry said. "What did the sergeant have to say?"

"He's out on patrol," Trapp said. "I left a message that there's a free drink waiting for him here."

"We'll just have to wait for him, then, and see what he has to say."

"Uh, how about another?" Blake asked, smacking his lips.

"Here," Trapp said, putting the price of a drink on the table. "Go and buy it yourself."

"You're a good man," Blake said, grabbing the money. "A very good man."

Blake got up and wandered over to the bar.

"What do we do in the meantime?" Trapp said.

Fry looked around. The place was filling up, and he knew that sooner or later a poker game would start up. He didn't mention it to Trapp, though. The memory of what happened the last time he played poker would be too fresh in the old mountain man's mind.

———

KELLER KNEW THEY WERE THERE.

There were about three or four braves stalking him from behind. He wasn't spooked enough, yet, to mount up and ride. In fact, he might never get that spooked, because so far they had made no move to close the gap between them. It was possible they were just going to watch him, playing some sort of cat-and-mouse game. He knew that if he displayed no fear, the game would go on longer.

Maybe long enough for him to get where he was going —alive!

———

"WAS I YOU," Sergeant Caleb Nichols said, "I'd leave tonight."

Trapp and Fry had sat together in the saloon for hours waiting for Caleb Nichols to show up, and when he did, they knew him immediately. Apparently, the sergeant had come as soon as he'd returned from patrol, without even cleaning up. He was covered with dust and dirt from head to toe, and had a thirsty look on his face.

Sergeant Caleb Nichols was in his late forties, with a huge belly that hung down over his belt. He was badly in need of a shave and a haircut, but Fry suspected he always looked like that. If he really did have the experience they'd heard about, he probably got away with a lot of things other soldiers wouldn't.

"There some fellas in here who promised me a free drink?" he asked, addressing the entire room.

Fry hesitantly raised his hand. Nichols moved toward them quickly and stared down at both of them eagerly.

"I'm here to collect."

They got the sergeant to sit down, fixed him up with a beer, then put their question to him.

"Why tonight?" Fry asked. "Because Indians don't fight at night?"

"That's a crock of shit," Nichols said. He took a quick drink, spilling some on the front of his dusty uniform. "Naw, I'd leave tonight because Quanah will think you're two crazy white men, traveling in the dark. He'll probably leave you alone."

Trapp and Fry exchanged a glance.

"You mind traveling at night?" Fry said.

"I just want to get going," Trapp said, "and if we have a better chance at night, let's get moving."

They both stood up and the sergeant said, "Hey, where you going?"

"Thanks for the information, Sarge," Fry said, patting the man on the back. A dust cloud leaped up and spread out, causing Fry to lean away.

"We'll pay for two more beers on the way out, Sergeant Nichols," Trapp said. "You've earned them."

"Well, all right—" Nichols said, but Trapp and Fry were out the door already and on their way to the hotel to get their gear.

CHAPTER TWENTY-NINE

Keller walked into Fort McAdams at first light, looking as if he'd been dragged all the way.

"Looks like you had a rough trip," a soldier said to him.

Keller ignored him and continued to walk, his horse trailing behind him. He walked through the fort and out the rear gate, then asked someone where the livery was. When he had directions, he walked his horse over there.

"He's got a stone bruise," Keller said to the man. "I'll need another mount."

"You can wait three or four days and this here one will heal up," the man said. "He's a good horse."

"I'll need another horse," Keller said. "I'll trade with you."

"If that's what you want," the liveryman said with a shrug.

"Where's the hotel?"

"You passed it on the way here," the man said.

"I must have missed it," Keller said.

"Uh, just go back two blocks. It's on the right."

"I'll be back later today for that horse."

"You staying the night?"

"I doubt it," Keller said, and left.

When he got to the hotel, he signed the register. Four names above his he saw the name "Trapp."

"Is this man still here?" he asked the clerk.

The man had to turn the book around to read it.

"Oh, him. Big fella, he was. Came in here filthy as you and walked out clean, with new clothes."

"He left?"

The man nodded.

"Last night, him and his friend."

"Who's his friend?"

"He didn't sign in," the clerk said. "The big fella asked for two rooms."

"You don't know the other man's name?"

"No."

"Would anyone in town know it?"

"Sure," the clerk said, "the sheriff. Those two fellas were involved with a killing."

"I see," Keller said. "I'll be needing a bathtub."

"Down the hall behind me."

Keller nodded and accepted his key.

He took a quick bath, changed into some clean clothes, then went looking for the sheriff.

———

"SURE I REMEMBER THOSE TWO," Sheriff Keeper said. "Couldn't rightly forget them. One of them, Trapp, was a big fella, although he looked kind of sickly, like he'd lost some weight recently."

"And the other one?" Keller said. "Do you recall his name?"

"Sure," Keeper said. "Fry, Kid Fry. He's got himself a little reputation. It was him the three yahoos were after in the saloon. He got two of them and the other fella, Trapp, got the other one with his buffalo gun. Nearly cut him in half, too."

"I've heard of Fry," Keller said. He was already composing his telegram to Sam Train, telling him that there was an "extra consideration."

"About this big fella, Trapp?" he went on.

"Yeah?"

"Kind of on the old side, isn't he?"

"I suppose so," Keeper said, "but you wouldn't know it to watch him move. Witnesses in the saloon say he moved pretty quick to gun that fella down. He and his friend have a history, too, a recent one. They were involved in killings in Littlesworth and Portsville."

Keller had been in Littlesworth and heard about the shooting there. No one had given him Fry's name then. He had bypassed Portsville, so this was the first he was hearing about the shooting there.

"Those two seem to attract trouble," Keller said.

Keeper laughed.

"That's what I told them when I asked them to leave."

"And did they?"

"What?"

"Did they leave when you asked them?"

"No," Keeper said, "funny thing about that." He went on to tell Keller about the telegrams to and from Denver about a Mr. Sam Train.

"You ever hear of this fella Train?" the lawman asked.

"No," Keller said, standing up, "never."

"Tell me something," Keeper said from his seat behind his desk.

"What?"

"Why are you so interested in those two? Bounty hunter?"

"You guessed."

"I've been a lawman a long time," Keeper said. "You get so you can smell bounty hunters."

Keller knew the man was trying to insult him, but he let it slide. He didn't need trouble with the law at this point.

As he left the sheriff's office, he changed the address of his mental telegram from Sam Train to a "Mr. Oliver."

————

"YES, OLIVER?"

Sam Train was sitting in his "hot room," thinking about times past when Oliver entered.

"We've heard from Keller."

"Where is he?"

"In Fort McAdams."

"Did he get him?"

"No," Oliver said. "Trapp and Fry were gone when he got there, but it seems this Fry has something of a reputation as a gunman."

"Keller wants more money."

"Under the circumstances," Oliver said, "he thinks it's fair."

"Actually," Train said, "it is. Wire him back and tell him he can have another ten thousand. That should satisfy him, don't you think?"

"I'm sure it will, sir."

"When you come back, Oliver, come in here and smoke a cigar, will you?" Train said. "I feel like smelling some cigar smoke."

"Yes, sir," Oliver said.

————

KELLER LEFT THE TELEGRAPH OFFICE, pocketing the reply from Oliver. The extra ten thousand would be wired to him when he gave them an address. He'd do that as soon as he got to a decent sized town, with a real bank.

He went to the hotel and checked out.

"But you just checked in," the clerk said.

"So charge me for a half day."

Nervously, the clerk explained he couldn't do that, and Keller didn't argue.

He went to the livery and asked the man if he had a horse picked out for him.

"You want me to pick one out?" the man asked.

"Sure," Keller said, "I trust you, because if I have any problems, I'll be back."

"Er, come with me," the man said nervously.

Keller followed him to a corral in the back.

"That dun's a good horse," the man said.

Keller eyed the animal and decided that it would be a fair trade for his roan.

"All right," he said, "put my rig on him and bring him around front."

"Now? You're leaving now?"

"That's right," Keller said, "I'm leaving now."

While the horse was being saddled, he went to the general store for some supplies. He bought some coffee and bacon, and some dried beef. He figured that Trapp, being from the mountains, would be traveling light, so he wanted to do the same to keep pace.

When he got back to the livery, the dun was saddled and ready.

"You won't have any problems with this animal, mister," the liveryman promised him.

"I hope not," Keller said, mounting up. "For your sake."

The liveryman swallowed heavily.

Keller turned his mount so that he was facing the man.

"Two men left here last night. Were you here?"

"Sure was," the man replied. "They woke me up to open the doors."

"Did they say where they were going?"

"No," the man said, "only that they weren't looking forward to trying to outrun Quanah Parker."

"Quanah won't bother us," Keller said. "We're not carrying anything he wants."

Keller had been stalked all the way to the fort, but since he was walking, it had to be clear to the Indians that he didn't even have a decent horse for them to steal. They had left him alone.

He hoped they would continue to do so.

Part Five

ORDEAL

CHAPTER THIRTY

Trapp and Fry rode all night without incident. They were not attacked by any Indians; their horses did not step into any chuckholes. As first light dawned, they decided to stop and give the horses a much deserved rest.

They dismounted and broke out some dried beef for breakfast. They did not want to take the chance of making a camp and relaxing.

"I don't see anything," Fry said, staring out at the flat land around them. "Could they be out there and we don't see them?"

"I suppose so," Trapp said. "In the mountains there are more places to hide. I'm not used to land this flat, this...barren."

"When I look at this," Fry said, indicating the flatness around them, "I can't wait to get to your mountain."

"Well, finish your breakfast and we'll get under way," Trapp said.

They chewed the dried beef without enthusiasm, both of them squatting down for comfort. When they rose and reached for their horses, they both saw them at the same time.

"Where the hell did they—" Fry started.

"It doesn't matter," Trapp said. "They're there."

Ahead of them, sitting astride their horses and watching them, were at least a dozen Indian braves. They could only assume that they were Comanches, and that they were Quanah Parker's men.

"Mount up," Trapp said.

Once they were mounted, Fry said, "Should we turn around and make a run for the fort?"

"We'd never make it," Trapp said. "Let's ride straight for them."

"What?"

"Right up to them."

"Are you crazy?"

"No, I'm scared. Are you?"

"You're damned right I am."

"Well, we can't let them see that," Trapp said. "If they even think we're scared, we're dead."

"I thought you didn't know anything about Comanches," Fry said.

"I don't, but I have dealt with Indians."

"Mountain Indians, not plains Indians," Fry said. "They're different."

"There must be some similarities," Trapp said. "They must all respect courage."

"I hope so," Fry said. "If they kill us on the spot, I am going to be very disappointed in you."

"I'll keep that in mind," Trapp said. "Let's go."

They kicked their horses' ribs and started forward. The twelve braves did not move as the two white men approached them.

It seemed to take forever to close the gap between them, but finally they were there and had to rein their horses in. Trapp had a secret hope that they would simply move out of the way and let them pass, but it didn't happen that way.

He studied each of the braves and none of them had blue eyes, so Quanah was not among them.

"Do any of you speak English?" Trapp asked, preferring to make the first move.

All twelve of the braves stared at him.

"Maybe we should try and take them," Fry said.

"No," Trapp said, "some of them have rifles."

"A wise decision," one of the braves said. He was sitting his horse right across from Trapp.

Trapp and Fry looked at each other, then at the brave who had spoken.

"I have never seen a rifle such as that one," the brave said, looking at Trapp's Sharps.

"It is very old," Trapp said.

The brave stared at it a little longer, then looked at them both. "You will come with us."

"Do we have a choice?" Fry asked.

The brave did not answer.

"I guess we don't," Fry said.

The other braves moved now and in seconds had formed a ring around Trapp and Fry. When the braves started moving, Trapp and Fry had no choice but to move with them.

"They haven't even taken our guns," Fry said, leaning over and speaking softly to Trapp.

"I don't think they feel a need to, Kid," Trapp said. "Do you feel a need to prove them wrong?"

"Not me," Fry said.

"Well then, I guess we're about to get an education of sorts," Trapp said. "Let's sit up straight and pay attention, and maybe we'll get out of this alive."

———

THEY RODE for a couple of hours and none of the braves ever spoke to them or even looked at them. They were hopelessly penned in by the Indians, so they simply rode along, keeping pace and never trying to slack off.

Finally, they spotted some movement ahead of them. As they drew closer, they saw that it was a village of teepees and fires and people—men, women, and children.

As they rode into the village, they became the center of attention. Children came running up for a closer look, and the circle around them broke to allow it.

Trapp looked down at their open, curious, often dirty faces and wondered suddenly why white men did not think of Indians as people. These were children—*real* children—with a child's curiosity and needs.

He reached down and chucked one black-eyed little boy under the chin. Most of the children were looking at Trapp because they had never seen anyone of his size. Astride his horse he looked like a giant to them.

"They are curious," the lead brave said, looking back at Trapp.

"That's okay," Trapp said. "I don't mind being stared at."

The brave dismounted, and Trapp and Fry followed as the others did the same thing. The little boy Trapp had chucked beneath the chin came running up, then stopped and stared up at him and said something Trapp couldn't understand.

Trapp looked at the brave and asked, "What did he say?"

"He said that you are a giant, even when you are not on a horse."

Trapp towered above everyone in the village. The brave he was speaking to was a half a foot shorter, but he was built along strong lines with a deep chest and thick thighs. Trapp would not have liked to face him in hand-to-hand combat, even thirty years ago.

The boy was still looking up at him with wide eyes so Trapp reached down, took the boy beneath the arms, and lifted him up on his shoulders. The boy shouted, but the smile on his face made it clear that he was not afraid.

"What did he shout?" he asked.

"He said that he is a giant, too," the brave said.

"I hope his father doesn't mind this," Trapp said.

"No," the brave said solemnly, "I do not."

———

QUANAH PARKER CAME out of his teepee to greet his "guests."

He saw two white men walking toward him with Strong Hawk. One of them was very tall and was carrying Strong Hawk's son on his shoulders. Both white men still had their weapons, which indicated that they had not tried to resist when they were taken.

If they had, they would be dead.

Trapp saw the man who had stepped from the teepee. He was tall, not as tall as Trapp, but he would not be as dwarfed by the mountain man as others were.

The boy sat quietly on his shoulders, totally relaxed. Fry walked beside him, anything but relaxed. Trapp hoped that the

Kid would be able to hold up and would not make any foolish move.

As for himself, he found that he was curiously at ease in this camp. Certainly more at ease than he had been in any of the white men's towns he'd visited since being released.

As they came closer to the man, Trapp could see clearly that he had blue eyes.

This was Quanah Parker.

CHAPTER THIRTY-ONE

"Why are we here?" Trapp asked.

He and Fry were seated inside Quanah's teepee. The only other person there was the brave who had brought them there. His name, they discovered, was Strong Hawk.

"Strong Hawk brought you here," Quanah said in almost perfect English.

"I know that," Trapp said. "I mean, why did Strong Hawk bring us here?"

"Would you rather he had killed you right away?"

"No," Trapp said, "but I am still curious."

"He watched you ride all night," Quanah said, "and he thought you were"—he groped for the word, then found it—"crazy white men."

"I see."

"He was also *curious*," Quanah Parker said. "He wanted to see what manner of men traveled at night."

"Careful men," Fry said.

Quanah looked at Fry, because these were the first words he had heard the younger man speak.

Quanah himself was in his early thirties, an impressive figure of a man with broad shoulders and powerful arms and legs.

"This is your son?" he asked Trapp.

"No," Trapp said, "my partner."

"Partner?"

"We ride together."

"He is very much younger than you are."

"Yes," Trapp said, "he is."

"It is odd for two such as you to be…partners, is it not?"

"Some people might think so."

Quanah looked at Strong Hawk and said something, and the other brave replied.

"What did you say?" Trapp asked.

Quanah looked at him sharply. Trapp guessed that he wasn't used to being questioned.

"I asked him what he wanted to do with you."

"And he said?"

"He did not know," Quanah said. "He has not decided yet."

"Is that for him to decide, or you?" Trapp asked.

"He brought you here," Quanah said. "It is for him to decide."

Quanah stood up.

"Strong Hawk will show you to your teepee."

Trapp and Fry stood up.

"Before you leave," Quanah said, "leave your weapons there." He pointed to a blanket lying on the floor.

This is it, Trapp thought. Fry might think that he had a chance in here, with only two of them, to do some damage. Trapp had to head him off.

Before Trapp could say anything, though, Fry said, "Sure, why not? After all, we're your guests, right? What do we need guns for?"

Fry unbuckled his gun and dropped it on the blanket. Trapp laid his Sharps down next to it.

"Go with Strong Hawk," Quanah said, and turned his back.

Strong Hawk stepped outside and they followed.

"Nice move, Kid," Trapp said.

"What did you think I was going to do?" Fry asked. "Draw on them? We'd still have the rest of this village to deal with."

"We're just going to have to wait and see what they have in mind for us," Trapp said.

"What *he* has in mind for us," Fry said, pointing ahead of them to Strong Hawk.

"Quanah seems to be a leader who doesn't mind letting his people think for themselves."

"I just wish we knew what this one was thinking."

"Maybe we should just ask him," Trapp suggested.

"Do you think he'd tell us?"

"No."

"Do you think he'd take our asking as a sign of weakness?"

"Probably."

"Then maybe we shouldn't ask," Fry said.

"Maybe you're right."

Strong Hawk stopped at a teepee and said, "This is yours."

"Mine?" Trapp asked.

"Both of you."

Fry looked at Trapp and said, "Ours."

"Right."

"Quanah says you are our guests," Strong Hawk said.

"And we want to thank him—" Trapp began, but Strong Hawk wasn't listening.

"Do not try to escape," he said, and turned and walked away.

Trapp and Fry looked around and noticed that there were several braves watching them.

"So much for being guests," Trapp said.

"Yeah."

"Come on, let's get out of the sun."

They went inside the teepee, which was not as large as Quanah Parker's. There were a couple of blankets on the ground, but they weren't needed at the moment.

They each picked out a place on the floor and sat down.

"I don't know how we're ever going to get to my mountain if we can't even get out of Texas," Trapp said glumly.

"Well, there ain't much we can do about it now," Fry said. "We're in Quanah's hands."

"Maybe we can escape."

"Without our guns and horses? You think this land is flat now, wait until you try to walk it."

Trapp's shoulders slumped and he said, "I'll take your word for it."

———

KELLER KNEW there wasn't much chance of tracking Trapp and Fry through the hard plains. There was a scuff mark here and a cold campfire there, but much of the time he simply traveled in a straight line, hoping he was going in the right direction.

There was something else he used, though, and it was something he had developed over years of hunting men. It was called *instinct*.

His instinct was attuned to John Henry Trapp, and he *knew* that he was heading in the right direction. It also helped to know that Trapp was a mountain man, and was surely heading back to the mountains. Even if Keller was *not* on Trapp's trail, they would both end up in the same place.

The Rockies.

According to the information he'd gotten from Oliver, Sam Train's butler, Trapp came from the Green River country of the Central Rockies.

He would continue to travel in a straight line until he reached there.

Hopefully, he'd get to Oklahoma without running into any of Quanah's Comanches.

That hope was dashed quickly enough.

He was walking his horse, resting it without stopping, studying the ground. When he looked up, there was suddenly a row of Comanches in front of him. At least he *assumed* they were Comanches.

He reined his horse in and watched them, but all they did was watch him. He correctly guessed that they were waiting for him to run. If he did, they would probably ride him down and kill him.

He took his pistol from his holster and very deliberately dropped it to the ground, then followed with his rifle.

They approached him and formed a circle around him, and one brave retrieved his weapons. After that, they herded him to their camp.

He had made the right decision, and he was alive —for now.

———

"SOUNDS LIKE SOME COMMOTION OUTSIDE," Trapp said.

Fry had heard it also. They both rose and moved to look outside. It was the first sound of activity in the hours they had been there, other than the one time an Indian girl had come to them with some food.

"What are we eating?" Fry had asked, chewing some of the stringy meat.

"I may be wrong," Trapp said, "but I think it's dog."

"Dog?"

"Tastes like some wolf meat I once had."

Fry had stared at the meat for a few moments, then shrugged and said, "What the hell," and continued eating.

Now Trapp said, "Looks like we're going to have some company."

"Know him?" Fry asked, then said, "No, of course, you wouldn't. You've only been out a matter of weeks."

"I take it you don't know him?"

"No, I've never seen him before."

"Looks like he made the right decision, too," Trapp said.

"I guess Strong Hawk is going to have another decision to make."

"I wonder what he was doing out there all alone."

"Maybe he wasn't alone," Fry said. "Maybe the people he was with didn't make the right decision, like he did."

"I guess we'll find out," Trapp said. "They're bringing him over here."

"Gonna bunk him in with us, huh?" Fry said. "They don't have real private accommodations around here, do they?"

They backed away from the entrance as the man and his escort reached the teepee. The flap was thrown back and the man entered. He stood up straight and stared at Trapp and Fry.

"Do you two know what's going on here?" he asked.

"Apparently," Fry said, "we are the reluctant guests of Quanah Parker."

"Ah, so they *are* his men."

"Yeah," Fry said, "we've seen him."

The man studied them both for a moment, and Trapp had the impression that he was being measured for...something.

"My name is Flynn," the man finally said. "Douglas Flynn."

"How do you do, Mr. Flynn," Trapp said. "I'm John Trapp."

Trapp shook hands with the man and was impressed by the confidence of the grip. The man was powerful, but felt no need to prove it. That indicated a confident man.

"Fry," Fry said, shaking hands briefly.

"How long have you fellas been here?" the man asked.

"Just a few hours longer than you have," Fry said, although it was more like six or seven hours. "They took us this morning."

"Without a fight?"

"We were slightly outnumbered," Trapp said.

"Yes, so was I," the man said. "Was it just the two of you?"

"Yes," Trapp said, "just us two."

The man nodded.

"Yeah, I was alone," the man said. He rubbed his hands together and looked around at their somewhat cramped quarters.

"Well, what are we supposed to do now?"

"I guess we just wait," Trapp said, "and see what they have in mind for us."

"I suppose they intend to kill us," the man said. "They're just deciding whether to do it slow or quick."

"That's a possibility," Trapp said. "My guess is they intend to test us."

"Test us?"

Trapp nodded.

"Test our courage."

"Well," the man said, "I hope we're all up to it."

Yeah, Trapp thought to himself, so do I.

Keller couldn't believe his mixed luck. He'd been captured by the Comanches, and then thrown in together with the very men he'd been hunting. Standing in front of him was thirty-five thousand dollars, twenty-five of which he had already collected.

He still intended to earn that money, and he had no intention of letting the extra ten thousand get away.

All he had to do was figure out a way for the three of them to get away alive, so he could kill both of them.

————

THE NIGHT PASSED WITHOUT INCIDENT.

No one came to take any of them away, and no one came to bring them any more food. They gave what they had left to the new man, Flynn.

"This tastes like dog," he said, after taking a nibble.

"That's what I thought," Trapp said. "You've eaten it before?"

"Mr. Trapp, I've eaten almost everything there is to eat," Flynn/Keller said. "Dog, mule, snake, rat—"

"You sound like you've had a rather...interesting life," Trapp said.

To Trapp, Flynn looked to be in his forties. He was a healthy specimen, so he hadn't had to eat any of those things lately.

Fry noticed that the man called Flynn's holster was well worn, but also well cared for.

When they had a chance, they could compare notes about him.

Just before they decided to turn in, someone did come along, but it was only a man's arm poking in and dropping another blanket on the floor.

"Kind of them," Keller said, picking up the blanket.

"They don't want us to freeze to death," Fry said, "but they don't want to feed us too much, to keep our strength up."

"I think we'd better get a good night's rest," Trapp said. "Whatever they have in store for us, we're going to have to be ready."

"I agree," Keller said.

Fry nodded and they all lay down and made themselves as comfortable as possible.

———

IN THE MORNING they were awakened abruptly. Five braves rushed into the teepee and hauled them to their feet without warning. They were pushed outside, where they all stood shielding their eyes from the bright sun.

"What the hell is going on?" Fry demanded, but no one was answering.

Suddenly, they were seized again, this time from behind, and their shirts were stripped off.

"This is not looking good," Keller said.

Next they were lifted off their feet and their boots were removed.

"This is definitely looking bad," Fry said.

"If they try to take my pants, I'm leaving," Keller said.

Trapp thought that the humor on both their parts sounded a

bit forced. He also hoped that their nerve would hold up, no matter what they had in front of them.

Trapp considered that he was probably calmer because, being a lot older than the Kid and Flynn, he had less to lose. Maybe being sixty-four was finally going to work in his favor.

Finally, Quanah stepped out of his teepee, but he did not approach them. Instead, Strong Hawk came over to talk to them.

"You will have a head start," he said, "and then my braves will hunt you down."

"I don't understand what I'm doing here—" Flynn/Keller began, but Strong Hawk silenced him with a quick look.

"You are being tested," Strong Hawk said, then he smiled thinly and added, "I am interested in seeing how much courage you have."

"Well, I was riding through your land alone, wasn't I?" he asked.

"That could have been foolishness," Strong Hawk said, "even stupidity. Now we will see how truly courageous you are."

"And how sound the soles of our feet are," Fry said. Already the ground beneath his feet was starting to heat up from the sun.

Strong Hawk moved over in front of Trapp and stared at him.

"You are quiet."

"I have nothing to say."

"You interest me most of all," the brave said. "You are older, but are you wiser?"

"I don't believe wisdom is what will get us through this," Trapp said.

"Of the three," Strong Hawk said, "I believe you will survive —if any of you do."

"Him?" Keller asked. "He's an old man. He'll never survive out there. When the sun gets real hot—"

"Silence!" Strong Hawk said. "You are wasting what little time you have."

"What are we supposed to do?" Keller asked.

"Run," Strong Hawk said. "Just...run, and keep running until nightfall. Whichever of you returns here after dark will go free."

Keller looked at Fry, who looked at Trapp, who said, "I suggest we start running."

"Here," Strong Hawk said, and handed Trapp a knife.

"What about me?" Keller asked.

"One knife for the three of you," Strong Hawk said. "Go."

"Maybe I better hold the knife, old timer," Keller said.

"Trapp's a mountain man, Flynn," Fry said. "If anyone knows how to handle a knife, he does."

"Let's get moving," Trapp said.

———

THEY STARTED RUNNING, each with their own stride.

Trapp had a long, loping, easy stride.

Fry's stride was shorter, but no less fluid.

Keller was used to riding, and running had never been a strong point with him. His stride was short and choppy, and of the three he was sure to tire first.

"I wonder why they gave us one knife," Fry said aloud.

"Two reasons that I could think of," Trapp said.

"What...are they?" Keller asked. They had run maybe two hundred yards, and he was beginning to labor already.

"First, I think they wanted to see if we would fight over it," Trapp said.

Fry gave Keller a glance, and the man looked away.

"What's the second reason?" Keller asked.

"I think they're hedging their bets," Trapp said. "I think they feel that the one knife will keep the three of us together. That way, we'll only be as fast as the slowest runner, and we'll be easy to find, and catch."

"Then what you're saying is that we should split up," Fry said.

"Exactly."

"Who gets the knife?" Fry asked.

"I do," Keller said.

"Why you?" Fry asked.

"That's easy," Keller said. "I'm the one they're gonna catch first. I mean, already my lungs are burning. Look at Trapp. He's not even breathing hard."

"Yeah," Fry said, "not bad for an old man, huh?"

"All right," Keller said, "I'm sorry for that. Maybe I panicked a little."

"None of us can afford to panic," Trapp said. "If we do, we're dead."

"Hey, who are we kidding?" Keller asked. "We're dead anyway, it's just a matter of when."

Trapp reached across Fry's chest and handed Keller the knife. Keller looked at Fry before taking it.

"Good luck, fellas," Trapp said, and veered off to his left, increasing his pace.

"That guy's unbelievable," Keller said. "How old is he?"

"Sixty-four."

"Living in the mountains must do wonders for you," Keller said. "Jesus...I've got to stop and rest."

Fry stopped with him as Keller leaned over to catch his breath. He held the knife in his right hand, and it would have been very easy for him to kill Fry right there and then. All he had to do was bring the knife up into Fry's belly, twist it, and leave him on the ground, gutted.

"We don't have time to rest, Flynn," Fry said. "I'm gonna keep going, and I suggest you do the same."

"Yeah," Keller said, looking up at Fry as he tried in vain to catch his breath. "Yeah...sure...good luck, Fry."

"Good luck," Fry said. "Maybe we'll all make it back."

CHAPTER THIRTY-TWO

T rapp was surprised.

He had expected to feel tired, but he didn't. In fact, he felt almost invigorated by the simple act of running. It was *pleasure* to be able to run again, after so many years—but he knew it wouldn't last. As the sun got higher and hotter, it would drain his strength. He might last longer than the others, but not as long as he might have twenty-five years ago.

The sun on his neck and back felt hot already, and the ground beneath his feet did as well. Fry would be all right for a while. After all, he was twenty-five years old. It dawned on him that Fry may not have even been born when he himself first went into prison.

The man who called himself Flynn had looked done in almost immediately, and might have already been run down by the fleet-footed Comanches.

Trapp couldn't afford to think about Flynn now, or even Fry. They were going to have to look after themselves, just as he was.

He didn't know how far he was from the border into Oklahoma, but he doubted he could make it on foot. His only chance was to survive until the sun went down and then return to camp. He'd have to hope that Strong Hawk—and behind him Quanah Parker—were men of their word.

He looked around and noticed for the first time that the plains terrain was not quite flat. There were rises and depressions—surely nothing like the mountains, but not quite as flat as a desert either. He might be able to put those rises and depressions to use. However, surviving would be a lot easier if he had a weapon.

He started to check out the ground as he loped over it. The only thing he was likely to find was a sharp rock, something sharp enough to inflict damage. He wondered briefly what would happen if he killed any of Quanah's braves. Would he still be allowed to go free upon returning to camp?

His feet were starting to burn. He looked around and saw *some* vegetation, but there was nothing he could use to cover his feet, except his pants.

He stopped running and sat down on the hard ground. He tried to tear one of his pant legs, but the jeans were too tough. Quickly he removed the pants and started gnawing at the leg with his teeth. When he'd managed to chew through, he tore it and went to work on the other leg.

Eventually he had enough material to wrap both of his feet. He tore some thinner strips from the pants and used them to tie the cloth around his feet. He then slipped on what was left of his pants. The legs now barely reached his knees.

He stood up and ran a few steps and then stopped to tighten the strips. Satisfied that his feet were protected at least from the heat, he started running again. Of course, the material would not protect his feet from getting cut on something sharp, so he was just going to have to watch his step.

———

FRY WAS LIVID, and the pain brought tears to his eyes.

He had stepped on a sharp piece of rock and cut his foot. He was angry at himself for his clumsiness.

Sitting on the hard ground, he inspected the wound. It wasn't deep, but it was bleeding a lot. He pulled his handkerchief from his pocket and tied it tightly around the wound. He looked behind him and wondered just how much of a head start Strong Hawk had given them. He still could not see any Comanches—but he realized that he *wouldn't* see them if they didn't want to be seen. Maybe they had him well within their sights but were playing with him.

Maybe standing up and running on the cut foot would be a waste of time.

He stood up and tested the foot. It still hurt, but he realized that he couldn't feel the heat of the ground through the handkerchief. If he'd had another one, he could have bound the other foot as well.

He sat down again and tried to tear one of his pant legs. When that didn't work, he took off the pants, tore one leg with his teeth, then continued to tear until he had what he wanted. He did the same thing with the other leg and double wrapped his wounded foot. He did not know that Trapp had done the same thing, but what other way was there for them to protect their feet?

———

IT WAS EASIER for Keller to protect his feet. He simply cut the strips he needed from his pants with the knife and then tied them to his feet. He sat where he was longer than was wise, but he had to get his breath back.

He wondered how many braves would be after them, and how they'd split up when they figured out that the three white men had separated.

Would they figure that out? Of the three of them, Fry was the one who had continued on. Trapp had veered off to the left, and Keller to the right.

Maybe they'd have to run Fry down and kill him before they realized the white men had separated. That would give Keller and Trapp more time to survive. Once Fry was dead, it didn't matter who had killed him. Keller could collect the ten thousand dollars anyway.

The thought surprised Keller. In the past he never would have claimed payment for a job he didn't do. Being in this predicament had made him realize how much he wanted to live. With thirty-five thousand dollars, maybe he could retire from manhunting and enjoy the rest of his life.

If he *had* a rest of his life.

———

TRAPP FOUND A ROCK FORMATION, and it presented him with a dilemma.

It was certainly the kind of thing someone would use for cover, and he *would* have used it if he'd had a gun. The way things stood now, if he tried to hide behind it, the braves would catch up to him. They'd *know* that he was behind it and would have to try and get him out.

What would happen, he wondered, if he managed to survive until dark? If the braves got to him in the dark, would they kill him anyway? Probably. The deal was that he had to *return* to camp in order to survive.

He reached the formation and found it was quite large. It could have easily afforded three men with guns ample cover to hold off a group of Indians.

For him it simply represented a place to die.

FRY WONDERED how many square miles Texas had. That was something he'd like to find out if they got out of this. He also wished he knew how many miles he had run already. He was sure it wasn't as much as his aching legs were telling him. Ah, it was probably better if he didn't know.

KELLER STILL COULDN'T SEE any of the Comanches. For a moment he wondered if it was all a joke. What if Strong Hawk really didn't send anyone after them at all? What if they were running around out here for no reason?

Keller decided that wasn't the case. He didn't know all that much about Comanches, but he didn't really think they had a sense of humor.

HE COULDN'T SEE THEM.

That worried Trapp. If they were on his tail, he should have been able to see them by now.

He stopped running as something occurred to him. He didn't know how well even a Comanche could track over this terrain. Would they know that the three white men had split up? Or would they simply keep running away from their camp —in which case they would eventually run down Fry, or Flynn, whichever had continued to run in a straight line.

Trapp turned around and started running back the way he'd come, but on a diagonal course. He hoped that he would intercept either Fry or Flynn, and he hoped he was right and he wouldn't run headlong into a bunch of Comanches.

———

FRY COULD HEAR THEM.

They were making sounds like animals on a hunt, and maybe that's what they were. He turned his head and saw them. There were half a dozen of them, and they were all running his way. Was six all Strong Hawk had sent out, or had they split into three groups?

Fry's lungs were burning, and now his feet were burning, even through what was left of the material he'd wrapped his feet in. The cut foot hurt like hell and all he wanted to do was sit down and rest.

If he sat down, he'd get a lot of rest, all right.

He'd rest *forever*.

———

KELLER STOPPED RUNNING and looked back. He couldn't see anyone, and he became convinced that no one was coming —not for him anyway. That meant they were trailing either Trapp or Fry. Trapp and Fry were white men, just like him. Keller had never had friends, not in his whole life, but if he had to pick between a red man and a white man, he'd pick the white man every time.

Maybe—just maybe—if they stuck together, they'd get out of this alive.

He turned around and began to run back, but he chose a diagonal course. Maybe he'd cross paths with Fry, and maybe they should then turn and face the Comanches. At least they'd die fighting, and not running.

Keller was nothing if not a fighter.

TRAPP LOOKED AHEAD and wasn't quite sure he was seeing right. Maybe his eyes were playing tricks on him. The heat was coming up from the ground, creating a haze, but it looked to him as though he was running up on about six Comanche braves—and farther ahead of them was the figure of a running man.

It was either Fry or Flynn.

During his run back, Trapp had stopped several times to pick up likely-looking stones, big enough to fit into his hands but not so heavy he couldn't carry them. Now he wanted only to get close enough to the Indians to chuck the stones at them. With a little luck he might be able to knock out one or two of them. That would leave four for him and the other man to handle.

Fighting and dying was a better idea to him than continuing to run and run and run, and then maybe dying anyway.

At least this way he was in control of his own destiny.

Sort of.

KELLER STARED AHEAD OF HIM, through the heat haze that was drifting up from the ground. Was he seeing right? It looked as if there were six Indians ahead of him.

His right hand tightened on the knife and he wondered if he could close on them and dispatch at least one before they saw or heard him.

How good was a Comanche's hearing anyway?

FRY TURNED and looked over his shoulder once again. They were closing on him. A few hundred yards more and they'd be on him, and he'd probably be too tired to fight them.

He stopped running abruptly and turned around.

"Come on, you ornery redskins, come and get it!" he shouted—at least, he'd intended to shout. What came out of his dry mouth could not have even been called a whisper.

Damn, and all he had gotten for the effort was cracked lips.

———

TRAPP SAW FRY STOP RUNNING. For a moment he thought his friend was giving up, but from the way Fry was gesticulating at the Indians, that was the farthest thing from his mind.

At the same time he saw Flynn coming from the other direction, brandishing the knife in his right hand.

Great minds, he thought.

He wondered which of them the Comanches would notice first, himself or Flynn.

By some wild coincidence they were all coming together at the same place at the same time.

He wondered what the final outcome would be, and let fly with a rock.

CHAPTER THIRTY-THREE

The stone struck one of the Indians on the head, knocking him down, and maybe even out—but that was not all it accomplished.

As the Indian fell, a couple of his cronies turned their heads to see where the stone had come from. Naturally, they saw Trapp running toward them and shouted to the rest of their friends.

They were now aware of Fry ahead of them, waving his arms and trying in vain to shout, and Trapp behind them, chucking the rest of his stones.

They were sufficiently distracted by both men that they never saw Flynn/Keller until it was too late. He was on them, hacking at them with his knife.

Fry, seeing what was happening, stopped waiting for the Indians to reach him and ran forward.

Trapp, stoneless now, reached the group and picked up the knife that belonged to the Indian he'd stoned. Everything that came after that was instinct.

He stepped forward, took hold of one brave's chin from behind, and pulled his head back. He brought the sharp edge of the knife across his throat, slashing it wide open. As the brave's blood stained the ground, he released him and went on to the next one.

Fry reached the fray and literally threw himself into it without hesitation.

Keller, on the ground with two Indians, slid his knife between the ribs of one of them and lashed out at the other with his elbow.

Trapp slid his arm around the throat of another brave, grasped his chin with the other hand, and broke the red man's neck.

Fry fronted the last standing Indian and hit him as hard as he could in the face with his fist.

The last conscious Indian was the other one on the ground, struggling with Keller, whose knife had somehow become wedged in the body of the Indian he'd stabbed. The second Indian he was struggling with raised his knife and started to stab downward. The arc of his knife was intercepted by Trapp's hand, which clamped down on his wrist.

Fry came over, pulled the knife from the Indian's hand, and drove it down into the back of the man's neck. The Indian shuddered once, then fell still, his dead weight pinning Keller to the ground. Trapp and Fry pulled him off and assisted the man they knew as Flynn to his feet.

"What took you guys so long?" Fry asked.

————

AFTER CHECKING ALL THE BODIES, Trapp said, "Four dead and two knocked out."

"We can fix that easy enough," Keller said. He leaned down to slit the throat of one of the unconscious Indians, but Trapp's big hand stopped him.

"What's wrong?" Keller asked. "You want them to get up and come after us again?"

"We don't have to kill them."

"Trapp," Fry said, "I think I have to agree with Flynn here. We don't even know if these six are all Strong Hawk sent out. There may be more. We have to make sure these two don't get up and come after us again."

Trapp was still dubious, but he realized that they had already killed four of Quanah's men. If the Comanche leader was going to kill them for that, they wouldn't be any more dead for killing two more.

"Shit," Trapp said, but he released Flynn/Keller's hand.

While Keller slit the throat of one, Fry leaned over and took care of the other one.

"You fellas better take a pair of moccasins each," Trapp said. "We still have a long time to spend out here."

"What about you?" Fry asked, removing the footwear of one brave and trying them on.

"None of these fellas had feet my size," Trapp said.

"These fit," Flynn/Keller said happily.

Fry also found a pair that fit, and stood up.

"Let's take their knives," Trapp said. He picked up two and stuck them in his belt, and the others followed. They now had seven knives between them.

"We're going to have to assume that there are other Comanches out there looking for us," Fry said.

Trapp looked up at the sun and said, "We've still got a good five hours left before we can even start thinking about getting back to camp."

"Are your feet going to be all right?" Fry asked Trapp. He hadn't told either of the other men about his cut foot. The moccasins were going to make that a lot easier to handle.

"I'll be fine," Trapp said.

"Considering how well we did here," Keller said, "maybe we should stick together this time."

Trapp and Fry agreed.

"I know a place we can hole up for a while," Trapp said, thinking of that rock formation he'd passed. "We might as well just wait and see what else we're going to have to deal with."

"Does it offer any shade?" Keller asked.

"It does."

"Then lead the way, partner," Fry said.

———

WHEN THEY REACHED the rock formation, they sat on the shady side and kept a sharp eye out for Comanches.

"You know," Fry said, "I'm starting to think we might get out of this alive."

"If Quanah and Strong Hawk are men of their word," Trapp said. "I just hope the death of six braves doesn't outweigh that."

"We didn't have any other choice," Keller said. "I think we all had the same thing in mind."

"To die fighting," Fry said.

"Exactly."

Fry turned to Trapp, but the older man was staring off into space.

"What's he thinking about?" Keller asked.

"His mountain."

"Mountain?"

"The Rocky Mountains," Fry said. "That's where we were headed when we got caught."

"What for?"

"That's where he lives."

"What was he doing all the way out here?"

Fry looked at Keller, whom he knew as Flynn, and said, "It's a long story."

"I've got nothing but time," the other man said.

Fry was about to reply when Trapp said, "You fellas better get some rest. I'll keep watch. If we have to take on the whole Comanche nation when we get back, we'd better be rested."

"Good point," Fry said. He looked at Keller and said, "I'll tell you about it another time."

"If there is another time," Keller said.

"There will be," Trapp said. "I'm not going to let even a bunch of Comanches keep me from getting back to my mountain."

Part Six

SHOWDOWN

CHAPTER THIRTY-FOUR

F ry woke to find Trapp shaking him.

"Horses," Trapp said.

Fry remained still, listening intently. Trapp must have had incredible ears, because he didn't hear a thing. Moments later, he did hear it.

"Wake Flynn," Trapp said.

"I'm awake," Flynn/Keller said, opening his eyes.

They all got up and began to look around.

"They can't be Indian ponies," Trapp said.

"Why not?" Fry asked.

"That would mean that Quanah broke his word."

"Is that so hard to believe?" Keller asked.

"For some reason," Trapp said, "yes."

"Look," Fry said.

Both Trapp and Keller looked in the direction Fry was pointing—the opposite direction from where they might have expected the Indians to come.

"Three riders," Fry said, "and they're white."

"They're soldiers," Trapp said.

All three of them stepped out from the rock formation and began to wave. After a few moments the riders spotted them and changed direction. When they reached the three white men they stared, for they made a strange sight with their tattered clothes, their skin red from the sun, and their lips cracked.

"What the hell are you three doing out here?" one soldier

asked. He was wearing sergeant's stripes. The other soldier was a private. The third man was not a soldier, but a civilian scout.

Quickly, Trapp explained their predicament.

"Well, we're riding in advance of a supply train," the sergeant said. "You can ride double with us until we reach the wagons."

Thanks," Trapp said, "we appreciate it."

"Any sign of Comanches, Jeter?" the sergeant asked the scout.

"No, sir," the man said, pausing to spit tobacco juice, "nary a sign."

"Let's go, then," the sergeant said, "before we run into them."

Trapp got up behind the sergeant while Fry climbed up behind the private, and Keller rode double with the scout.

"I'd say you fellas were pretty damn lucky we came along," the sergeant said to Trapp.

"And I'd say you were right, Sergeant," Trapp said. "Some good luck was just what we needed."

———

WHEN THE SUPPLY train reached Fort McAdams, Trapp, Fry, and Keller climbed down from the wagons and again thanked the sergeant, whose name was Casey.

"The major's going to want to talk to all three of you," Casey said. "Your information might finally lead us to Quanah's camp."

"We'll be happy to tell the major all we know, Sergeant, after we clean up a little," Trapp said.

"Surely," the sergeant said. "Just come over to the fort and ask for me, and I'll take you boys over to see him."

The three of them started walking to the rear gate and stopped there.

"Where you headed?" Trapp asked Keller.

"Well, there's a stop I'd like to make even before the hotel," Keller replied, "so I guess I'll be seeing you boys around."

As Keller walked away Fry said, "I wonder what's more important to him than getting cleaned up."

"Maybe he's going to buy some clothes."

"We're going to need some clothes also," Fry said. "We have

to have something to change into."

Luckily, while leaving them their pants, Quanah had also left them their money, which was in their pockets.

They walked over to the general store to buy some shirts, jeans, and boots, and thought it odd that they didn't see Flynn there.

After that they went to the hotel and asked the clerk if they could have their rooms back.

"Sure," the clerk said. "Ain't filled them yet."

He turned the register around so they could sign in.

"By the way, did your friend find you?"

"What friend?" Trapp asked.

"Fella who came in here yesterday asking for you," the clerk said. "There's his name, right there."

Trapp looked at Fry and then they both looked at the name on the register.

"Keller," Fry said. "Why does that sound familiar?"

"What did he look like?" Trapp asked.

The clerk described Keller, and both Trapp and Fry realized that he was also describing the man they knew as Flynn.

They backed away from the desk so the clerk couldn't hear them talking.

"What's going on?" Trapp asked.

"Wait a minute," Fry said. "I know a Keller. He's a bounty hunter, a killer for hire."

Trapp rubbed his jaw and said, "He must have been hired by Sam Train."

"But why didn't he kill us out there when he had the chance?" Fry asked.

"Because out there we needed each other to survive," Trapp said. "My guess is buying a gun was more important to him than clothes or a hotel room."

"Good point," Fry said, "and that means we'd better get some guns, and fast."

It was then that Trapp realized that his Sharps was still back in Quanah's camp.

"You take your bath and get changed," Fry said. "I'll go and get a gun."

"You'd better be careful you don't run into him on the street," Trapp said. "Maybe we'd better go together."

"One would be less noticeable than two," Fry said.

"All right," Trapp said, "but why don't you see if this fella here behind the desk has a gun you can borrow, just for now."

They went back to the desk and posed the question to the clerk.

"Well, I do have an old Walker Colt back here," the man said, "but I keep it in case of trouble."

"I'll rent it from you," Trapp said.

"How much?"

"Two dollars, for an hour."

The clerk brought out the gun and handed it over. Trapp gave it to Fry and paid the man.

"Is it loaded?" Trapp asked.

"Yeah, and I think it'll even fire."

Fry tucked the gun into his pants.

"Here," Trapp said, "put on one of these shirts, or you'll attract everyone's attention."

Fry slipped into one of the clean shirts and tucked it in, so it wouldn't lie over the gun.

"I'll be back soon," Fry said.

"Get me a rifle," Trapp said.

"What kind?"

"It doesn't matter," Trapp said. "Something cheap. I just wish I had my Sharps."

"Too bad," Fry said. "It was a beautiful old gun."

Fry left and Trapp turned to the desk man.

"I'll need a bath," he said, "a hot one."

———

AFTER LEAVING TRAPP AND FRY, Keller went directly to the gunsmith's store.

"Well, what happened to you?" the man behind the counter asked.

"I need a gun and a rig."

"You look like you need a bath, a room, and a doctor, not necessarily in that order."

"First a gun," Keller said, staring at the clerk.

"Well, er, sure...that's what I'm here for."

Keller felt naked without a gun, now that they were back in civilization. Once he had one, he'd get cleaned up, then he'd take care of Trapp and Fry, and get started on his retirement.

CHAPTER THIRTY-FIVE

F ry walked down the street quickly and as he was approaching the gunsmith shop he saw Keller, looking ragged and beat, step out. For a moment Fry considered bracing him, but the man was wearing a brand new rig on his hip, and all Fry had was the old Walker Colt tucked into his pants. He stepped into a doorway and watched Keller cross the street. When he reached the other side he started walking, but not in the direction of the hotel. Fry waited until Keller had gone a full block, then stepped out of the doorway and made for the gunsmith shop.

Trapp would have liked to soak in the hot tub longer, but he kept thinking that Keller was going to break in on him any minute. He soaped off, washed his hair and beard, then got out of the tub. He changed into his fresh clothes and pulled on his new boots. It felt odd to have boots on again after all the barefoot running he had done that day.

He wondered idly what Quanah Parker would do when he and Fry and Keller did not return that night—and neither did his six braves.

He stepped out into the hall cautiously and walked back to the lobby. As he came out from behind the desk, Fry came walking in, wearing a gun on his hip. The holster looked worn, as did the gun in it.

"Here," Fry said, handing Trapp a rifle. "It's an old Winchester, but the shop wasn't exactly well stocked with new guns. I had to settle for this used Colt, but I took it because it's in good working order. Oh, yeah, here," Fry said, handing the Walker Colt to the desk clerk. "Thanks."

"Any time," the clerk said, putting the gun back beneath the counter.

"Why don't you get a bath and I'll watch for Keller," Trapp said.

"Come on back with me and we'll talk while I wash," Fry said.

They went into the back and Trapp sat in a straightbacked wooden chair by the door while Fry took a considerably more leisurely bath than he had.

"It's getting dark," Fry said. "I wonder what Quanah Parker's going to think."

"He's going to think that the three white men got clean away," Trapp said, "and we did—with a little help."

"When I get out of the bath, let's go and talk to the major. Maybe now that we have valuable information for him, we can get an escort tomorrow."

"First I think we'll have to deal with Keller," Trapp said. "He's probably been on our trail for a while. That was what he was doing out there alone. Now that we're all here together, I don't think he'll want to let the opportunity pass."

"Maybe he'll wait until tomorrow," Fry said hopefully, "when we've rested up some."

"You know, Fry, there's no reason you have to get involved with Keller—"

"Stop right there," Fry said. "We're partners, remember? Besides, Keller must know all about me by now. My guess is he's made separate arrangements with Train to cover my presence."

"I guess you're right."

"I'm coming out," Fry said, standing up. "I want to talk to that major before it gets much later."

As Fry was drying off, Trapp saw a deep, livid scar on his left buttock, but didn't ask about it right then. There were other things to be settled, first.

———

Trapp felt odd walking with the Winchester in his hand instead of the Sharps. This gun was so much lighter than the Sharps that he almost felt unbalanced.

They went to the fort and asked for Sergeant Casey. They were asked to wait by the corral while a soldier went to fetch him.

"Well, Trapp and Fry," Casey said, coming up on them. They had exchanged names while riding double. "Where's your friend?"

"Actually, we never saw him before they brought him into Quanah's camp, so we're not friends," Fry said.

"We don't know where he is," Trapp said.

"Well, that doesn't matter," Casey said. "You two can tell the major everything you know. Come on. He's waiting in his office."

They entered the major's office and Casey spoke to his aide, the young lieutenant who had admitted Trapp and Fry to see the major the first time.

"I'll tell him you're here," the lieutenant said, and went into the major's office.

"That shavetail is a real asshole," Casey said.

The lieutenant came back and said, "The major will see you now."

"No kidding," the sergeant said under his breath. "Come on, gents."

Casey led the way into the major's office.

"These are the men I told you about, Major."

"Well," the major said, recognizing them, "you two again."

"You've met?" Casey asked.

"Oh yes," the major said. "These fellas were interested in getting through the Staked Plains without running into Quanah Parker."

"It doesn't look like they did it, sir."

"If I didn't know better," the major said, "I'd think you fellas got yourself caught so you'd have something to trade. All right, have a seat and let's go over this."

Using a map on the wall, Trapp and Fry related their experience to the major. With the information they gave him, the commanding officer felt that he had finally pinpointed the location of Quanah's camp.

"If this works out, you fellas will be heroes," the major said.

"We'll settle for an escort off these plains," Trapp said.

"You'll have it," the major said. "Casey will be taking some wagons over the plains at the end of the week."

Trapp and Fry looked at each other. If they had to stay here until the end of the week—four more days—Keller would have plenty of time to do what he was hired to do.

"I'll send out a patrol tomorrow," the major said. "In fact, I'll take them out myself. I'm grateful to you men for this information."

"And we're grateful to Sergeant Casey for finding us," Trapp said.

"By tomorrow afternoon we should know something," the major said. "Will you be in the hotel?"

"We will."

"I'll send a soldier to find you when we get back."

"We'd appreciate it, Major," Trapp said, standing up.

They left with Casey, who clapped them both on the back outside.

"If you fellas are in the saloon later, I'll buy you a drink."

"See you there," Fry said.

When Trapp and Fry came out the back gate, Trapp said, "Four more days. That gives Keller plenty of time."

"Maybe we shouldn't wait for him," Fry said. "Maybe we should make the first move."

"What if we're wrong?" Trapp asked. "What if he isn't working for Train?"

"Well," Fry said, "we'll just have to find out for sure."

"How do you propose we do that?" Trapp asked.

"The easy way," Fry said. "We'll ask him."

CHAPTER THIRTY-SIX

"What do you mean he's not here?" Fry asked.

The hotel clerk looked at Trapp and Fry and said, "I'm sorry, but the man did not check in here."

"Is there another place he could get a room?" Trapp asked.

"Uh, yeah, as a matter of fact," the clerk said, "there's a rooming house on the other end of town."

"They have a bathtub?"

"I suppose so."

"That's where he is," Fry said, banging his hand down on the desk.

Trapp closed his hand over Fry's forearm and pulled him away from the desk.

"After he gets a bath and a change of clothes, what's he going to want?"

"Same things we want," Fry said. "Some food and a drink."

"Let's go and get those things and maybe we'll run into him in the saloon."

"Not another incident in the saloon," Fry said. "The sheriff wouldn't be able to believe it."

"We might not have so much trouble," Trapp said. "Remember, we've got the military on our side."

They left the hotel and went to the small cafe, Maria's. They each ordered the same thing, steak and potatoes.

"I've been thinking about what you said."

"About what?" Trapp asked.

"About the military being on our side," Fry said. "Quanah's not stupid. When he realizes that we've escaped, is he gonna keep his camp where it is, or move it?"

Trapp's heart dropped as he realized that Fry was absolutely correct.

"Of course he'll move it," Trapp said. "Probably take my Sharps with him."

For the first time Fry realized that Trapp was hoping the soldiers would be able to recover the Sharps.

"What about buying another Sharps?" Fry asked.

"Where?"

"How about when we get back to the mountains?"

"You know, I've been thinking a lot about the mountains," Trapp said.

"What about them?"

"They will be the same, but what about the area around them? Will the plains be different? Will there be towns like this one where I remembered grassy fields? And what about the people?"

"Trapp, you'll find out about all that when we get there, so why worry about it now?"

Trapp stared at the younger man for a moment then said, "Yeah, I guess you're right."

They finished their dinner and headed over to the saloon for a beer. The bartender recognized them, but did not comment on the condition of their faces, which were still red from the sun. They took their beers to a table against a wall and both sat so they could see the rest of the room.

"Maybe we should go and talk to the sheriff," Trapp said. "Tell him what we suspect."

"Ah, he'd just think we were trying to cover ourselves in case of trouble. No, if something happens here, Trapp, we'll have plenty of witnesses afterward."

"That's supposing that we're both around afterward," Trapp said.

"Why shouldn't we be? I mean, I've heard that Keller is good, but there are two of us."

"You mean you'd have us both go against him at the same time?"

Fry stared at Trapp and asked, "Why not? If he comes in

here looking for the both of us, it's his choice. Are we going to be gentlemen about it and say 'Here, Mr. Keller, face me first, and if you kill me, then you'll have to face my friend'? That doesn't make any sense, Trapp."

"It just...doesn't seem right."

After a moment Fry said, "Look, if it bothers you I'll take him alone."

"Can you?" Trapp said.

"Can I what? Take him? Sure."

"Have you ever seen him—I mean, you've never seen him before."

"Don't worry about it, Trapp," Fry said. "The important thing isn't having seen his move before, the important thing is having confidence in yourself."

"Which you obviously do," Trapp said. "How can you be so confident that you can outshoot everyone?"

"I can't outshoot *everyone*," Fry said. "I'm not dumb enough to think that. Somewhere out there is a better hand than me with a gun. I just have to hope that he and I never find ourselves in the same place at the same time."

"And if it's Keller?"

Fry shrugged.

"If it's Keller and he kills me, you better get acquainted real quick with that new rifle of yours."

Trapp looked down at the Winchester leaning against the table.

"I don't even know if I could fire it now."

"Lift it up here," Fry said.

Trapp put the rifle on the table.

"It's a lever action. Just work the lever to load a round, and fire. Then you lever next time to eject the spent shell and load a live one. See?"

"It's simple," Trapp said, somewhat surprised.

"Much easier than having to reload that Sharps of yours every time you fire, isn't it."

"Yes, it is," Trapp said, touching the gun.

"Okay, get it off the table before we attract attention."

Trapp took the gun and leaned it against the table again.

"Now drink your beer and get used to waiting. Once we find him—or he finds us—we can flat out ask him if he's hunting us, but that could be in the next hour, or three days from now."

———

KELLER GOT up off his bed in his room at the rooming house and strapped on his new gun. It was a piece of shit, but it was the best weapon the gunsmith had in his shop. When he got to a real town, he'd buy himself a brand new one. He liked the idea of going into retirement with a brand new weapon.

His intention now was to go to the saloon and get a beer. He knew that if there was one place in Fort McAdams that he'd be likely to run into Trapp and Kid Fry, it would be the saloon.

Unbeknownst to Trapp and Fry, Keller bad heard that Sergeant Casey would be taking some wagons across the Staked Plains in four days' time. Keller figured that Trapp and Fry would wait and leave with the wagons. That gave him four days to play games with them and unnerve them. He wasn't sure yet if he wanted to take the two of them at one time. As a hand with a gun, he didn't anticipate much trouble from Trapp, although he was otherwise impressed with the man and the things he had done out on the plains.

Kid Fry, on the other hand, had a reputation as a hand with a gun. Keller knew he could handle a gun, but that was not where his reputation lay. His reputation was as a hunter of men. Rarely did he face a quarry fairly when he caught up with them. Not that he shot them in the back, but he didn't quite play fair with the boys who thought that standing out in the street and shooting it out fair and square was the measure of a man.

The measure of a man was in surviving and that is what Keller was good at—and the reason he was good at it was because he always survived...no matter what the cost.

CHAPTER THIRTY-SEVEN

They saw Keller as soon as he walked in.

He walked to the bar, got himself a beer, and looked around the room, apparently without seeing them. When he'd finished taking the room in, he pushed away from the bar and walked right over to their table.

He *had* seen them as soon as he'd walked in.

"You boys mind if I sit down?" he asked.

"I don't see why not," Fry said, "after all that we've been through together...Keller."

Keller smiled.

"I guess I should apologize for that little lie."

"I don't see why," Trapp said. "Wouldn't do for you to introduce yourself to a man you were hunting, would it? I mean, that's sure as hell not the way you've made your reputation in your business, is it?"

"No, it isn't," Keller said. "You know, I'm real sorry that I am hunting you, because after what we went through together, none of us should have to kill the other."

"Then you admit that you're hunting both of us?" Fry asked.

"No," Keller said, and made them wait for clarification while he sipped his beer. "I'm hunting him." He pointed to Trapp, and was talking to Fry. "You just happen to be with him."

"And I ain't goin' away," Fry said.

"I didn't think you would."

"I suppose you've made arrangements to be compensated?" Fry said.

"Oh, yes," Keller said. "I've made all my arrangements—and now I'm giving you two time to make yours."

"I haven't got any arrangements to make, Keller," Trapp said. "I'm going to my mountain, remember?"

"I remember hearing something about that," Keller said, "but I'm here to tell you you ain't gonna make it."

"That's you talking," Trapp said.

"I usually mean what I say."

"So do I," Trapp said. He leaned closer to Keller, stared him in the eyes, and said, "Don't get between me and my mountain. I don't think I can make myself any clearer than that."

Keller held Trapp's eyes for a few moments, then looked at Fry.

"You know, if he was ten years younger—even *five* years—I'd be afraid, I surely would."

"Be afraid," Fry said. "You saw him out there, Keller. This ain't no normal man."

"Out there," Keller said, nodding. "Out there, I saw a man running on fear. Fear can make you do things you can't normally do."

Fry laughed.

"Fear? It was you and me running on fear, Keller. This man never showed an ounce of it, and you know why? Because he never felt it."

"Everybody feels fear," Keller said.

"I'm glad you said that, Keller," Trapp said.

"Why?"

"Because it tells me that you're not a stupid man. When you make your decision and it turns out to be the wrong one, I'll be glad to know that it wasn't based on stupidity."

Trapp put his hand on Keller's left forearm and closed it. Keller tried, but he couldn't move it from the table.

"I just figured out a way to be clearer," Trapp said urgently. "Don't get between me and my mountain, or I'll kill you."

He released Keller's arm, got up, and walked out of the saloon.

"He means it," Fry said.

Keller flexed his left hand to work the blood back into it and said, "I know it, but I've been paid to do a job, Fry, and I've never failed to complete one."

"There's always a first time," Fry said. "Why don't we just put that to the test now?"

"Now?" Keller asked. "I haven't finished my beer."

"I could wait for you outside."

"You'd be waiting a long time, Fry," Keller said. "No, I think I'll decide when we put that to the test. After all, I *am* the hunter."

"We could go to the sheriff."

"And tell him what? That I'm hunting you? He knows what happened to us out there. It's all over town. Everybody thinks we're good buddies. Besides, going to the law isn't your style, Fry, just like it isn't mine."

They both worked on their beers for a while and it was Keller who broke the silence.

"You know, you've got a pretty good reputation. If you stood back and let me take Trapp, you and I could then square off and find out who's better."

"Who are you kidding?"

Keller looked wounded and said, "What do you mean?"

"You ain't no gunman, Keller, you're a killer. A fair fight ain't your style."

Keller held up a finger warningly and said, "I never shot a man in the back."

"There are other ways to fight unfairly than shooting a man in the back," Fry said, standing up. "I'd hazard a guess that you've perfected almost all of them."

Keller stared at Fry and then laughed as the younger man walked away and out of the saloon.

They were more alike than young Fry knew.

————

WHEN FRY LEFT THE SALOON, he found Trapp standing outside.

"What happened after I left?" Trapp asked.

"I hope you don't think you scared him."

"Nah, just maybe made him think a little. Why, what did he say?"

"He said if I stood aside while he took you out, then he and I could see who the better man is."

"And what'd you say?"

"I told him he'd never fought a fair fight in his life, and I didn't expect him to start now."

"Can we prod him?"

"No," Fry said, shaking his head. "He's gonna make his move when he's ready, and not before."

"What makes him think he's got the time?"

"He must know about the wagons that are leaving at the end of the week," Fry said. "He don't have to be the smartest dog in the pack to figure out that we'll be leaving with them. Last thing we want to do is visit Quanah Parker again. I don't think he likes the way we left the last time."

"Probably not," Trapp said. "It *was* rude of us."

"To say the least."

"Well," Trapp said, "I'm going to turn in. I've had a rough day, for a man my age."

"*We've* had a rough day for a man any age," Fry said, "but I think I'll stay out here and watch Mr. Keller for a while."

"Why?"

Fry shrugged.

"You thinking of trying to scare him?"

"No," Fry said, "he won't scare for sure, but maybe I can make him think a little."

"Well, be careful," Trapp said, and started to walk away. He took two steps and turned back.

"What's the matter?"

"I just got a nasty little thought."

"About what?"

"You wouldn't be thinking of trying anything alone, would you?"

"And make you miss the fun?" Fry asked. "You'd never forgive me."

"You're right," Trapp said, "I wouldn't. Try to remember that."

"I'll remember it, Trapp," Fry said. "I'll remember it."

———

TRAPP WENT BACK to the hotel, but he was uncomfortable about doing so. Fry may have had a little—or big—reputation, but he was still twenty-five years old. Trapp remembered being really headstrong at twenty-five, and although Fry had shown no signs of it yet, that didn't mean that it wasn't there.

Leaving him on the street alone may not be the right thing to do.

Fry watched Trapp walk away, then moved into the confines of a dark doorway to await Keller. Once Keller came out, Fry would let the man see him, and would follow him back to his rooming house. There would not even be an *implied* threat, but just the simple fact that Fry was there would have to make Keller think twice...and thinking twice was a hazard in his business.

As soon as Fry left the saloon, Keller got up and went to the bar and caught the bartender's attention.

"Another, sir?"

"No. Is there a back door out of here?"

"Yes, sir, right through that curtain and down the hall, but we don't allow customers...uh, sir? You can't go back there. Sir!"

CHAPTER THIRTY-EIGHT

Keller slipped out the back door, ignoring the words of the bartender. After all, the man had made no move to physically stop him. Smart man.

It was dark out and he stopped for a moment to allow his eyes to adjust, then began to move along the rear of the buildings until he came to an alley. He moved down the alley, came to the main street, and stopped. He peered around the corner and found that he was only one building away from the saloon. Across the street the doorways were dark, but he knew if he was patient—ah, there it was. Just enough movement to tell him that someone was there, in one of the doorways.

He wondered if it was Trapp or Fry. His money was on the younger man, Fry. Trapp would have more patience.

That *lack* of patience was going to get the young man killed.

———

FRY WONDERED how long he was going to have to wait. He'd be the first to admit that patience was not his long suit. Maybe that was something he could learn from Trapp. The older man had really impressed him out on the plains. He wondered what kind of man John Henry Trapp was twenty-five years ago.

He would like to have met him then.

Keller eased himself out of the alley, keeping to the sides of the buildings, where the shadows were deep. Somebody would actually have to be looking for him to see him. Fry was probably waiting for him to come out the front door so he could tail him. He probably felt that he'd unnerve Keller by doing that. It was the kind of foolish decision a young man would make.

Keller moved carefully, so he wouldn't bump into anything and give himself away.

He knew what doorway Fry was in. All he had to do was get himself into position to make his shots count. If he put two or three into that doorway, he was sure to hit his target.

There was plenty of moonlight, which lit the center of the street, but it was that very moonlight that made the shadows black as ink.

Finally he slid into a doorway which gave him an excellent vantage point of the other doorway across the street. He settled in and waited. He wanted one more indication that he had the correct target.

He waited and waited but there was no movement. Either Fry had suddenly become very, very still...or he was no longer there. If he had moved, firing a shot into the doorway would only give away his own position. Maybe the young man was better than he thought.

———

IT WAS QUITE by accident that Fry saw the movement across the street. He had looked away from the saloon entrance for a moment, just long enough for his eyes to adjust to the shadows. He caught some movement, as if someone was moving in the shadows across the street.

The back way, he thought. Keller had probably used the saloon's back exit to get out.

It looked as if they both had the same idea, to make something happen tonight.

As quickly and quietly as he could, he slipped from his doorway and moved farther down, away from the saloon. He found an alley and took refuge in it, peering around the edge.

Now he'd *have* to show some patience, or end up dead.

———

KELLER DECIDED to retrace his steps, going back down the alley and moving along the rear of the buildings until he was farther down the street, where he could safely cross without being seen.

Once on the other side he found another alley, which led him to the rear of the buildings on that side of the street. He now felt confident that he was *behind* Fry.

All he had to do now was find him.

———

FRY KNEW that Keller had moved—but where would he have moved to? He decided that there were two options. The man had either gone to the rooftops, or had somehow crossed the street and was now on the same side.

Suddenly he looked behind himself, into the darkness of the alley. Keller could be moving in behind him.

Now he had a tough choice to make. He could move farther into the alley and risk running right into Keller, or he could slip out of the alley and take a chance on exposing himself.

Although it was dark it was still early enough for there to be *some* street traffic. Every so often a man, or two men—sometimes soldiers—would pass by. Fry wondered if and when the sheriff made his rounds. He could always ask the man for help, but somehow that went against his grain. He was used to taking care of his own problems.

Gun in hand, he decided to risk moving deeper into the alley.

———

KELLER WAS MOVING ALONG behind the buildings, and every time he came to an alley, he peered into it. At the end of each alley he could see the moonlit street. If there was someone in the alley, he kept to the side of the building on either side.

He gave each alley a few minutes, then passed it and moved on to the next, always keeping a sharp eye behind him.

He was approaching the third alleyway when someone came out of it, moving slowly.

It had to be Fry.

Keller raised his gun and fired.

———

FRY FELT the impact before he heard the shot—or at least, that was the way he remembered it.

The bullet hit him in the hip and spun him around, but he held on to his gun and squeezed off a shot, just for the scare value of the noise. When he hit the ground, he scrambled and crawled until he found cover behind some crates.

———

KELLER KNEW he had hit his target, but there was a flash and a shot as Fry pulled his trigger, and Keller hit the ground. He heard some scrabbling on the ground and correctly deduced that Fry was crawling to cover.

"I know I hit you, Fry," he said. "I can smell the blood. As of now, as you run out of blood, you run out of time." He paused then said loudly, "I'm gonna kill you, Fry."

Keller knew that it would take time for anyone to figure out where the shots had come from. There had been only two and they were close together. Some people—especially those in the saloon—would still be listening, to make sure they had heard right.

He had time to make his killing shot.

———

FRY WAS TRYING to stop the bleeding.

He knew the wound wasn't serious, but he had to stop the bleeding or he'd be in big trouble. He pulled his shirt out of his pants, tore off a large piece of it, and wadded it up. He unbuttoned his pants and slid the wadded cloth in until it covered the wound, then he buttoned the pants again. That would slow down the bleeding—unless he had to move.

He knew that Keller was right. Where they both once had time and mobility on their side, he now had neither. Keller could wait or move, at his leisure—unless the shots brought somebody, which wasn't likely. He made the same assumptions that Keller made about the shots being too close together and difficult to pinpoint.

Of course, if there were *more* shots…

When the shots came, Keller ducked, but then realized that Fry was not shooting at him. The kid was firing to bring help.

Keller knew that he had to move fast now. He stood up and moved quickly toward Fry, who now fired another shot in the air.

He had two shots left.

———

TOO LATE, Fry realized how Keller would respond to his shots. He turned too quickly, pain lancing through his hip. He put his left hand down on the ground to brace himself and it slid on the sticky blood. Keller was moving toward him fast, and as Fry raised his gun to fire, Keller kicked out. His foot struck Fry's hand and the gun went flying.

Keller was standing over him, his gun pointing down at him.

"Like I said before," Keller said, "it's too bad I have to do this, after we saved each other's lives from Quanah Parker."

"I can see you're real upset about it."

Keller smiled and cocked his gun.

"Keller!"

It was Trapp's voice. Both Keller and Fry looked around and finally saw Trapp, standing ahead of them. Fry wished Trapp had come up behind Keller.

"You're next, Trapp," Keller said. "Just let me finish here."

"I'm first, Keller," Trapp said. He had already left the hotel and was looking for Fry when he heard the shots. Even so, it wasn't until the second volley that he was able to pinpoint their location. "You've got to kill me before you can kill him."

Keller looked down at Fry. If he shot Fry, Trapp would shoot him. His only chance was to get Trapp first.

Trapp was holding his rifle in front of him, not pointing at Keller. Fry hoped that he had already levered in a round.

"Your call, Trapp," Keller said.

Keller started to bring the gun up, shifting his feet at the same time. He stepped in a sticky, slippery patch of Fry's blood and his foot slipped. As he was trying to regain his balance, Trapp shot him.

The bullet struck Keller squarely in the chest. Fry heard Trapp lever another round, but it wasn't needed. Keller's gun fell from his hand and the man hunter toppled over onto his back.

Trapp moved forward as they heard some people coming down the alley.

"What's going on—" the sheriff demanded, coming into view. He saw Trapp and Fry and said, "Oh no, not you two again."

Trapp ignored the lawman and crouched down by Fry.

"Are you all right?"

"I am now," Fry said. "I'm glad you remembered how to use that rifle."

"So am I. Can you stand?"

"I think so."

Trapp helped him to his feet and supported him.

"This one's dead," the sheriff said, crouched by Keller. He stood up and said, "You two want to explain this to me?"

"As soon as we get my partner to a doctor, Sheriff," Trapp promised, "I'll tell you the whole story."

EPILOGUE

"What do you think?" Trapp asked.

Kid Fry looked up at the majestic Rocky Mountains and said, "Is that snow?"

"It's snow, Kid," Trapp said.

"White as pearls," Fry said, remembering what Trapp had said.

Fry winced and Trapp said, "How's the hip?"

"Sore," Fry said. "The doc said riding would do that to it for a while—maybe forever."

"Well, you're lucky that bullet lodged in your hip, or it would have tore a bigger hole going out and you'd have been laid up even longer."

The rest of the trip, after leaving Texas, had been uneventful for the most part. Of course, they'd crossed paths once or twice with trouble, but never with the same result as in Texas. Sometimes Trapp thought that if they had been able to avoid crossing Texas, the trip would have been faster and easier—and certainly less painful.

Trapp hefted the weight of his Sharps, wondering when they'd catch their first sight of buffalo—or if there were even any buffalo left, or beaver.

Crossing the plains at the foot of the mountains, he had already seen the changes he'd been afraid of. Settlements, even the beginnings of real towns. Already there were too damn many people around.

Up top, though, that's where he felt it would be the same.

"Up there," he said, pointing. "When we get up there, we won't have to worry about people, about anybody."

"That'll be a nice change."

Trapp looked down at his Sharps. He'd gotten it back the day after the shooting, when the major returned from his search for Quanah's camp...

———

THE SOLDIER HAD HAD MIXED luck. They had found the camp and killed themselves some Indians—among them, Trapp was quite sure, some women and children—but Quanah and his warriors had not been there.

"Not your fault, Mr. Trapp," the major said magnanimously. "Even though we didn't get Quanah, we hurt him. Maybe it'll make him think twice about showing his face again for a while."

"Well," Trapp said, thinking of the little black-eyed son of Strong Hawk, "that's something, isn't it?"

"We did find something you might be interested in, though," the major said. "Sergeant Casey?"

Casey came running over then, and in his hand he was carrying Trapp's Sharps.

"Well, I'll be—" Trapp said, grabbing for it.

"I don't think they even knew how to work it," the major said. "It's a beautiful old weapon. I thought you might like to have it back."

"Thank you, Major," Trapp said. "This means a lot to me."

———

WHEN FRY WAS ready to ride, they had hit the trail again, and now, finally, they were here.

Trapp was home again.

The air was the same, clean, fresh, and cold enough to freeze your piss.

They came to a stream and Trapp made Fry drink the water.

"Oh, my God," Fry said after sipping some, "that's the coldest thing I ever drank."

"How do you like it?"

"It's also the best thing I ever drank," Fry said. "Do you know how beer would taste if you put it in a barrel and dropped it in there?"

"Delicious," Trapp said. "Delicious."

At that point a Blackfoot party had come along and chased them across the stream halfheartedly. After a couple of hundred yards the Indians gave up the chase. They probably could have run them down if they'd really wanted to, but back in one of those plains settlements they had already picked up a pack horse and extra supplies.

"After the Comanches," Fry said, "that was easy as pie."

"Take it from me," Trapp said, "they're not always that friendly."

———

THEY CAMPED that night just below the snow peaks. In the morning they'd go up higher, where Trapp wanted to be for a while. He wanted to wash all the poison of the past twenty-five years out of his system, and the only way he knew to do that was to get as high as a man could get without flying.

They made bacon, and some coffee, and Trapp looked across the fire at Kid Fry.

"Before I take you up there," Trapp said, jerking his chin upward, "up to my mountain, I want to know something from you."

"What?" Fry asked warily.

"What are you running from?"

Fry stared at Trapp, then looked up at the snow peaks that looked as if they were getting ready to poke holes in the sky.

"I was gonna tell you, Trapp," Fry said. "I think I was gonna tell you up there."

"Well, tell me down here, Kid," Trapp said. "Tell me now."

"It's no big deal, really," Fry said. "I just fudged a bit on my reputation."

"How little?"

"Well, you asked me if I'm wanted by the law. Fact of the matter is, I am. There's probably paper on me reaching Texas and Oklahoma right now."

"Paper?"

"Wanted posters."

"From where?"

"New Mexico. You see, my reputation isn't all that small, and I've been trying to get away from it of late. But it seemed that in the three or four months before I met you, I was being challenged more and more. Every time I came out of a hotel or a saloon, there was somebody there wanting to try me out."

Trapp remained silent when Fry paused, and waited for him to continue.

"Well, I was in a town in New Mexico, having a drink in a saloon. It was late, and I guess I'd had one or two too many. I came out of the saloon and suddenly somebody called my name, real loud. I reacted instinctively. I turned and fired, all in one motion."

This time when Fry paused, Trapp became impatient.

"And?"

"And...it was a kid," Fry said. "Fourteen, and he had no gun."

"He was dead?"

"Dead," Fry said. "I killed an unarmed kid just because he called my name."

"What happened after that?"

"Well, people started pouring out of the saloon and when they saw what I'd done they started some lynch talk right away. I don't mind telling you, I ran. I was running when we met, and I'm still running."

"That was why you never wanted to use your name on telegrams, or talk to a lawman?"

Fry nodded.

"It takes paper some time to circulate, but I was playing it safe," Fry said. "You'll recall I wanted to leave Texas earlier than we finally did."

"You would have killed yourself, trying to ride on that wound."

"Yeah, I might have," Fry said, "but I was afraid that paper would catch up with us."

"Well," Trapp said, "it won't catch up to you up there."

Fry looked at Trapp and said, "You'll still take me, even though you know I'm wanted?"

Trapp shrugged.

"You forget, I'm wanted, too," Trapp said. "When Sam Train

finds out that we killed Keller, you don't think he's going to quit, do you? He'll send somebody else."

"And he'll send them here," Fry said. "It won't be hard for him to figure that you'd come back here, to the mountains."

"Well, also don't forget," Trapp said, "this is my mountain. I know every inch of it, and the terrain will be unchanged even after twenty-five years. Nobody will find us up here, or up there, Kid. It'll just be you and me."

"You, me," Fry said, "and our pasts."

"Well," Trapp said, "what do you say we leave our pasts down here and only take our futures up there."

Trapp stuck his hand out and Fry smiled and took it.

"Just one thing," Fry said.

"What?"

"I don't know what we'll do with our time up there, but just don't ask me to play poker with you."

A LOOK AT: BUTLER'S WAGER

Gambler Book One

Award winning, best selling author Robert J. Randisi delivers the goods in this classic action and adventure Western series starring Ty Butler, a gambler extraordinaire.

Ty Butler came from Eastern wealth—but ruthless killers destroyed everyone—and anything—who shared his name. Seeking a safe haven in the open West, he discovered refuge among the outlaws and fugitives who staked their claims at the gaming table. His remarkable, and at times uncanny skill at reading faces and cards has kept Butler flush with cash and living comfortably—but it has also kept him sharp and ready for the numerous assassins hunting him, eager to finish the job of wiping the Butler name and legacy from the pages of history.

Arriving in Dodge City, Butler finds the place in chaos. A new type of law is in play here where Bat Masterson carved his legend. Old and powerfully dangerous grudges are about to explode, and Ty Butler is caught smack dab in the middle. When the smoke clears and the undertaker has cleared the corpses, Butler will have friends and enemies in all the wrong places.

"Classic old west as a gunman begins settling scores for good people..." Amazon reviewer on *Lancaster: The Complete Series*

AVAILABLE NOW

ABOUT THE AUTHOR

Randisi was born and raised in Brooklyn, N.Y., and from 1973 through 1981 he was a civilian employee of the New York City Police Department, working out of the 67th Precinct in Brooklyn. After 41 years in N.Y, he now resides in Laughlin, NV, 90 miles South of Las Vegas, on the Colorado River, with his 25-year partner-in-life-and-crime, Marthayn Pelegrimas.

He is the author of the "Miles Jacoby," "Nick Delvecchio," "Joe Keough," and "Dennis McQueen," mystery series, and the co-author of the "Gil & Claire Hunt" series. He has been nominated four times for the Shamus Award from the Private Eye Writers of America, in the Novel and Short Story categories.

www.ingramcontent.com/pod-product-compliance
Lightning Source LLC
Chambersburg PA
CBHW010117070726
47497CB00022B/3235